Harley wondered how she could *feel* someone so completely when she wasn't even touching that person.

"I have to go," M...... ....ed to the door. Harley fo..... ....en he left. She sta.... .... She felt as if her fle... ....bone, had come alive, as ... .ns or other chemical entities we.. ....rough her system with tiny sparks of re. ...t fire. He had to leave, otherwise she'd embarrass herself.

But she didn't really care.

Still, he was right. They needed time. Just because they could hook up didn't mean they should forget that there were consequences to any deed, even if neither had any expectations.

At the door, he turned to her.

She walked forward, her eyes on his, until she was touching him, and when she did, he backed into the door. At the same time, his arms came around her.

She let herself touch his face. Stroke his cheek, feel the power in his arms as he drew her close. She shuddered with delicious abandon as she felt the heat of his body, the texture and strength in his muscle... ....g hers, a.. ....

cascades. And then she felt his mouth, crushing...
...and she returned the kiss with equal passion

SHADOWS IN THE NIGHT

BY
HEATHER GRAHAM

First Published in Great Britain 2017
By Mills & Boon, an imprint of HarperCollins*Publishers*
1 London Bridge Street, London, SE1 9GF

© 2017 Heather Graham Pozzessere

ISBN: 978-0-263-92930-0

46-1117

Our policy is to use papers that are natural, renewable and recyclable products and made from wood grown in sustainable forests. The logging and manufacturing processes conform to the legal environmental regulations of the country of origin.

Printed and bound in Spain
by CPI, Barcelona

New York Times and *USA TODAY* bestselling author **Heather Graham** has written more than a hundred novels. She's a winner of the RWA's Lifetime Achievement Award and the Thriller Writers' Silver Bullet. She is an active member of International Thriller Writers and Mystery Writers of America.

For more information, check out her website, www.theoriginalheathergraham.com, or find Heather on Facebook.

Prologue

The Mummy
A Year Ago

"Sir!"

The word was spoken softly and with respect.

Dr. Henry Tomlinson, renowned Egyptologist, turned. One of the grad students had just slipped through the inner flap of the air-controlled prep tent and was smiling benignly, awaiting his attention.

He hadn't actually taught in about five years, but he still loved it—and working with students. He'd retired to spend all his time in the field, and he'd recently been hired by Alchemy, an Anglo-American sponsoring company, to head this dig. Alchemy was into all kinds of tech and had become a Fortune 500 company. Every year, they sponsored an exceptional archeological event, followed by a public exhibit. Recent ones had been centered around the Amazon River, central China—and now ancient Egypt. Their resources were phenomenal and Henry still couldn't believe his good fortune. But no matter what monetary resources had been offered, he was thrilled about having grad students involved.

This one was Harley Frasier. Just twenty-six, she was tall, shapely, honey blonde, with a face crafted in perfect classic symmetry and enormous green eyes that seemed to take in everything. She was serious and brilliant and could nail the crux of information with laser-like acuity. She also had a sense of humor and the most delightful laugh he had ever heard.

Of the five specialty graduate candidates, she was, beyond a doubt, his favorite. He often felt like a grandfatherly mentor to her—and the idea made him happy. He'd had no children of his own. He'd never even had a wife. No time for a family. He hadn't intended it be that way forever, but there was always so much to do. If he'd had the chance to be a father, he would've been pleased and proud to have had Harley as a granddaughter. She seemed to feel the same closeness to him.

Perhaps their bond was odd since, of the five grad students, she was the one who was different, the only one not majoring in Egyptology—though she was minoring in it. She had no plan to go into Egyptology or even archeology or history for her life's vocation.

Harley was with him, first of all, because of her knowledge regarding the field and her love for it. But she was also there because her work was going to be in criminal psychology and forensic science. Henry had been baffled when he was approached by her university. Professors at the Maryland college Harley was attending—which was arguably the top school for criminology and it also offered majors and minors in Egyptology and archeology—had explained to him the importance of having a student like Harley on this expedition. He had been on the hunt for the tomb of Amenmose for nearly a decade; for that entire decade, he'd been finding more and more clues about the location—and, of course, with the permission and blessing of the Egyptian government—finding other ancient tombs and treasures in the process. This allowed for his continued excavations. But the discovery of the tomb of Amenmose was the main focus of his work.

Many others had searched.

Some of them had died or disappeared in that effort.

History suggested that Amenmose had been murdered. As a criminology student, Harley was to be in on the discovery and would seek and find whatever evidence those who had managed his secret burial might have left behind.

Not that, to Henry's mind, Amenmose hadn't deserved murder. He had usurped power every step of the way. He'd abused officials below him. It had even been intimated that he had attempted to kill those in power above him.

"I think we've gotten all the manual labor done for the evening and we're going to pack it in, maybe drive to that little town for some dinner. Want to come with us? You should. You'd enjoy it. Or shall we bring you back something?" Harley asked him.

"Next time, Harley, I'll come with you all," he promised. "There's so much in here! I'm not going to go touching anything until we've had a chance to work with the preservation measures, but I do intend to look at everything."

Earlier that week, they had finally discovered the secret site of the tomb of Amenmose. And, of course, since then, Henry Tomlinson had been on cloud nine. This was a dream come true, a fantasy realized, the culmination of a lifetime of love and dedication.

Harley laughed softly. "Yes! You did it, Dr. Tomlinson."

"I did, didn't I?"

The Amenmose find was among the most important ancient Egyptian discoveries of the past few years; he couldn't have been more excited about being a major player in that discovery. And even now, at the end of an exhausting day—and even though he truly enjoyed the young people working with him—he was far too fascinated to leave. There were a dozen or so coffins to be studied, one of them presumably that of Amenmose; the group wouldn't consider opening them until everyone was back at the museum in Cairo. But he *could* study the canopic jars they'd found thus far. There were also other artifacts that had been carefully moved into the prep tent. So much to observe and to describe! And there were the broken coffins, which had probably been as meticulously set as any of the others, but had been in the section where a partial cave-in had taken place. Several of those outer and inner coffins had split and exposed their mummies. Henry Tomlinson was fascinated to see what study was possible before the mummies were packed and crated and prepared for the trip to Cairo, where options for preservation were far more sophisticated, and where the mummies could be X-rayed and DNA could be tested.

Oh! It was all so monumental.

Amenmose had been a priest in the days when another priest, Ay, had ruled Egypt as regent. Ay had done so for a well-known pharaoh, the boy king, Tutankhamen. As regent, Ay had wielded immense power. He'd gone on to become pharaoh in his own right—after the death of Tut at the age of nineteen.

Amenmose, according to ancient texts, had tried to usurp some of that power. And he'd had his own followers in the court, making him a dangerous man. Because of this he had feared for his immortal life—and his wife had kept his burial plans a complete secret, shared only with members of his family. Naturally, legend had it that many of his most loyal followers—rather than give away any secrets—had been willing to die with him, sealed alive in a grave for eternity.

"Dr. Tomlinson, you worked so hard. And wow! You triumphed. You should celebrate. Come out with us. Is there nothing I can do to convince you?" Harley asked. She still had that wonderful smile, as if she were the one who was far older and wiser. "Nothing's going to disappear. We'll go have some dinner and drinks and come on back. There are plenty of men on guard here. And," she added, "you really deserve a little celebration with us. Think of it—you researched and imagined and looked into the ancient Egyptian mind and you made the discovery. It's your shining moment. You're another Carter with his Tutankhamen, Dr. Tomlinson. Do you realize that?"

"Oh, no, no," Henry demurred. He shook his head firmly. "A celebration is tempting, but I couldn't leave. I couldn't. I do promise that I'll come with all of you on another day. Harley! Look at this! I feel like, as the song says, I have treasures untold."

Harley laughed. "You saw *The Little Mermaid*?" she asked.

He stared at her, feeling a bit chagrined. "Oh! Yes, I get it, you wouldn't think that I'd see a children's movie…" He laughed, too. "Remember, I do have great nieces and nephews! Anyway…"

He started walking as he spoke. "Harley, these are such treasures! This broken coffin." He gestured at it. "Damaged by time and by that cave-in, however many centuries ago. And this fellow, Harley. It almost looks as if he was buried alive. Wrapped up alive and screaming."

"I don't think you can embalm anyone and have that person come out of the process alive," Harley reminded him, amused. "That's only in fiction. We both know what was involved in Egyptian embalming, and just how many factors could've had an effect on the mummy's appearance. Screaming mummies belong to B movies, right? And when you think about it, weird mummies are all the more reason you should come with us."

"Why is that?"

Harley didn't answer. The flap opened again and Jensen Morrow, another of the students, poked his head in to answer.

He'd obviously heard the question.

"Ooh! 'Cause you shouldn't be alone with scary old stuff when you have cool kids like us to hang out with!" Jensen said.

They all laughed. Jensen was a good-looking, dark-haired young man who loved the study he was involved in, and Dr. Henry Tomlinson liked him very much, as well. Jensen played hard, but he worked harder. He came from money; his father was an inventor who'd come up with a special cleaning product. And yet Jensen never acted like money, never acted pretentious or entitled the way some rich kids did.

"Tempting, tempting, tempting," Henry said again. "But I'm going to stay."

Jensen raised his eyebrows at Harley. "Hey, girl, then it's you and me heading out. The old man here isn't coming. That's okay. We're bringing back the goods. Just the two of us, since Belinda Gray is waiting for a video chat with her fiancé—military, as we know!— in Iraq. Roger Eastman agreed to help one of the tech guys investigate some computer info they're picking up. I hate to say it, but we're getting chatter about an insurgent group starting up. And Joe Rosello said he wants to learn more about the excavation equipment. He's working with that pretty Egyptian girl, our trans- lator, and learning about hoists."

"Hoists? Yeah, right!" Harley said. "Satima. She *is* pretty, and thank goodness we have her. I'm just grate- ful she filled in at the last minute when the older gen- tleman we'd hired wound up ill. If I know our friend Joe at all, I know he's very happy!" she said to Henry. "We won't go far, since we seem to be feeling a wee bit nervous! And we won't be late. We'll bring you some- thing to eat and see if you want to be social when we get back, okay? If, and only if, you're absolutely posi- tive you don't want to take a ride with this handsome, if ridiculous, guy and me?"

Henry laughed. "Oh, Harley, you're a sweetheart, but give it up. You know I'm not coming."

She grimaced, a delightful movement of her face. "Yes, I do," she admitted. "But we—your devoted stu- dents—have to try. I'll bring you a special treat for dinner."

"Don't worry about me, guys. I'll be fine."

"Sorry, we *will* worry about you. At least we can make sure you eat. I'm willing to bet you're going to be up all night—and you won't even notice that you haven't slept," Harley said.

He smiled and made a shooing motion with his hands. "Go! Get on out with you. Be young and have fun and don't become an obsessive old curmudgeon like me. Jensen, get her out of here!"

"Yes, sir!" Jensen said.

Harley still hung back. "You're neither obsessive nor old," she insisted. "Okay, wait. Maybe you are obsessive. Anyway, we'll be back by nine or so, and like I said, I'll bring you something delicious."

"Sounds lovely! See you soon."

And at last, Harley and Jensen left.

Dr. Henry Tomlinson turned his attention back to Unknown Mummy #1 for several long moments. Many pharaohs and royalty and even esteemed but lesser men, like Amenmose, ended up with unknowns in their tombs—servants needed in the next life.

Almost the entire lid of the coffin had been torn open. That afternoon, two of the students had painstakingly cleared out the rubble around the mummy. But Henry felt as if he was indeed looking at remnants featured in a B horror flick; the thing really did appear to be a man who'd been wrapped up with his mouth open in horror, left to silently scream into eternity.

Mummies weren't wrapped like this alive. Unless, of course...

He'd never been intended to be a mummy?

He'd been a murder victim.

Could this unidentified mummy be Amenmose himself? he wondered excitedly. They hadn't identified the man's tomb.

Great question, but it wasn't scientific to jump to

conclusions. X-rays would give them an image of the insides—and that would probably tell them if the facial contortions had happened because of some accident in the drying process or if he *had* somehow been wrapped alive!

No, it couldn't be Amenmose, Henry decided. According to the ancient texts and all the information at his disposal, Amenmose had died before burial. Besides, they'd discovered one coffin in an inner tomb, deep in a hidden recess—again, just as the ancient texts had said. Amenmose's enemies might have defiled his tomb if those who loved him hadn't concealed his remains. The mummy here, found in the outer chamber, couldn't be Amenmose—not unless there was a great deal they were missing! "Sorry, old boy. Lord only knows what happened to you," Henry told the mummy.

"Hey!"

The inner flap to the preparation tent opened again. Henry looked over to see that it was Alchemy's director at large, Ned Richter.

He was smiling. As he should have been. Their day had been fantastic.

"Hey," Henry said. He liked Richter okay. Although not an Egyptologist himself, the man was studious and yet always ready help out with manual labor when needed.

Henry didn't like Richter's wife, Vivian, so much. She was an Egyptologist, too—at least in her own mind, he thought with a snort. Okay, so she did have her master's degree from Brown; she was just annoying as hell and she didn't think clearly or reason anything out. She was an attractive enough woman with short dark hair and dark eyes, and she claimed the maternal side of her father's family had been Egyptian.

She liked to pretend that she knew what she was talking about.

She seldom did.

"Just checking on you!" Richter said.

Henry heard Vivian speaking behind her husband. "Tell him to come with us. We'll get some food and drinks."

"Hey, Viv!" Henry called out. "I'm good tonight. Going to work. And a couple of the students are picking me up something to eat. Listen," he added in a more affable voice, "can't wait till you and I have a chance to talk tomorrow. We can compare notes then!"

"Can't you make him come?" Henry heard Vivian whisper.

"No," Richter said flatly. "He's head of the examination and prep all the way through the removal to Cairo—by Alchemy and the Egyptian government. As you know," he muttered.

"See you in the morning!" Henry called pleasantly. Yes!

But he'd barely turned around before he heard the inner tent flap opening again.

This time, it was Arlo Hampton, the Egyptologist who'd been employed specifically by Alchemy to watch over their investment.

Arlo was young—tall, straight and a little skinny. He preferred his thick glasses to contact lenses. Good thing for Arlo that nerds were in; he was, beyond a doubt, a nerd. But a friendly and outgoing nerd. He loved Egyptology, and yet, unlike certain other people, he wasn't full of himself or convinced that he knew everything.

"Hey, I knew you'd be alone with the treasures, snug as a bug in a rug!" Arlo told him cheerfully. There was something slightly guilty in his voice. "I wanted to make sure you were okay, though."

"I'm great. And, of course, if you want to join me…"

"I'm beat, Henry. I'm what? Thirty years younger than you? I don't know how you do it. I'm going to have a sandwich with the grad students when Harley and Jensen get back, and then hit my bunk until tomorrow. If that's okay. I mean, I should be like you, hard at work… Oh, I did just meet Belinda's boyfriend on Skype. Seems like a decent guy. So Belinda, Roger and Joe are taking care of their personal business, and then we're all going to meet and after that—"

"I saw Harley and Jensen. They'll bring me food. You're fine, Arlo. Have a nice night."

"Yeah, thanks. Strange, though. Something doesn't feel right his evening. Am I just being paranoid?"

"Yes. And shoo. Go on, Arlo. You worked hard today. And I'm an obsessive old bastard. Get out of here!"

Arlo grinned. He lifted his hands. "I'm gone!"

And, at last, he was.

Henry was thrilled. He even began singing Ariel's song from the Disney movie *The Little Mermaid.*

He walked back over to Unknown Mummy #1. "Strange," he said, shaking his head with perplexity as he studied the mummy. "Just who was he? And what brought him here in this state?"

But then he shrugged. He'd found "natural" mummies at other sites—servants who'd stood guard after burial rites and died where they collapsed after the tombs were sealed and they slowly asphyxiated.

Henry walked back over to his desk to dictate notes into a recorder for the exhibit, which would one day be based on this project. "The earliest Egyptians buried their dead in small pits in the desert sand. The sand and the heat naturally 'mummified' the dead. Later, to prevent animals from digging up the bodies, they resorted to creating coffins. Coffins kept out animals, but they didn't allow for the natural mummification that had been occurring when the bodies had gone straight into the sand. So the Egyptians began to learn the art of embalming. They quickly discovered that the 'wet' parts of the body needed to be removed. That included the heart and lungs, brain and liver and other organs. These were stored in canopic jars, where they were guarded, just as the body was guarded, so the dead were protected and ready as they entered into the afterlife. The process became forty days of drying with natron, a form of salt. Of course, a body was never simply dried. It was adorned with oils at various stages and also treated with religious rites."

Henry stopped speaking; he thought he'd heard something moving in the preparation tent. That was odd. The local guards and the staff who worked for Alchemy were weary and bored with the findings. Egyptians had been unearthing mummies forever and ever, and even the security force of Americans and Brits was more bored by the ancient than intrigued. Most of them had worked around the world. They were, in a word, jaded—and far more interested in the pay scale than the work itself.

He looked around the tent. Nothing. Everything as it had been. Crates and boxes and mummies and treasures!

He shook his head, impatient with himself. He was incredibly lucky to have this time alone in the preparation tent. He'd been the one to do the research and the calculations; he'd been the one who'd garnered the sponsorship that had provided the money for this expedition. His papers had raised significant interest. It was—yes, indeed—his baby.

But eventually Dr. Arlo Hampton would want his time here, his chance to study these mummies, these treasures. So would Yolanda Akeem, their liaison with the Department of Antiquities. Then, of course, there was Ned Richter…and his wife. He'd bet that Richter couldn't care less if he got any time with the mummies and ancient treasures or not. Richter was there to guard Alchemy's interests and, Henry suspected, to ensure that they looked as if they were being incredibly magnanimous to the Egyptian government. After all, Alchemy financed these expeditions, he was almost certain, for tax breaks—and the media attention and promotion they provided.

Fine. The excavation was a great success. And this was *his* time. His time alone with all his treasures!

He started to go back to his work, but he could've sworn he'd seen movement from the corner of his eye.

He stood up and walked around.

Nothing.

Henry sat back down and continued his recording. "Ancient Egypt—"

There *was* something behind him!

He tried to spin about.

And he saw nothing but binding, the linen binding

that had been used on the ancient dead, saw it wrapped around fingers and a hand, saw the fingers and the hand circle his neck and—

Fingers, like wire, clutching his throat, so powerful, so strong...

He fought their hold. Wriggled and squirmed. He tried to rise; he couldn't. The pain was terrible. The world began to blacken before him; little dots of light exploded in the darkness. And all he could think was that—

The mummy!

The mummy had risen to kill him!

It was impossible. Impossible. Impossible...

He was a scientist. Rational. He didn't believe.

He was a scientist...

And as the last electrons exploded against the stygian pit of his dying mind, he couldn't help but think...

He was a scientist.

Being killed by an ancient Egyptian mummy.

It didn't make sense. It wasn't right.

Chapter One

One Year Later
The New Museum of Antiquity
New York City, New York

The moon that shone down through the skylights in the temple region of the museum created a stunning vision. Opalescent light shimmered on the marble and made it appear that the ribbon of "Nile" river by the temple was created of crystal and glass. The lights in the area were dim, designed to look as if they were burning torches set along the walls.

The exhibit in the New Museum of Antiquity was impressive—even to Harley, despite all the time she'd spent in the real Sahara. In designing this space, the organizers had also borrowed heavily from another famous NYC museum, all to the benefit of the Egyptian displays. Harley felt a sudden breeze from an air-conditioning vent, and she shivered.

"Mummy thing getting to you, huh?"

"Pardon?" Harley turned quickly to see the speaker. The words had been teasing; they'd also been spoken in a pleasantly deep, masculine voice.

The voice aroused a strange memory she couldn't

quite reach—and seemed to whisper to something inside her, far beneath her skin.

She hadn't seen the speaker before, despite the fact
that his voice seemed oddly familiar. Here, on opening night, she should've known most of the invited
crowd. But she didn't know him, and—as her chosen field of criminology had taught her—she studied
anyone she didn't recognize in a situation such as this
evening's event.

A soiree to celebrate the exhibition. This was opening night for the traveling exhibit that would, in the
end, return to Egypt, where the precious artifacts of
that country would then remain. But tonight they celebrated the very first time the exhibit had been seen! It
would open to the public in the morning. It had, quite
properly, been named in honor of Henry—the Henry
Tomlinson Collection of Egyptian Culture and Art.

There would be toasts in his honor, of course.

This phenomenal display would not have been possible without him.

But Henry was gone, as much a part of history as
his treasures.

She sensed that this man—with his deep, somehow
familiar voice—was connected to Henry.

She definitely hadn't seen him before.

He wasn't the kind of man you forgot.

He was tall—well over six feet, she thought. Because she'd recently taken identification classes that
taught criminologists to look for details to include in
descriptions, she also noted that not only was he about
six foot three, but he had excellent posture. Nicely mus-
cled, too. She had no doubt that he was the kind of man
who spent time in a gym, not to create impressive abs,

but to train the complex human machine that was his most important tool.

How could she be so sure of this? she asked herself. And yet she was.

He wore a casual suit, no jewelry. He was freshly shaven, and kept his dark hair cropped close to his head.

Someone's bodyguard?

Beneath the glimmer of the moon that showed through the skylights, she couldn't quite ascertain the color of his eyes. She had a feeling they were light, despite the darkness of his hair.

Thirty-three to thirty-six years old, she estimated. Carefully nondescript clothing—dark blue suit, dark blue shirt, pin-striped tie in shades of blue and black. Sunglasses resting on head.

He moved closer to her; she was certain he'd been doing the same kind of study on her that she'd nearly completed on him.

No, she'd never seen him before, but she *had* heard his voice.

"Sorry. I didn't mean to interrupt. You're not afraid of mummies, right?" he asked again, his expression quizzical.

"No, not at all," she assured him. "Ah, well, that's a bit of a lie. I might be afraid of some of the bacteria that can be found in old tombs, but as for the mummies themselves…no. My dad was a cop, a very good one. He taught me to fear the living, not the dead."

"Sounds like a bright man," he said. He stepped toward her, offering his hand. "Micah. Micah Fox."

She shook his hand. "Harley Frasier. How do you do? And pardon me, but who are you? Do I know you?"

He smiled. "Yes, and no. I'm an old student of Dr. Tomlinson's," he said. "I was at Brown when he was teaching there. About twelve years ago, I was lucky enough to join him on one of his expeditions. Back then, he was looking for the tomb of a princess from the Old Kingdom, Fifth Dynasty." He paused, still smiling, and shrugged. "He found her, too—right now she's in one of the display cases in a room not far from here, near the temple." He stopped, studying her again, and asked, "Are you surprised by that?"

"No, no, I'm not. You don't look like an Egyptologist," Harley said. "Sorry! It's not that Egyptologists look a certain way. I just—"

"It's okay. I'm not an Egyptologist," he told her. "I meant is it surprising that he found his princess? No, of course not. Henry was the best. But even though I began in archeology, I changed my major. I'm with the government now."

"FBI?" Harley guessed.

He nodded.

"Something seems to be coming back. I'm not sure what," she said. "I know your voice, but I don't know *you*. I mean—"

"Yes, you know my voice. I guess I should start over. I called you soon after the incident when you were staying in Rome. Your group was shipped from place to place, and we were trying to get a handle on what happened. I'm the Fox from those phone calls. Special Agent Micah Fox—though I admit, I was working on my own, and not as assigned by the bureau. And I apologize, because I do know a lot about you, although it wasn't appropriate to bring that up at the time. You're Craig Frasier's first cousin, and Craig and I have actually worked together. Of course, we're in different offices now. Naturally, you've met a number of the men and women with the New York office. Craig told me you finished grad school, and you're deciding what to do with all your education—join up with NYPD's finest, remain with the private agency employing you now, or go into a federal agency. But tonight, you're here for the same reason I am, honoring our old professor. For one summer, you were an unofficial Egyptologist. And, as I just explained, you recognize my voice because we spoke on the phone. I'm Criminal Division, FBI. Right now, I'm assigned down in DC. I've taken some leave to be here."

"I...see," she said.

Did she?

No, not really.

Wait. Fox—yes, that was the name of the man she'd spoken with about Henry Tomlinson, just once, what now seemed like a lifetime ago.

These days, that time was mostly a blur. Maybe because she didn't *want* to think of it. But she couldn't stop her mind from rushing back to the night they'd returned to the camp, laughing and loaded down with food and drink for their professor, only to find him on the floor, along with the broken coffin and the "screaming" mummy. He'd been garroted by his own belt, eyes open and bulging, throat blackened and bruised, a swatch of ancient linen wrapped around it.

There'd been an immediate outcry. Security was convinced that no one from outside had been anywhere near the expedition tents; they kept a tight perimeter around the work area, which included the tents that had been set up for the staff. Egyptian police had come out, ready to help with the investigation.

Then, all hell had broken loose. The computer had picked up more chatter. And word had come that the fledgling, unaffiliated militant group calling themselves The Ancient Guard was bearing down on the expedition. Perhaps they intended to steal the artifacts to finance their cause. Not an uncommon scenario... It meant that everyone and everything needed to go as quickly as possible. Government forces were being sent out, but no one wanted scientists from around the world caught up in an exchange of gunfire.

Security forces from Alchemy, along with the Egyptian police, did their best to preserve what they could from the expedition, as well as the body of Henry Tomlinson so they could discover the circumstances of his death.

Much was lost. But at least no one else was killed. The final inquiry, conducted by the Egyptian police and the Alchemy security force, concluded that the brilliant archeologist Dr. Henry Tomlinson had driven himself mad and committed suicide. According to their conclusions, he believed a mummy had come to life with the intention of murdering him... It was suspected that some unknown bacteria had caused the temporary fit of insanity, and everything from the expedition would be scrutinized using proper precautions.

Harley had fought the verdict—vociferously. She was a criminology student; she knew what should have been done and a lot of it wasn't. Pretty much nothing had been done, really, not as far as a crime scene examination went.

Not in her opinion, anyway.

How many men committed suicide with their own belts in such a manner? She sure as hell hadn't seen or read about any. And she was *studying* criminology.

Nope, never heard of it!

Her friends backed her up, at first. And then, one by one, it seemed, they all decided that the poor professor—so caught up in his love and enthusiasm for his work—had gone mad, even if only temporarily. No one could find a motive for murdering him. Henry Tomlinson had been respected and dearly loved by everyone. No one could find a clue.

The police assigned to them had been incompetent, to Harley's mind. Authorities in Egypt and in the United States hadn't done enough.

And the Alchemy people…

They wanted it to be a suicide. They didn't want to deal with a murder. They accepted the verdict without a whimper.

They were so sorry and sad, they'd claimed, and in hindsight, they could see so many mistakes.

They should've known to be more careful!

Henry should've known to be more careful!

But in fact, they said, the professor's enthusiasm for the project had caused them all to bypass modern safety regulations that might have kept him alive.

A great company line, Harley thought in disgust.

And what was the matter with her? They might all have been killed by a crazy insurgent group that hadn't defined exactly what it was fighting for or against. It was a miracle that they'd gotten out, that they were all alive.

Well, most of them. And Henry, poor Henry, he'd done himself in—according to the authorities and to

Alchemy, who went on to say that now they'd never completely understand the biology of what had gone on. They weren't allowed back on the site; the Egyptian government had stamped a foot down hard.

And that night...

First, they were shuffled to Cairo, then, almost immediately—on the orders of the Egyptian authorities and the US State Department—they were put on planes to Rome, and from Rome they were flown to New York City.

But, thinking back, Harley recalled that it was while she'd been staying at the little Italian hotel near the Spanish Steps that she'd spoken with this man. Fox. He'd wanted to know whatever she knew about the situation, and she'd told him everything, adding that she didn't believe a word of the official explanation.

There was no way Henry had killed himself.

Special Agent Fox had seemed to accept her version, but apparently he'd been just as stonewalled as she had.

Like her, he'd been forced to realize in the end that no one was going to believe him. Or her.

And even if the authorities had believed him, they didn't care enough to make a killer pay!

Here, tonight, for the first time in a year, everything about that horrible occasion was suddenly coming back.

Tonight was about honoring Henry Tomlinson. This would be an event during which people would shake their heads sadly, missing the professor who'd done so much, declaring it tragic that he'd lost his mind because of what he'd loved so deeply.

"Ms. Frasier?"

She blinked, staring at the man in front of her, wondering how long she'd been lost in her own thoughts.

In a way, she did know him. They'd just never met in person. She'd left the Sahara before he reached it. Then she'd been flown out of Cairo, and soon after that she was back in New York.

"I'm sorry!" she said softly.

He shook his head. "Hey, it's all right. I know you really cared, and that you tried to do something. It must have been hard to maintain your own belief that he'd been murdered when everyone else was telling you otherwise," Micah Fox said.

It had been and still was. "Oh, don't you know?" she muttered. "'Henry went crazy. Bacteria in the wrappings. He just *had* to dig in before proper precautions were taken. It's so tragic—don't make it worse by rehashing every little thing!'"

Her tone, she knew, was heavy with sarcasm.

They were alone in the temple area—or so she believed. Still, she looked around and repeated, "I'm sorry. I tried... I do believe he was murdered. They did find bacteria, but not enough. Henry was murdered. And I couldn't do a damned thing to prove it."

Micah nodded at her. She liked his face. Hard-jawed, somewhat sharp-boned. His eyes, she saw now, were actually blue—sky blue—and they seemed to see a great deal.

"Remember, I was a student of his, too. And now I'm an FBI agent. And I couldn't do anything, either. You have nothing to be sorry for." He paused. "I should explain. I knew about you through Craig, of course. And also through Henry. We kept in touch when we could—he'd let me know what was up, what was going on. I went into law enforcement, but I still love Egyptology. Henry thought the world of you." He shook his head. "I can only imagine what it was like that last night. I hope you're okay now. Time…heals, so they say."

"So they say."

"It heals when you're at peace with the past."

"And I'm not," she said grimly, and added, "And neither are you."

"No. Anyway, I'd like to find out about the last time you saw him. If you don't mind."

"There won't be a chance tonight," she said.

"I know. At a later date."

Harley nodded. "I'll be happy to speak with you. I'm not sure what I can tell you, though."

"You found him."

"Yes."

"I'd just like you to go over it with me. I realize it's painful, but…"

"The verdict was ridiculous! You know what the ME said! That he killed himself."

"An Egyptian ME, who wanted out of there as quickly as possible, with armed insurrectionists about to attack the place."

True!

But then…

"The company, Alchemy, brought in a medical examiner, too. He agreed with the Egyptian ME's findings."

"I'm sure that all happened in about two minutes in Cairo or Rome. And as soon as they made their decision, Henry was shot through with preservatives and packed into a box. So anything that could be con-

strued as evidence was compromised. I could be way
off base. *We* could be way off base. Thing is, I'd feel
better if we could talk."

"Yes, of course," she said.

Of course?

She didn't want to remember that night!

And yet, here was someone—someone in law enforcement—who agreed with her, the only person who
did. Like her, Fox believed there was a truth out there
that everyone else had denied.

They looked at each other awkwardly for a moment.

"Well, a pleasure to meet you in person. I guess
I'm going to head over to the party area," Micah said.
His voice softened. "I didn't mean to interrupt you.
You might want more time here. On your own. By
the way, as I said, I really do know your cousin fairly
well. We worked together years ago on a case in DC.
He's a great guy."

"Yes. Craig's great," Harley agreed.

She sensed that he wanted to say more.

Like maybe when or where they could meet again?
But he didn't speak. They weren't alone anymore.

Jensen Morrow came striding through the temple
area. He apparently saw Harley, but not Micah Fox,
probably because he stood in the shadow of a carved
obelisk.

"I knew I'd find you here!" Jensen told Harley, heading toward her for a huge hug.

He'd written his thesis, gotten his graduate degree
and taken a job here as an assistant curator, making use
of his doctorate in Egyptology. He'd been her friend
through her suspicions, her anger, her demands—and

her final defeat, when she'd realized that nothing was going to be done.

No one was ever going to make her believe that Henry Tomlinson had been convinced that a mummy was attacking him—while strangling himself with his own belt.

Jensen, she was certain, had just given up. He'd been told the lie so many times that to him, it had become truth.

Harley accepted Jensen's hug; she still cared about him. When they'd first met, they'd hit it off as friends. They might have become more at one time; he was fun, energetic and thoughtful, not to mention tall, dark and handsome. But everything had changed the night Henry Tomlinson died.

Even though she didn't see the friends she'd made in Egypt very often—they were all busy working, getting on with their lives—they had all stayed friends. They were, in fact, oddly close; they had shared the experience of the dig, Henry Tomlinson's death and the escape from the desert under dire circumstances in the middle of the night. All of that meant they had an emotional bond few people shared.

And yet it was a closeness stained with the loss of the man they'd all adored. Stained, too, by the way they'd fled on the very night he died, swept up in a reign of terror.

She'd gone on to finish her own graduate work, head bent to her studies, and had taken part-time work with a prestigious investigation firm in the city so that she could still take classes when she chose while deciding what path to take for her future. It felt right, for the time being. But she had to make some real decisions soon.

And yet, even as she'd worked toward her educational and career goals, she had felt that she was waiting. A temporary post—with flexible hours!—was all she'd been willing to accept at the moment.

"They're about to start," Jensen said, pulling away from her to study her face. That was when he rather awkwardly noticed there was someone else in the temple exhibit.

He offered Micah Fox a hand. "I'm sorry. How rude. I didn't see you. I'm Jensen Morrow."

"Micah Fox," the other man returned. "And actually, we've spoken. Over the phone."

"Oh! Hey, that was you?" Jensen said. "Wow. Was I vague when I talked to you? Or worse, rude? If I was, I didn't mean to be. It's just that...well, you had to be there that night. We found Henry—or, I should say, Harley found Henry—and by the time the medical examiner arrived, they were screaming that the insurgents were a few miles out and we had to break camp ASAP! I know Harley and I were going crazy with concern and disbelief and...well...hey," he finished lamely.

"There wasn't anything you could have done to change the situation," Micah said.

"Well, you're FBI, right? I guess if you couldn't prove anything different from what was said or get anything done. Harley and I, who had no law enforcement power, couldn't have done more than complain and question. Which we did. Who knows? The thing is—thing that got me, anyway—we weren't in a closed or confined space. I mean if bacteria were going to get him, you might've thought someone else would've had a reaction or... Anyway, had you been assigned to the case—officially? The FBI works in Egypt? Or does it?"

"The FBI works all over the world, as necessary," Micah replied. "But… I was there because of Henry."

"Special Agent Fox was another of Henry's grad students, but years ago," Harley quickly explained.

"Ah," Jensen murmured. That was obviously enough of an explanation. "I guess you were crazy about him, too."

"I was. Brilliant man. Horrible circumstances."

Jensen glanced at Harley. "I think we were the last people who saw him. Alive, I mean. Harley was trying to get him to come out with us. But you knew him. There was no way he was going to leave his work that night."

"No, Henry wouldn't want to leave his work." He paused, clearing his throat. "Well, I think they must be about ready to start."

"Let's go." Harley slid her fingers into Jensen's and they left, nodding to Micah. It was ludicrous, but she was suddenly afraid to be too close to the man. He not only projected strength—he was someone warm when the world had been cold. Too confident, too attractive…

She could easily give in to her feelings of sadness and loss and even anger on a night like this. With a man like this.

She was aware of Micah watching them leave.

And she wondered what he was thinking.

HARLEY FRASIER, CRAIG'S COUSIN, was certainly a beautiful young woman, Micah thought, watching her leave, hand in hand with Jensen Morrow. He'd been studying her intently for some time before he'd spoken with her. It was evident that she had really cared about Henry. And he knew how Henry had felt about her.

According to Craig, she had wonderful parents and a great older brother, living grandparents, all kinds of family life. Micah's parents had been lost in a bridge accident when he was a child; his aunt had raised him. Auntie Jane. He loved her and she was a talented and compassionate woman. But she was it as far as family went. He had no siblings, no cousins—no one else anywhere that he knew about. His family went far back in Virginia history; it had simply winnowed down to him and Jane.

His father had been FBI. People had feared the dangers of his job. They'd never imagined that he might die young because of a bridge collapse.

Henry Tomlinson had treated him like a son or grandson. He'd shared his enthusiasm for Egyptology with Micah. Henry had a family he adored. He hadn't married, but he had a loving niece and nephew-in-law, and he was crazy about their kids.

He'd send Micah pictures of an unusual canopic jar right alongside ones of the kids with their new puppy. That was Henry.

Micah followed the pair who'd just left, wondering if he was indulging himself in an exercise of futility. Was the truth about Henry Tomlinson's death ever going to be uncovered? Henry had been murdered, which was terrible enough, but it had happened on a night when both the Egyptian government and the US Department of State had been determined to get all the workers away from the site and out of the country. The group who'd planned the attack had called themselves The Ancient Guard.

Apparently, they hadn't believed that Alchemy intended that the treasures they'd found would merely go on loan to the United States and other countries—and that they'd remain Egyptian property. Maybe they hadn't cared. And maybe, like most militant groups, what The Ancient Guard wanted, religious and political ideology aside, was a chance to fight and stave off frustration. And probably steal the treasures to finance their fighting.

They'd either been beaten back or dissipated quickly when met with armed resistance.

Micah had gone to Cairo to investigate Henry's death on an unofficial basis, and then to Rome, where the Alchemy crew had briefly stayed. Their communication had been by phone—he'd been a day behind each time everyone had moved on. And by the time he'd reached the States, it had all been too long.

Henry had been cremated, just as he'd instructed his niece to arrange in the event of his death. Then, of course, it was too late to bring in any experts.

But Henry had never suspected that he might be murdered.

And why would he?

Why the hell kill an academic like Henry? The man had never wanted or kept anything for himself—he'd never tried to slip away with even the smallest, most insignificant artifact. His work had always been about sharing treasures with the world.

Tonight... Well, tonight, Micah could watch. He could see the people who'd been close to Henry in his last days.

The grand foyer of the museum had been chosen for the site of the private gala opening. The center monument here was a massive replica of a temple from Mesopotamia that sat in the center of a skylit rotunda. The museum was beautiful, and just down the street from its larger cousin, the Metropolitan. Many design ideas that worked well in the first had been used in this newer museum. The offices were deep in the basement, for the most part. The museum was dedicated to the ancient world; it was divided into sections that concentrated on the earliest humans to the rich, ancient civilizations of Greece, Egypt, Persia, Mesopotamia and more.

The exhibition hall that would open to the public in the morning was an admirable addition to the museum. Exhibits didn't stay forever, but the hall itself would continue to thrive because of the work of Henry and other archeologists and scholars; right now, however, it was all about Henry.

Men and women in pairs and groups stood around the room, chatting, while waiters and waitresses in white-and-black attire moved about with trays of hors d'oeuvres and flutes of champagne.

Many of those invited were here because they were sponsoring patrons of the museum. There were also a number of politicians, including the mayor.

None of them interested Micah.

He scanned the crowd, taking note of those he did find intriguing.

Arlo Hampton, young, pleasant, eager. Tall and slim, but handsomely boyish-looking in a suit, speaking with an Egyptian dignitary. Ned Richter and his wife, Vivian. He so robust, she so tiny, both smiling, standing close, chatting with the mayor. And there—between an aging Broadway director and his latest ingénue—Belinda Gray, sans her fiancé, who was still serving in the military. He saw Roger Eastman, wiry and lean, wearing thick-lensed glasses, talking with his hands as he loudly discussed a technical innovation for dealing with the security of priceless historic objects. Across the room, in the midst of a few young female museum apprentices, was Joe Rosello. Joe seemed electrically energetic; he was a square-shouldered guy who could've been a fullback. He had a full head of curly dark hair and a very white smile.

Micah had done research on everyone involved with the last stages of the dig. Every one of the workers who'd had access to the tent. It hadn't been easy finding out about the Egyptian workers. Since they weren't archeologists or preservation experts, they hadn't been allowed into the inner sanctum of the camp, where the preparation tent was located. Still, he'd done his best. But everything in him screamed that the guilty party was not Egyptian, but someone among those who should have loved and honored Henry.

Why? he asked himself again. Why the hell would anyone kill Henry? If he could come up with a *why...*

"Micah?"

He turned. He hadn't expected to know many people here tonight. His name had been softly voiced by one of the few people he did know, and he knew her fairly well.

Simone Bixby, Henry Tomlinson's niece.

Simone was in her midthirties, a sandy-haired woman who looked eternally like a girl. She was small and slim and wide-eyed. She was accompanied by her husband, Jerry, a banker, who was equally slim and wide-eyed.

Micah greeted them both.

"Thank you for coming. And thank you for caring so much," Simone said. "It's still so hard to accept what they say."

"Yes, it is," Micah agreed.

"But tonight," Jerry said brightly, "tonight we honor his body of work."

"Yes. An incredible body of work," Micah said. "How are the girls?"

"Getting big!" Simone answered. "Ten, eight and five now."

He nodded. "I've seen pictures. They're beautiful."

"They are. Thank you. They loved their uncle Henry, too," Simone said.

"We all miss him."

"Oh, look—there's Arlo Hampton," Jerry said. "Micah, we'll talk later? Simone, we need to find out what he wants us to do when he speaks."

"Excuse us," Simone said.

"Of course!" Micah told them. They moved on.

He continued to survey the room.

Hail, hail, the gang's all here. Grad students. Administration staff. Egyptologists. City officials. Museum people. And there…

An exotic woman with dark skin and almost inky black hair was speaking with Simone and her family. Arlo stood beside them.

Yolanda Akeem. They'd met briefly—very briefly—in Cairo. She was the Egyptian liaison with the Department of Antiquities. Naturally, she'd be here tonight.

She saw him looking at her. She elegantly lifted her glass a few inches in acknowledgment.

She'd given him whatever information she'd had in Cairo; it hadn't been much. A two-second autopsy report and a lecture on the dangers of the Middle East. He didn't listen to much of it. Henry's body was gone by then and the members of the expedition had been shuttled off. He'd been ready to follow them as quickly as possible when they'd been in Egypt—and through their escape from the trouble that had befallen the expedition that night.

Tonight, they were all here.

And there was Harley Frasier. She had a smile on her face as she spoke with Gordon Vincent, director at large for the museum. Her smile was forced. Jensen was with her, smiling and chatting, as well. He seemed to be putting a little too much effort into being charming.

Which didn't seem necessary, since he was already employed by the museum.

Harley didn't; she worked for Fillmore Investigations, a large security and investigation company that served the civilian market, but was known for its close affiliation with the New York City PD and other law enforcement agencies. The founder of the company, Edward Fillmore, had barely survived a kidnap-for-ransom scheme as a child. He had founded his company on the premise that all agencies, public or private, should work together for the benefit of victims. Since Micah's job with the FBI had come about because of similar circumstances, he liked the man without even knowing him. Micah was pleased that Harley Frasier had chosen such a reputable company. None of his business, of course. But…

He'd felt something for her, just from hearing her voice over the phone a year ago.

And now…he'd seen her.

Anyone awake and breathing would find her attractive and charming.

He was certainly charmed by her and impressed by her—and so much more.

Even though he hardly knew her…

He forced himself to look away from Harley and objectively observe the other people in the room.

He was standing back, watching, when he became aware that a friend had arrived.

"I have to admit I was definitely expecting you to be here," Craig Frasier told him.

Micah smiled without glancing over. "And I guess I'm not surprised that you're here," he said.

"I can't let you get into too much trouble," Craig murmured.

"I'm just here to honor an old friend," Micah said.

"Like hell." Craig smiled grimly, studying the crowd milling in the foyer. "But I don't know what you think you can discover at this late date."

Micah turned to face Craig at last, a rueful half smile on his face. "Right. Well, it would help if someone suddenly had a guilt attack and admitted going crazy—from the bacteria in the wrappings, of course—and murdering Henry."

"Not going to happen."

"I know."

"So?"

"Don't worry. I'm not going to harass your cousin," Micah said.

"I'm not worried. I think you two can actually do each other some good it you get a chance to really talk. Maybe you can figure something out, late as it might be. There was so much done so quickly and so politically. State Department, international bull. A cover-up. Yeah, it'll be good for the two of you to talk."

"You say that as if you doubt the official line, too," Micah said quietly.

"Because I do. I believe it was a cover-up."

"Not by the government," Micah said.

"By?"

Micah looked at him and said, "By Alchemy."

Craig didn't get a chance to respond.

Arlo Hampton took the microphone on a small portable dais set in the center of the foyer. He cleared his throat, then said, "Ladies and gentlemen, friends of the museum, friends of science and exploration, and friends of the City of New York!"

It took a moment for everyone to stop talking and start listening. Someone tapped a champagne flute with a fork or spoon. Then the room fell silent.

"We welcome you to our amazing new exhibit, brought to us through the genius of the man—the brilliant, kind, ever-giving man—whose name will now grace our museum walls, Dr. Henry Tomlinson. Those who knew Henry loved him. He was a scholar, but he was also a very human man who loved his family and friends. No one knew Egyptology the way Henry did…"

A sudden gasp from the crowd silenced him. Everyone turned.

Someone had come up from the basement steps, and was now staggering through the crowd.

Someone grotesquely dressed up in a mummy's linen bindings, staggering out as if acting in a very bad mummy movie.

A performance for the evening?

No.

Because Arlo grunted an angry "Excuse me!" and exited the dais, walking toward the "mummy" now careening toward him.

"What the hell?" Micah and Craig were close enough to hear Arlo's words. "Richter, is that you? You idiot! Is that you?"

It wasn't Richter; Micah knew that right away. Richter was far too big a man to be the slight, lean person now dressed up.

Or at least Ned Richter was!

Micah burst forward, phone out and in his hand. As he neared the mummy, he was already dialing 9-1-1.

"Get those bindings off her! Get them off her fast!" he commanded.

The mummy collapsed.

Micah barely managed to catch the wrapped body sagging to the floor.

As quickly as he could, he began to remove the wrappings.

He heard the sound of a siren.

Then Vivian Richter looked up at him, shuddered and closed her eyes.

The wrappings, Micah knew, had been doused in some kind of poison.

Chapter Two

Chaos reigned.

Harley was stunned and horrified that Vivian Richter was so badly hurt—so close to death.

She was wrapped tightly. The outer wrappings were decayed and falling apart; they'd come from a historic mummy. The inner wrappings were contemporary linen, the kind the museum used in its demonstrations, made to look like the real deal.

Vivian was gasping and crying, completely incoherent. One woman in the room was a doctor—a podiatrist, but hey, she'd been to medical school. She was kneeling by Vivian, calling the shots, talking on the phone to the med techs who were on their way.

Special Agent Fox had already taken control of the room. No one was to leave; they were all in a lockdown.

She was incredibly glad that Craig was there. And, of course, he was with his girlfriend or fiancée—Harley wasn't sure what Craig and Kieran called each other, but she *was* sure they were together for life. Kieran was standing near Harley, ready to comfort her, as the slightly older and very protective almost cousin-in-law. Harley appreciated that, even though she didn't really need it. She worked with criminals all the time, as well as people who weren't so bad but still wound up in the criminal justice system. She was calm and stoic; Micah and Craig were questioning people, grouping them, speaking to them, both digging for answers and assuring them all that they were safe.

"She's going to die! She's going to die!" Simone Bixby, Henry Tomlinson's niece, cried out. Harley saw that Micah Fox hurried over to her, placed a comforting arm around her shoulders and led her to a chair.

By then, of course, museum security had arrived. So had the police—New York City and state police.

People were talking everywhere. Micah and Craig had herded everyone into groups, depending on their relationship to the museum. Some were employees of the museum; some were special guests. The people who'd been on the expedition were in a corner. Harley was with Belinda Gray, Joe Rosello, Roger Eastman and Jensen Morrow, as well as the Alchemy Egyptologist, Arlo Hampton.

Ned Richter was crouched on the floor, at his wife's side.

All of this seemed to go on for a long time, yet it was a matter of minutes before more sirens screamed in the night and the EMTs were rushing in. Ned Richter was allowed to go with his wife; Arlo Hampton and others more closely associated with the exhibit were now gathered together in a new group. Guests who'd only recently made it through the doors were questioned and cleared.

Anyone who had anything to do with prep for the evening was in another group; every single person would be questioned before being permitted to leave for the night.

Officers and crime scene techs were crowding through the museum, heading to the Amenmose section—and to the staff office and prep chambers beyond.

"Too bad we couldn't continue the celebration," Joe said, hands locked behind his back, a look of disappointment on his face. "What a waste of great food and wine."

"Joe! What's the matter with you?" Belinda chastised.

"Come on! Vivian Richter's a drama queen," Joe said.

"She might die," Roger said very softly.

"You mark my words. She will not die," Joe insisted.

"They're saying it's poison," Roger pointed out. "Some kind of poison on the wrappings."

"She's going to be very, very sick," Jensen said. "Those wrappings decaying and falling all around her... Who the hell knows where they came from—or what might be on them?"

"Or if something was *put* on them," Roger said. "That's how she would have been poisoned."

They were all silent for a minute.

"And then dead—like Henry Tomlinson," Belinda said.

Again, they were silent.

"Great. But at least now, maybe someone besides me will start fighting to figure out what happened to Henry," Harley said quietly.

She'd actually discovered that night that someone *was* on her side. The agent with the great voice. Craig's friend. Micah Fox.

"Okay, okay," Belinda said. "I didn't push it a lot at

the time. I mean, it didn't make any difference, did it? The cause of death—two medical examiners said—was the fact that bacteria made him crazy and he killed himself."

The reaction to her comment was yet another bout of silence.

"What were we going to do?" Belinda wailed. "We had no power. Insurgents were bearing down on the camp, and everyone wanted us out! So, what *could* we do? Henry was dead," Belinda said.

"And back then, none of us believed he killed himself," Jensen said at last.

"But we all let it go." Roger sounded sorrowful as he spoke. "Except Harley, and we all kind of shut her down," he added apologetically. "But, seriously, what were we going to do? There were some whacked-out insurrectionists coming our way. I'm sorry, but I've got to admit I didn't want to die. I really didn't care if anyone was collecting evidence properly—all I wanted was out of there! And in the end, I guess we bought into the official—" he made air quotes with his fingers "—version. It was just easier and—"

"Ms. Frasier!"

Harley was being summoned. She saw that it was the plainclothes detective who had apparently been assigned to the case. He was lean and hard-looking; his partner was broader and had almost a baby face and a great smile. They were McGrady and Rydell, Rydell being the guy with the smile.

She wasn't going anywhere alone. She was never sure how Craig could home in on her problems so quickly, and tonight he was with Micah Fox, the agent who had called her before—and approached her at the beginning of the evening. What if she *had* talked to him when he'd wanted to?

Could tonight's disaster have been avoided?

Did it have anything to do with what had happened before?

She was led into one of the museum offices that had been taken over by the police. She felt, rather than saw, her cousin Craig and the enigmatic Micah Fox come in.

They didn't sit; they took up stances behind her.

McGrady took the seat behind the desk and asked her sternly, "Ms. Frasier, what exactly is your association with the museum, the expedition—and the injured woman?"

"I was on the expedition. I don't really have an association with Vivian. It's not like we have coffee or hang around together and do girls' night," Harley said. "Vivian is married to Ned Richter, the CEO of Alchemy. Alchemy financed the expedition. Alchemy is the largest sponsor for this exhibition. We were all pretty close in the Sahara—not that we had much choice."

"So you did know her well!"

"I didn't say I knew her well. We were…colleagues."

"But you like mummies, right? All things ancient Egyptian?" McGrady asked.

"Yes, of course. I find the culture fascinating."

"And it would be a great prank to attack someone and lace her up in poisoned linen. Like a mummy?"

"What?" Harley exploded.

McGrady leaned forward, wagging a pencil at her. "You were the one who discovered Henry Tomlinson—dead. Correct?"

Harley had never thought of herself as particularly

strong, but his words, coming out like an accusation, were too much.

She heard a guttural exclamation from behind her. Craig or Micah Fox, she wasn't sure which.

But it didn't matter. She could—and would—fend for herself. She leaned forward, too.

"Yes. I found Henry. A beloved friend and mentor. I found him, and I raised an outcry you wouldn't believe. And no one in a position of power or authority gave a damn. First, it was oh, the insurgents were coming! Saving our lives was more important—and yes, of course, that was true—than learning the truth about the death of a good man. I could buy that! It's an obvious decision. But then, no decent autopsy, and his niece, bereft, had him cremated. And now you're asking me about Henry—and about Vivian Richter. You have nerve. I was here tonight in honor of Henry. I didn't see the exhibit before tonight. I haven't been associated with Alchemy since we returned. I suggest you speak with the people who *were* involved there and worked on the exhibit."

McGrady actually sat back.

Everyone in the room was silent.

Then Harley thought she heard a softly spoken "Bravo."

McGrady cleared his throat. "Sorry, Ms. Frasier, but you do realize that Vivian Richter is dangerously close to... Well, we might have a murder on our hands."

"You *do* have a murder on your hands. Dr. Henry Tomlinson was murdered. Now we have to pray that Vivian comes out of this, but still, you've got a killer here. Do you have anything more to ask me?" Harley demanded. They did need to hope and pray for Vivian, but by now, surely they had to recognize the truth of what had happened to Henry!

"Did you see Vivian this evening?"

"No."

"But you arrived early, didn't you?"

"Only by a few minutes. I walked out to the temple area."

"Which is off-limits until after the exhibit officially opens tomorrow."

"I was allowed to go back there because I'd been on the expedition."

"And you were close to the backstage area where exhibits are prepared?"

"Yes."

"Where Vivian would have been?"

"Possibly."

"But you didn't see her. Who did you see?"

"Just Jensen. Jensen Morrow. He's working here, with the exhibit. This is actually his field of work. I saw Jensen—oh, and Special Agent Fox." She glanced back at him. He and Craig were flanked behind her like a pair of ancient Egyptian god-sentinels. They almost made her smile. Not quite. She couldn't believe that this detective was quizzing her—when she couldn't get any help before, no matter how she'd begged and pleaded!

"Special Agent Fox?" McGrady said.

"I arrived within minutes of Ms. Frasier. I was told she'd just headed for the temple. I wanted to speak to her about the death of Henry Tomlinson. I went straight there. We were speaking when her colleague Jensen Morrow appeared. Exactly as she indicated," Micah Fox said.

McGrady stood up. "Fine. Ms. Frasier, you're free to go."

Harley stood up and glared at him. "I'm delighted to leave. But perhaps first you'd be kind enough to let me know how Vivian's doing. We might not be close, but we were serious associates."

McGrady sighed. "She's holding her own. The doctors are combatting the effects of the poisoning."

"What was the poison?"

"It's an ongoing investigation. That's information we can't give out right now, even if we had it."

"I see. Thank you."

Craig opened the door; she marched out. He and Micah followed. She thought she heard McGrady mutter, "And take your Feds with you."

"Not the usual helpful attitude, at least not in my association with the NYPD," Craig said. "Usually, we have an excellent working rapport."

"Maybe he's resentful because he's not sure what this is yet. It's impossible at this time to say what happened," Micah said.

Harley spun around to stare at him. "What are you, a fool?" she snapped. "We both know—not suspect, but *know*—that Henry Tomlinson was murdered. Then Vivian Richter comes out wrapped in mummy linens, screaming and poisoned with some kind of skin toxin, and we don't know what happened? Obviously, someone tried to kill her!"

Craig grabbed her by the shoulders. "Harley! Stop. Micah's on your side. What are you?" he asked. "A fool?"

She flushed uneasily. They were just outside the door. The nicer cop, the quiet one with the baby face,

Rydell, came out and approached Jensen Morrow. He was next on the block, Harley thought. And how stupid of the cops. Jensen had been with her, away from the camp, when Henry Tomlinson was killed. They just didn't seem bright enough to realize that there was a far bigger picture here. They needed to see it—before someone else died.

But Craig was right. She shouldn't be taking it out on Micah Fox.

Why was she being so hostile, so defensive?

Pushing him away on purpose.

He was trying to help her. He was…

He was a promise she was afraid to accept. He claimed he wanted the truth, and he seemed to have all the assets needed to get at that truth. He was too damned good to be true, and she didn't dare depend on someone like that when the very concept of an ally, someone to depend on, was still so…

Foreign to her! He was law enforcement—and on her side. It was good. After all this time, it felt rather amazing.

"Sorry," she murmured.

She'd barely spoken when Kieran Finnegan came hurrying up next to her. "I have a car outside. Come on, I'll get you home."

"But—"

"There's nothing else you can do here tonight, Harley," Micah said.

"Remember, you came to me."

"Yes. And there's nothing else you can do here tonight," he repeated.

Harley stiffened.

"Let's go," Kieran said gently.

So she nodded. "Thank you," she said to Craig and Micah, and then she allowed Kieran to lead her out the door, to the front of the museum.

A light-colored sedan was waiting, just as Kieran had promised. Kieran wasn't driving; Harley assumed the driver was FBI and that Micah or Craig had made the arrangements.

Once in the car beside Kieran, Harley regretted the fact that she'd already left. "I should still be there. I should be back with the exhibits. I should see the prep rooms. I was with them on that expedition and I know what we discovered. I saw the tomb when it was opened. And I… Lord, yes, I'm the one who found Henry."

"Logically, there isn't a damned thing you could've done tonight. They won't let anyone back by the exhibits, the prep rooms, the offices—anywhere!—until the crime scene people have gone through it all. Naturally, everyone's hoping that Vivian Richter pulls through. If she does, maybe she'll be able to remember something that will help. For now, well…"

"McGrady is NYPD. He isn't letting Craig and that Agent Fox in on anything."

"They'll get in on it. Trust me. Craig will talk to his director. His director will call the chief of police or the mayor or someone, but they'll get in on it," Kieran said with assurance.

Harley leaned back for a moment, suddenly very tired. She closed her eyes and then opened them again, looking over at Kieran. She liked her cousin's girlfriend. Really liked her. She wasn't sure why they weren't engaged or married yet, but…

Kieran, of course, knew all about what had gone on

during and after the expedition out to the Sahara in the search for Amenmose's tomb. Considering what she did for a living—a psychologist who worked with law enforcement—nothing much surprised her or rattled her. Besides, she'd met Craig during a period when the city was under siege with a spate of diamond heists.

"So tell me—what's your take on this?" Harley asked Kieran. "Who would kill Henry Tomlinson? Or rather, who'd dress up as a mummy to kill him, and then dress Vivian Richter like a mummy to try and kill her?"

"The incidents might not be related," Kieran said.

"Oh, please! Don't tell me Henry wasn't murdered! Don't tell me I want that to be the case because I don't want to believe he went crazy and committed suicide."

"I'm not saying that at all. Here's the thing. You were in the desert, so it had to be someone there. Henry's dead and maybe this would-be killer is playing on that. Or maybe the two are related. The problem is, I don't know anyone involved. It's hard enough to make judgment calls when you've had a chance to speak with people and question them."

"Yeah, yeah, I'm sorry."

"That said…"

"Yes?"

Kieran smiled and shrugged. "You've had as much education as me, if not more."

"Ah, but in different courses! I need more in psychology."

"Specifically in human emotions. Like jealousy."

"Jealousy? As in…someone who wanted to be a famed Egyptologist?"

"Possibly. Some people kill because they're deranged. They're psychotic, or they're sociopaths. Then, of course, you have the usual motives. Love, greed, hatred…jealousy. Think about everyone involved if you're convinced that the two situations are related. The rest of us weren't there. Only you know the dynamics among all the people who were on that expedition."

"I can't imagine anyone who would've wanted Henry dead. I just can't."

"It's not that you can't. It's that you don't want to," Kieran told her.

They'd reached Rector Street and the old warehouse apartment that legally belonged to Harley's uncle, who was mostly out of state now and had generously given the large, rent-controlled space to Harley while she finished her degree and decided on her permanent vocation.

The driver hopped out of the car, opening the door for Harley. Kieran leaned out to say goodbye and thank the man.

"Get on home, get into bed, go to sleep," Kieran said. "Much better to start fresh in the morning."

Harley gave her a quick hug and a peck on the cheek. "Thanks. Thanks for getting me here. But… I'll be back on it in the morning."

Kieran grinned. "We'd expect no less." She leaned back in the car and the driver shut the door. He offered Harley a grave nod, and waited until she was safely at the door to her building.

Harley keyed open the lock and waved to the night clerk on duty at the refurbished twenty-floor building. Then she took the ancient elevator to the tenth floor. It wheezed and moaned, and she wondered if Mr. Otis himself had seen it installed in the building. However, it worked smoothly, and she was soon on her floor and in the spacious area she knew she was incredibly lucky to have in New York City. The building had once housed textile machinery and storage. She had over a thousand square feet with massive wall-length windows that looked out on the city with a special view of Grace Church. Harley knew she was blessed to have this space, and reminded herself to send Uncle Theo another thank-you. A counter separated the kitchen from the dining area and living room, while wrought iron winding stairs led up to the open loft space that was her bedroom. Her mom had told her that the apartment had once been Uncle Theo's bachelor pad, but at the ripe old age of sixty-five, he'd met Helen, the love of his life, and they were happily enjoying the pleasures of Naples, Florida, year round. Helen, a spring chicken of fifty-five, was delighted that Harley was watching over the place, just so they'd have a place to crash when they came up to see friends.

Harley found herself staring out at her view of Grace Church.

Home, bed, sleep.

Impossible.

Henry Tomlinson, an Egyptologist by trade, had loved Grace Church. The church itself dated back over two hundred years, although the current building went back to the 1840s, with new sections added along with the decades. Gothic and beautiful, it was the kind of living history that Henry loved.

She wondered if Vivian Richter was still hanging on. She thought about calling the hospital, but they probably wouldn't give her any information.

Home, bed, sleep.

She could try.

Climbing up the stairs to her bedroom, she quickly changed into a cotton nightshirt and crawled beneath the covers. She realized she hadn't closed the drapes.

She stared out at the facade of Grace Church.

Yes, Henry would have loved a view like this.

What was Henry's niece, Simone, thinking tonight?

And Micah Fox? How had he arranged time off? How had he managed to be there? Would he figure something out?

She prayed for sleep, but her mind kept returning to that time in the Sahara. Being part of the expedition had been such a privilege. She remembered the way they'd all felt when they'd broken through to the tomb. Satima Mahmoud—the pretty Egyptian interpreter who had so enchanted Joe Rosello—had been the first to scream when the workers found the entry.

Of course, Henry Tomlinson was called then. He'd been there to break the seal. They'd all laughed and joked about the curses that came with such finds, about the stupid movies that had been made.

Yes, people had died during other expeditions—as if they *had* been cursed. The Tut story was one example—and yet, by all accounts, there had been scientific explanations for everything that'd happened.

Almost everything, anyway.

And their find...

There hadn't been any curses. Not written curses, at any rate.

But Henry had died. And Henry had broken the seal...

No mummy curse had gotten to them; someone had

killed Henry. And that someone had gotten away with it because neither the American Department of State nor the Egyptian government had wanted the expedition caught in the crosshairs of an insurgency. Reasonably enough!

But now...

For some reason, the uneasy dreams that came with her restless sleep weren't filled with mummies, tombs, sarcophagi or canopic jars. No funerary objects whatsoever, no golden scepters, no jewelry, no treasures.

Instead, she saw the sand. The endless sand of the Sahara. And the sand was teeming, rising up from the ground, swirling in the air.

Someone was coming...

She braced, because there were rumors swirling, along with the sand. Their group could fall under attack—there was unrest in the area. Good Lord, they were in the Middle East!

But she found herself walking through the sand, toward whomever or whatever was coming.

She saw someone.

The killer?

She kept walking toward him. There was more upheaval behind the man, sand billowing dark and heavy like a twister of deadly granules.

Then she saw him.

And it was Micah Fox.

She woke with a start.

And she wondered if he was going to be her salvation...

Or a greater danger to her heart, a danger she hadn't yet seen.

Chapter Three

Micah did his best to remain calm and completely in control. That was definitely a hard-won skill from the academy.

It was the crack of dawn, the morning after the event, and he'd been called in to see Director Richard Egan. Alone.

Egan was Craig's immediate boss. The man was Hard-ass, Craig had told him, but in a good way. He had the ability to choose the right agent for the right case in the criminal division.

He'd also fight tooth and nail when he thought the agency should be involved. He'd take a giant step back, too, when he thought he'd be interfering with the local authorities.

They were often part of a task force, but it didn't seem there was going to be one in this situation. Hell, there might not even be any official FBI involvement. At the moment, they were looking at what might have been a murder thousands of miles away, and what might have been an attempted murder at a museum opening. It might also have been some kind of bizarre ritual or prank.

Several morning newspapers—among the few still

available in print—were on Egan's desk. The front pages all held stories with headlines similar to the first one he read: Mummies Walk in New York City!

Egan glanced at the papers and shook his head, dismayed, Micah thought, more by people's readiness to believe such nonsense than he was by the disturbing headlines.

"You see? Everyone will be going crazy. Thank God that woman didn't die—thank God she didn't die, no matter what—but with this mummy craze…there'll be pressure. The press will not give it up. So. Let me get this straight," Egan said. "You have lots of leave time?"

"Yes, sir. I'm on leave now."

"But you started off taking some of that leave and traveling to Egypt."

"Yes, sir." He hesitated. "That was a year ago. I took several weeks then, and I'm taking several more now. I'm never sick. I've accrued other time as well and work with a great group. So, last year…"

Egan was waiting.

"I came back. I'd heard that Henry Tomlinson, an old friend, had died under unusual circumstances. I tried to reach the site, but when I got there, it had been cleared out. I tried to track down his body, but I was behind by several steps. But you know all this." He hesitated. "I'm a bit of a workaholic, sir. Like I said. I put in a lot of time, and wind up owed a fair amount of time off."

"And you use your leave working, I see."

"I flew all over last year, being given the runaround. Our people in Cairo helped, but they were stonewalled, too. And a lot of the time, certain Egyptian officials acted as if I was an idiot and an annoyance. According to them, they were trying to keep people alive and I was making waves about a dead man. It was too late for them to do anything, of course. I pursued it as far as I could, but Henry's niece had been told that her beloved uncle had died in a horrible accident and, abiding by his wishes, had him cremated. Can't autopsy a pile of ashes."

"Our people in the Middle East would've done exactly what you did," Egan assured him.

"Yes, sir."

"But?"

"But I knew Henry Tomlinson," he said. "He was a friend. He was also a good man. His death deserved a decent investigation, which—due to the circumstances, I know—he did not get."

Egan was quiet for a minute.

Then he said, "And you just happened to be at the museum tonight when a woman, wrapped in would-be old linen tainted with nicotine poison, came crashing into the ceremony."

"So that was it, nicotine poisoning. Hmm. But I didn't just *happen* to be at the event, sir. I was there purposely. As I said, I knew Henry Tomlinson. I loved the guy. I was there to honor him."

"But Craig Frasier has an involvement because his cousin Harley was on the expedition."

Micah shrugged, but kept his eyes steady on Egan's.

"You're a good agent, Micah," Egan said after a moment. "I've seen your service record. I know your supervisor."

Micah lifted his hands. "Sir—"

"Yeah, whatever, forget about it," Egan said flatly.

"Begging your pardon, sir, but—"

"I heard the cop on the case is a dick." He grinned. "In more ways than one."

Startled, Micah raised his brows.

Egan laughed. "The guy's partner, Rydell, actually called me. He wanted to apologize for McGrady's behavior. I guess the guy was hoping it would turn into a murder case and that it would be his—and he wanted the FBI out of it."

"I see."

"Don't worry. The FBI is in. Taking lead."

"Really?" He'd decided to stay calm, so made a point of not betraying his surprise and delight.

Egan leaned back, studying him. "The case began in the Middle East. It entails far more than the City of New York."

Micah felt his pulse soar, but he still maintained his composure.

"That's excellent, sir. And..."

"Yes, I've spoken with your office. You and Craig can take lead on the case. Mike—you know, Craig's partner, Mike?—he needs some vacation time, and if you're here and we're taking this on, I'm going to go ahead and give it to him. So it'll be the two of you. Work with the cops, though, and any other agencies that may become entangled in this. We'll have State Department and embassies involved, too, I imagine. Anyway, our victim from last night regained consciousness thirty minutes ago. I've asked that they let you and Craig do the talking. You are no longer on leave. I suggest you get moving."

"Yes, sir, absolutely. Thank you."

"Just get the son of a bitch," Egan said.

Micah nodded and started out.

"Hey!" Egan called, stopping him.

"Sir?" Micah walked back.

"I didn't hear much about that whole mess in Egypt. What ever happened with the insurrection?"

"Over before it began, from what I understand," Micah told him. "By the time I landed in Cairo, the expedition people were on planes headed out. And the military had routed the coup—it was more of a student protest than anything else. Sadly, it's a fact that there's a lot of unrest in the Middle East, for various reasons. Anyway, it was over, but the expedition was gone. I went out to the site, but...by then, there was nothing to find. Everything had been cleaned out."

"And the insurgents?"

"A few arrests. Most of them dispersed when the military came on the scene."

"In retrospect it might look like overkill, but better safe than sorry," Egan said.

"Of course, always," Micah agreed.

But as he left Egan's office, he found himself wondering, for the first time, whether the insurgent event had been planned to ensure that Henry Tomlinson's death wasn't investigated.

Maybe he was pushing it, getting paranoid.

Maybe he was taking a conspiracy theory too far.

And yet...

Had there been some kind of conspiracy?

"What do you think?" Jensen asked Harley.

She was back at the museum, in the Amenmose exhibit; she hadn't been able to resist. Jensen had called her, saying that with Vivian in the hospital, he could use some extra help, so she'd come.

"They've delayed the opening by a day," he'd told her over the phone early that morning. "But with Vivian out of the picture—temporarily, of course!—and especially since you were there and have a memory like a camera, you can help me with loose ends, tying things up, paperwork."

She'd assured him that she'd be there.

Jensen had told her he'd never left the museum the night before. He didn't look tired, but he was one of those people who could work for days, then sleep twenty-four hours, party a night away, and work a full load again. Jensen could be absolutely tireless.

"I think the exhibit is so special. Just like Henry," she said quietly.

They were standing in the temple area, right where she'd stood the night before when Micah Fox had come upon her. But she wasn't staring at the exhibit, which was surrounded by the glass-and-concrete walk and the "river"; rather, she was looking back at the hall that led to the temple.

One broad corridor led here, with six smaller chambers off the main hall. The temple faced east, in the direction of the sunrise, since it was dedicated to the sun god, Ra. It wasn't filled with statues. Instead, it was open to the glass that revealed the sun.

"The earliest known temple to Ra," Harley said, smiling.

Jensen nodded. "Info on Ra, on Tutankhamen, Ay and Amenmose are on the side there. Near Amenmose's mummy." That was on display in a small room, which it had all to itself. "The hallways feature a lot of the fabulous funerary art we found," Jensen continued.

"Which is surprising, don't you think?" Harley asked.

"How do you mean? That we have anything left—after running out with our tails between our legs?"

"Running out with our tails between our legs was the only thing to do," Harley replied. "No, of course, the historical assumption is that Amenmose was murdered. By someone under Ay, who knew that Amenmose wanted to usurp his power with the boy king, Tutankhamen. Our discovery proved that he *was* murdered, once we were back in the States and the body was properly identified through the DNA testing."

"He'd been strangled!" Jensen said.

"Like Henry," Harley murmured.

"Well, we don't really know about Henry."

"I do."

Jensen shrugged. "In this case," he said, "when it comes to Amenmose, X-rays that show fractured hyoid bones don't lie."

"But we have no clue who did it."

"I'm willing to bet Ay did it himself."

"Oh, today, in one of our courts, Ay would be guilty. He'd be guilty of *conspiracy* to commit murder. It was his idea, I'm sure. But that's just it. Somehow, Amenmose still ended up being properly mummified and placed in an inner coffin and several sarcophagi and laid to rest in his tomb. So who killed him? And who got the body and managed to bury it with such honor?"

"Hey, I'm the Egyptologist here!" Jensen reminded her.

"Yes, and I'm the criminologist. We've got to know who did it and why," Harley said lightly.

"I think we can rest assured that the murderer has long since gone to his own reward," Jensen said, grinning.

"Amenmose's murderer."

"Ah! But not whoever murdered Henry, right? Is that what you mean?"

She nodded.

"Your cousin's FBI and that other guy, Micah, he is, too. They'll get to the truth. And now, because of what happened to Vivian, they'll keep going," he said with confidence. "And guess what? We sold out. We didn't open today as planned, obviously, but we will tomorrow...and it's a total sellout. Not that sales weren't good before, but now that we have mummies walking around, we're a real hit."

"I've seen the news and read a few of the papers. Yeah, what a great story. But there was no mummy walking around. That was Vivian. And speaking of her, how's she doing? Have you heard anything?" Harley asked.

"Doing well, I understand. Awake and aware and lording it over the hospital staff. She's going to be fine."

"Thank God. But what's she said?"

"Nothing. She remembers nothing. Who knows what'll happen eventually? They'll have shrinks in there and everything. At the moment, though...nothing."

"But she'll be okay. That's the most important thing."

"Of course," Jensen agreed. Then he said, "So, what are you doing tonight?"

"What am I doing?" Harley repeated. She felt a strange tension. She'd almost dated Jensen when they were on the expedition. Almost. There was nothing to dislike. He was good-looking, he was smart, he was alpha-fun and...

She did like him.

But she suddenly dreaded the fact that he might be asking her out. There wouldn't have been anything wrong with dating Jensen. They'd teased and they'd flirted and come close. But now she wanted to retreat; she wasn't sure why. It must be everything that had happened, that *was* happening...

She didn't want to turn him down. She wanted to be friends. Maybe she even wanted the relationship option left open.

"I'm, um... I'm not sure," she said. "I came here this morning because you said you needed me, and I want to help."

"This is social."

"Oh. Well, um—"

He laughed softly. "Don't worry. I'm not putting you on the spot. Not tonight. We wanted the whole group to get together. Those of us who were the last people with Henry," he added.

"Oh. Okay. Well, you know that my cousin's girl-friend owns a place and—"

"Yes! That's right. What a great idea! Finnegan's on Broadway. We were planning on meeting somewhere midtown, but once you're on the subway, who cares? We talked, Belinda and Joe and Roger and I. And we thought we owed it to ourselves and to Henry to have our own private little event. Can you get us a corner at Finnegan's? A reserved corner?"

"Anyone can make reservations. But—"

"But you'll be someone they care about when you make the reservation."

"It's a pub. That means hospitality. They care about everyone."

"But more about you."

She gave up. "No problem. I'll make the reservation."

"Cool. So you'll join us all?" Jensen asked her.

"Sure. It'll be great."

Would it be great? she wondered. What was going on with Vivian now? The woman hadn't died; she was doing well. If that had changed, surely they'd all know.

And the majority of the museum was open, although there was a little time left for the cops to come back and look over the new stuff for the Henry Tomlinson section. Still...

"Love ya!" Jensen said, grabbing her by the shoulders and planting a quick kiss on her lips. "I'm so glad you're in for tonight! I was afraid that you wouldn't be."

"Nope, I'm in," Harley assured him. "Anyway, I thought there was work you needed me to do?"

"Yeah, look around the exhibit. Some of the work here is yours, like the prep stuff you were writing up before we even found the tomb. For someone who was going into criminology, you were quite the Egyptologist."

"Hey, lots of people do more than one thing in life. I love Egyptology. It was my minor, just not my major."

"That's my point here. Thing is, check it all out. Make sure there are no imbecilic mistakes."

"Okay. But I'm not the most qualified person to be doing this."

"Oh, come on! You *should've* been an Egyptologist. You were so good at all the stuff we delved into. You knew who thought what, all about the argument over the gods, everything. And you cared about what we were doing. You just wanted to do more with fingerprints and DNA and the detecting part of it. But this exhibition is your baby, too. Check it out for me. You're going to love it!"

He waved and started walking in the direction of the temple, then apparently decided he should go the other way. The temple was a dead end, except, of course, for museum employees. There was a back hall that led to the stairway and a number of museum offices.

"Where are you going?" she asked.

"To clean up—after the cops!" he told her.

"Clean up what?"

He didn't hear her or pretended not to. But he wasn't heading to his office. She had no idea what he was up to.

She glanced at her watch.

That was all he wanted? For her to verify exhibits? He'd said he'd needed help because Vivian wasn't there. And yet he didn't really need much.

Did it matter? She'd never get a chance like this again.

She wasn't even part of it all anymore; she was Jensen's guest and she was a guest because once, she *had* been a part of it all. She didn't embrace Egyptology with the same wonder that drove some of the others, but she did love ancient Egyptian history.

Nope, she probably wouldn't have another opportunity to wander the exhibit entirely alone.

For a moment, she stood still, and then she smiled. She hurried to the right, slipping into one of the rooms where the social and political climate of Amenmose's life and times were explained. She'd done a great deal of the research work and prepared a number of the papers from which the story in the exhibit had been taken.

Entering the first room, she looked around. Display cases held many items of day-to-day life; sure, there were fantastic necklaces and beautiful jewelry, but Harley had always been most fascinated by the storage jars, the pans and other cooking implements that told more about a basic everyday lifestyle.

The center in this exhibit was an exceptionally fine statue of the god Ra, depicted with the head of a falcon, the sun disc above him.

She read softly aloud. "'Ra—ancient Egyptian sun god. By the fifth dynasty, in the 25th to 24th centuries BC, he had risen to prominence, and would be joined by others at various times. Tutankhamen's great changes after his father's reign and his own ascension to the throne involved bringing back the old religion. Under Akhenaten's rule, the old gods had been disrespected; many statues and other honorary sites were destroyed. His dedication to his religion—he wanted to see the deity Aten, the disc of Ra, the sun god, worshipped above all else—caused a weakness in the Egyptian military and a lack of action that was seen as a betrayal by a number of the kingdom's allies. Tutankhamen meant to undo the harm, as he saw it, his father had done. He wanted to bring back all the old gods, including Amun and Mut and others who made up the hierarchy of ancient Egyptian power. Amun-Ra, as Ra was often called, and the others would return. Tutankhamen felt his father's legacy was one of destruction, and under *his* rule, the world would improve. To that end, he looked to the priest Amenmose, despite the fact that the priest Ay was in power as the boy king's regent.'"

She let her words settle in the empty room. "Pretty good," she said with satisfaction.

There was an inner sarcophagus of a handmaiden, buried with Amenmose, in the last of the horseshoe-shaped displays. The woman, at least judging by the artist who had painted her face for the sarcophagus, had been beautiful.

"What do you think?" she asked the image of the long-dead woman. "The New Kingdom, Middle Kingdom, Old Kingdom—it can all be so confusing. Not to mention the dynasties! Anyway, I think the display works, and I had a lot to do with that. It's simple enough to be understood, without leaving out any important facts. Of course, in my view, young King Tut was probably murdered, too. But we'll never find out now, since Howard Carter found that tomb so long ago!"

She read the little note beneath the sarcophagus. The young woman's name had been Ser. She'd served Amenmose in his household. She hadn't been killed for the purpose of being placed in his tomb. She'd succumbed to a fever before his death, and had been moved here to lie with the man she had served so loyally.

Next to her was a servant, Namhi. Like Amenmose, Namhi had been strangled. There was no explanation anywhere on his wrappings or in the tomb. From all that she had read, Harley suspected that either Namhi had been used as an instrument of murder, or he had belonged to the cult of Aten-Aten, a secret society pretending to agree with Tutankhamen's return to the old religion while trying to undermine it at the same time. It had been suspected during Amenmose's lifetime that Namhi was a leader of the cult. That alone would make Ay want to murder him, as well as Amenmose. But Amenmose might also have been murdered by Tutankhamen's half sister or brother-in-law.

Ay had actually been the grand vizier. And, upon Tutankhamen's death, he would become pharaoh.

"You all had motive," Harley murmured.

Yes, just as it seemed everyone did today in the murder of Henry Tomlinson and the attempted murder of Vivian Richter. No one had a solid motive—or, rather, they all had the same motives! Fame, position in life, in society. But...was that enough to make someone kill?

Harley turned to look at the case where mummified animals were displayed. She was staring at a mummified cat when she heard the bone-chilling sound of a cat screeching as if all four paws and its tail had been caught in a car door.

She froze; she felt goose bumps forming all over her body.

There were no cats in the museum. Not living cats, anyway!

A complete silence followed the sound. And then Harley became certain that she heard movement in one of the side rooms off the Amenmose exhibit main hall.

She remained still, listening.

She'd spent her life priding herself on her logic. Obviously, a mummified cat had not let out a yowl. It was more than possible that someone else was in the exhibit. And possible that a cat had somehow found its way in. There might well be police in the prep areas and in the offices behind the public areas of the museum.

Despite her logical reasoning, there was no way to explain the sensations she was feeling. They were different from anything she'd ever known.

She quickly slipped from the side room where she'd been, the first one next to the temple. She thought she saw movement at the end of the hall.

A person, wearing something dark.

That hall was a dead end for visitors. There was a magnificent podium that held the giant-size lion sculptures that had guarded the inner door to the Amenmose tomb. You walked around it and saw the second side of the exhibit before exiting to the rest of the museum.

She told herself she had no reason to be afraid that someone was there. People worked here, for heaven's sake! The cops and crime scene techs were probably still trying to figure out how Vivian Richter had been assaulted with nicotine poison.

But...

There'd been something furtive about the dark figure.

Well, at least it hadn't been a mummy walking around. The person had definitely not been in decaying and frayed linen wrappings.

Whoever it was wore black. Head-to-toe black. Slinking around.

Crazy!

The room she was in displayed different stages of mummification. There was a life-size display in which a mannequin was being dried with natron on a prep table, while priests said their prayers and sprinkled him with some kind of herb water or oil. In the next window, the wrapping process itself was displayed.

The next room was filled with sarcophagi and mummies, wrapped, half-wrapped and unwrapped. And among them...

She paused again, gazing at Unknown Mummy #1. She suddenly, vividly, remembered the night Henry had died. She could see the interior of the prep tent, could see Henry, his face reflecting his enthusiasm.

Somebody brushed by something out in the hallway.

Anyone might have been there! Working, investigating, exploring.

No. The person was moving...

Furtively.

She hurried to the door and looked outside. She could run back to the statues and escape into the back to the offices and prep rooms behind the scenes.

She could demand that whoever it was show him or herself.

And wind up with a belt or other object around her neck, or poisoned linen wrapped around her body?

She realized that her heart was thundering. In a thousand years, she could never have imagined being so frightened in the middle of the day in a museum. She wasn't sure she'd been this frightened even when they were forced to flee the Sahara.

Harley flattened herself against the wall, waiting.

She was startled to hear the scream of a cat again.

That was no damned mummy! There was a living cat in the museum—fact!

But she wasn't staying to search for it.

She burst out into the hallway, racing toward the exit.

"Harley!"

She heard her name; it was a heated whisper. She sensed somehow that it wasn't a threat, but by then she was propelling herself forward at a frantic pace.

"Harley!"

That whisper of her name again.

She wasn't going to make the exit.

She turned and saw Micah Fox standing there.

One minute she was running, her feet barely touching the floor.

The next...

She'd fallen flat on her back, blinking up at the man straddling her.

"Harley! Damn!"

Fox. Micah Fox. Special Agent Micah Fox.

She stared at him blankly. For a moment, she wondered if *he'd* been stalking her through the Amenmose exhibit.

"There was someone in here!" she said. "Watching me."

"Yes," he said flatly. "And thanks to you, that someone has gotten away."

Micah rose to his feet and helped Harley to hers. "What?" she demanded. "How?"

"I had him—or her. I don't even know which it was. Then you made enough noise to raise a legion of the dead—"

"Oh, no, no, no! *You* were the one making the noise!" Harley told him.

"Harley, if you'd just stayed where you were..."

"And let someone get me? What a bright comment from a law enforcement officer!"

"Harley," he began, then broke off and halfway smiled, lowered his head and shook it slightly. "Sorry.

I guess I think of you as Craig's cousin, and as a student of criminology, and I suppose..."

"You suppose what?"

"That you'll behave as if you were trained in criminal behavior and...well, working a case."

She stood there, still staring at him, pursing her lips. Then she offered him an icy smile. "Okay, let's put it this way. Take doctors. Some are great practitioners and others are diagnosticians. My training helps us to figure out what happened—not to bulldoze our way into a situation with guns blazing!"

He listened to her speak; his reaction was undeniable amusement.

"Okay, whatever. Let's go to the offices here and see who we can see, yes?" he asked her.

She turned and headed for the doors marked Cast Members Only—as if they were at a theme park rather than a museum—and pushed her way in. She feared for a moment that the doors would be locked. They were not.

A long hall stretched before her. To the left were offices; to the right were the labs and prep rooms.

She could see that one door was marked with the name Gordon Vincent. She hadn't really met him, she realized, and he wasn't just in charge of the Amenmose exhibit, but the entire museum. His appearance was perfect for the part; he was solid, about six feet even, gray-haired and entirely dignified. The office beside his bore a temporary name; that was obvious from the way the name placard had been slipped over another, the name being Arlo Hampton. Next to his office, the jerry-rigged nameplate read Vivian Richter.

Jensen Morrow had his own office, since he was now an employee of the museum.

No one was in the hall. Looking through the large plate-glass windows to the lab, they could see that Arlo wasn't in his office; he was in the lab. He was working with one of the unnamed mummies they'd found in the tomb, running the X-ray machine over the remains. Harley waited until he'd completed his task. Then she tapped on a window. Arlo raised his head, startled. He saw Harley and offered her a large smile—then noticed Micah and didn't seem quite so pleased. He disappeared for a moment as he walked through the changing area and then opened the hallway door to let them in.

He beamed; in fact, he seemed to come alive as he met Harley's gaze.

He did not seem concerned that a woman, a colleague, was in the hospital. That someone had attempted to murder her in a particularly grotesque manner.

"Harley, nice to see you. Jensen said he asked you to come in. I believe he was going to ask you to work with him on a few last additions we're thinking of adding. I'll tell you the truth, I wish you'd been one of ours. I want a room on what we've discovered from the mummies—and what we know about their deaths. Oh, the whole Tut thing is still speculation, and that's not ours to tear apart. This is!"

"Thanks," Harley said, wondering why Jensen hadn't mentioned that. "I'm happy to help with…whatever's needed."

"Great. And you, Agent Fox." Arlo turned to him. "Are you part of the police investigation? They were here all night. They found nothing. Of course, they still have Vivian's office closed off and we won't open this section until tomorrow, but…wow."

"Yeah, wow," Micah said, his tone flat. "So, what do *you* think happened to Vivian Richter?"

"Her husband's with her now," Arlo said. "I mean, needless to say, we care most about the living. It's just that…well, the world can't stop because something bad happened to someone."

"Yeah, but that bad thing happened right here," Micah reminded him.

"Of course," Arlo said. "But…it had to be a prank, right? She didn't die. I'm thinking some college student who suffered some kind of slight at our hands was in here and played a prank on her."

"Nicotine poisoning is no prank."

Arlo looked truly perplexed. "Someone definitely came in through the back, to get to her. Otherwise, whoever it was would've been on the cameras. The only people picked up on the security video cameras in this section were the two of you and Jensen Morrow. But, of course, there are entrances from the basement on up—a few secret entrances. Did you know the building itself was originally erected by Astor as a bank? That's why there's the gorgeous foyer and all. But speaking of secret entrances, the cops are looking at everything. Oh yeah, you're a cop. Okay, sort of a cop. Do you want a tour?"

"I would love a tour," Micah told him. "But first, who else is working today?"

"Well, define 'working.' I think everyone's been in. The only one not really part of the new exhibit is Harley. Belinda, Joe and Roger have been giving it about ten hours a week. Jensen is here full-time, which I'm sure you know. Joe and Belinda both have full-time jobs with two of the other major museums in the city, and Roger is teaching now. They were all in at one time or another this morning, checking out their space. The cops tore through everything, looking for the source of the wrapping and the poison. But honestly, I don't think we even have any natural linen back here. And any idiot knows that's not how you make an ancient Egyptian mummy. But—"

"So who else was here this morning, Arlo?"

"Let's see. Ned Richter was in. Left the hospital, popped over here and went back. But he was here."

"And the others?" Harley asked.

"Yes, like I said, at one time or another. I've been busy, as you can see. We still have a wealth of remains and artifacts. There was the mess with that so-called insurgent group, but then the company and the government sent guys with big trucks and equipment, and they emptied the tomb—including all the mummies—before thieves could. Oh yeah, some people see the Western world as one giant thief, but everything we have is cleared through the Egyptian government and will be returned, and that was common knowledge from the get-go."

Arlo seemed to consider it more important to honor international agreements than to worry about anything else.

Admirable.

But Henry had died. And Vivian might have died, too.

"I'd love that tour now," Micah said, smiling. Harley saw the way his face moved when he smiled. Ob-

viously, despite his work, he smiled a lot. He had the
kind of smile that made her wonder what it would be
like if they were just talking together at a restaurant,
in a class...

"I can't give you a tour of the entire place. We're
going to concentrate on this exhibit. You'll notice that
our offices are in this section with the directors, with
Gordon Vincent. He's a very smart, well-educated and
supportive guy. He purposely keeps his office over
here. That way, whatever is new, he's in on it."

"So he might have been in his office before Vivian
came out screaming?" Micah asked.

"I suppose so," Arlo replied. "But are you suggesting Gordon was involved? Really? I don't think so."

Harley didn't, either. He hadn't been on the expedition. She could tell that Micah didn't think Vincent
was guilty of anything, either; he was just covering
his bases.

"Show me around, please. That would be great,"
Micah said.

"Okay, let's go!"

Arlo ripped off his paper lab coat and set out. "As
you can see, that's a lab—a 'clean room' lab, if you
will. You have to coat up, glove up and mask up before going in. You never know what might've been in
the ground for millennia! And over there, the museum
offices. Now, we're on the ground floor, or so you'd
think. Directly beneath us is the cafeteria and there's
another rotunda-like area for international exhibits.
That one's a bit different. International, of course, but
Egyptology has always had a place in the higher echelon of what people find fascinating in a museum. And,
sadly, museums are bottom-line—everyone needs do-

nations and funding and numbers—and mummies are a draw. Always have been. Even though they were so plentiful in Victorian times that people used them for kindling! Yes, those good religious uptight folk used human remains as kindling."

He kept talking, pointing out different research rooms and more offices. Then he came to a staircase. It was an old stone circular staircase, high and steep. "This led down to the vaults at one time. It wouldn't have been easy to steal from this place when it was a bank!"

They followed him down to the basement and then the sub-basement.

"Does this bypass the actual basement?"

"Yes, these stairs do. And…" Arlo turned, shining a flashlight at them, although they were still receiving ample light from above. "It'll get dark in here!" he warned.

Harley took a penlight from her purse at the same time as Micah drew one from his pocket. She was rather proud of herself for never leaving home without one!

"You can still kind of see. There was emergency lighting put down here before the place went belly-up during the Great Depression," Arlo told them. "As you can tell, the design of the hallways is almost like a perfect cross, and each of them opens out to five vaults. The elite of the elite had their treasure down there. The museum will use the space eventually, but at this stage, it's not really needed yet. Anyway, the quality of the exhibits means more than the quantity."

Arlo was quite happy to keep talking. They saw

what he meant about the cross design, and each section held vaults of slightly different sizes.

"And there's a way out?" Harley asked.

Arlo didn't get a chance to answer. There was a narrow area that simply looked like an empty space at the end of the vault area facing Central Park. Micah headed that way.

Harley followed Micah, and Arlo followed her.

"What's going on?" Arlo asked when Micah came to a stop.

Micah had found something. Harley could hear metal grating and squealing; she realized he'd come to a door. That he'd gotten it open.

She came up behind him and looked over his shoulder.

All she saw was black.

"Abandoned subway tunnel. They're all over the city," he murmured.

"I guess that's one way out. Or you can just walk out the door that leads back up to the park and picnic area at the side of the museum," Arlo said, pointing to the right. "But an abandoned subway. I think I'd heard rumors, but never really knew if they were true of not. Cool!"

"Yeah. Cool," Micah said wryly. "So, does everyone know about that way out—to the park area?" he asked Arlo.

"Oh, I wouldn't think so," Arlo replied. "Just people who work here. And maybe people they've told."

"We might want to get a lock on the door to that exit," Micah said. "And to the subway tunnels. The info could easily have been tweeted across the country. Maybe it has." He paused, studying Harley. "We'll get a few of our people down here," he told her. "I need to go over to the hospital. I've been told that Vivian is conscious and speaking. But I'll need to find you later. Do you know where you'll be?"

Harley hesitated. Then she shrugged. "Finnegan's," she told him. "Finnegan's on Broadway."

"Kieran's family's place?" he asked her.

"It's the only Finnegan's on Broadway."

"You'll definitely be there?"

"Oh, yes. I'll be meeting my colleagues from the expedition."

"Including me!" Arlo said happily. He sighed. "Well, we won't have Vivian there, and I doubt we'll have Ned Richter with Viv in the hospital."

"Henry. We won't have Henry," Harley said.

"No, we won't have Henry," Arlo agreed. He tried an awkward smile. "But at least we won't have any mummies running around at Finnegan's. A banshee or two, maybe, but no mummies!"

Neither of them managed even a small smile for his attempt at humor.

As they left, Harley remembered the cat she'd heard earlier. There'd been no further sound after Micah had appeared—claiming she'd frightened off the person who'd apparently been stalking her. The person he, in turn, had followed. And lost.

Chapter Four

"I was in my office," Vivian Richter said. "I was in my office…"

Her voice trailed off. Her face was set in a concentrated frown.

"In my office and then…"

"And then?" Micah pushed gently.

Vivian was in her hospital bed, in a seated position. Craig Frasier and Micah stood at the foot of the bed, patiently waiting.

Micah knew that the local cops had already been in. But it had only been a short time since the lead on the investigation had been handed over to the federal government. Vivian had let them know that she'd spoken with McGrady and Rydell. The nurse in the hallway had informed them that McGrady had brought Vivian to tears, demanding that she remember what she just couldn't.

Micah had received a call from Rydell, since it was still a joint task force, if a small one. Rydell had apologized for his partner.

For the most part, I work with great people. No one is better than the NYPD, Rydell had assured him.

Micah had told him not to worry; any agency in the

world could come with a jerk or two—and McGrady was that jerk. He hadn't said that in so many words when he'd spoken to Rydell, but they both knew exactly who he was talking about.

"I'll bet you were excited about the exhibit," Micah told Vivian. "All the work that had been done. And then the discovery—and the terror in the desert, with Henry Tomlinson dead and the fear of armed rebels coming at the camp. But now, here, you have the culmination of your dream of getting the Amenmose exhibit up!"

"Oh, I was excited. So excited. And we were going to have all our grad students and Henry's niece and her family at the opening. And...oh! Those children. Henry's great-nieces and nephews. And there were probably other children there. And they saw me coming out like—?"

"A mummy. Vivian, think. Did anyone come in to see you in your office when you were getting ready for the grand celebration?"

Her frown deepened.

"Everyone had been there. Everyone. Ned, of course. We were excited together. He's administration and I'm an Egyptologist, but we're a married couple, and that made it an incredible night for both of us. Arlo, darting in and out with last-minute things. The grad students...they were all there. Belinda wanted me to look at her dress and Joe—that boy is such a flirt!—asked if he looked both dignified and handsome. Let's see, Jensen. He's full-time here now, you know. He was in more than once. And then..."

She went silent, dead silent, her mouth falling open in an awkward O of horror.

"What?" Craig asked.

"One of the mummies came in. It was walking. Yes, yes, that was it! There was a mummy. Oh, my God! A mummy... I remember now. It...stared at me!"

She began to shake. Micah and Craig glanced at each other, deciding it might be time to hit the nurse-call button.

But first they both moved close to her, each man taking one of her hands.

"It's going to be all right," Micah said in a soothing voice.

She shook her head. "Mummies don't walk. Except in really bad movies. Okay, even good movies... *The Mummy* with Brendan Fraser was good." She paused. The shaking had stopped, and she looked at Craig. "You any relation?"

"I'm afraid not. My last name's actually Frasier," Craig told her.

Vivian suddenly stared hard at Micah. "That was it, yes. I saw the mummy. I stood up—I'd been at my desk. I stood up, and I couldn't believe what I was seeing. It had to be a joke, a prank...but then the thing came at me and I tried to scream, or I think I did, and it kept coming...and..."

"And?" Micah asked.

"That's it. That's all I remember. A mummy came to life," she whispered.

"Vivian, you of all people know that a mummy didn't come to life. Whoever was pretending to be a mummy wrapped you in linens that had been soaked with nicotine. That person wasn't a real mummy," Micah said.

"But...it seemed so real. Or surreal. But terrifying!" Vivian said.

"Vivian, someone who was in the museum at the time dressed up as a mummy to attack you. Do you have any idea why? Were you having an argument with anyone? Is there any reason— Well, I'll be blunt," Craig said. "Is there any reason anyone would want you dead?"

Vivian gasped. "Oh, God!"

Micah glanced at Craig. She must have just realized that someone had tried to kill her.

"No, no, no!" Vivian said. "I know I'm not the nicest human being in the world. I'm not a Pollyanna of any kind, but... I don't hurt people. I've never fired anyone, not that I have that kind of power. I'm not mean to people, I don't scream at them to work harder. I'm a decent person, damn it! No, there's no reason anyone would want to kill me!" she declared.

"Did you have a fight with anyone—anyone at all?" Micah asked.

She sighed. "Every once in a while, I get into it with Arlo. But that's just because...well, when Henry was alive, we all acknowledged him as the real guru. He had the experience. He was chosen by Alchemy to head up the exhibition, and he was chosen because all his research on Amenmose was so good and so thorough. With Henry gone, I think maybe Arlo and I have a bit of a rivalry going. But a healthy rivalry!"

"Arlo was working today."

"Of course he was. There's still much to be done. You have to understand that the tomb was *filled* with mummies, including that of Amenmose. And, as with Tut, some of the funerary objects appear to have been reused. We have every reason to believe that Amenmose was murdered—and it must've happened quite

suddenly. He was entombed with all the rites by someone who really loved him, but it was all hush-hush and
under the radar. Ay did become the ruler after Tut died.
Anyway, there's still so much to determine about our
find! I'm sure everyone's working." She was quiet for
a minute. "Including my husband. Bless Ned. He was
so torn! But I've assured him that I'm on the way to
being just fine and that the museum—at this moment—
is the most important thing in our lives right now. And
I'm getting great care here, so it's fine that he's gone."

Micah wasn't sure she was telling the truth. He
wasn't convinced she didn't feel hurt that her husband
wasn't with her.

But he didn't want to rub salt into any wounds.

He glanced at Craig. They would move on. Craig was
probably doubting her words, too, but they wouldn't
get different answers to what they'd asked—not at the
moment. Time to ask other questions.

"What about the grad students? Any arguments with
any of them?"

"Well, they're not grad students anymore, are they?"
Vivian asked a little sharply. "I told you, I saw Belinda
and Joe and…" She paused, sighing deeply. "I was a bit
worried about seeing your cousin, Agent Frasier. She
was so committed to Henry. We all loved him, but it
was as if he saw her as a grandchild and she saw him as
a wonderfully brilliant grandpa. She never got over his
death. Then, of course, there's Jensen, and he's taken
a permanent position with the museum. He helped her
fight for Henry up to the end, and then… Henry was
cremated. We had two different medical examiners
give verdicts that suggested suicide, possibly brought
on by a delirium caused by bacteria. Anyway, we'll

probably never know just what was going on in Henry's mind. And. ." She broke off again, looking from Micah to Craig. "Someone wanted me dead, too. But how did I get out in the foyer? How did I get help? Oh, it's all so terrifying!"

She began sobbing quietly.

Micah squeezed her hand. "Hey, you're going to be fine. So if there's anything, anything at all, please call one of us. We intend to find the truth. We *will* find the truth."

She nodded and squeezed his hand back. "Thank you," she said.

"Of course," he told her.

He thought she smiled.

THERE WAS A lively crowd at Finnegan's on Broadway that night, but then again, it was Friday.

New Yorkers had a tendency to be "neighborhood" people. On the Upper East Side, you found an Upper East Side hangout. There were lots of bars and pubs around Cooper Union, St. Mark's Place, the Villages, East and West, and any other neighborhood you could think of in the giant metropolis.

But Finnegan's drew people from everywhere. For one thing, it was one of the longest-running pubs in the city, dating back to pre–Civil War days. For another, it was run with a family feel, and somehow, people knew the right time to bring their kids and the right time not to. The kitchen was as important as the bar. It was simply a unique place, and Harley was delighted with Craig's association with the Finnegan family— and through him, her own connection to them.

She'd been able to reserve a corner near the entrance, against the wall and across from the actual bar tables.

Jensen got there first, greeting her with a hug and a kiss on each cheek. She wasn't sure just how far he would have gone; a waitress—a lovely girl who'd just arrived from Ireland, came by to take their order. That was when Joe Rosello walked in.

He had to flirt. But he couldn't seem to decide whether to flirt with Harley or the waitress.

He opted for both, which got him a punch on the shoulder from Jensen. "Hell, you can't take him anywhere."

"You are atrocious," Harley told him, shaking her head.

"Hey! I just admire people and make them happy. I don't do anything evil!" Joe protested.

"We'll let it slide this time," Jensen said. "Lay off Harley, eh? She's seen you with the ladies. She knows your MO."

"Harley, do you really mind me telling you that you're gorgeous and mysterious and desirable in black?" Joe asked, sounding wounded.

"No, just don't slobber on my hand, please."

"Slobber? That was an elegant kiss!"

"Ah-ha! A very wet and elegant kiss!" Jensen said. By now, Roger had come in; he listened to the ongoing conversation, rolling his eyes. "And every one of us has a doctorate!" he murmured. "Pathetic. What is this world coming to?"

"I think the world was a mess long before we came along!" Belinda said, joining them.

It was then that Harley noticed Micah Fox; she hadn't seen him come in. He was standing at the bar with her cousin Craig. The oldest Finnegan, Declan, who ran the family establishment, was talking to the two men.

She had a feeling they were all watching her and her friends.

A minute later, Micah walked over and joined the group.

Harley wasn't the first to greet him; Belinda was. Harley was busy greeting Arlo, who had just arrived, and Ned Richter, who had apparently chosen to join them rather than stay with his wife at the hospital.

They were seated around two of the big mahogany tables in the corner, Ned Richter, Arlo, Joe, Roger and Belinda crowded in against the wall, and Craig, Micah, Harley and Jensen perched on the chairs across from them. There was ordering of drinks and meals, with casual conversation at first. And then Ned Richter raised his glass and said, "In memory of Henry Tomlinson, the greatest Egyptologist I ever knew and one of the finest men to have ever walked this earth, as well."

"Hear, hear!" the others chimed in.

They all raised a glass to Henry, and then Ned continued with, "And to the bastard who hurt my Vivian—may these agents and cops find him, and may he rot in hell!"

"Hear, hear!" another cry went up.

"That's harsh," Jensen teased. "At least you're among friends."

"That's what an Irish pub is all about," Richter reminded them all, drawing a round of laughter. He went on, saying, "Sorry, I can't help it. I hope the bastard dies a hideous death."

Harley wondered why he wasn't with his wife, since he was so devastated by what had been done to her.

But she was wedged between Jensen and Micah, and she was very aware of both men being so close to her. She found herself wondering, too, just what connected people. She was seated between two very fine men. Both exceptionally good-looking and bright—and both engaged with the world...in completely different ways.

She liked them both.

And yet, sitting there, she knew why she wasn't with Jensen, why they hadn't gone out. Each man's interest was unmistakable.

But only one man's seemed to matter.

She was attracted to Micah Fox. She barely knew him, and yet when she'd seen him again, just the sound of his voice had aroused her senses.

"Seriously, who would've done such a thing? Harley, what do you remember?"

Harley realized that her mind had completely—and inappropriately—wandered. Belinda was staring at her, brown eyes wide, and waiting for an answer.

Harley took a sip of her drink—a Kaliber nonalcoholic beer by Guinness, since she'd decided she couldn't risk losing an ounce of control tonight. She hoped someone would say something that explained Belinda's question.

She felt Micah's eyes on her. Maybe he knew she'd been distracted. Hopefully, he didn't know that her mental absence at the table had been due to him.

"About that night...that night in the Sahara," he said.

"We were all so excited," she began, and around her, Jensen, Joe, Roger and Belinda all nodded.

"And we were rewarded!" Ned Richter said.

"A find beyond measure!" Arlo agreed.

"We'd started to bring some things from the tomb into the prep tent," Harley said. "It's a special tent, temperature-controlled. Everyone's careful there. Amenmose's tomb turned out to have more than a dozen mummies and sarcophagi—all in different states of disrepair and decay. We've proven that Amenmose was murdered, so after it happened, someone who loved him borrowed—or stole—funerary objects from the dead who'd passed on before him. They also brought together people, dead and alive, who'd served him."

"Why would they do that? Why go out and find people who'd already died to bury with him?" Micah asked her. "I studied Egyptology," he said sheepishly, "but, I don't understand—taking people who have already died and their things. It's like robbing the dead. It *is* robbing the dead."

"He would need servants in his next life. Servants, women... He would need people and animals, just as he'd need his bow and shield," Harley explained.

"I know about objects needed for the next life. I guess I never heard of them being taken from somewhere else...dead, or still alive."

Micah seemed to move even closer to her. She could feel his eyes; she could almost feel his touch. His elbow was on the table and his fingers dangled near her lap.

She forced herself to concentrate. "We worked really hard that day—for hours and hours. I'm pretty sure it was close to eight o'clock. There was a little village not far from the dig and the people there were incredibly nice. We'd go sometimes to have dinner and maybe sit with coffee at a place there, something like a family-run restaurant or cantina. But we decided in the end that Jensen and I would go by ourselves and bring back food. Jensen came to get me while I was trying to talk Henry into coming with us. We were all tired, of course." She glanced over at Belinda who was still watching her with wide brown eyes. "Belinda was Skyping with Al. he was in Iraq at the time, I think."

"Iraq, yes, just about to leave," Belinda said.

"And Roger was working on tech and communications because we were hearing rumors about an upstart hate group, so he didn't go." She turned to Joe and couldn't help grinning. "Joe was still moving some of the artifacts. We had a lovely young Egyptian as our interpreter. Satima Mahmoud. They were...working."

"Working, right!" Belinda mocked, then laughed affectionately. "Joe was flirting."

"What? I don't flirt!" Joe protested.

"You're a flirt!"

Harley was sure they all said the words at the same time.

Joe flushed and shrugged. "She's really pretty. And smart."

"That she is," Harley agreed.

"So, Jensen," Micah said, looking past Harley, "you and Harley went out together that night. How long were you gone?"

Jensen thought it over, raising a brow at Harley. "Hour and a half maybe?"

"Somewhere in there. An hour to an hour and a half," Harley said.

Micah nodded, then swiveled around to look at Ned Richter and Arlo Hampton. "Neither of you checked on Henry during that time?"

"There was no need to check on Henry!" Ned Richter said. "We had security on the outskirts of the camp. Henry was completely in his element, like a kid in a candy store. I wouldn't have interrupted him."

"And you?" Micah asked Arlo. "Shouldn't you have been in there with him?"

"No, because I—"

Arlo turned beet red and stopped speaking.

"You what?"

"I was working," Arlo said.

"On what?" Ned Richter demanded.

Arlo looked guiltily around. "Well, I had one of the funerary tablets in my tent."

"You took a tablet from the find into your tent?" Ned repeated, his tone grating.

"Well, you see, I was interpreting, trying to figure out just what had happened at this site and how. It wasn't usual, having that many dead in a tomb. I was transcribing the tablet."

"What did it say?" Harley asked. She'd never heard about the tablet.

Arlo flushed miserably again. "I don't know."

"No artifacts in private tents," Ned told him, irritated. "I'm not going to fire your ass or anything over it, but damn it, that's the last time, Arlo. We follow the rules at Alchemy."

"What did the tablet say?" Harley persisted.

"I don't know,' Arlo said again, his expression peevish.

"You didn't translate?" Harley asked.

"I didn't have time. I got through a zillion lines of how wonderful Amenmose had been and then...you started screaming."

"I'd just found a friend—dead!"

"Well, yes, you screamed, and then everyone had to come and look at Henry. Then we heard we were about to be attacked, and *then* we were all helping when it came to loading up what we could, trying to get to the airport in Cairo."

"Yes, but where—"

"Harley, I haven't the faintest idea where the damned tablet ended up!" Arlo said. "I thought we were getting together tonight to be supportive, and you're all accusing me of terrible things!"

"We didn't *accuse* you," Ned pointed out drily. "You admitted you took an artifact."

Arlo sighed. "Where were *you*? What were you doing? Why wasn't Vivian with Henry? She's the one who loves it all so, so much!"

"I had gone to get dinner to bring with Jensen. And, then, of course, when we got back, we were busy making plans to get everyone and everything out of the desert! That was a nightmare. What the hell? We're going to attack one another now?"

"Hey, guys, you all came here to honor Henry!" Micah reminded them.

Jensen laughed. "You're the one who started this."

"Yes, I am," Micah said seriously. "Henry died out there that night. Now Vivian's been attacked. I wonder if you realize just how lethal nicotine poisoning can be."

"I certainly realize," Ned Richter said hoarsely.

"We all do. It's just that...we wouldn't have hurt Henry!" Belinda said. "And... I have no idea what went on with Vivian. No idea," she repeated softly.

"Nor do I. She was in her office," Jensen said.

"And you last saw her when?"

"I told the police—I told anyone who asked. I saw her about an hour before the celebration started. She was in her office, said hi, then waved me out. She seemed too busy to worry about the opening ceremonies, although she definitely showed up later. She loves the exhibit, you know."

"The rest of you? Did anyone see her before the celebration?" Micah asked.

"I saw her at about four o'clock," Ned Richter said. "She came to my office. She wanted permission for more expensive testing. I told her we had to hold off for a while." He paused and then added, "Every once in a while, I have to make her understand my position. I'm a CEO. I can't give in to her just because she's my wife. *Especially* because she's my wife. She's a highly qualified Egyptologist, but she didn't even work for Alchemy at first. She has her position due to me, so…"

"I waved to her," Arlo offered. "I was working in the lab. She didn't wave back. She was concentrating on whatever she was doing. Then again, that's Vivian's way."

"I didn't see her at all," Belinda said. "You know, not until…"

"Me, neither," Joe said.

"Nor me," Roger chimed in.

"Thanks." Micah lifted his glass. "So, to the evening, then, huh? To Henry, our mentor, a man we all loved dearly… I assume?"

Assent was quickly voiced by everyone in the group.

"To Henry!"

Their waitress came by; Harley noted that Micah

made a point of dropping any questioning at that point. Instead, he ordered the pub's very popular shepherd's pie.

He clearly had the ability to be very charming when he chose. He got Belinda to speak about her upcoming marriage—she was supposed to have a Christmas wedding—and he got Arlo talking about the way he'd fallen in love with mummies at the Chicago Field Museum as a kid. Joe, in his turn, became enthusiastic and wistful talking about the beautiful Satima Mahmoud and what an excellent interpreter she'd been, helping whenever anyone needed it. They'd come this close to having an affair, he admitted, and then, of course, everything had gone to hell.

Roger talked about his love for the desert—and his happiness over the fact that they were home. There was no place like New York. He loved being home, he said; he loved his job.

Ned didn't stay more than an hour, since he was going back to the hospital to be with his wife.

No one else seemed to want to break up their get-together, but it was growing late. The fine Irish band playing that night announced their last number.

The evening inevitably came to an end.

"So who sees to it that our lovely companions get home okay?" Joe asked, rising and indicating Belinda and Harley.

"No need to worry about me," Harley assured them. "Seriously. The tall, dark, handsome and deadly-looking guy at the bar is my cousin."

"Oh, Craig's here! I didn't realize. He should've joined us," Belinda said.

"Maybe he didn't want this to look like an inquisition," Jensen said, staring at Micah.

"Maybe," Micah said casually. The two men were almost the same height, both about six-three. Micah was smiling, not about to get into it—and not about to back down.

"If you're tired, I can take you to your place," Jensen told Harley.

"I'm fine, really," she said. "My cousin, remember? Craig is my cousin."

"Yeah, he is," Jensen said. For a moment, his eyes fell on her, and she thought he might be feeling something like jealousy over her preference for Craig's company rather than his. But although they'd teased and flirted, they'd never dated; they'd never been more than friends. She liked that he was protective. However, he didn't have any grounds to be jealous. At least not of Craig...

"Fine. Belinda?" Jensen said.

She laughed. "I'm a native New Yorker. I've been taking the latest subway most of my life. But sure."

"Your fiancé is a man serving his nation, Belinda. It's my privilege to see you safely home. And," he added, "I'm damned good with the subways myself."

"Okay, thanks. Come on. I'll make tea when we get to my place—so you can get yourself safely home after that!" Belinda left with Jensen's arm around her.

Harley realized that, as the others trailed out, she was still standing near the exit with Micah.

"Strange," he muttered.

"What is?"

"He's the one person who can't be guilty."

"Who? You mean Jensen?"

Micah turned to look at her, studying her eyes thoughtfully, his own pensive. "Yes. He was with you in the desert. The two of you saw Henry alive together, and then you left together, and when you came back, Henry was dead."

"Yes. Why do you find Jensen suspicious?"

"Something about him."

"They teach you that at the academy?" Harley asked.

"Actually, yes. But never mind." He took her elbow. She was startled by the way she reacted to his simple touch.

"Shall we join Craig?" he asked.

They did. Craig stood politely to offer Harley his bar stool, but almost on cue, the cuddling couple who'd been taking up the seats next to him rose, hand in hand, seeing nothing but each other. They began to wander from the bar and toward the exit. Craig gestured at the three stools conveniently left for them and they all sat down.

Micah went over the conversations at the bar and Harley knew that Jensen had been right; Micah really had been grilling all of them.

If Craig had joined them, it wouldn't have been a get-together.

It would've been an inquisition, just as he'd said.

Kieran came from the back office, sliding in comfortably with her back to Craig's chest, leaning against him on his bar stool.

"Make any headway?" she asked.

"Ah, yes, Special Agent Fox has had a gut feeling," Harley replied.

"I don't trust the guy," Micah said mildly. "Jensen."

"Hmm," Kieran murmured.

"The psychologist's deep, dark 'hmm'!" Craig said. "There must be a Freudian meaning there!"

"No, I don't think there's a rational explanation for a gut feeling." Kieran shook her head. "But perhaps if there's dislike involved…"

"Don't dislike the guy. He seems okay. But I sense that he's not quite trustworthy," Micah said.

"Ah." Harley shrugged. "I have a hard time seeing Jensen as a criminal. And in our group, Joe's the one who tends to go off on tangents, not that it means he's guilty of anything. But he's easily distracted."

"By the beautiful Egyptian girl," Micah said. "Satima Mahmoud."

"Yes, and she's still in Egypt, so I doubt she had anything to do with last night," Harley said.

"You know for sure that she's still in Egypt?" Micah asked.

"I, um…"

Harley was forced to pause. "No. Of course I don't know *for sure* that she's in Egypt. I assume she is. It's where she lives and works."

"Worth checking on," Micah said. He was, however, aiming the remark at Craig, who nodded in agreement.

"I think I need to go home." Harley stood up, yawning.

"I've got a car today. We'll get you home," Craig said. "Kieran? You ready?"

"You guys go ahead. I promised Declan some help figuring out an invoice."

"No, it's okay! I go home alone all the time," Harley said. "You—"

"Micah, you take the car," Craig interrupted. "Pick me up in the morning. I'll wait here with Kieran. Declan can drop us off or we'll grab an Uber."

"I can grab an Uber, too. I'm really close, just by Grace Church," Harley said.

"No," Craig insisted. "Let Micah take you, please. This whole mummy thing is…creepy."

"I'm not afraid of mummies."

"You should be. But only of the living ones," Kieran said. "Living people who are pretending to be mummies. Or having other people dress up like mummies. Anyway, get home safely, okay?"

Arguing would make her appear…argumentative, Harley thought.

"Thanks," she said simply. She turned away, aware that she was trembling slightly. It was a ride—a ride home. She wasn't afraid of Micah. She was afraid of herself.

She felt intensely attracted to the man. She'd sat at their table in the bar, wondering how she could be seated between two men with all the right stuff—and feel such an attraction to one and not the other.

She knew nothing at all about Micah Fox, except that he was with the FBI, that he'd worked with Craig and that Craig seemed to like him. And that he'd also been a student of Henry's.

That was the sum total of her knowledge. Was it enough of a basis for…anything?

Or had she spent the past year drifting, trying to develop an interest in someone, and not managing to find any kind of spark, any reason to pursue a relationship, even just a sexual one?

But if this was sexual, did it matter?

It did! He'd loved Henry, too. He was friends with Craig.

What if she threw herself at him, and he turned her down?

She was afraid her thoughts were making her blush, so she kissed her cousin and Kieran good-night and led the way, with Micah right behind her. She explained that it was ridiculous that he felt he had to drive her; it was maybe a mile away at most.

"Yeah, but it's late," Micah said.

She knew that the cars Craig used that belonged to the bureau could be parked just about anywhere. Except that parking wasn't easy in Lower Manhattan—or pretty much anywhere in Manhattan!

"You can drop me off in front of the building, and thank you again," Harley told him.

"I don't think so." He gave her a smile. "Sorry, even if you weren't Craig's cousin, it wouldn't be my style."

"You'll never find parking."

"Yes, I will. The academy also taught us how to summon our individual parking witches," he said, his tone droll.

She pursed her lips and sighed. "Great. Witches? I thought people had parking fairies."

"Not in the academy. Witches are scarier. They get rid of the other cars, frighten them off, you know?"

He did have a parking witch—or damned good luck. She was surprised at how close he got to her building.

He walked her there, and stepped inside with her. He saw the security guard and nodded in approval.

And, of course, he could leave her right there. She was obviously safe; her building had keyed entry and security! The push of a button summoned the police in the event of any trouble.

She found herself staring at him, waiting.

"Good building," he told her.

"Thanks."

She hesitated. She wanted to kick herself. She was standing here so casually—surely she was standing casually; surely she could speak casually!—but she didn't want to let him go. Something was alive inside her, something burning, hot, shaking, nervous...something that made her feel as if she was in her teens again. She'd done very little except study and work over the past year, trying to struggle up from the strange void Henry's death had created.

"Did you want to come up for...tea?" she finally ventured. "Or something stronger? And a view of Grace Church?" she asked. She had to sound like an idiot. "I'm keyed up tonight. I don't know why. I keep thinking we should all be exhausted..."

"Yes."

"What?"

"Sure, I'd love to come up."

"Oh! Um, great." She turned and headed for the elevators, praying that her flushed face wouldn't betray the way she suddenly longed to forget every propriety, every word, and just fall into his arms.

Preferably naked!

Chapter Five

"This place is incredible!" Micah said, looking around her loft. He glanced at her with a curious frown. "Did I miss something about you? You're a trust fund baby?"

She laughed. "I happen to have an uncle who isn't living here right now. He was a snow bird, but these days he's spending most of his time in Florida. He's had the place for fifty years, and I'm pretty sure his dad had it before him. They were both in construction, so they did a great job with the space. However, only in NYC, Tokyo, Mexico City and a few other cities around the globe would this be considered a big space. You must've tried to rent in New York at some point."

He nodded, staring out the windows at Grace Church.

"I went to Brown, and then to Columbia University, so I lived here for a while," he told her. He grinned drily. "I think I lived in a closet."

"Ah, Columbia," she murmured. "But you knew Henry at Brown, right?"

"Yep. I knew Henry. I went on to Columbia, where I was a grad student. I didn't particularly intend to be an Egyptologist, but I was considering anthropology or archeology. And then…"

His voice trailed off. He shrugged and then turned

to look at her again. "My senior year as an undergrad, a friend of mine was kidnapped. The FBI tracked down the kidnappers. My friend's family was rich, and yes, they were going for a ransom. But...well, one of the guys admitted after they were caught that they hadn't intended to let him live. I guess I kind of fell into a bit of hero worship for the FBI. So, I switched to criminology. I knew I wanted to do what those agents had done."

"I'm sure you made a great choice. I know how Craig feels. Of course, my whole family worries about him, but we all believe he made a great decision."

"Yeah. Sometimes, though, the bitter truth is that you lose, too. Things don't always work out the way you want them to."

"You didn't lose with Henry. You were never in the fight," Harley said quietly.

He nodded. "Yeah? Thanks. Well, I suppose I should get going."

"I'm still wide-awake. Um...can I get you something to drink? I was going to make tea. Oh, it's not decaffeinated. I mean, that's never made much of a difference to me, but..."

"Caffeine. Sounds good."

"Okay."

She turned in her little kitchen area and put the kettle on. He perched on one of the bar stools. Facing her, he also faced the kitchen. Spinning around on any of the stools, you'd still have the great view of Grace Church. She waited for the water to boil, aware that he watched her as she got out mugs and tea bags.

She needed to let him go. And she needed to let go of her interest in him—emotional and physical!

"How's it going with Officer Friendly?" she asked.

"McGrady?" he asked. "He's kind of irrelevant. The powers that be have gotten the NYC office put in charge," he told her. "Henry's death may not be related to what happened at the opening ceremony, but on the other hand, it might have been. That makes this not just national but international, and luckily the FBI does work out of an office in Cairo. It was my first avenue of investigation last year when I heard about Henry. I wasn't officially on the case, but I went to Cairo. I knew our guys would be sympathetic. This might be a terrible thing to say, but I think Detective McGrady might've been disappointed that he wound up with a live victim. He wanted a murder case."

"You still have to deal with him, though?"

"Yes, but he's not really interested now. Rydell's a good guy, and he keeps apologizing for his partner. We haven't made any complaints. We're trying to keep it all copacetic."

"Where would someone get nicotine for a poisoning like that? I gather the linens were soaked in it and only the fact that they got them off her so fast saved Vivian's life, right?"

"Right."

The kettle whistled, and Harley poured the water into two mugs. Their fingers nearly touched as she pushed his toward him, as they both dipped their tea bags in the hot water. She flushed, catching his eyes on her.

She really, really needed to let him go.

That or...

Give in. Spit out the truth that she was incredibly attracted to him. Totally inappropriate under the circumstances, but they *were* adults, after all. It could just be sex; she could handle that. And they could try to figure out what was going on between them after this case was solved.

"We have people looking into large purchases of nicotine, but—"

"Insecticide," Harley interrupted, thinking of the most obvious place to buy commercial nicotine.

He sipped his tea and nodded. "I forgot. Research for an investigation agency is what you've been doing."

"Part-time. I've been trying to sort out what to do with my career. And this job pays well." She shrugged. "Only a few of the cases I've worked on have actually been criminal. Mostly civil suits. A lot of my time's been spent monitoring bad behavior. People trying to get a relative to leave money to one person or another, husbands and wives behaving poorly and, very sadly, in one case that did become criminal—stopping a blood relative from preying on a young boy. The job's been interesting, but I haven't been sure what I want to do, which way I want to go. But since I met Kieran, I've come to like the psychology part. I think I'd like to get into profiling."

"You certainly have the right degrees."

"It all looks good on paper. I'd have to see how I do in practice."

"Want to practice?" he asked her.

"What do you mean?"

He was suddenly very serious. "Think of all the people you know who were involved with the Amenmose expedition and exhibit. Who would have a reason to kill Henry? Was money ever an issue?"

"Not that I know of—other than the fact that an archeologist's prestige means more money the next time he or she wants to go out on a project. But I'm sure you're aware of that."

Harley realized she was leaning against the counter. He was seated in one of the stools, so that meant she was leaning closer and closer to him. Their fingers, wrapped around their mugs, were only inches away.

It was hardly champagne and strawberries.

It was...

She needed to move back.

"Ye olde process of elimination," he murmured, apparently unaware of their closeness. "So, who can you eliminate?"

"Everyone!" Harley said.

He shook his head. "That won't work. You most probably know the killer."

"Any of the students would benefit from prestige. It would make a radical difference as far as their careers in Egyptology, archeology and anthropology are concerned," Harley said. "It was impressive to work with a man like Henry, but to take his place would be even more impressive. Still..."

"Process of elimination," he repeated, then abruptly stood up.

"I have to leave."

"Oh. Okay. If you have to."

"Yeah, I do."

But he was still standing there. He smiled suddenly. "Yeah, I have to go," he said again.

"You really don't."

His smile deepened. "I do."

"Because I'm Craig's cousin?"

He shook his head, his eyes never leaving hers. "Because you're you. I don't know what it is… I guess we can't define attraction, but… Anyway, I'm being presumptuous, but—"

"No, actually, you're not," Harley broke in. She wondered how you could *feel* someone so completely when you weren't even touching that person.

"We have to give it time and thought."

"I wasn't thinking everlasting commitment. I'm not FBI, but I can help a great deal and we're going to…be together. Differently. I—"

"That's not what I meant," Micah said.

"Yes, okay. I guess I know what you mean. I believe… I believe we'll see each other tomorrow and the next day, and if…"

"Yes," Micah said. Then, neither spoke; they looked at each other.

"We're adults," Harley whispered.

"Yes, and so… I'm heading out."

He walked to the door. Harley followed him, ready to lock up when he left. She stayed a short distance behind him. She felt as if her flesh and blood, muscle and bone, had come alive, as if neurons or atoms or other chemical entities were flashing through her system with tiny sparks of red-hot fire. He had to leave; otherwise, she'd embarrass herself.

But she didn't really care.

Still, he was right. They needed time. Just because they could hook up didn't mean they should forget that there were consequences to any deed, even if neither had any expectations.

At the door, he turned to her.

It could have all ended there—as it should have.

She could've stayed where she was.

But she didn't. She walked forward, her eyes on his, until she was touching him, and when she did, he backed into the door. At the same time, his arms came around her.

She touched his face. Stroked his cheek, felt the power in his arms as he drew her close. She let herself shudder with a delicious abandon as she felt the heat of his body, the texture and strength in his muscles. And then she felt his mouth, crushing hers, and she returned the kiss with equal open-mouthed passion. They stood in the doorway, fumbling with each other's clothing. Micah pulled away for a second, removing his holster and Glock from the back of his waistband, setting them down on the occasional table.

Then he paused, breathing heavily. "Wait. Is there... someone else? Is there that kind of reason?"

She shook her head. "No. No one else. There hasn't been anyone else in well over a year." She felt her cheeks turn a dozen shades of red. "But it's all right. I'm on the pill."

He drew her back into his arms for a very long, very wet, hot kiss.

Then they moved through the apartment, half disrobing themselves, half helping each other.

They stood in the center of the loft, next to the plate glass windows looking out on the night, on the gothic structure of Grace Church. They both hesitated a minute.

Not that anything was wrong; rather she felt blessed.

The light that came in and bathed them together was beautiful and romantic. Micah smiled and said, "I have this great image of me sweeping you into my arms and carrying you up the stairway...but it's winding and it's iron and..."

Harley laughed. She turned and ran up the winding stairway to the loft. He quickly joined her.

The loft seemed to be aglow with light in the most glorious colors—pastels with bursts of darker blue and mauve, probably from some vehicle moving down on the street. They found each other's mouths again, kissed forever, and then Harley rolled over and straddled him. They twined their fingers together and looked at each other again, and she couldn't help wondering if it was possible to not really know someone—but to believe that you did.

You could be fooling yourself! a voice nagged.

But she didn't care. She'd been spending the year since Henry's death biding time, waiting...

For what, she hadn't known.

Until now? Until this? And maybe it was just sex...

But at this point in her life, that was fine, too!

She felt his hands moving over her body, touching and teasing, exploring and giving. They turned on the bed, facing each other, laughing, kissing, their lips roaming, intimate. They shared kisses that caused sensation to soar, cries to escape into the night...

Then at last they were together, moving with the brilliant colors of the night. She caught his eyes and they were beautiful.

His hands were electric, his movement fierce and erotic, and it seemed that they'd joined in something wonderful that captured the pulse and beat of the city... agonizing in its wonder, lasting too long, and yet over too quickly.

She lay beside him, breathing desperately. She could hear her own heartbeat as if it shook the very foundations of the building.

And she felt his knuckles, gentle on her cheek. He pulled her to him. She prayed her heartbeat would slow...

"What are you thinking?" he asked her quietly.

For some reason, she couldn't resist being honest.

"That you're very, very good. Or that everyone else in my life of the boyfriend variety has been bad. Disappointing, anyway. I mean, as a lover..."

He laughed. "I'm going to take the 'very, very good.'" He hesitated, drawing a line gently from her face to her collarbone. "Why?" he asked.

"Why are you good at this?" she murmured, perfectly aware that wasn't what he meant.

"Why have you been...alone?" he asked her.

She shook her head. "I haven't been alone. My world is very rich with family and friends. I'm lucky. I've been out there. I've even waited tables a few times at Finnegan's when they were short on people. And I actually like working for Fillmore Investigations. I'm not out on the street much. I like to think I'm kind of a little like Sherlock Holmes. Field agents with the company bring me information and I figure things out from the bits and pieces. I often talk to Kieran, and discuss my people with her, put them in hypothetical situations."

"That's work. Not personal."

"Yes, true. I've been to Florida to visit my family. And I've gone to tons of shows with Kieran's family. Her twin brother, Kevin, is an actor and—"

"I know. So why did you suddenly need me so badly?" he asked her.

She turned toward him, drawing the sheets to her shoulders as she answered the question. "Why are *you* here—needed or just as needy?" she asked.

He laughed softly. "Ouch. Hmm."

"It's a fair question. I was in criminology, probably because of Craig. I've lost family members, but I hadn't ever seen anyone die the way Henry did. And I was so crazy about him, as if he'd been a relative. You know...yeah, you know what he was like. Anyway, I tried to do something about his death. I failed. I never expected this, though!"

"You mean me?"

"No, sorry! No, I meant Thursday night, at the gala. Vivian! Why kill Henry and wait all this time to attack Vivian?" Harley asked.

He rolled onto his back and stared at the ceiling. "Maybe the killer's triggered by events."

"You mean—"

"Henry died the day your team made the discovery. Vivian was attacked the day you were all about to celebrate that discovery."

"The mummy's curse?"

He groaned.

"No! I don't believe it, but... Micah, there were Egyptian workers who told us we were going to be cursed."

"None of the Egyptian workers were here at the gala," Micah reminded her.

"Yolanda. Yolanda Akeem," Harley said.

"Ah, Yolanda."

"You know her?"

"I do. I met her in Cairo."

"So...would you say you're friends?"

"Oh, I don't think that word describes our brief time together. No, she got me out of Egypt, helped me chase after you guys," Micah said. "We're having some problems reaching her, although I assume she's still in the country. McGrady tried to get her to stick around after the night of the celebration, and he managed to talk to her for a few minutes, but in my mind, she hadn't been properly questioned yet."

"What? Why?"

"She has some kind of diplomatic immunity. And, of course, she had nothing to do with what happened to Vivian."

"How do you know that?"

"She was always within range of cameras," Micah said. He smiled. "The FBI's taken the lead, so we have footage, prints, you name it. Sadly, even with all the crime scene evidence that was collected, we don't have answers. But as far as Yolanda goes, we're almost positive she wasn't anywhere near the museum before the gala. She arrived just in time for the party, and she was on camera the entire time. She didn't even take a trip to the ladies' room."

"Why do you think she doesn't want to talk to police?"

"Apparently, she believes that the entire expedition was run by a bunch of idiots, and she's tired of all the bad press involving archeological work in her country." He grinned suddenly, and ran a finger from her collarbone to her abdomen. "There's something wrong with this picture I'm lying here, next to you, seeing you, feeling you and..."

"And we're talking about work. But with your kind of job, it's what you do all the time, right? Is that what you mean?"

"No," he said, laughing. "What I meant is that I'm obviously not so good or you'd be more intrigued by us being together here—naked in bed!—than by the puzzles that will return in the morning."

"Morning, evening…"

Harley felt almost giddy and worried about herself all at once. It was too natural to be here with him. Too easy, too sweet.

She crawled on top of him, her breasts just teasing his chest. "Don't worry. I'm not at all distracted. Like I said, you're very, very good. Of course, feel free to reinforce such a notion at any time."

"Of course!"

He drew her to him. They were locked in a hot, wet kiss again, then disengaged to shower each other with featherlight touches, brushing with their lips and fingertips, delicate brushes that turned urgent and became fierce, passionate lovemaking that left them both breathless, hearts pounding once again.

It was incredible. Being together was incredible. She lay curled next to him as he held her. They were both silent for a few minutes.

"Okay, we know that while Yolanda Akeem might conceivably have had something to do with Henry's death, she couldn't have had anything to do with what happened to Vivian," Micah murmured.

Harley laughed softly. "So, *I'm* not that good, eh?"

He turned to her. "Good? Good? 'Good' is a total understatement. You are spectacular. And beyond."

They both went on to prove just how much they appreciated each other.

WHEN MORNING CAME, and they'd both showered and dressed, he sat on the bed next to her, adjusting his sleeves while she buttoned her blouse.

"Amazing, huh?" he said. "And that's not a word I use lightly."

"What is?" She grinned; she couldn't help herself. "'Very, very, *very* good'? Now, as to amazing…"

"Hey!"

"Okay…amazing."

"I meant that it was special to have a night like this, to be focused entirely on another person, without losing focus on the rest of your life."

"But remember, neither of us has a hold on the other. How awkward! What I mean is…you didn't become forever committed."

He gently kissed her lips.

"No hold. I have to meet up with Craig at the office. I'll see you later, right?"

Harley nodded. "I'll be at Finnegan's this evening. I've gotten together with Kieran and Craig for Sunday roast the last few weeks. I imagine that if you're going to be with Craig, you'll end up there, as well."

"Excellent."

At the door, he lingered, kissing her goodbye.

He left and she leaned against the door.

Then she reminded herself that he'd been nothing but a forgotten voice until two nights ago. That she'd wanted to believe she'd be happy with just one night.

Except that now…

She wanted far more than a night.

MICAH SAT IN the New York office with Craig and one of the computer techs.

He stared at the security footage from the museum over and over again.

It didn't matter how long he studied the footage, it didn't change. He saw everyone involved with the exhibit as they arrived that day. Administrators and other key people got there early, heading straight over to the area that was about to be unveiled.

He saw the coming and going of visitors to the main part of the museum during the day.

The caterers arrived. Everything looked just as it should for the evening that would welcome a special group for the official opening of the Henry Tomlinson Collection.

"Whatever went on with Vivian, it was planned way before the event. There are security cameras just about everywhere except for the offices, and they reveal nothing and no one out of the ordinary. Of course, there are the subterranean so-called 'secret access' areas that Arlo showed Harley and me," Micah said. "There's no question in my mind that whoever did this planned it well ahead of time. The linens would've been on hand in the prep room. Even before the Amenmose exhibit, the museum offered Egyptology and they have classes for high school kids in which the religious and funerary rituals are demonstrated. As to the nicotine poisoning, it's easy enough to get hold of insecticide."

"We'll need warrants," Craig said, "if we want to check out credit card purchases. Although I sincerely doubt we'd find what we're looking for. And I'm not sure we can even get warrants unless we have information or evidence we can use to designate suspects."

"Whoever bought the poison didn't use a credit card. And he or she didn't buy it all at the same place," Micah said. "It's one of them," he added. "I know that one of them killed Henry. The same person apparently tried to kill Vivian. Either that or…"

"Or?"

"We've been chasing the wrong dog," Micah said

thoughtfully. He looked at Craig. "Everyone involved in that exhibit and in the expedition knows that a lot of people didn't believe a verdict of death by accident— that Henry killed himself in a state of delirium—no matter what official reports said. I realize that most eventually gave up and accepted the verdict, or pretended to."

"What if someone was trying to kill Vivian, and trying to make it *appear* that it was Henry's killer coming after her?" Craig suggested.

"I don't know," Micah said with a long sigh. "Maybe that's far-fetched. I'm still suspicious about the entire thing that went on in the desert. The insurgency—the supposedly violent insurgency that killed no one and led to nothing but a few demonstrators being arrested. Also, there's another name that keeps coming up, that of Satima Mahmoud. The translator."

"She's in Egypt."

"I'd like to talk to her. If we can reach someone in our Cairo office, perhaps they can arrange a meeting."

"All right. I'll give tech a call. We'll see if they can get through to our people over there now. And if so, if the staff can bring Satima in and set up a satellite call."

"That's great. Either a video meeting or, if I have to, I'll fly back over."

"Alone?" Craig asked him.

"You're welcome to join me."

"I wasn't thinking about me. To be honest, I don't like the idea of Harley going back there—not now, and not in relation to this case."

"I wouldn't bring Harley," Micah said quickly.

"You're going to make damned sure you keep her out of danger, right? I know she'd say she can look after herself, and of course, that's true. But she's my cousin and I love her, so I can't help feeling this way. You understand?"

Micah nodded. He understood.

Craig was still looking at him. "Yeah, you do understand. Thank you," he said quietly.

And once again, Micah nodded.

Chapter Six

Edward Fillmore was an exceptional boss.

In many ways—although he was less on the slightly crazy academic side—he reminded her of Henry Tomlinson.

They were both decent men. Not on-a-pedestal wonderful; they had their moments. But they were both good people. Or, rather, Henry *had* been good until his unfair and untimely end.

Edward had founded his company years earlier. They handled private investigations, such as finding lost family members, searching for missing children and were certainly happy to participate in any "silver" alert, as well. He seldom took on divorce cases in which one spouse was trying to trap the other. In fact, he'd only take on such a case if he met with someone he saw as an injured party first, and then only if it meant getting suitable support for any children who might be affected.

When Harley had first gone to work for him, he'd told her to feel free to use her own time and whatever resources the company had to look into Henry's death. She'd never used work hours—say, when she was tracking down a credit card report or some lead on a missing person—to pursue her own investigation. But she'd accepted his offer, although she hadn't come up with anything yet. Henry was gone, had been cremated. And there was no lead to follow; it was all a stone wall. It was somewhat comforting to know that the FBI had encountered the same stone wall. No one had been able to crack the defenses established when the Amenmose expedition had ended, Henry had died and they'd all left the site.

Now, of course, she had a new crime to pursue— the poisoning of Vivian Richter.

She called Edward Fillmore and asked if she might have his blessing to head into the offices and search through info on various people.

Edward was quick to allow her access to his computers and databases.

So Harley spent her Sunday morning going through everything she could find on everyone she knew—including her colleagues on the expedition, the people she'd never suspected. Her search yielded little.

Ned Richter had been a CEO with a pharmaceutical company for nine years before joining Alchemy, where he'd been in charge of "Exploration" for over a decade.

His work record was spotless. He'd graduated from Harvard.

He'd married Vivian Clifford, a graduate of Cornell, a decade ago. When not working, the couple loved to vacation in historic places, including Peru, Mexico, Egypt and Greece. The couple had no children, but seemed devoted to each other.

Arlo Hampton had no criminal record, not even a parking ticket. He'd received his doctorate in Egyptology from Brown. He'd been with Alchemy for nearly eight years and had been hired by Ned Richter.

She looked up Jensen next. He'd gone to NYU. He was a New Yorker through and through.

He had a ton of parking tickets.

Nothing else on him.

Roger Eastman had been arrested once; he'd been protesting commercial testing on animals.

He'd received probation.

Belinda had no parking tickets—she didn't drive. She'd never been arrested. She'd been valedictorian of her high school class and had gone to Northwestern before arriving in New York for graduate work.

Joe—Joseph Rosello—had also been born in New York City, in the Bronx. He'd gone to Ithaca, in Syracuse, and then finished at Brown. However, she found something she hadn't known or even suspected. He'd paid his way through college by working as an extra in movies and doing a stand-up comedy gig at a place in Times Square.

According to his social media pages, he still enjoyed dressing up and playing parts.

She should have known this. And, of course, she would have—if she'd just spent more time on social media. So…he played roles.

Would that include the part of a mummy?

HARLEY WASN'T EVEN sure what she was doing at first when she reached for the phone; then she knew. She called Kieran and asked for Kevin's number, since Kevin was a working New York actor.

Naturally, Kieran wanted to know what was up. Harley told her.

"Kevin's performing at some kind of zombie walk today in Times Square. What's your guy's name? I can see if he's taking part," Kieran said.

But Harley didn't need Kieran to check it out for her; she'd keyed in some more information and had come up with Joe's status for the day.

"Yes!" she exclaimed. "They're both taking part in the zombie walk. The walk's for charity, and Joe's one of the performers doing pictures with people. Hey, do you feel like heading down to be in a zombie walk?"

"Sure," Kieran said. "I'll be a good sister. What the heck, we can support a charity and investigate what's going on. Sounds like a plan to me."

They agreed to meet at a restaurant off Times Square—quieter and not as much of a tourist attraction—and get lunch before joining the zombie walk.

And watching the players.

A waste of time? Harley wondered.

A lot of investigative work was a waste of time; that was part of the process of elimination, as Micah had described it. But Kieran was right. If nothing else, their entry fees would go toward charity.

MICAH HAD NO intention of denying anything; he really cared about Harley—and Harley certainly behaved as if she cared about him. Was it forever and ever? How could they tell? Did he want to see her again?

Touch her again, breathe in her scent, be with her again and feel her, naked, against him?

Well, yes. That was a definite yes.

But he'd never been in precisely this situation before.

Was Craig supposed to ask him about his intentions?

Or maybe he was supposed to give Micah a good left hook to the jaw.

"You're sleeping with her, right?" Craig asked.

"Define sleeping," Micah said. "I only knew her as your cousin and a voice on the phone until two days ago. Last night, yes. We were together." He hesitated and then admitted. "I actually tried to leave. Probably not hard enough."

Craig lowered his head, obviously amused.

"Just keep her safe," he said.

And then, before either one of them could say any more, the phone in the conference room rang.

Craig picked it up and frowned as he listened to what was being said. He hung up slowly, rising as he did. "Come on, Egan's office. He's got a video call up with one of our agents in Cairo."

"Already? They have Satima Mahmoud?" Micah asked.

"No, but they have some kind of information," Craig replied.

They strode rapidly down the hall. Egan's secretary waved them in and they entered his office. He was speaking with someone via his computer; they both walked around behind his desk.

Micah had met the agent on the screen. His name was Sanford Wiley, and Micah quickly greeted him. Egan introduced him to Craig.

"So, we got your inquiry just now and I happened to be in the office," Wiley said. "I don't know whether it means anything or not, but I wanted to get back to you right away with what I have. The local police are looking for Satima Mahmoud. Now, they're not always entirely forthright with us, but from what I've been able to gather, she's suspected of having something to do with agitating trouble—and insurrection. She was under suspicion by the Egyptian police, who are now helping our people with the investigation, we believe, as well. They've been searching for her for several days. We'll start our own line of investigation, since she's a witness or person of interest to you all. Fox, I know you had some interaction with her. Do you suspect her of being involved in Henry Tomlinson's death?"

"When I saw her, she informed me that the others had left. She had just gotten to Cairo herself when I was trying to head out to the expedition site," Micah told him. "I'm very interested in what she may know. Or more specifically, what she knows that she didn't share at the time. She was the one who first sounded the alarm about the uprising. Everything was pure chaos when I was there, which I'm sure you remember, Wiley. But, yes, if you find her, I'd very much like to speak with her."

"We're on it from this end—with the Egyptian police, of course."

"Of course."

"We get the impression that they're perplexed about the situation. She's disappeared."

"Thanks for letting us know," Micah told him.

There were a few more exchanges, and then they ended the video call.

Egan looked thoughtfully at Micah. "To be honest," he said, "I'm not sure what you can learn from this woman—or what you could prove—this late in the game. Crews are still going through whatever evidence they could find at the museum after Vivian was attacked, but…"

"I know, sir," Micah said. "But it's only been a matter of days. And I'm pretty convinced that Vivian Richter's attack relates back to Henry's death. And if not, well, we still need to know who the hell would attempt to murder a woman with nicotine-soaked linen wrappings."

"Yes, and we *will* find the truth," Egan said with conviction. "I'll inform you of anything we learn through our people here and in Egypt, and through any chatter they pick up." He hesitated. "If they can't find this woman..."

"There's always the possibility that she's dead," Craig finished.

"Why kill an interpreter?" Egan mused.

"There's also the possibility that she's alive—and more of a player than we'd imagined," Micah said. "Or that very fact could account for her death. If that's what happened."

"When you talked to her, did you get the feeling that she was involved in any way?" Craig asked.

"She seemed harried, frightened and glad to be back in Cairo. But I was still trying to catch up with the Americans involved. Now I realize I should have given her more attention then. The entire situation was terrifying, so of course it seemed reasonable that she'd be upset. And I still don't see her with a motive of any kind to strangle Henry."

"You never know," Egan told him.

"Except we do know that she's definitely not in the States," Craig said. He suddenly began to feel his pocket, which was apparently vibrating. "Phone," he muttered. "Excuse me, two seconds. This may be important." He answered the call, taking a step back from Micah and Egan.

"She's not in this country that we know of, anyway," Micah said to Egan. He hesitated, speaking carefully. "I still don't think she killed Henry."

"But you think she might know who did?"

"I think she knows *something*," Micah said. "She's Joe Rosello's alibi for the time Jensen Morrow and Harley Frasier were away from the camp. What if she lied because he either cajoled her or bribed her?"

Egan nodded. "That's a possibility."

"You're talking about Joe Rosello?" Craig asked, putting away his phone.

"Yes," Micah said.

"That was Kieran. She's going to Times Square with Harley. And it's about Joe Rosello. The man's an actor, and he's in a zombie walk today. Not sure I actually get it, but Kieran knew about it because of her twin, Kevin. He's one of the performers hired on as an improvisational actor and guide for the walk."

"Sounds like a good time for us to get to Times Square and see just what he's up to," Micah said.

"Zombie walk?" Egan asked, shaking his head.

"They're all over the country now," Micah told him. "The power of television and mass media today. The popularity of certain television programs can create some strange circumstances."

"There's a show on TV about mummies?"

"Mummies, zombies, walking dead. Close enough, I think. Let's head on out," Micah said to Craig. "With your blessing, sir, of course," he added, addressing Egan.

"Go, sir, with righteousness!" Egan said. "And get

the whacked-out son of a bitch, will you? Speaking of media—they're having a heyday with this. Mummies! As if we didn't have enough of the plain old walking, living, flesh-and-blood kind of criminals!"

A MAJORITY OF the "zombies" there for the walk and to support the charity were dressed up.

They wore zombie makeup, tattered clothing and many looked as if they'd rolled in the dirt.

Luckily, not all the participants were dressed up, and since it was a charity walk, whatever one chose to wear was fine. Joining the walk cost ten dollars. The fee included a comedy "zombie" performance at the end, with the bleachers reserved for those who'd paid. Anyone could see the show, but since the entry fee went to charity—three of the major children's hospitals— virtually no one was going to mind paying.

"This would've been fun no matter what," Kieran told Harley, surveying the crowd. "A lot of the costumes on the walkers are really cool. Oh, there, at the sign-up tables. There's Kevin."

Kieran started walking ahead; Harley quickly followed.

Kevin Finnegan was an exceptionally good-looking man, tall, with great bone structure, a toned body and broad shoulders. He and Kieran were clearly related, but of course, they weren't just siblings—they were twins. Like Kieran, he had deep auburn hair and his eyes were a true blue.

Harley waited while Kieran greeted her brother with a hug and a kiss; she then greeted him, as well.

"I'm so glad you came out. I know how you feel about crowds in Times Square," Kevin told his sister.

"It's...well..." Kieran began.

"Ah. I'm being used," Kevin said, but his smile was affectionate. "What do you need? How can I help?"

"We signed up legitimately, don't you fear," Kieran said. "But do you know a Joe Rosello?"

"Not that I'm aware of."

"No? Oh, I guess you don't know everyone working here today," Harley said.

"Actually, I do."

"Oh! Well, supposedly, Joe's working."

"Maybe he works under a different name. SAG rules mean you can't use a name if someone else has it already. Or even if he's not SAG, he might be using a stage name," Kevin said.

"That's him! That's him right there!" Harley exclaimed.

"Oh, so that's your guy. His name is Robbie. At least when he's here it is. Nice guy, or so it seems."

Joe—or Robbie Rosello, as he was calling himself for the day—was standing over by one of the tables. As Kevin had been doing, he was posing with people who wanted their pictures taken with a zombie.

He was dressed in tatters. Not like a mummy, just in tatters. His skin was painted white and he had very effective makeup that darkened his eyes and made his cheeks sink in.

As Joe so often did, he was flirting.

"Yep, that's him!" Harley said again.

The girls with whom he'd been posing moved on, and Harley ran over to him. He turned to look at her and his eyes widened with surprise, alarm—and wariness.

"Harley!" he said. "Um, what are you doing here? You're a zombie fan?" He sounded skeptical.

"It's a good cause, right? You know, I was shocked to find out that you're an actor."

"Oh, well...?" He smiled at her awkwardly. "I'm not really an actor, more of an 'I love the movies' kind of guy who likes to get work as an extra. I don't hide it, but I guess I don't talk about it at work. There are people who don't think you can be a serious academic if you...if you do things like take part in a zombie walk."

"That's silly."

"Yeah? Well, we both know the world can be full of silliness, some of it malicious."

She nodded. "I guess, but if this is something you love, you shouldn't have to be afraid that others won't approve."

He frowned. "I agree."

"I guess we have to work on convincing the rest of the world."

"The academic world, anyway. How did you even find out about this?"

"You remember Craig Frasier, my cousin? He's dating Kieran Finnegan. And her brother, Kevin, is an actor—"

"Kevin is a *serious* actor. He actually makes a living at it," Joe said. He grimaced. "I don't think I'd be able to do that, so I have to be a serious academic instead."

"By the way, you look great," she told him.

"Thank you."

"Is the costume yours? Do you have many...costumes?"

"Oh, no. No," he said firmly, apparently figuring out just where she was going with her question and why she was really there, "No! Emphatically no. I've never dressed up like a mummy." He hesitated. "I swear, I'd never have hurt Henry, and I did nothing to Vivian Richter. I swear!"

"Hey, Robbie! Zombie dance thing starting up," someone called.

"Excuse me, gotta go. Don't worry. I'll have thousands of witnesses for my every move today," he assured Harley.

"Have fun!" she said.

He gave her a thumbs-up and joined a number of other actors, Kevin Finnegan among them. Someone struck a chord on a guitar, and the group went into a shuffle dance, akin to the one in the music video for Michael Jackson's old "Thriller."

The song was very clever, and the words had to do with giving generously to fight disease.

And when it was over, Kevin—the head zombie, apparently—stepped out from the group and announced they'd be walking down Broadway. Volunteers with water were positioned along the route. The walk would end at the bleachers, where some of the entertainers would then be performing.

Harley turned and looked around until she finally saw Kieran. Kieran saw her at the same time and hurried toward her as a sea of people—some in zombie rags and makeup, some not—came between them. They were almost carried along by the crowd. Kieran shrugged and waved at her from a distance, then laughed as they were both pushed along.

Harley tried to thread her way through the would-be zombies.

Kieran did the same.

Now and then, they'd come across another kind of creature, something from Disney or perhaps one of

Jim Henson's characters from his movies or television shows.

Harley ran into some comic characters she didn't recognize. A man in a very large banana suit struggled to maneuver to the side.

He fell over.

She tried to reach him, but he was helped up by a group of grapes. Police were everywhere on the street and they also tried to help the banana; the grapes were just faster.

It was Times Square, after all.

And Times Square on an especially crazy day. It reminded her why she usually avoided the area. But a lot of the theaters were down here, too, and she did love going with Craig and Kieran to see plays when Kevin was in them—and even when he wasn't!

But today...

"Hey there!" Kieran called. She was walking parallel with Harley, a few feet to the left.

"Hey!" Harley called back, grinning.

But then she saw the mummy.

On a day like this, it was difficult to discern the differences between costumes; many were tattered white, and appeared to have been made from linen strips.

But this...

This was a mummy.

It was a mummy that looked exactly the way Vivian Richter had looked when she'd staggered into the midst of the gala. It might've been created by the same costume artist! Or would-be costume artist...

The thing was behind her, lurching along. Harley scanned the crowd. The mummy seemed to be walking alone.

And walking in a casual manner that brought it closer and closer to Harley.

"Kieran!" she screamed.

At first, her friend turned to her with a broad smile. Then she saw the mummy. And she began to stride aggressively over to Harley—with the mummy between them.

The mummy sensed pursuit and headed toward Kieran. But then, it headed back in Harley's direction with a purpose and a vengeance, no longer staggering.

"Come on, come on, I'm ready for you!" Harley thought. "Police! Police!" she cried.

And then the thing was upon her, placing a hand on her chest. It looked right at her, but she couldn't see its eyes. They were covered in the same linen gauze that stretched over the body, dirtied and rendered old, as if—mummy or zombie—the creature had long been dead.

THE THRONG OF people was impressive, particularly for a charity event.

Micah assumed many people were out just for the entertainment value and, of course, the fun of dressing up as a zombie.

But it made for a massive crowd—tens of thousands at the very least, and maybe many more considering the size of New York City.

"I see Kevin Finnegan," Craig said.

"Where?"

"Leading the zombie charge."

"You're sure that's Kevin?"

"Yes, and if so, Kieran is near him, and if she is…"

"Then Harley's near Kieran. Let's go!"

Wending their way through the horde of people wasn't easy. Apparently, no one had thought to tell the regular performers who thronged Times Square daily in costume, charging for tourist pictures, that zombies would be ruling the day.

Maybe it didn't matter. As they hurried past the Times Square Marriott, Micah saw a zombie posing with a Disney figure and with one of the imitation "naked" cowboys who'd staked a claim on the street.

He kept up a brisk pace, saying "excuse me" almost every other second.

And then he saw Kevin Finnegan, laughing, talking, making announcements through a speaker and pointing to the bleachers ahead.

He also saw Joe Rosello dancing along with a group as he moved forward in costume—ragged jeans, ripped rock band T-shirt and heavily made-up face and body.

And there…

A mummy!

A mummy, standing in the street, touching Harley, touching her with wrapped hands that appeared to be wet, soaked in something.

"Stop now!" he shouted.

He barely avoided knocking over a teenager playing zombie-on-a-crutch. In a circuitous route, he cleared a number of teens. As carefully as he could without losing speed, he continued to press forward through and around people.

The mummy saw him—and turned to run.

He heard Harley shout. She was starting to run after the thing.

"No!" He caught up with her.

"We have to catch that mummy!" she said.

"No, no—get your shirt off!"

"What?"

"Your shirt. Get your shirt off."

"Here? In Times Square?"

Craig, gasping for breath, had reached them. "Get your shirt off! The hands—the mummy's hands were covered in something. Get it off *now*. Harley, damn it, there could be poison on your shirt. Get it off before..."

She cried out, all but ripping the shirt from her body. It fell to the ground.

There were creatures of all kinds gathering around them.

"Way cool!" a passing zombie said.

"Yeah," said another. "It's legal, you know. Men can go topless, and women can go topless! New York City, man. What a great place."

"Maybe she'll take off her bra!"

"Moron!" Harley breathed, swinging around.

"I've got the shirt," Craig said, slipping into gloves and reaching down.

"The mummy's probably shedding poison with every step," Micah said. "Cops. Get cops over here. Warn them there's a hazard...gloves, bags..."

He didn't need to talk; Craig knew what had to be done as well as he did. Micah had already begun moving, and as he did, he swore. The "mummy" was indeed shedding, leaving what was likely poisoned and hazardous material every few steps.

But the trail of wrappings at least gave him a direction to take, as clear as tracking any animal, human included, in a forested wilderness.

"Look!" a girl cried. "It was a mummy! A mummy!"

She'd picked up some of the shredded linen that had

been cast on the ground. Micah swore again, using his gloved hands to snatch it from her.

"Hey!" she protested.

"Get to a cop. Get to a doctor. That might be poisoned material," Micah said. A man quickly appeared at the child's side, holding her, and taking Micah more seriously than she did, apparently.

"Cop! Doctor!" Micah ordered.

"Yes, sir!" the man said, clutching his daughter.

Micah hurried on.

Cops were filling the area. Craig had gotten to Kevin Finnegan, and Kevin was announcing the problem, warning people not to touch the linen, to get to a cop, hospital, or doctor if they had.

Micah kept running. He saw more of the linen along the road. Swearing, he knew he'd have to stop and add it to the growing cache he stuffed into a large evidence bag as he hurried along.

The "mummy" had planned well, knowing that the police and FBI were fully aware that poison—using poisoned linen—was his or her talent.

And that they'd definitely be delayed in their pursuit, trying to keep others from becoming victims of possible illness or even death.

The last piece of linen was in front of an alley that led from Times Square down one of the side streets.

Micah swung around the corner, racing down the street. And then he stopped.

The street was filled with massive office buildings; there was also a massage place, a Chinese restaurant and somebody's bar and grill.

And there was no one on the street.

It was New York! Where was everyone?

But it was Sunday. Offices were closed. Whoever was getting a massage was already inside; any diners at the Chinese restaurant were already seated.

Micah hurried along the street. The mummy couldn't possibly have changed so quickly.

Or maybe it had. Maybe the linens had been shed completely and the mummy was just a normal person now, enjoying a delicious bowl of lo mein.

Micah moved on down the street.

Yeah, by now, the mummy might be just a "normal" person.

But Micah was sure it was going to be a normal person he knew. And he was determined to find that person. This time, he was chasing the damned mummy—person, whoever it was—to Jersey or Connecticut if he had to.

There! Up ahead.

The mummy was turning onto Fifth Avenue and heading north.

Micah started to run.

"Do you know who it was? Do you have any clue who it was?" Kieran asked Harley.

It had been a ridiculous, uncomfortable day. She was still half-naked, feeling embarrassed and exposed. Just because one *could* go topless according to NYC's equality laws, didn't mean she had any desire to do so! She was running through the crowd, Kieran keeping pace beside her, anxious to get to a car so she could go home and have a shower.

A taxi stopped for them when they made it over to Eighth Avenue. The driver grinned wolfishly at Harley, nodding when they gave him her address. A quick conversation with one of Craig's ME friends had assured them that Harley's going home for a shower would be fine; if the poison had touched only her clothing, there should be no problem, and of course, once the contaminated linen was analyzed, they'd know what they were looking at.

"We aren't even sure there *is* poison on the wrappings," Harley said.

"What do you want to bet?" Kieran asked her.

Harley didn't want to bet.

The mummy had taken her completely by surprise. She'd wanted to knock the thing in the head and rip the linen wrappings from it.

And instead…

It had touched her, and only Micah's arrival had kept her from contact with linen that was possibly doused in nicotine.

"How the hell is that damned mummy wearing poison and not dropping dead?" she demanded. The driver was staring back at her in his rearview mirror, even more interested than he'd been earlier. She leaned forward, ready to snap at him—and then didn't.

What the hell. She dropped back against the seat.

"Kieran, how is he or she doing it? All that poison?"

"Wearing something underneath the wrapping, I guess. We don't have anything analyzed yet, although I'm convinced that was actually an attempt on your life—or a warning for you to back off."

"Okay, so the mummy found me. But it looked as if the mummy was running through the crowd, touching anyone and everyone," Harley said.

"That was to stop the police or anyone in pursuit," Kieran told her.

"Hey!" Harley snapped. The taxi driver was grinning; he was about to take a roundabout route to her building. "No, go straight and then turn right!" she said.

"One-way street," the driver said in a singsong voice.

"And it's going the way we want it to!"

They reached their destination and Kieran paid the cabbie as they stepped out; Harley realized she was being rude.

"I'm sorry. Didn't mean to make you pay that!"

"Harley, that's the least of our concerns at the moment," Kieran said.

"They haven't called? Micah or Craig?"

"Harley, Micah was in hot pursuit and Craig was headed in to get those wrappings to the lab. It takes time. We're here. Listen, just smile at the clerk or security guy on duty," Kieran advised. "He's staring at you just like the taxi driver was. Now let's get up to your place."

Harley did manage a nice smile for the security guard on duty. He was staring at her, as Kieran had said, but at the last minute sent her a confused smile in return.

Upstairs, Harley told Kieran to make herself comfortable, and Kieran said she would. Harley showered.

And showered, nearly scrubbing herself raw in the process.

She emerged from the shower, wrapped in a robe, and hurried downstairs.

Kieran was on the phone. She turned to look at Harley.

"Good call on Micah's part. Yes, those wrappings were soaked in nicotine.

There was something odd about the way she was speaking.

"What is it?"

"Micah followed the mummy on foot—all the way up to Central Park and the museum."

"The New Museum of Antiquity?" Harley said.

"Yes. And he found a mummy...half-dead."

"Mummies *are* dead."

"No, I mean... I'm sorry, Harley. Arlo Hampton is probably going to die. He was found on the floor, stretched out in wrappings, right in front of the Temple of Ra."

Chapter Seven

The same day Vivian Richter was released from the hospital, Arlo Hampton was rushed in, swiftly ripped out of torn swaths of mummy wrappings.

This whole thing was his fault, or so it appeared.

He was both the would-be killer—and his own victim, in the end.

At least, Harley thought, that was how it appeared. Or how it was *supposed* to appear.

It seemed evident that he'd dressed up as a mummy but carefully gloved his hands in plastic before soaking a number of loose and shredded strips of "decayed" linen in nicotine and then heading out to assault a "zombie" crowd. Afterward he'd returned to the museum, only to collapse there.

Perhaps he had started back in the Sahara. Perhaps his jealousy, his determination to rise in his field, had caused him to attack Henry Tomlinson back at the expedition prep tent. He must have attacked Vivian as a mummy. She'd blacked out and he had dressed her up and when she came to, he'd sent her, crazed, into the crowd, where she'd been saved.

Today...

No one really knew his intent. Had he just meant to poison a bunch of random "zombies"? Had he known, perhaps, that Joe Rosello was going to be among the actors? Had he thought Joe knew something and needed to be silenced?

He'd come up to Harley.

He had touched her with his poisoned linen rags.

But he couldn't have known Harley would be there; Harley hadn't even known that herself until the last minute. That seemed to make Joe the chosen target.

Unless, of course, Arlo Hampton had just wanted to indiscriminately poison people in the crowd. None of them could determine the truth as yet. And if Arlo died, they might never find out.

Arlo might be accused of killing Henry, or the attempted murder of Vivian—and intent to attack Joe Rosello and a number of innocent "zombies" in the crowd. But he'd calculated wrong; he hadn't taken the right care. He had not been immune to the poison he'd been trying to administer to others.

They knew this, because Craig gave them whatever information he could over the phone. He and Micah had managed to get to the museum quickly; in fact, Micah had reached it just minutes after everything happened. He'd pursued the mummy from Times Square!

Harley insisted that she and Kieran needed to get to the museum.

She didn't know why; she just knew the whole thing simply didn't feel right.

They got there fairly fast. Officers in uniform were maintaining crowd control—the entire museum had been closed down—but someone on duty recognized

Kieran. Craig was summoned, and the two of them were let through with Craig leading the way past more officers, spectators, and a sea of media at the entry.

Arlo Hampton no longer there, of course; he'd been rushed to the hospital. Photographers and crime scene technicians were still at work. Apparently, Arlo had been discovered by a pair of teenage girls who remained in a corner of the room, huddled together. They were still in shock. According to them, Arlo had grunted and tried to reach for them when they'd first found him, nearly giving them joint heart attacks. They'd now told their story a few times and were waiting for their parents.

Rydell and McGrady were there; it remained, after all, a joint investigation. They were with Craig and Micah, trying to create rational scenarios as to what might have happened.

Micah was looking at crime scene photos on his phone, photos snapped by the security guard first on the scene.

McGrady tried to stop Harley when she stepped forward to reach Micah.

"Ms. Frasier, I'm sorry, but you're in the way."

Micah immediately came to her defense. "She's got more degrees in criminology than the rest of us put together. She knew Arlo. She was stalked by him earlier and he tried to get to her at the zombie walk. Ms. Frasier may have something useful to say."

"What's there to say?" McGrady muttered. "He's probably going to die. We weren't there to get him to a hospital fast enough. Nicotine poisoning. Doc just said so—it's all over the wrappings. Jerk dressed up as a mummy for that damned zombie walk, and now he's dead by his own hand."

"It's not him," Harley said.

"What?" McGrady spun on her.

"That's not him—"

"Harley, it *is* Arlo Hampton," Craig interrupted, his tone firm as he frowned at her.

"Yes, Micah, I know Arlo's the one who was found here, but that's not the mummy who was at the zombie walk."

"Harley," Micah said slowly, "trust me. I've been running after him. Olympic-style running. I saw him when he turned north on Fifth. I followed this mummy from the zombie walk, and then I followed him down a bunch of streets, and I saw him go through the tunnel entrance to the museum. By the time I got through the maze down there and back up to the exhibit, those two teenagers were screaming." He was quiet for a minute. "Harley, it *had* to be him. We can't find any other mummies in the museum."

Harley blinked, looking at him.

"Yes, sorry, I know," Craig said, sounding aggravated and weary. "The museum's full of mummies. I mean living mummies. Living people dressed up as mummies. This place is crawling with security and we—"

"You're being an ass!"

He winced, and quickly apologized. "Yeah, sorry. I just don't see—"

"There are so many rooms and tunnels, and I'm telling you, this isn't the same mummy."

"What's different?" Craig asked her.

She didn't know! She couldn't tell. Judging by the photographs Craig and Micah had shown them, the wrappings appeared the same. True, the mummy walking through the crowd had been stripping off pieces of his wrapping, but that wasn't what bothered her, since Arlo's wrappings looked quite disheveled.

Somehow, this mummy—the mummy in the pictures, the Arlo Hampton mummy—was different. Not the wrappings so much, but…something.

"You think the cops are incompetent, Ms. Frasier?" McGrady turned his back on her.

Rydell shrugged apologetically.

"No, Detective, I think the cops are great. I've worked with lots of cops, including some of the ones here right now. Like I told you, I think they're great. You're not great. You've got a chip on your shoulder a mile wide."

"Harley," Micah said quietly.

"He's not just being patronizing and rude, he's jeopardizing an investigation!"

"Yes, that's true, but for the moment…"

"We're lead on this," Craig said.

"We need to start another search!" Micah announced, his voice booming.

"This is going to be reported," McGrady threatened.

"You bet," Micah promised him.

"Rydell, you saw it all."

"Yeah, I did," Rydell said.

Furious, McGrady stomped off. He seemed to be heading for the exit.

"Sorry," Harley murmured.

"No, you were in the right," Micah assured her.

"Someone find me a blueprint of this place. Let's get on it. Every room, every display, every office. It's going to be a long day, folks. We're going to have to get down to the basement and below. Search everywhere."

A man in one of the crime scene jumpsuits approached Micah and Craig; they spoke for several minutes, and then a group of people in crime scene jumpsuits began to emerge from various corners of the exhibit. They were given instructions and dispersed, everyone going in a different direction.

"Micah?" Harley asked. "May I go to the museum lab? I'd like to see what's been going on there. I swear to you, I'm not sure how I know, but I'm convinced that the mummy who confronted me in the street didn't look the same as those pictures of Arlo. Maybe I can find something in the lab."

"I'll keep her company," Kieran volunteered.

"All right. I'll inform the crime scene people," Micah told them. "I'm going down below. Arlo was the one who showed us all the basement tunnels and entrances and exits." He watched Harley as he spoke. She wondered if he believed her; he'd stood with her against McGrady, who was being such a jerk, but she had to wonder…

Just how many mummies could there be running around?

Living mummies, rather than the dead ones.

Micah turned away and spoke with the crime scene people again. She noticed that Detective Rydell hadn't gone with his partner; he was awaiting a discussion with Craig and Micah.

"Come on through. We're going to be searching the

offices," one of the crime scene women told Harley and Kieran. "Just follow us."

As they left the exhibit space behind and came into an employee hallway, Harley saw that Gordon Vincent, director of the museum, was arguing with the crime scene people. He looked at Harley with annoyance and then pointed at her. "This whole exhibit has turned into a disaster."

Harley looked back at him, startled. "Mr. Vincent, I'm sorry you feel that way. I don't think the exhibit can be blamed for what this person's doing. The artifacts that were discovered are amazing, sir, and law enforcement will get to the bottom of this."

Kieran stepped forward, offering Vincent a hand, "How do you do, sir? We haven't actually met. I'm Kieran Finnegan, a psychologist with the offices of Fuller and Mira. They're psychiatrists who spend a great deal of time working with law enforcement. From my field of study, I'd guess that—sad though it is—these horrible events won't hurt your museum. On the contrary—this will cause an influx of membership and tourism. People love mummies…and mysteries. You're receiving unbelievable media attention, and while these days may be hard to weather, I believe that in the end you'll find that the museum itself is in an excellent position, no matter how discouraging a comment that might be on humanity."

Vincent turned to Kieran, blinking. "Fine. It's all closed for the day. Make sure the powers that be within the FBI and NYPD let me know if I can or cannot open my museum in all or part tomorrow!"

He strode on by them.

Harley looked at Kieran and laughed. "I'm not even sure what you said myself!"

"It worked, though. I guess that's what matters."

"You were excellent."

"You can be more excellent in this situation. You're so involved. You need to really think about the people who are connected to the exhibit, and how and why they might be acting a certain way. You know all the players, Harley, and you have to think about every one of them."

"Well," Harley said, "I guess we can let Joe Rosello off the hook. I'm almost positive that he was the intended victim today. But then I happened to be there. And who knows what was really planned, since—"

"Harley, are you absolutely sure that Arlo Hampton wasn't the 'mummy' who came up to you at the zombie walk?"

"Kieran, I'm telling you, it wasn't him. And remember, Vivian Richter said a mummy came to her, and then, apparently, that mummy dressed her up as a mummy, too, in poisoned linen."

"I know," Kieran said. "But—"

"But that's the point, right? Vivian Richter was working in her office. A mummy came in and suddenly she's a mummy. Isn't it possible that the same thing happened today?"

"Of course," Kieran said. "But everyone's been searching...and they haven't found the stash of nicotine that's being used."

They reached the lab and walked through the outer entry; there were paper gowns and caps and booties to be worn inside the room.

"Really? Do we have to do all this?" Kieran muttered.

Harley laughed. "Yes! It helps prevent the spread of anything, any bacteria, that might be on antique, long-buried objects from getting out into the world. And it keeps us from bringing in anything that might be harmful to very old stuff."

"Okay, makes sense," Kieran said grudgingly.

"What I really want to do is get to Arlo's desk over there. The small one. See?"

Kieran nodded and followed Harley's actions as she suited up, donned gloves and booties, and then headed into the actual lab.

"What bothers me about this is the lack of clear motive," Kieran said. "It should be obvious, right in front of our faces. These people are dedicated to their work. It means as much to them as anything else in their lives. Maybe more. Most of us live for our mate, spouse, and so on, first—or our children. The instinct to protect a child is strong, except when you're talking about a person who's truly mentally impaired. But in our type of science, in psychiatry and criminology, you come across people who are more devoted to their work than to family or friends."

"Yes, and we think someone was terribly jealous of Henry—which is why he was killed. Now it seems that someone is trying to kill Vivian and Arlo—who are also hardworking and respected members of the Egyptology community. But…"

"But what?"

"I know I keep saying this, but I don't believe that Arlo and the mummy on the street were the same per-

son. I just don't believe it. And Arlo was the one to
walk Micah and me all around this place the other day.
Do you think…?"

"Think what?"

"There's another motive? There's something we're
missing?"

"Of course. That's always possible."

"Love, hate, greed, jealousy. Vengeance," Harley
murmured.

"Ah, vengeance. For what? And against whom?"

Harley made her way to the small aluminum desk in
the far corner of the room. It was made so it could be
constantly sterilized, but still allow for a notepad, pens,
tablet, computer or whatever else the scientists and lab
techs might need to accurately notate their work.

She opened the first drawer, which held a large plastic container of sanitary wipes.

She opened the second drawer. There was an un-
used notepad and a case of pencils.

There should've been a computer somewhere. A
tablet. Even a voice recorder.

There was not.

Harley opened the third drawer. And there she saw,
shoved against the back, a small, almost archaic, flip
phone.

She pulled it out and studied it carefully. It had the
look of a phone that might be bought at any convenience or drug store—pay as you go. She hit key after
key; nothing on it denoted ownership. She went to con-
tacts.

Her own number was there, along with the numbers
of others who'd been on the expedition.

"Kieran," she said slowly.

"You found something?"

Harley looked up at her. "Maybe. I think I may just have found a way to reach our liaison, Yolanda, who hasn't been seen since the night of the party. And I think we might have a connection to our long-missing interpreter, Satima Mahmoud."

"In 1524, New York was called New Angoulême by the Italian explorer Giovanni da Verrazzano," Micah said to Craig as they traveled deep into the underbelly of the museum. "The first recorded exploration by the Dutch was in 1609. In 1664, English frigates arrived and demanded the surrender of the city. Peter Stuyvesant sent lawyers to arrange the capitulation—the Dutch and the English liked to go at it in those days. Well, come to think of it, over the years most European powers went after one another. Anyway, it was in 1665 that the city became New York under English rule."

"A lecture on New York history while we're looking for mummies—which happen to be a good bit older than the city," Craig said.

"True, but my point is that although it's not old in comparison with some cities in Africa, the Middle East, the Far East and Europe, New York *is* old. And while it all started downtown—Wall Street, Broad Street and so on—it's been many years since people came up to this area by subway. And down here in these tunnels, especially with so many routes now abandoned, it's just a jungle."

"Yep. And hey, love my city and all…but you just

gave away the fact that you were some mean historian before you were a special agent."

"Actually, I'm complaining. This is like looking for a needle in a haystack," Micah said, and he sighed, leaning back against a wall to catch his breath.

He nearly fell backward.

"What the hell?"

"Hey!"

Craig made a grab for Micah's arm; Micah caught hold of him just in time to keep from plunging through a decayed section of wall.

They both half fell and half stumbled into the remains of an old subway tunnel.

The posters on the walls were peeling, but they were magnificent; they advertised Broadway shows opening in the 1930s. There were stairways to nowhere crafted of wrought iron and beautifully designed.

"There!" Micah said, gesturing with one hand at something extremely modern that marred the time-travel look of the place.

In a corner where plaster and paneling had decayed with time, there was a pile of insecticide containers.

At least fifty of them.

Enough poison to kill… God alone knew how many people.

"THERE HAS TO be some evidence there, right? *Something?*" Harley asked anxiously.

She was seated at a corner table at Finnegan's, along with Micah, Craig and Kieran. Crime scene crews had gone into the offshoot of the abandoned subway station, and they were studying every piece of evidence—primarily the containers of insecticide—with every technique available to them to find out who had used them. Or at least where and when they'd been purchased.

No one had answered when they'd tried to reach Yolanda Akeem or Satima Mahmoud; Egan had people working the phones as well, trying to find a way to pin down the locations of the women's phones via the contact information.

Now it was a matter of waiting.

And it was still Sunday. Although it was late, they had friends in the kitchen, so they were able to enjoy Sunday's traditional roast.

"Here's the thing. We've known that Yolanda Akeem was here in New York. She was at the museum when everything happened with Vivian," Harley said. "And after they questioned her briefly, she left."

"She was visible on security footage," Micah reminded her.

"I think we definitely have a problem, and everyone's part of it—the museum and the Egyptian Department of Antiquities, as well as our government and their government," Craig said. "The truth was left to slide."

"Murder is ugly. No one wants a part of it," Micah murmured to Harley.

"Were any artifacts stolen?" Kieran asked.

"No. Not that I know of," Harley replied. "And what about the motives for any of this? Jealousy, as we already discussed? I keep thinking that a longing for glory seems obvious. Too obvious? The people who would've been jealous of Henry were Arlo and Vivian—and they were the ones who were attacked."

"And you don't think I was an intended victim?" Joe Rosello asked. "Rather than you?"

Harley looked up and smiled. Joe and Kevin had arrived together, all cleaned up and out of their zombie makeup.

Micah and Craig had risen; Kevin brought a couple of extra chairs to draw up to their table and then left telling Joe he was going to arrange for two more meals.

"You *were* an intended victim," Micah told Joe flatly. "Had to be. The culprit couldn't have known that Harley was going to be there. Harley didn't know it herself until she talked to Kieran and found out about the zombie walk and that *you'd* be there."

"But...we should be safe, shouldn't we? I heard Arlo was the culprit and that he's in the hospital—and they don't know if they can save him or not."

"It's true that Arlo is in the hospital. And many people believe he was the mummy and that he was guilty of trying to kill Vivian. She did, after all, say that a mummy had come to her."

"Was there time for the mummy to have reached the museum and attacked someone else to create a new mummy?" Kieran asked.

"You did say that you were right behind him, getting to the museum," Harley said.

"I'm afraid that yes, there was time. I followed the mummy, but I was still some distance away when I saw him go down to the basement area of the museum. Then, of course, I stumbled around down there myself for a while. They need to wall all of that off, because if they don't, they're going to lose some curious fifth-grader down there one day."

"I'm taking a leave from my job," Joe said. "I'm getting out of here tomorrow morning. When this is all over, I'll come back. I called the museum I'm working at and they understood."

"That might be your best move," Micah told him.

Joe let out a long sigh. "Thank God! I thought you were going to tell me I wasn't allowed to leave town."

"We'll need your contact information. However, you were in full sight of thousands of people most of the day. It would be very hard to prove you had any involvement," Craig said.

"Thank God," he muttered again.

Kevin Finnegan returned to the table. The talk shifted back and forth between the zombie walk and the situation at the museum.

Suddenly they all seemed to realize it had grown very late.

"I'm going home so I can get out of here in the morning," Joe said. "You all take care."

"We need to know where you'll be and how to reach you," Craig said.

"You bet. Just no sharing anything that's gone on," Joe said.

"No sharing," they all swore at once.

"I take it you're getting Harley home?" Craig asked Micah.

Kieran looked at Harley—who refused to look back at her.

She didn't know. *Was* he seeing her home? She'd thrown herself at him last night; maybe he'd changed his mind about her during the very long day.

"Yes, I'll make sure she gets home safely," Micah

said. He managed to keep a straight face. Harley was surprised that he could.

Actually, she was surprised that she didn't flush. She just smiled sweetly at Kieran, who was obviously amused, intrigued and, Harley hoped, glad that she and Micah seemed to be getting on very well, indeed.

As he drove her home, there was so much to say; so much speculation in which they could indulge.

But they didn't talk at all.

The minute they reached Harley's place and closed the door to her apartment, they were in each other's arms. Micah impatiently shed his Glock first; Harley shrugged out of her jacket, grabbing for his shirt as she tore at her own buttons.

Micah drew the shirt over her head before she could get to the last of the buttons. She had her hands on his waistband and his belt buckle, while their lips merged in a deep and fiery kiss that was also sweet and breathless and filled with laughter.

There was a fair amount of awkwardness that went along with stripping so quickly, with wanting nothing more than to touch, to feel, to kiss…

Clothing wound up strewn all over the floor.

Harley hoped there was no one on the street as she raced past the windows and headed for the stairway.

Micah caught up with her. He swept her into his arms.

"Oh, no! You can't…they're winding stairs. We'll end up—"

"I can do it this way!" he assured her, tossing her over his shoulder.

And he could. He made it up the winding stairway.

Dropped her naked on the bed and fell beside her. Still panting, he raised himself on one elbow.

Harley pushed him back down.

She rained kisses over his naked body, reaching all around, taking him into her mouth.

He lifted her up, pulled her to him, rolled with her, kissed and teased and took his kisses everywhere until she cried out. They kissed and laughed in the tangled sheets, and then they were locked together again and the laughter was gone. They were too breathless, too desperate…

This was new. So new. It had been a long time since she'd chanced a relationship with anyone. It was wonderful because…

Because it was wonderful.

She knew with an indefinable certainty that it would always be good with him. They were so easy together. They could laugh, even do silly things, and those things somehow became erotic. She wanted to forget the world and curl up next to him forever, except that one could never really forget the world.

And, of course, that was it.

She could be with him—as if he were an oasis—and still talk about the burning sands and the desert around them. She could make love, hot and wickedly wet and exciting—and she could still tell him what she was thinking. They could share confidences and exchange opinions without any risk of betrayal.

She was in lust…and maybe falling in love.

"She knows something," Micah was saying. "I'm sure she does."

"She? Which she? Vivian, Belinda, Yolanda or

Satima?" Harley asked. She propped herself up on an elbow to look down at him.

"Satima. I mean Satima," he said. "As for Yolanda, I think she just wants to keep her nose clean. She hates it that something connected to the Department of Antiquities has negative baggage attached to it. I'd swear she just doesn't want to get involved with the ugliness of it. Egan is working the diplomatic channel to get her to come and talk to us. As far as we can tell, she's still in the States. She may not have anything for us, but I'd still love to talk to her myself."

"McGrady could have turned her off American law enforcement forever and ever," Harley said.

"Sad thing is, he might have been a decent cop. You don't get to be a detective unless you come up through the ranks or know someone. He has no patience."

"And no ability with people," Harley put in.

Micah shrugged. "I want to talk to the missing girl, Satima, as well. And now we have a number for her that we didn't have before—thanks to you knowing where to dig. So to speak."

"Ah, yes…dig. The crime scene people would've found that phone. I don't know why Arlo had it where he did—or why he thought he needed a special phone."

"It's a chip phone, good around the world. Maybe that was the intent," Micah suggested. He sighed, bringing her closer. "I keep feeling we're looking at a giant puzzle and we should be able to see what it is, what the whole picture represents. Except there's one piece missing. If only we had that piece."

"We will have that piece," Harley said confidently.

"You and Craig, the FBI, NYPD. You'll find that piece. It's like…"

Her voice trailed off.

"Like?"

"Well, you know my main role in the expedition was to find more clues as to what might have happened to Amenmose. He was murdered. He was buried hastily by someone who loved him. There are many suspects, of course. He was a threat to Ay, who was regent for Tut, and who did become pharaoh in his own right. He was also despised by Tut's sister and brother-in-law. But nothing I've found in any of the ancient stories or records suggests that one of those people killed him. He had a family, and servants, so I guess the suspects are endless. I feel the same way about that as you do—as we both do—about our current case. Suspects everywhere, but it seems impossible to get the real motive pinned down. Or to determine the whereabouts of each suspect at the crucial times."

"Process of elimination," Micah said. "Joe Rosello. People did see him all day long."

"Vivian Richter. She got out of the hospital late that morning."

"I'd still like to find out if she was home the rest of the day!"

"But…"

"Something might occur to her," Micah said.

"Everyone, including you, seems to believe that Arlo Hampton is guilty. That he poisoned himself trying to poison others."

"Hey, I keep an open mind! You say the mummy

who touched you on the street was someone different. I believe you."

"We don't know where Jensen Morrow was today. Or Belinda."

"Or—at this moment—Vivian or Ned Richter. Or Roger Eastman. But we'll know soon."

"We will?"

He smiled at her. "Of course. Craig and I are just cogs in a giant machine, a machine that doesn't stop. Anyway, I agree with you. Something still isn't right. First thing I want is a conversation with Satima Mahmoud. Then Ned and Vivian Richter. Then…"

"It's about motive," Harley said.

"Motive," he repeated.

He was done talking.

He pulled her back into his arms.

And she lost herself in the feel of him against her.

Chapter Eight

Micah woke to the sound of his phone ringing—somewhere.

He remembered that he'd shed his clothing downstairs.

He leaped out of bed and hurried down the winding wrought iron staircase, glancing at the picture windows that looked out over the night, the city and Grace Church.

He sped across the room, thinking they had to remember to buy drapes—major drapes—before night fell again. Of course, that was being presumptuous, but...

He couldn't force his thoughts in any other direction.

His phone. He dived for his jacket and caught it on the eighth ring.

"Fox."

"Fox!" It was Richard Egan. "We have Yolanda Akeem down here. She's going to be returning to Egypt later this morning. She's with a friend of mine from the State Department. I suggest you get in quickly. I'll inform Frasier, too."

"Yes, sir!"

Micah turned off the phone and ran around finding the rest of his clothing. He tore up the stairs.

Harley was sleepily beginning to rise.

"What is it?" she asked anxiously. "It's not even seven," she murmured. "I guess that's not so early."

"I have to go. Now. They've got Yolanda down at the FBI office. She's leaving for Egypt, and she's with someone from the State Department."

"Go!"

He ran for the shower. She didn't follow him.

They both knew why that wouldn't be a good idea.

In a few minutes he was dressed and heading for the stairs. Harley had slipped into a robe to accompany him down. "We should've set coffee to brew last night," she murmured, opening the door so he could leave.

He paused to kiss her quickly on the lips.

"We weren't thinking about coffee. Personally, I'd forgo the coffee for what we did last night. I'll call you as soon as I know anything. You're not working today, are you?"

"No, nothing for Fillmore," Harley said. "Maybe I'll hang around and read for a while."

"Sounds good. Talk soon," he promised.

Then he was out the door. The office wasn't far, and once there, he could leave the car with a young agent in the street. No more than thirty minutes had passed since he'd answered his phone to Egan, but he couldn't help being a little afraid Yolanda might already have left.

She was returning home; this was his chance.

To his great relief, she was there. He learned from the receptionist that Egan was with her in the conference room. He hurried there—just in time to fall in step with Craig Frasier, who'd arrived, as well.

"Think she has anything?" Craig asked hopefully.

"Your guess is as good as mine." Micah shrugged. "But anything she does have might be worthwhile."

"Too true, when we keep stumbling in the dark. Literally. In the basement and below at the museum."

"Someone knows the museum—and knows it well."

They'd reached the conference room. When they entered, Egan and the handsomely dressed man who had accompanied Yolanda Akeem rose to meet them. Yolanda started to rise; they quickly urged her to remain seated.

"Gentlemen, Ms. Yolanda Akeem and Mr. Tom Duffy from the State Department," Egan said. "Special Agents Craig Frasier and Micah Fox."

Everyone sat then.

"Thank you for being here," Micah told Yolanda. "We know you don't have to speak with us. We're grateful that you're willing to do so."

Yolanda Akeem was an attractive woman, probably approaching fifty. Her eyes and skin were dark, a testament to a rich and diverse background. Her appearance was dignified, almost regal.

She nodded. "I would have spoken earlier, if I'd thought I had something of value to say," she said. She wrinkled her nose. "I spoke with that silly policeman when Vivian Richter was attacked. He wanted to know if I believed that mummies could come to life—if I thought that curses were real! They *are* real, of course, when we are cursed with foolish people!"

"We weren't in charge of the investigation then, Ms. Akeem," Egan said.

"Yes, I know. And I spoke with Special Agent Fox before, when we were both reeling from the loss of a dear friend." Yolanda Akeem looked over at Micah and smiled sadly. "So, so sad. So much trouble. Such a terrible time."

"Yes, a terrible time," Micah agreed.

Yolanda waved a hand in the air. "Everyone running and rushing—and Henry barely cold. And then, of course—the insurrection! Children mewling that they are not privileged enough. A mountain out of a molehill. But…safety first, always. Yes, it's a tough world and there are very real terrors and threats. But in this case…"

"Yes."

"My friend, Special Agent Fox, believes that something about this entire situation, and about the tentative conclusions we've managed to reach, isn't right," Craig said. "Frankly, we may be looking too hard at the wrong suspects."

Yolanda Akeem hesitated. "I wish I could say, 'No, you're wrong.' But, you see, there's a bad taste in my mouth, although I don't understand why. The expedition was going well, or at least I thought so. Henry had worked in my country many times before. We loved him. And his students…they were charming. I was happy to work with them, too. The people from Alchemy…well, I overheard them having arguments with each other over money now and then. How much was being spent, where they needed to save. Of course, it was funny because Mr. Richter was the on-site CEO for the company and he was watching pennies, while his wife… She's a true dreamer and scientist, I believe. Money meant nothing to her." She grinned. "Henry ignored them all. Arlo Hampton tried to remind everyone that *he* was the main Egyptologist for Alchemy. Still, despite the little spats, it all seemed to be going well enough. But then... Henry died."

"You were at the camp that night?"

"I was. Belinda was going to go into town with Harley and Jensen, but she's engaged, you know. They will marry soon, I hope. Video chatting with her fiancé was a highlight for both of them. Belinda used my equipment for her chats. I was doing paperwork, and she was with me."

Micah glanced at Craig. It seemed that they could definitely scratch Belinda off any list that had to do with Henry's death.

"But you saw Henry."

"I saw Henry. Just for a few minutes early in the evening. I also saw our young interpreter, Satima Mahmoud, with Mr. Rosello. Joe, yes, Joe Rosello."

Micah nodded. Joe was already off their list. He'd been on the zombie walk—and he'd been costumed as a zombie, not a mummy.

He couldn't believe he was even thinking that way!

Yolanda suddenly frowned. "Perhaps trouble was in the air. I heard Satima arguing with Joe. They didn't usually argue. They were beautiful people, you know? Both of them. But that night Satima was tired. She just wanted to go home. Joe kept saying that he wanted to finish the work. She said the work wouldn't go away, and she had family she had to see. So it was...a hot, troubled evening. Yes, hot in the desert, of course. But the Richter husband and wife were arguing, and Satima and Joe were arguing. Henry was busy with his new treasures. Arlo wanted a bigger role, and I think he saw

Henry as a means to that end, but he knew he had to leave him at some time. He was testy... That evening I wanted nothing more to do with any of them. Satima was...almost nasty to me! If I'd hired her, I would have fired her right then and there. I speak many languages. My father was Egyptian, but my mother was Mexican and French. I can interpret nicely. I wish I'd been the one doing that job."

She looked at them all and released a long breath.

"I will admit that I wasn't crazy about Vivian Richter, but I'm sorry she was hurt. Arlo... I'm sorry he was hurt, too. After Henry's death, he got his own way with Alchemy and the exhibit, but he did not seem like a bad person. Did he do all this? Why? For position? For glory? They say that he is going to die, most likely. He was not found as quickly as Vivian."

"We don't know if he was guilty," Egan said. "Or if he was a victim."

Yolanda shook her head. "I'm sorry. I know nothing more. And I did not mean to be...unhelpful. You may feel free to call me with more questions if you wish. I am returning to Cairo, but I will be accessible to you, if I can be of any more help."

Everyone rose, bidding one another goodbye.

Then the man from the State Department and the Egyptian liaison were gone. Egan, Craig and Micah were left to look at one another.

"This is the first I've heard of everyone fighting," Micah said. "Even when I was in Cairo, it didn't come up. Of course, everything was chaos then."

"That could explain," Craig began, "why Ned Richter wasn't sitting at his wife's side the entire time she was in the hospital. If they'd been fighting, I mean."

"And maybe he wasn't with her yesterday," Egan said. "Check into it. And also, we've got people hot on the trail of the interpreter, Satima Mahmoud. Let's hope they'll be able to find her. They work hard at keeping up good communications with the police, here and abroad."

"What about Arlo Hampton?" Micah asked. "Anything? He made it through the night?"

"He's alive, yes, hanging on. Unconscious," Egan said. "Doctors… Well, I'm used to speaking with medical examiners. Seems I understand them a lot better than the guys who treat the living. Anyway, Arlo Hampton's still alive but they're not sure about neurological impact."

"The guy could end up a vegetable," Craig said.

"He could pull through all the way. They had to put him in a medically induced coma. When they bring him out of that, we might learn something. Anyway, he's alive, but he's sure as hell not going to be working soon," Egan said.

"Let's trust that he makes it," Micah said quietly.

"I guess maybe we should try speaking with Ned Richter and Joe Rosello again," Craig said.

"Rosello came out squeaky clean," Egan reminded them.

"Yes, but I don't think our missing interpreter is so squeaky clean," Micah said.

"You really think this Egyptian woman—who isn't even in this country—is involved?" Egan asked, puzzled.

"Yes. But I haven't figured out how. She can't be found. I'm hoping that doesn't mean she's dead," Micah said.

"Joe wasn't playing a mummy yesterday. We know

that. But I agree with Micah," Craig said. "It'll be interesting as hell to find out what was going on between him and Satima Mahmoud."

"I'M SO SORRY. You sound terribly depressed," Harley told Jensen.

He'd called early, right around eight. Of course, by eight, half of New York was already bustling, but with no real plans, Harley had actually thought she'd be able to sleep in.

And simply enjoy the fact that she lay in sheets where they'd been together, where Micah's scent still lingered.

But she was glad to hear from Jensen; he was still trying to function, despite all else.

"Well, of course, I'm depressed," Jensen Morrow said over the phone. "Cops all over the place. It's necessary, I guess. Vivian came around fast—got better, survived!—but I understand Arlo's in bad shape. On the other hand, if Arlo did kill Henry and tried to kill Viv, he deserves whatever's happening to him."

"I don't think he did it, Jensen. He didn't commit any crimes yesterday, at any rate. I saw the mummy in the street, or *a* mummy in the street, and—"

She broke off. She suddenly knew what had been different about the mummy in the street and the pictures of Arlo Hampton as a mummy, passed out, almost dead, on the museum floor.

She wasn't sure it would be wise to share that information with anyone other than Micah, Craig and the police.

Jensen didn't seem to notice that she'd abruptly stopped speaking. "I'm here at work," he continued.

"Let's see, Ned Richter is due in, and—you're not going to believe this!—Vivian Richter is coming with him. She's barely out of the hospital. She may be a bitch on wheels, but she's a trouper, I'll give her that. The woman loves her Egyptology! Needless to say, Arlo won't be here. And it's lonely without him. None of our buds are around. Belinda and Roger are busy with their own work. Talked to Joe—he left town this morning. He's scared. He thinks the mummy in the crowd was after him. And that might be true. Who knows? But if the mummy *was* Arlo, then none of us has anything to worry about. Right?"

The mummy in the street had not been Arlo Hampton. Arlo was tall. The mummy hadn't been very tall.

"Jensen, I don't think Arlo was guilty of anything."

"Some criminologist you are! You want to believe the best about everyone," Jensen muttered. "Are you going to come in and keep me company and help me ward off mummies?" he asked.

"I—I was going to spend some time with Craig's girlfriend."

"The lovely Kieran. So the two of you are going to dig deep into all our minds and figure out which one of us is the sicko? Whoever it is has to be crazy as a bat. I can see the defense in court. 'The bacteria made me do it!'"

Harley couldn't help smiling. "Defense attorneys. It's their job. But, yes, bacteria. It can affect the mind."

"Should I leave town?" Jensen asked her seriously. "Man, I love this place. I know I can come off as a jerk sometimes, but I love this city and this museum. I loved the expedition, too—until Henry was killed. But I can't let all our work fall apart, Harley. It meant too much to Henry. And it's too important for future generations."

"You're right," Harley agreed. "The cops—"

"Are idiots. Whoops, sorry. Maybe the Feds are better."

"Killers make mistakes—and they get caught," Harley said.

"And sometimes they don't."

"This time, they will."

"You haven't seen the half of it. The stuff here, Harley, it's ironic that it all started with a murder, isn't it? Amenmose, I mean. Maybe you can figure out who killed the guy. That was the major thing for you on our expedition, right?"

"Yep. I still find it incredibly interesting that he was killed, and yet he was rewarded with the kind of tomb that would allow him to move into the afterlife," Harley said.

"Come in today! I'll meet you at the doors. You'll be safe. Lots of cops around. I'll get you any piece of research material you want that I can find! I'll be like your apprentice!" Jensen said.

"Okay," Harley agreed. "I'll text you when I'm at the entrance."

She ended the call and glanced around the room, running her hands over the sheets. So much for luxuriating in memory.

She hurriedly showered and ran out, anxious to get to the subway and up to the museum.

Despite herself, she found that she kept scrutinizing the crowds of people who thronged around her. It was still morning rush hour. People were everywhere, on their way to work and school.

She was looking for a mummy, she realized.

That was ridiculous, she thought. And yesterday, it didn't seem bizarre at all that there'd be a mummy around; a mummy fit right in with the zombies.

Rush hour on Monday. Not likely that a mummy would be running around. Then again, it was New York, and people might see a mummy and merely shrug.

No mummies appeared—and she had to admit she was grateful.

As she neared the museum, she texted Jensen. He texted back that he'd meet her at the entrance.

Jensen and an NYPD officer were at the door; Jensen explained who she was and Harley showed the officer her ID.

She was allowed to come in.

It felt strange to walk through the entry with Jensen when everything was so empty. He told her there were at least ten police officers in the building, along with what he believed were "fledgling" FBI agents— probably bored to tears, but assigned to watch over the museum. Jensen talked about the museum itself with great enthusiasm; he just couldn't resist. She already knew that the facility was devoted to ancient civilizations, from Mesopotamia to Rome to Greece and ancient Egypt and other societies. He explained that he considered it a homage to humanity creating civilization; there was even a wonderful new section on the development of humans, back to the hominidae or great apes speciating from the ancestors of the lesser apes. "When this is...when this is solved, when things are back to normal, when life at least *feels* normal, you really have to come and spend a day here, just touring around, checking out the exhibits. It's a phenomenal museum. And I'm so happy to be here, except now the rest of the scientists, curators, historians—and even the café and gift shop employees!—hate us."

"Oh, I doubt that."

"Nope. It's true."

"When life does get back to normal, they won't hate you. And, as we've noted before, I'll bet all the insanity's going to make the museum more popular than ever. It has a really wicked mystery story now," Harley reminded him.

"Well, anyway, let's head back. In one of the prep clean rooms, there are some papers Henry'd been working on. Plus, there are a number of mummies in the room—still in their coffins, for the most part, except for our 'screaming' mummy, the one we saw with Henry before he…died. Anyway, I have a meeting with the museum director in a few minutes."

"Gordon Vincent," Harley murmured.

Jensen nodded. He glanced her way and sighed. "Yeah. They don't know if Arlo's going to make it or not. If he does, I heard he's probably going to be arrested."

"He didn't do it," Harley said again.

"But—"

"I'm telling you. He was a victim. Like Vivian."

"Well, from your lips to God's ears, right? Anyway—and honestly, I wouldn't want something to come about this way—I believe I'm going to be promoted to curator director for the Amenmose exhibit."

"Oh. Wow." Harley murmured. "Congratulations. Well, I guess… I mean, I understand, no one would want things to work this way, but wasn't Arlo employed by Alchemy?"

"Yes, but he was being offered the permanent position here," Jensen said.

They walked by the temple and the exhibits that were usually open to the public, then went to the employee section of the museum and one of the rooms next to Arlo's lab.

"It's mainly artifacts," Jensen said. "But that desk has boxes of Henry's notes. No one could read his scribbled handwriting as well as you could. Maybe you'll find something. I'll come back as soon as the meeting's over and we can go to lunch. Not in the museum, I'm afraid, since everything is closed down today. But I'm sure we can think of someplace you'll like."

"How about the sandwich shop over on Sixth?" Harley suggested. "It's a five-minute walk."

He gave her a thumbs-up and left. She listened as the door clicked shut.

This room didn't require "clean" suits, but it was climate controlled. Harley assumed it would be taken for granted that anyone in the room would have complete respect for ancient sarcophagi, bodies and other artifacts.

For a moment, she just looked around.

Many things were still crated. There were just so many artifacts that they were switched in and out of the display. Some of the sarcophagi—the magnificent, beautifully designed and painted outer coffins—had been unpacked. They'd withstood time and climate well, since they were made of hardwood and precious metals.

Shelves on the wall held numerous canopic jars; others were heaped with jewelry. One shelf contained dozens of statuettes and, carefully set in a corner of the room, was a pile of chariot wheels, the body of a chariot and a set of harnesses.

Another shelf held several mummified cats.

Yet another held weapons, some of them simple, having belonged to rank-and-file soldiers. There were maces, shields, daggers, swords, knives and more. Some were inlaid with precious jewels and gold.

They were worth a small fortune.

But to the best of Harley's knowledge, nothing had ever disappeared from the museum.

The motive for murder wasn't for treasure. So it seemed, anyway. Then why...?

She shook her head. It was like a puzzle, as Micah had said—with one crucial missing piece. But if you could find all the pieces and put them together, a picture would emerge.

A picture from the past? Perhaps. And what might that have to do with the present? Probably nothing at all. But then again, sometimes just turning one's mind to a different puzzle helped solve the one that was more pressing.

Harley examined the many offerings in the room that would eventually be catalogued and join other treasures on the museum floor. Then she moved to the cheap aluminum desk—with the cheap aluminum chair in front of it—that was piled high with cardboard boxes of Henry Tomlinson's observations and recordings. They ranged from his calculations as to where they would find the tomb, to his reactions the day they discovered it. If she knew Henry, the boxes were also stuffed with research papers and anything else he'd found or received that complemented his own work.

Harley sat down and began to read.

Surely, museum staff had at least scanned them before this.

But maybe they hadn't read everything. Maybe they hadn't known Henry.

Maybe they hadn't been determined to catch a killer.

NED AND VIVIAN RICHTER had a house—a Victorian manor in Brooklyn, in the Williamsburg area, not far from Pratt Institute.

"Swanky," Craig murmured, ringing the bell.

"It is nice," Micah agreed. "When I was around here several years ago on that special assignment I worked with you, this area was still kind of sketchy. Lots of drugs and crime—and 'swanky' places like this were usually turned into frat houses or apartment buildings with dozens of closet-size apartments."

"This area has come up in the world—and someone's put real money into this house. But Richter's been a CEO on expeditions with Alchemy. I guess he's earned plenty of bonuses and more through the years," Craig said.

"I guess so."

Craig rang the bell again.

"What do you want to bet a maid's going to answer?" Micah asked.

"I wouldn't bet against you!" Craig replied.

"Nothing wrong with being rich," Micah said. "I'd love to try it one day."

They were right; the door was opened by a pretty

young woman in a maid's outfit that would've done any movie set proud.

"May I help you?" she asked. She had a strong accent, possibly Slavic.

They showed their badges.

"We need to see Mr. and Mrs. Richter, please," Micah told her.

The woman pursed her lips. "You are aware, sir, that Mrs. Richter is just out of the hospital," she said.

"Yes, we are aware. We plan to be brief," Craig assured her.

She led them into a parlor that looked like a furniture showroom. Micah wondered if anyone had ever been in the room before.

But they were only there a minute or two before Vivian Richter made an appearance. "Gentlemen. What can I do for you? I'm about to head into the museum. With everything that's been going on... Well, I keep thinking that maybe someone's out to sabotage the exhibit. I keep going over our books, our notes—and, of course, our artifacts. I'm saying 'our.' They aren't ours, as I'm sure you realize. Everything we discovered will be returned to Egypt. We're not thieves anymore. There was a time, though... Did you know that during the Victorian era, mummies were so plentiful they were often used as kindling? That's shocking, isn't it?"

"I think I've heard that somewhere," Micah said.

"Well, anyway...how can I help you? Would you like to come into the museum with me?"

"Actually, we'd like to know where you were yesterday, once you got out of the hospital, and if you were with your husband all day. We'd like to speak with him, too."

"Ned's already gone to the museum. But in answer to your question, he was with me all day. He's a devoted husband."

"When did he leave?" Micah asked. "This morning, I mean."

"A little while ago, I believe," Vivian said.

"You *believe*? You didn't actually see him?" Craig asked.

"I spent yesterday and this morning sleeping, resting. I know when my husband's with me. I can feel his presence. Are either of you married? No? You see, after years of marriage, you don't need to *see*, gentlemen—you *feel*. You're both still young. Wait until you've been married for years. You'll understand what I'm talking about."

Vivian Richter was dressed in an attractive, businesslike pantsuit; she looked very thin and a little flushed, but otherwise well.

"Agents, why exactly are you questioning me?" she said to them. "I'm a victim. And you can't possibly suspect Ned of any wrongdoing! The whole expedition rested on his shoulders. He wouldn't want anything to go wrong."

"Our apologies, but questioning is necessary, under the circumstances," Micah said.

"Part of the job," Craig added ruefully.

"Oh, please!" Vivian said. "Agent Fox, I heard that you saved my life! And you, Agent Frasier, have been hard at work on the case. I'm grateful to you both, although—due to my recent bout with near death—I haven't had much chance to socialize with law enforcement."

"Mrs. Richter, I can't take credit for saving your

life. Anyone there would have dialed 911," Micah said. "We're just glad to see you looking so well."

"Yes! I thank God!" she said. "Great hospital staff, wonderful EMTs… I'm a very lucky woman. I understand I was poisoned with insecticide but apparently, according to the doctors, there's been an upsurge in problems of that kind because of the liquid nicotine used in electronic cigarettes. They hit me with activated charcoal, and they monitored me for seizures. I was lucky, so lucky. I hear Arlo may not fare as well, that he was exposed to a heavier dose of poison and that he was unconscious when he was found. But I also heard that the police believe Arlo was guilty. That he might've been the 'mummy' who attacked me. Who meant to kill me!" she ended in a whisper. "Arlo and I… We worked well together. I thought so anyway. I wonder if he was worried because I'm married to Ned. Maybe he was worried that would put me in a better position for a raise at Alchemy. And I realize that some people are convinced that Henry was killed… I never knew what to think. I mean, we had to run! There was death coming at us from the desert!"

"Of course," Micah said sympathetically. "So, you believe we'll find Ned at the museum now?"

"Yes. He should be there working."

"But he didn't actually tell you he was going in. And you didn't actually see him," Craig said.

"No, as I was telling you…"

"Yes. You *felt* him. When's the last time you *saw* him?" Micah asked.

"I, uh… Yesterday's a bit of a blur for me. We left the hospital and then—"

"He came to the hospital to get you," Micah inserted.

"I told you! He's a loving and devoted husband," Vivian said. "Yes! He came to get me. I'm going to call your superiors, gentlemen, if you suggest once more that he's anything less than a wonderful man."

"You still didn't answer the question," Craig pointed out.

"All right! I don't know what time he left this morning. I know he was going to the museum. And he knew, of course—" She suddenly stopped speaking.

"Yes?" Micah prompted.

"I knew he was going into the museum, and he knew I was coming in later today. With everything that went on, and cops, technicians, crime scene people everywhere... I need to see to the integrity of our entire exhibit—especially in light of what happened to Arlo!"

"We'll see that you get there safely, Mrs. Richter," Craig offered. "We have a company car, so we can drop you off at the museum. However, considering what you've been through, I recommend you contact one of the policemen on duty there today. I think you should be under protection."

"I'll make a call," Micah said.

"It's not necessary to request protection," Vivian said. "Honestly, I'll be fine. Now I know to watch out for people coming near me."

"I'll make a call," Micah repeated firmly.

Vivian smiled. "Thank you. It's so lovely that you're watching out for me."

"We'll wait here until you're ready," Micah said.

"Well, then...thank you! Excuse me. I'll be right with you."

She left the room. "You'll take her in?" Micah asked Craig.

"You're going to speak with the housekeeper?"

"Yep."

"You think she's an illegal?"

"Yes. Okay, right now I'll call Egan and get him to talk to whoever's in charge of guarding the museum. They need to keep an eye on Vivian and get eyes on Ned Richter, too. Then I'll come back here and talk to the housekeeper. Find out the last time she saw Ned Richter."

"Okay. I'll get her to the museum," Craig said. He hesitated. "Richter. I just don't see him as a player in this game. He's in big with Alchemy, but he's not a fanatic Egyptologist."

"Maybe, this time around, jealousy isn't the motive," Micah said.

"Then what the hell is?" Craig murmured.

Vivian reappeared, a heavy bag over her shoulder. Craig politely took it for her, and they exited the house.

Micah opened the passenger door of the agency sedan for Vivian. She looked at him, obviously a little confused. "I don't mind riding in the back."

"Ah, but we'd rather have you ride up front with my partner. He'll enjoy your company," Micah said.

"You're not coming?"

"I have some things to do," Micah said vaguely. "Don't forget, Mrs. Richter—I'll get a cop assigned to you. Stay safe and take care of yourself."

When he started to close the car door, she stopped him. "Agent Fox, don't be suspicious of my husband. I know I'm repeating myself, but he's a very kind man.

People love him and that's why he's good at his job. He'd never hurt me."

"Stay with an officer, Mrs. Richter," he said, and he managed to close the door.

He glanced back up at the house.

He thought he saw the drapes move and, as soon as the black agency sedan with Craig and Vivian Richter turned the corner, he went back up the walk to the door.

The housekeeper was afraid; he was certain of that. Her immigration status was probably not legal, as he and Craig had guessed.

She might try to hide.

But he wouldn't leave.

And he knew that—whether it was face-to-face or through the door—she would listen to him when he threatened her.

He hated threatening people, especially a young woman like this, working hard to get into the country.

But he had to know the truth.

Because someone else could die.

Standing there on the steps, waiting, Micah realized that he was afraid for more than just an elusive *someone.*

He was afraid for Harley. She'd been on that expedition, she'd been determined to voice her suspicions. Harley was poking her nose into everything.

And Harley Frasier was among those who might be targeted by a mummy. A living mummy armed with deadly poison.

Chapter Nine

Harley lost track of time.

She'd known for years, ever since she was a teenager and saw Craig join the FBI, that she wanted to solve crimes. She hadn't wanted to run around the streets with a gun, although she'd been more than willing to partake in classes at a shooting range. What she loved was the puzzle part of crime-solving. She also loved the concept of profiling, and was extremely glad of her friendship with Kieran Finnegan and, through her, Dr. Fuller and Dr. Mira. They were giving and generous with their time, and they'd talked to her upon occasion about criminal profiling. She'd considered going through still more school and entering the field of profiling.

She'd been part of the Amenmose expedition because of her fascination with figuring out motives, clues, possibilities. The puzzle aspects of a crime.

Not that solving the murder of a mummy could help with a present-day case.

Still, solving what might be considered an *extremely* cold case was certainly a useful exercise.

That afternoon, in the room with the mummies and the artifacts and Henry Tomlinson's notes, she found herself even more fascinated with the crime—committed thousands of years ago—because, despite time and place, people were people.

She was familiar with Tutankhamen, but read more about him, including some material that was new to her. She read about Ay. There were numerous references to Amenmose, as well. He knew the stars; he could navigate by them. He knew the heavens and the earth.

And he knew about Ra, about the dishonor Tutankhamen's father had done the ancient gods.

She reviewed the facts about Tut and Akhenaten in Henry's notes and translations, as well as those prepared by other scholars. The discovery of Tutankhamen's tomb by Howard Carter in 1922 had opened their ancient lives to investigation, leading to years of speculating. Some of that speculation had proven to be true; Akhenaten had tried to create a monotheistic society, his one god being Ra, the sun god. When Tutankhamen came to the throne, his father's efforts had been completely erased. In fact, his father's reign had been erased from records, and his mummy had disappeared.

Among Henry's papers, Harley found a research document dated 2010, of which he was a coauthor. It was about the discovery, in a cache of royal mummies, of one who'd proven through DNA testing to be Akhenaten.

But in Tut's time, there must've been many people who still believed what Tut's father had believed. Perhaps there were people prepared to kill a man like Amenmose, a man so ready to help Tut and Ay obliterate his father. Or not. Most experts concluded that Ay had ordered the murder.

Then Harley came across the translation of a letter mentioning a woman named Skrit; more digging showed that she was Amenmose's wife.

Harley rose and walked around the room for a moment. Was one of the mummies there Skrit?

She saw nothing that would indicate such a thing.

Why wasn't the woman buried with him? Of course, the tomb had been a secret. Had she, his loving wife, planned it, planned the burial? Amenmose had been murdered, but he'd been given all the correct funeral rites such a man would have required.

Frustrated, Harley sat back down. She began to read and research again, referring not just to the notes they had, but looking up entries online made by scholars through the ages.

She stopped looking for Amenmose. She started looking for Skrit.

And what she found was truly fascinating.

MICAH KNOCKED AGAIN.

He knew the housekeeper was in the house.

He'd been there for nearly ten minutes, and she had yet to answer the door.

But he knew she was in there. And that she was hovering close to the door.

"I just have a few questions," he said loudly. "If you don't care to answer them…well, I can have some people from Immigration come down here in a few minutes. I can call Homeland Security, too."

The door finally opened. The pretty housekeeper stepped back. Her eyes were huge and wet with tears she was trying not to shed.

Micah felt like a real jerk. "I'm sorry," he told her.

"I don't want to hurt you in any way. I just have to ask you a few questions. And I need you to answer me honestly."

She nodded, looking anxiously out at the street, then pulled him quickly inside.

"I am Valeria. Valeria Andreev. I don't want to go back, please. I want to be legal. Mr. Richter has said he will help me. He pays me well. He is a kind man."

"I don't want you to be sent back, either. You obviously want to be here, and you seem to know the language well."

"I want to be American."

"We can try to help you. But I need your help."

She nodded again, an earnest expression on her face.

"Did Mr. Richter go to the hospital to bring Mrs. Richter home yesterday?"

"Yes, that is true. It is not a lie."

"What time was that?"

"Close to noon."

"Okay, thank you. And then?"

"And then Mrs. Richter asked me for juice and some food, and told me that she would sleep, and she didn't want to be disturbed."

"And?"

"I did not see her again until this morning."

"Okay, thank you. And what about Mr. Richter? Did he stay with her? Talk to her, take care of her and make sure she was all right?"

Valeria looked stricken. She didn't want to tell the truth.

"I saw him… I saw him bring her home."

"He went into her room?"

"Yes."

"But he didn't stay there."

Valeria bit her lower lip and shook her head unhappily.

"I don't think so. I think…they argued. I think she was angry with him. I heard their voices, and then I heard nothing, and I thought…"

"Yes?"

"I thought I heard the door slam."

"Did you see when Mr. Richter left today?"

Valeria shook her head. "No… I… I saw him yesterday. I didn't see him at all today. But, of course, that means nothing. I do not sit here and stare at the door, you know. I don't mean to be a—what do you say?—wiseass. But I don't know."

Micah smiled. "It's okay. I don't think you're trying to be a wiseass. What you do know is this—Mr. and Mrs. Richter fought. They came home from the hospital yesterday at about noon. You saw them both go to her room. You haven't seen Mr. Richter since—and you saw Mrs. Richter for the first time today when you went to get her for my associate and me?"

Valeria nodded, wide-eyed.

Micah handed her one of his cards. "If you need help, call me."

Her eyes brightened and she held the card close to her chest.

Micah headed out to the street. He saw a taxi and grabbed it, pulling out his cell phone as he did.

They were nearing the bridge when he got through to Craig.

"The maid didn't actually see either of the Richters after about noon yesterday," he told Craig. "Until she brought her to the door this morning."

"Interesting," Craig said. "Because Ned Richter isn't at the museum. I talked to the officer in charge. No one's seen him since yesterday, sometime in the afternoon. In fact, right around the time Arlo Hampton was found."

HARLEY JUMPED UP, determined to find Jensen. She was almost certain that she'd discovered the truth about Amenmose. She'd put well-known facts together with information from less well-known sources—and had come up with her theory.

She wondered if there was a way to prove what she believed she knew.

Not easy.

Because, of course, if the murderer was Ay or any other person with power, he or she wouldn't have performed the deed himself—or herself. He—or she—would have had lackeys.

But Harley was convinced her theory made sense. Perfect sense.

Amenmose had been killed. He'd been killed because he'd secretly been a far greater fan of Tutankhamen's father than he'd ever let on. Ay had probably known that Amenmose whispered in the boy king's ear. Amenmose had been skilled at playing the political game. He'd pretended to listen to every word that left Ay's mouth; he'd proclaimed himself a man of the future, not the past. But in his heart, he'd felt certain that Tut's father had been right. And because of that— because those closest to him had known and others might have suspected—anyone connected to him, related to him, or even just a friend or servant to him, might have been in danger.

She left the room and glanced quickly down the hall. There was no one to be seen; not a police officer, not an employee, no one.

"Jensen?"

No answer.

"Jensen, where the hell are you?" she wondered aloud.

She hurried down the hall, past the lab. No one there, either. Of course, Arlo was the person who usually worked in the lab. And Arlo...

She hadn't heard that he was dead. Maybe he was still clinging to life, even if his poisoning had been worse than Vivian's. She hoped so.

Because she just didn't believe that he was guilty.

"Jensen!"

Past the lab, she made for her friend's office and knocked. Once again, no answer. She tried the door and it opened easily, but Jensen wasn't inside.

"Damn you," she grumbled. "Bring me in—and then disappear!"

Harley closed the door and tried the offices of Vivian Richter, Ned Richter, Arlo—even the museum director, Gordon Vincent's. No one was in any of them.

As she stood there, she again heard the terrible screech of a cat.

Just as she had heard when she'd been looking at the cat mummy.

Nothing mysterious about that, she told herself. There was obviously a cat somewhere in the museum. She'd meant to ask someone. It had probably been a stray, and a museum employee, unable to stand the sight of the poor creature begging in the street, had brought it in. That person must have fed it and kept it hidden here somewhere.

Poor thing; it deserved better.

"Where are you?" she murmured aloud. "Little creature, where are you? Where's Jensen? Where's anyone?"

She went back into the hallway, listening for the cat.

She heard it meow. She thought the sound was coming from the walls—or from beneath her.

She guessed the cat was down in one of the old tunnels, maybe in a section of the abandoned subway.

Harley remembered the day she and Micah had been with Arlo, and she hurried to the stairway that led below.

It was dark, of course.

She had her flashlight—of course.

She turned it on and walked carefully down the steps, first to the basement, through rooms and rooms of storage, and then down another level.

To tunnels of nothing.

To darkness that led nowhere.

And then she heard it again. It wasn't a scream this time. It was a pathetic kind of mewling.

She hadn't even seen the cat yet, but she felt so bad for the little creature, which was obviously scared. It probably had no idea where it was, how to get out, how to find help or sustenance.

Maybe she could keep a cat. A cat would be a good companion.

She wondered if Micah liked cats.

She wondered if it mattered.

Harley knew she was definitely in lust and halfway in love, but she'd told herself it *was just temporary,* that she expected nothing. He was living and working in Washington, DC, and he'd go back there. He'd given her no hint, nothing to suggest Harley should go back with him.

And yet she couldn't accept the fact that he might walk away. They'd met and joined forces over Henry. They got along extremely well, but they were both determined and stubborn, and she didn't intend to forget that she wanted to pursue her career.

Everything had begun just a few days ago, and already she couldn't imagine her life without him in it.

She gave a little scream, startled when the cat let out another mew. The sound was very close.

"Kitty, kitty, where are you?" she called.

The pathetic squeaking began again.

"Where are you? Come on, kitty, kitty, kitty. I'll help you!"

She came around a corner and almost fell into a niche in the wall. She tried to steady herself and realized she was leaning on an old maintenance door.

It creaked open on very rusty hinges.

She heard the cat cry again, really loudly this time. She'd found it!

"Hey, there you are," she said. "Come on, little one. I'll take you somewhere safe and warm and get you something to eat."

What if Micah Fox was allergic to kittens? She'd never asked him about pets.

She'd never asked him about anything. She'd just fallen into something crazy, she'd wanted him so desperately.

She shone her light around again, seeking the cat.

"Hey, sweet thing, I'm going to find you," Harley said out loud.

And then she froze as her light fell on the crying kitten.

And on so much more...

"GET IN HERE. We've got Sanford Wiley, our man in Cairo, ready for a video chat in twenty minutes," Richard Egan told Micah. "He has some information."

"On Satima Mahmoud?" Micah asked.

"That's what I imagine," Egan replied.

Craig was doing the driving. He was a damned good driver, and as a New Yorker, he could maneuver the streets as few could.

Micah had a feeling that whatever Sanford Wiley had discovered, it was important to their case.

He put a call through to Harley, anxious to talk to her, to hear her voice.

She didn't answer.

Craig glanced over at him.

"She didn't say she was going out," Micah murmured. "Or, she might have said that she was going to be with Kieran."

"I wouldn't worry. Leave a message. If she's on the subway, she won't get it for a while."

"I'll bet she went to the museum. Jensen—that friend of hers—I think he keeps encouraging her to come in. I don't feel good about it, but I'm not sure why."

"At least Vivian Richter seemed fine. She seems to believe that Arlo tried to kill her and that he might've killed Henry Tomlinson."

"Yeah, well, I *don't* believe it, and I'm positive you

don't, either. Also, I know damned well that Harley doesn't believe it. And Craig, what I've said before is true—Harley's had more classes of all kinds than we have. Yes, in a classroom. She doesn't have much practical experience, not really. But she's smart as a whip. If she says something is off, it is."

"I'll call Kieran. She'll track her down. How's that?"

"Thanks. Tell her we'll join the tracking party as soon as we're done with the video chat," Micah said.

"Will do."

"She's at work, though, isn't she?"

"She won't have a problem. Tell them it's an active case and the good doctors will be more than happy to send Kieran off—or get into it themselves!" Craig assured him. He spoke to the car phone; it dialed Kieran.

"Anything new?" she asked. "What's going on?"

"Can you find Harley?" Craig asked her.

"Sure. I know where she is."

"You do?"

"At the museum. I talked to her briefly when she was on her way there. Jensen asked her to come in. They're good friends, you know, and I think he's feeling pretty lost and alone in all this."

"Yeah, lost and alone," Micah murmured. "Can you get over there? I tried to reach her by phone. She didn't answer."

"I'll go right over," Kieran promised. "I'll find her, don't worry. And when I do, we'll give you a call."

Kieran said goodbye and hung up; Craig looked at Micah. "Feel better?"

"I wish I did."

"You don't like Jensen."

Micah shook his head. "But he was with Harley when Henry was killed, so…"

"Yep." Craig was quiet for a minute, and Micah knew what he was thinking.

"Two people could've been involved," he said quietly. "It's a question of which two. Do you think maybe Ned Richter? Would Richter actually have done that to his own wife?"

"They fight quite a bit, or so we've heard," Craig said. "Yolanda told us she heard them arguing, and the maid told you that they were fighting yesterday."

"Yes, but…wrapping someone in nicotine-soaked linen?"

"She was found immediately. So she survived," Craig said.

They reached the office. Leaving the car, they hurried through the ground-floor security check and up to Egan's office.

Egan was already engaged in the call with Sanford Wiley.

On the video screen, they could see that Wiley looked glum.

"Did you find her? Did you find Satima Mahmoud?" Micah asked.

"Yeah, we found her," Wiley said.

"But you didn't bring her in."

"She's dead," Wiley told them.

Micah had been standing. He sank into one of the chairs in the conference room. "Dead? Not…as a mummy?"

"As a mummy? No. Right now, they have some of her friends in custody. She was likely killed by a member of her 'group'—although exactly who that is, I don't know—or by an enemy of this group. That's just what we're being told. The situation's complicated, but from what we've gleaned so far, there was no real insurrection planned for the night Henry Tomlinson died. We know this because the Egyptian police are questioning someone they pulled in. Some kid who didn't want to spend his life in prison. He says they were contacted by Satima Mahmoud. She had money, a lot of money. She was willing to pay them to get a fake insurrection going. That's why it was such a pitiable show. No one really wanted to bear arms, go against anything—or get caught," Wiley explained.

"So we've been thinking in the right direction," Micah said. "It was all a diversion to keep the police or any other authorities from discovering what really happened to Henry Tomlinson."

"Yes, that's what we believe on this end," Wiley said. "Satima Mahmoud was found with a bullet in her back. We think it could've been fired by someone in a group with a different political view for the future— or, as I said, someone in her own group. Many people were arrested for taking part in the so-called uprising. Perhaps someone wanted revenge."

"Still hard to understand," Craig said. "The Amenmose find was worth a fortune."

"Yes, there were priceless objects. And, yes, they might have wanted them for their monetary value to support their cause, whatever that was. Thing is, the black market is hard to navigate these days. And if you're caught...not good. Cash—cold hard cash—is far better than even a priceless object. Someone gave Satima a lot of cold hard cash. At the moment, that's all I know. If we get anything else..."

"Thank you, Wiley," Micah said. "You've been a tremendous help. I'm sorry the woman is dead," he added.

Egan finished up with Wiley, and they cut off the chat.

"Cold hard cash? Someone with access to a lot of it?" Egan mused. "That's not your average grad student."

"There's Richter," Craig said. "Or…well, some grad students come from family money. That's how they manage to study forever and ever. We have background checks on everyone. I've skimmed all the files…"

"Morrow, Jensen Morrow. His father invented some kind of cleaning product. He's got money," Micah said. But it was true, too, that they'd just left the Richter house, which had to be worth millions.

Craig nodded. "Yeah. But to be fair, it *could* be Richter. He'd have the money. He was supposedly with his wife when everything was going on back in the Sahara. We know now that the two of them fight, although Vivian Richter swears that her husband is totally loving and good."

"But the maid said differently," Craig pointed out.

"The maid?" Egan asked.

Craig waved a hand in the air and said, "Sir, I think we may have to help that woman out when this is all over. She talked to Micah about Richter's whereabouts."

"Go and get Vivian Richter," Egan said. "Bring her in. I think it's time we had a conversation here in the office."

"On our way!" Micah said.

They hurried back to the street where the car was waiting.

As they drove, Micah tried Harley's number again. "Still not answering," he muttered to Craig.

"We'll find her," Craig promised. "Don't forget," he said, "she's my cousin."

There was a grim set to Craig Frasier's mouth.

Micah was glad for it. That meant he wasn't alone; they were going to find Harley, and they'd damned well find her fast—and she'd be all right.

IT WAS RIDICULOUS, it was horrible, and it was like something out of a horror movie by a master of the genre.

Harley had found the cat.

And the cat was sitting on the head of a man.

The man was dead. It was Richter. Ned Richter.

She couldn't scream.

The last thing she *should* do was scream!

In fact, she was worried about having her flashlight on. But the whiff of gases or decay, some ghastly smell, that was coming to her made Harley think the man she was staring at had been dead for some time, probably at least twenty-four hours.

He hadn't been wrapped in linen. He probably hadn't died from any kind of poisoning.

Ned had been stabbed through the heart with an Egyptian dagger. He was shoved up against a wall; he'd probably died right there, she surmised, studying the pool of blood that surrounded him. Blood that had grown sticky.

He'd been killed yesterday. Either just before Arlo had succumbed to the linen wrappings and their nicotine, or just after.

If Arlo had tried to kill Ned Richter… Wait, that

made no sense. Why stab Ned with an ancient Egyptian dagger, and then dress up in linen wrappings himself?

And who the hell had that been on the street, the person shorter than Arlo who'd approached her, touched her with the poison?

"Harley? Harley, where are you?"

Jensen?

Jensen was calling her now.

Sure, Jensen was taller than the figure who'd come up to her. But what if he was working with someone? What if he'd gone with her that night in the desert just to throw suspicion off himself? He hadn't killed Henry Tomlinson; that would've been impossible. But he might have been in on it.

She forced herself to stay silent.

But to her great distress, the kitten took that moment to mew desperately for help once again—apparently deciding that help wasn't going to come from Harley.

"Kitty! Aw, here, kitty, kitty!" Jensen said. "Who the hell would be keeping a cat down here?" he asked himself.

He was coming in her direction.

He didn't sound like a killer.

To make matters even worse, Harley's phone began to ring.

It was on vibrate, but even vibrate sounded shockingly loud to her!

She saw that it was Micah, and that he'd called several times. The calls hadn't gone through. Suddenly, now—now!—they were.

She backed as close as she could against the wall. She almost let out an involuntary scream; she'd backed into the corpse. She was stepping in the sticky blood.

"Micah!" she whispered.

He was talking as she answered. She didn't think he'd hear her, and she didn't think he had any idea that she wasn't in a good situation.

"Harley, you're at the museum, right? Kieran's coming there to get you. Leave. Leave with her. Wiley, the agent in Cairo told us Satima Mahmoud's body was found. She was killed either by a rival political group or by her own friends, they don't really know. But here's what's important—there was no insurrection. It was staged to cover up Henry's murder. The killer could be Ned Richter or possibly Jensen Morrow," Micah said. "You need to get out of there—"

"It's not Ned Richter," she said in a hoarse whisper.

"How do you know?"

"I'm looking at him. He's dead. Dagger to the heart," Harley said.

"Where are you?"

"Subbasement, I think. Near the old subway station."

"What are you doing down there, Harley? Never mind, never mind. We're on our way. You need to get out!"

"Yes, but—"

"Get the hell out of there now! It could be Jensen. Get out, Harley!"

"I can't!" she whispered.

"Why not?"

"Jensen is down here, coming right at me."

Chapter Ten

There were a number of hallways and tunnels, entrances and exits down here.

Harley knew that because Arlo had shown her and Micah around the basement and subbasement levels. She had to think; she had to remember everything they'd learned that day. She needed to...

Find a way out.

The kitten was continuing to cry. He had jumped off the body of Ned Richter and was coming to Harley at last, trying to wrap around her ankles.

Harley swept up the kitten.

Poor little thing was sticky with blood; so was she.

Ned Richter's blood. Ned hadn't done any of this. He was innocent—and he was dead. It was almost as if they'd all been victims of a pharaoh's curse.

"Hey, kitty, kitty! Where are you?" Jensen called. "Harley? Damn it. Where are you, girl? Why haven't the police gotten these damned tunnels closed yet?" he muttered to himself. "Harley? Hey, anybody down here?"

He was coming closer and closer.

A weapon. She needed a weapon!

There was a dead man right next to her. A dead man with a dagger protruding from his chest.

She carefully put down the kitten and crept toward Ned to get the dagger.

It wouldn't move! It was stuck deep in his chest, as if the man's body, his flesh and blood and bone, refused to give up what had brought about its demise!

She would've sworn out loud except that Jensen was coming closer and closer.

Micah and Craig were on their way. They'd be here soon. Kieran was up in the museum somewhere, and it was crawling with police. Kieran wouldn't wait long when she couldn't find Harley; she'd insist that the police start searching the place, tearing it apart.

"Harley?"

Jensen couldn't be more than twenty or twenty-five feet from her.

"Jensen Morrow! Stop right where you are!" a male voice thundered.

Harley knew the voice—it was McGrady. Detective McGrady. He'd followed Jensen down here. She hadn't even seen him, hadn't known he was at the museum.

Harley switched off her penlight.

The darkness seemed overwhelming, except...

She could see Jensen. He had his own light. "McGrady, what the hell is the matter with you? I'm trying to find Harley. You can help me. Harley, where are you and what the hell... Jeez! What's that smell? Is it cat poop? If so, it's the worst damn cat poop I've ever smelled."

He was talking about cat poop. He didn't know he was smelling a dead man. But if he'd killed Ned Richter, he would know.

"Stop, Morrow, or I'll shoot you, you murdering bastard!" McGrady called out.

"What?" Jensen demanded, obviously thrown. "I stopped! I'm right here."

Harley straightened in the dark, letting out a breath. McGrady was here. He was a cop. He had a gun.

But Jensen wasn't guilty. He was just looking for her. Looking for a cat. She believed it with her whole heart.

Harley held her breath for a minute, afraid to speak, to cry out—to warn Jensen and the cop—and afraid not to.

She had solved one mystery that afternoon. The mystery of Amenmose's death. His wife, Skrit, had ordered him killed. She had hired the assassins. She hadn't hated him—well, maybe she had. But despite wanting him dead, she hadn't wanted him deprived of an afterlife. She'd seen to it that he'd died; she had done so to protect herself and their children from the growing power of Ay. She'd been no threat to Ay's position, but her husband had. Still, she hadn't denied him their form of heaven.

And now...

"Harley!" Jensen called, sounding desperate.

She stepped into the darkness of the hall, ready to call his name.

But just as she did, she saw a dark figure streak out from behind Jensen, coming straight at him.

"Jensen! Watch out!"

Harley screamed the warning just in time. He spun around, avoiding a lethal blow from Vivian Richter, who was wielding a jewel-encrusted pike. But Vivian was quick to double back, hitting him hard on the head with the end of her weapon.

Jensen went down. And as he did, his light went out.

"What the hell?" McGrady roared. "Mrs. Richter, are you all right? Are you all right?"

Something flew through the tunnel—heading directly for the cop. Harley cried out his name. "McGrady! Get down!" she shrieked.

She couldn't see what happened next.

Jensen's light was gone; McGrady's was, too.

Harley and Vivian Richter were both suddenly left in absolute, subterranean darkness.

CRAIG AND MICAH arrived at the museum just in time to find Kieran telling a policeman that she was going down to the basement, with or without him, but if he valued his employment, he would be accompanying her.

The policeman was telling her that an officer had already gone down, following Jensen Morrow.

"Detective McGrady is down there. He said there's no good reason for any of those science people to be running around in the basement."

Micah didn't wait; he had to get down to the subterranean levels.

Craig went to explain to the officer that they were FBI and to get Kieran, from where she had been speaking with the cop.

Micah ran, ran hard. He reached the stairs Arlo Hampton had so recently shown him. He stumbled down them, afraid to use his penlight.

When he got to the bottom, he paused.

He began to move slowly, feeling his way.

Then he smelled death.

Yes, as Harley had told him, Ned Richter was down here. And he was dead.

Had Jensen Morrow killed him?

"Help! Oh, my God, help me!"

He heard the cry. It came from ahead, down the long hallway before him. It was coming, he thought, from the abandoned subway section where they'd found the stash of insecticide. The nicotine poison.

The voice belonged to Vivian Richter.

"I'm coming!" he called. "Are you okay? Are you in distress?"

"No...he's going to kill me. Agent Fox? It's Jensen. He's going to kill me. He and Arlo...they killed Henry. The two of them. They tried to kill me. Jensen tried to kill Arlo because he had to make it look like Arlo had worked alone... Oh, my God! He killed my husband. Jensen killed Ned, my poor Ned!"

"Where are you?" Micah asked.

He was moving very slowly and very carefully, determined not to give away his position. But as he spoke, he ran into something with his foot.

Something hard—and soft at the same time.

He stooped down, his heart in his throat. A body.

Harley?

It wasn't Harley. He quickly realized it was a man.

Ned Richter? Jensen Morrow?

It couldn't be Ned Richter; he wouldn't be warm.

He wouldn't be...breathing.

"So that's it!" he said loudly, checking for Jensen's pulse. It was weak, but it was there. The man would need help, though, and fast.

"Vivian, where are you? You poor woman, attacked... Thank God Arlo was still so new at it. He ended up killing himself, but you're all right, barely touched! And Ned—killed by Jensen! Where are you? Let me help."

They were both playing a game, pretending they believed what the other claimed as truth.

Harley. Where the hell was Harley? Was the woman holding her somewhere? Was she down on the ground, dying...bleeding?

He heard a scream of rage.

Light suddenly filled the dank, dark space.

And he saw Vivian. She was bursting out of the old subway tunnel, a lantern in one hand, a dagger held high in the other.

She was coming right at him.

He stepped out of the way; she would catapult into the wall.

But she didn't.

Because there was another cry of rage that tore through the darkness and death and decay of the tunnel.

It was Harley. And she'd found a weapon of her own—an old paving brick. She flew at Vivian, encountering her before Vivian could close in on Micah.

Both women went flying down to the floor. Vivian's lantern rolled away as they fell, casting light and shadow everywhere.

Micah reached down, catching Vivian's arm, grasping it hard.

Vivian screamed and released the antique dagger from the painful pressure he'd placed on her arm. He kicked it far from her.

Footsteps pounded down the length of the tunnel hall. Craig was there, Kieran right behind him.

Micah walked away from Vivian and drew Harley to her feet and into his arms. He held her; he wanted to hold her forever in the strange darkness and shadows, keep her from the horrors.

But of course, he couldn't.

Time meant everything just now.

"We need an ambulance for Jensen," he said. "And..."

"McGrady's here, too. I don't know how badly he's hurt. He's here somewhere!"

"Here! Here I am!"

They saw a form stumble toward them. And as it did, the tunnel blazed with light. Police officers, all carrying lights, came surging toward them.

"It was her!" McGrady said, swallowing hard, shaking his head. "Her! The woman poisoned herself to throw off any suspicion. She killed Henry, and she killed her husband. Yeah?"

Craig had Vivian Richter up by then. She was in handcuffs—and spitting mad. "I shouldn't have had to kill the bastard! Don't you get it? That mealymouthed little snake, Arlo Hampton—he was supposed to kill Ned. I did away with Henry Tomlinson, and Arlo was supposed to kill Ned. He said he couldn't do it! But I got him...oh yeah, I got both of them!"

"Who the hell would have suspected this!" McGrady said.

Micah looked at Harley, and his eyes darkened with concern.

"There's blood on you!" he murmured.

"Not mine," Harley said.

"Thank God." Micah looked toward McGrady. "Then we're ready for the next step."

Harley smiled and nodded.

"McGrady, go ahead, do the honors. Bring Mrs. Richter in. We'll handle things down here. We'll get the medical examiner and the techs for Mr. Richter," Micah said.

"And an ambulance for Jensen. She got him pretty good," Harley said.

"Why don't you and Kieran go to the hospital with him?" Micah suggested.

"Yeah. Yeah."

They stared at each other for another long moment.

Then Harley turned away, bending down to Jensen. The EMTs arrived, followed by the medical examiner and the crime scene people.

And the night went on.

Light continued to blaze through the tunnels and the abandoned subway station as day turned to night, as the medical examiner came, as the body of Ned Richter was taken at last to the morgue.

Micah and Craig worked the tie-up in the tunnels. Long hours, a lot of waiting, a lot of speculating and figuring.

Meanwhile, Vivian had been questioned at the station—and confessed to everything, despite her attorney's cautions.

"The whole thing sounds like Hitchcock," Micah told Craig. "In a sick and twisted way. *Strangers on a Train*, except they weren't strangers. Vivian Richter was working with Arlo Hampton. Arlo wanted Henry's place as lead of the expedition. And Vivian was willing to kill Henry. It was an easy trade, or so it seemed. She'd kill Henry and Arlo would kill Ned.

And, of course, she was willing to pay so that Satima Mahmoud would get her political group of disenfranchised students to fake an insurgency to cover up the murder. But as I said, in return for Henry being killed, Arlo was supposed to kill Ned. He screwed up. Vivian was afraid that Joe Rosello might figure out that Satima Mahmoud had been paid, so she decided she should poison him, which was why she showed up at the parade. And it was how Harley knew it wasn't the same mummy. Vivian is nowhere near as tall as Arlo. But Arlo didn't follow through on his part of the bargain. And Vivian lost control. When she saw Harley, I guess she wanted to do her in. But she hated Arlo for leaving her in the lurch. She was ready to kill Ned without blinking—and poison Arlo."

"Yeah, so all that 'beloved husband' stuff was just an act. For our benefit," Craig muttered.

"In Vivian's mind, her husband never gave her the respect she deserved. She was bitter, says he constantly claimed that she only had a job because of him. I guess she grew to hate him. If Arlo had played his part properly, he would've been the big cheese and she would've held the second position. But Arlo failed her, so she poisoned him. Otherwise, what was he going to do? Blame her."

"So if Arlo does make it, he'll be under arrest. Conspiracy to commit murder—even if he chickened out on it," Craig said.

"Yeah," Micah agreed. "But…"

"But?"

"I'm glad that Jensen Morrow and the other grad students have been proven innocent. They're Harley's friends. For her, I'm happy."

"Yep. I'm going topside for a while. I'll try to find out about Jensen's condition," Craig told Micah. "I'll let you know."

Micah nodded. He hoped Jensen Morrow was going to be okay.

He was, Craig reported a short time later, upon returning to the tunnels. Jensen had a concussion, and they'd watch him at the hospital for a few days. After that, he'd be as good as new, according to the doctors.

Finally, just as dawn was breaking, they finished in the tunnels.

He and Craig left.

Craig didn't ask where he wanted to go. He dropped him off at Harley's.

"I should've called her, I guess," Micah said.

"She'll be waiting for you," Craig told him.

And she was.

The night security guard waved him in. He had no idea how Harley knew exactly when he'd reach her door, but somehow she did.

The door opened, and she hurried into his arms.

He held her tight. She was bathed and sweet and fresh, and the scent of her hair was intoxicating; he kissed her, a long and lovely kiss, then pulled away.

"The tunnels," he said with a shudder.

And the blood of a dead man and the rot of millennia, he might have said.

He didn't need to.

She drew him in and up the stairs, to the bedroom, where he tossed his gun and holster on the table, and undressed quickly with her help. In minutes, she got into the shower behind him, forgetting to shed whatever silky thing she was wearing.

The water was hot and wonderful. Sensual, erotic and yet comforting.

He wasn't sure when they left the shower; he wasn't sure when she shed the wet silky thing. He knew they were still damp when they fell onto her bed. The room was in shadows, dawn was breaking with a spectacular light, and nothing seemed to matter except that they were together, touching each other.

They licked, teased, breathed each other.

Made love.

And made love again.

And then they slept for hours and hours and finally awoke.

Just for good measure, they made love yet again.

Later, when another day was almost gone, Micah looked through the great windows at the beauty of the church beyond.

"We're going to get married there," he said.

And then, of course, he remembered that they'd really only known each other for less than a week.

"One day," he added. "Somewhere along the line."

"What a proposal," she said lightly. "So romantic!" But she smiled. "One day... Yes, I like it. I like it very much!"

As she replied, he suddenly heard a mewling sound. He looked at her with surprise.

"Oh!" she murmured.

She hurried away and returned with a little ball of gray fluff in her arms.

"Um, we have a kitten. I hope that's okay?"

He laughed. "How did you...?"

"I found him in the tunnel. With... Ned's body. I think he helped us, really. He...he needs a home."

"So where has the little guy been?"

"I guess he went into hiding while we were all down there."

"And then?"

"He followed me up to the ground floor, and one of the officers took him for me until I got back from seeing Jensen at the hospital," she said. "I was thinking of calling him Lucky."

"Lucky it is," he said, and he took her—and the ball of fluff—back into his arms.

Lucky.

Yes.

Epilogue

Two Weeks Later
Finnegan's on Broadway

"I was part of it all—and I still don't get it," Jensen said, shaking his head. "Okay, back to the beginning. Vivian Richter and Arlo Hampton made some kind of devil's bargain. She'd kill Henry. He'd kill Ned. And no one would suspect either of them because it wouldn't make sense. They wouldn't be guilty of the same crime. But Micah wasn't going to give up and they both knew he was coming to the opening of the exhibit. So she poisoned herself to throw off any possible suspicion?"

"Something like that," Harley said. She'd just finished up the last of the work she'd told Jensen she would do. With Arlo and Vivian gone, he'd fallen behind with the exhibit. She'd also been eager to finish what she'd written about the murder of Amenmose. Everything would be on record at the museum, but it was a museum specializing in the ancient world—and her job here had been to explain what had happened to Amenmose and how it had all fit in with that world.

For Henry.

Arlo was still in the hospital. He'd regained consciousness, but the poison had swept away a great deal of his mind.

He had no idea he was guilty of conspiracy. Sadly, he wasn't even sure who he was anymore, or what he'd done.

Vivian's attorney was still telling her to shut up. She, too, however, had apparently had some kind of mental breakdown, because she wouldn't stop talking to the press. She was going to go for an affirmative defense and claim that she'd been horribly abused by her husband and that he'd made her say things that weren't true. She also insisted that Henry Tomlinson had killed himself and that she'd long been a victim of chauvinism and abuse at the hands of both men.

"It's crazy. All crazy, huh?" Jensen asked her. "And you know what's even crazier? That horrible woman killed Henry and her husband, she tried to kill you and me and that cop—and I still love being at the museum."

"It's a good museum. Henry was a very special man, and loving the museum just honors him," Harley said.

"Hmm. And what about that cop? He was a jerk, and...well, you know, he came by to apologize to me."

"McGrady," Harley said. "Yep. He apologized to me, too. And thanked me for saving his life. He told me he's going to be a good cop—and that it'll be because of me! I sure hope that's true."

"You can find out, I guess."

Harley smiled. "Not for a while," she said softly. "For right now—"

She stopped talking and got up; she saw that Micah and Craig had come into Finnegan's. She waved, so the two of them could see her.

"Still don't see why you have to go to Washington," Jensen said.

Harley flashed him a smile. "Because I'm in love," she told him.

"Yeah, yeah. And okay, he's decent. And I'm happy for you both."

"Funny, he says you're decent, too. And he's happy we're friends."

By then, Micah had come to the table. He greeted her with a kiss and Jensen with a handshake.

Craig reached the table next, and then Kieran arrived from her day job. Kevin came over, then Kieran's youngest brother, Danny, and her older brother, Declan, joined them. Micah and Harley were surrounded by friends and family, and they were toasted. It was something of a goodbye party.

They might come back to New York eventually; a transfer was always possible for Micah. But Harley wanted to train with the FBI academy and work toward joining a profiling team.

Washington was best for both of them right now. Harley wasn't giving up her uncle's apartment; they'd be up visiting often enough.

Everyone talked; everyone had a great time.

Joe, Roger and Belinda came later—with Belinda being the happiest of the bunch. Her fiancé was back from his deployment overseas and their wedding was coming up.

"Will there be any kind of Egyptian motif?" Joe asked Belinda, smiling.

"No!"

"What about you guys?" Jensen asked Harley.

"No! Grace Church, and you're all invited. We'll let you know when."

"No zombies, mummies, or any form of ancient lore?" Joe asked.

"No!" Harley and Micah said together, the word emphatic.

They celebrated awhile longer. Then it was time to split up, and they hugged and kissed each other on the cheek and promised to stay in touch.

The most difficult thing for Harley was to say goodbye to Kieran and Craig, but they wouldn't be far away and they'd all go back and forth often.

"I know you don't have a firm date for the wedding yet, but what are you thinking?" Kieran asked Harley.

"We have no solid plans yet. We just know where," she said. "What about you two?"

Kieran laughed. "We have no solid plans, either. Not yet. All we know is that we *will* have a wedding, and oh, yes! The reception will be here!"

Micah caught Harley's hand. "We have a lot of dating to do," he told Kieran and Craig. "And apparently my proposal was lacking. I'm going to work on a better one. I'll fill you in on how that goes. We might take a honeymoon before we actually do the marriage thing. I want to make sure Harley knows we have some great history down Virginia way, too. It's not ancient, but it's pretty cool. I've got a friend who's working a dig in Jamestown. We can visit him for a while. And meanwhile, we'll date…"

They left. They went to spend their last night in the apartment with the great windows and the beautiful loft that they'd have for a while.

"Yes, we need to date…" Micah said.

Harley whispered in his ear.

He smiled. "Oh yeah. That, too. Lots and lots of that!"

The moon shone through the windows.

They hurried up the curving wrought iron stairway.

Tonight was an ending and a beginning.

And a beautiful night, made for love and for loving.

* * * * *

"How close were you to the car?"

"I'd gotten in and realized I hadn't closed the trunk. I was behind the car when it just—" Bellamy broke off, the disbelief still clear in her eyes. "When it just exploded."

"We're going to take a look at it but first I need Alex to sniff the rest of the cars that are still here so we can get these people out of here. Can you wait for me?"

"Where else am I going to go?"

For reasons Donovan couldn't explain, he sensed there was something more in her comment. Something that went well beyond a car bomb or the shaky aftereffects of surviving a crime.

Something terrible had taken the light out of her beautiful gray eyes.

And he was determined to find out why.

***

The Coltons of Shadow Creek:
Only family can keep you safe…

COLTON K-9 COP

BY
ADDISON FOX

MILLS & BOON

First Published in Great Britain 2017
By Mills & Boon, an imprint of HarperCollins*Publishers*
1 London Bridge Street, London, SE1 9GF

© 2017 Harlequin Books S.A.

Special thanks and acknowledgement to Addison Fox for her contribution to *The Coltons of Shadow Creek* series.

ISBN: 978-0-263-92930-0

46-1117

Printed and bound in Spain
by CPI, Barcelona

Addison Fox is a lifelong romance reader, addicted to happy-ever-afters. After discovering she found as much joy writing about romance as she did reading it, she's never looked back. Addison lives in New York with an apartment full of books, a laptop that's rarely out of sight and a wily beagle who keeps her running. You can find her at her home on the web at www.addisonfox.com or on Facebook (Facebook.com/addisonfoxauthor) and Twitter (@addisonfox).

For Max

You came into my life when I least expected it and
have colored my world with puppy cuddles,
cookie (mis)adventures and joy.

Always joy.

Prologue

Five years ago

She held the garland loosely in her hand as she slowly unwound the bright gold in steady, even rows. Turn by turn, the empty green branches filled with the shiny, vivid color as Bellamy Reeves enjoyed watching her handiwork come to life.

Her parents had asked her to work the store this evening, their annual holiday event with the local men's club a highlight of their year. She'd been happy to do it, the familiar work of managing the counter and ringing up purchases at Whisperwood's only corner store something she'd been doing since childhood. It was a far cry from her work in finance at Lone Star Pharmaceutical but it kept her in touch with her roots and she enjoyed it.

Add on that it gave her a shot at stringing up the decorations just to her personal specifications, and it was a job she was happy to take on.

Maggie had teased her about risking spinsterhood if she were willing to work the family store on a holiday Saturday night and Bellamy had ignored her. Her sister was fond of quoting all the pithy reasons Bellamy was doomed to a lonely existence and she'd learned to ignore it.

Or, if not ignore it, at least stop caring about it so much. Her sister was the resident beauty queen of Whisperwood, Texas. She'd had men wrapped around her finger basically since she'd crawled out of the womb and had learned to drape herself over their arms not much longer after that.

Bellamy was different.

She wasn't afraid of men. Nor was she afraid of dating or putting herself out there. She dated regularly but just hadn't found anyone who interested her. Or made her feel special.

She'd spent her life observing her parents' marriage and knew that was the type of love and companionship she sought. A deep, abiding commitment that bonded the two of them together.

Tonight was a perfect example.

Although it was the men's club event, both her parents enjoyed the evening in equal measure. It was *nice*, she mused as she dug in a large plastic container for another string of garland. And while the event might seem simple or unimportant—a dinner dance at the Whisperwood Lodge—it was something they looked forward to and talked about all year long.

The bell over the front door of the store jingled and Bellamy eyed the entrance as a well-built man pushed his way in, a puppy cradled in his arms. Her father was fairly laid-back about the store, but since they sold food, animals were forbidden unless in service. "I'm sorry, sir, but the dog needs to stay outside."

Dark brows slashed over even darker eyes and the guy juggled the black Lab pup from one well-formed arm to another, his biceps flexing as he shifted the limp bundle. "Believe it or not, he's a service dog. In training," the guy quickly added before reaching into his back pocket and pulling out a badge. "I'm with the Austin PD. I'm his handler."

The sight of the puppy—and the sudden delight she didn't need to kick them out—had her crossing the store to greet them. "He's sweet."

"And sick, I think. He's not very energetic and he won't eat."

"Oh." She reached out to lay a hand on the small head, the fur silky soft over the bony ridges of his skull. He was small, but the large paws that hung over the man's forearms indicated the puppy would be a big guy once fully grown.

"I wanted to pick up some chicken and rice and hoped you'd have what I needed."

"Would you believe me if I told you I had both already cooked in the stockroom?"

"Seriously?"

"Yep. They're my bland leftovers from lunch that I brought along in some vague attempt to offset Christmas cookie consumption."

Although he wasn't inappropriate, his eyes drifted over her body before settling back on her face. "You're dieting?"

Heat burned a path where he'd gazed, that steady appreciation lighting a fire. "I prefer to think of it as holiday calorie management. A goal I'm failing at miserably, seeing as how the bland chicken and even blander rice were horrible."

"Why not toss it?"

"Some vague notion of trying again tomorrow. You know—" she waved a hand as she headed for the back of the store "—to make up for the pizza I ate in its place today."

A hearty laugh followed her through the swinging door into the stockroom and she beelined for the fridge and the leftovers.

Her father's store carried all the basic necessities of a convenience store and boasted a fairly hearty kitchen out front to accommodate the breakfast and lunch crowds who buzzed in for coffee and portable meals. She'd nuke the chicken and rice out at the counter and be able to keep an eye on the front door at the same time.

She could also keep an eye on Officer Hottie.

Wow, the man was good-looking. His body, evident beneath the long-sleeved black T-shirt that seemed sculpted to his shoulders, was strong without being imposing. And the way he cradled the dog had pretty much put her ovaries on high alert.

He was hot *and* a dog lover. Did it get much better?

She pushed through the stockroom door, only to see the back of the guy's head disappear through the front exit. Spears of disappointment layered over the lingering heat until she saw him bend over through the glass, his small charge quivering before him on the sidewalk. She raced to the counter and grabbed a few bottles of water, then headed for the miserable little puppy getting sick on the front parking lot.

"Is he okay?"

The guy glanced up from where he crouched on the ground, his hand on the small black back. "I think so. Or he will be."

She passed down a bottle of water, touched when the guy twisted it open and poured some into his palm. "Come on, Alex. Here you go."

The small head bent toward that cupped hand, the sound of his tongue lapping drifting toward her in the cool night air.

"Poor baby." She didn't miss the three brightly colored plastic pieces that lay in the pile of vomit. "Legos strike again."

"What?"

She pointed toward the small pile. "Looks like a blue vase holding a single plastic flower and a two-piece."

Officer Hottie's gaze zeroed in on the offending irritants, his voice gruff. "Just the pieces my niece mentioned were missing from her masterpiece before we sat down to dinner."

He poured more water into his hand and the Lab lapped

it up, the trauma of his ordeal fading as his natural eager-
ness returned.

"He's looking better already." Bellamy opened the second bottle and poured it over the sidewalk, erasing the evidence and washing the Lego blocks aside. She'd come out
later and pick them up with a broom.

Or planned to, until the guy pulled out a hanky from
his back pocket and cleaned up the plastic, tossing the entire package into the trash. "That'll teach me to let dog or
child out of my sight together again."

"That's wise." She couldn't resist his rueful grin or the
clear relief in his dark eyes. Suddenly conscious of standing there staring at him, she shifted her gaze toward Alex's sweet face and the tongue that lolled out the side of
his mouth. "Why don't you come back in and we can give
him the food?"

"If you're sure?"

She smiled at that. "I'm certainly not going to eat it, no
matter how many vows I make to myself. It'll be nice to
see it go to a more appreciative recipient. Plus, he should
probably go easy on dinner based on his recent Lego binge.
The bland food won't hurt him."

The guy followed her back inside and she picked up the
discarded container to warm up the leftovers.

"Would you mind if I came behind the counter and
washed up?" He pointed to the sink beside her.

"Come on."

"Then I can introduce myself properly and shake your
hand." He settled the puppy on the ground, issuing a series
of commands that had the small body sitting up straight.
The little guy tried to move, his butt squirming on the floor
a few times, but ultimately gave in to the firm tone and the
unyielding command by sitting where he was told.

"He's good. How old is he?"

"About ten weeks."

"And he can listen already?"

"'Sit' is about all he can listen to, but he's coming along." Hands clean, the guy turned the full force of his attention on her. For the briefest moment, Bellamy could have sworn she saw stars, the sky around his face glowing brighter than the gold of the garland. Quelling the ridiculous impression, she focused on the moment and not making an ass out of herself, especially when that warm, slightly damp palm closed around hers.

"I'm Donovan Colton."

Colton?

The Coltons were well known in Texas; several branches of the family were scattered across the Hill Country. She thought she knew the entire family who lived in Whisperwood, but hadn't placed Donovan when he'd walked in.

Shaking off the sudden awareness when she realized she was standing there, staring at the man, she quickly shook his hand. "Bellamy Reeves."

"Thank you, Bellamy. I appreciate the help."

"I'm happy to help. And I'm glad the little guy's okay."

The microwave pinged and she pulled the food out, then transferred it to a paper plate before handing it over. The moment was oddly domestic, Donovan's close proximity and their joint actions to put food together for the puppy surprisingly intimate.

The bell over the store entrance pinged and she went to help her customer. One of the high school coaches, who came in regularly for his nightly dinner of soda and a meatball sub seemed unphased by the addition of a puppy behind the counter.

"Hey, Bell. Haven't seen you in a few weeks."

"I'm helping my parents out tonight. They're out cutting a rug at the men's club event."

"You doing well?"

"Yep. We're closing out a busy year at work."

"How's Magnolia doing?"

It happened often enough, she wasn't sure why she was surprised any longer. The small talk as a method to ask about her sister. The pretend friendliness that was really just a fishing expedition.

"Maggie's good. She had a hot date tonight so she abandoned me in favor of a night of dinner and dancing."

Bellamy handed over the sub, not surprised when the coach's face fell. And while she'd not-so-delicately delivered news he obviously didn't want to hear, it didn't make the facts of Maggie's plans any less true. The besotted coach paid and was on his way out without saying much more.

"Did he even notice Alex was back here?" Donovan marveled once the guy was gone, the scent of his spicy sub wafting in his wake.

"He deals with teenagers all day. I suspect it takes a lot to rile him."

"Maybe." Donovan bent and took the now-empty paper plate. "Guess Alex got his appetite back."

She dropped to her knee and rubbed the silky head. The puppy's gaze caught on hers, his brown eyes trusting as he stared up at her. "He sure is sweet."

"Don't let him fool you. He's a Lego thief."

Bellamy rubbed a bit harder before laughing when the puppy presented his belly for additional petting. "He's at risk of being spoiled." Pulling her hand back, she realized the potential danger of her lavish affection. "Should I be doing that? Am I going to put his training at risk?"

"There are hard-core guys among my numbers who may not agree with me, but I think part of his training is also knowing there's praise and affection. A few belly rubs after this evening's trauma shouldn't do too much damage."

When Alex's wiggles of ecstasy quickly faded to longer breaths and droopy eyes, she gave him a final pat and stood, coming face-to-face with Donovan.

Goodness, the man was attractive. His dark hair was cut close and showed off a sharply angled face and strong jaw. He was thick in build, but there wasn't an ounce of fat on him. Instead, he looked competent.

Capable.

And no one to mess with.

It made the warm eyes and sexy smile that much more powerful. Like she'd tempted him just the slightest bit to go against character.

"You mentioned closing out a busy year to that guy. You don't work here?"

"This is my parents' store. I grew up working here and can still be counted on to take a shift every now and again."

"This place is a Whisperwood institution."

She laughed at that, the description not quite how she'd have classified a small town corner store. "One they know about all the way up in Austin?"

"My family's here in Whisperwood. I grew up here and Mr. Reeves could always be counted on for a summer popsicle or a late night cup of coffee. I just came down for the evening for a family Christmas party and to put my dog at risk of my niece and her Legos."

She glanced at the clock and thought that eight was awfully early for an evening family party to end, but held the thought. Maybe they started early or maybe the kids had to go to bed. But…it raised questions.

"How long have you been a part of the APD?"

"I went in straight out of college, so a few years now. I've wanted K-9, and Alex is my first opportunity."

She did the quick math, estimating he was about four or five years younger than her. The thought was briefly unsettling—she usually went for older guys—but there was something about him that made the question of age seem more arbitrary than anything else.

Perhaps you've been looking in the wrong places, Bellamy Reeves.

Catching herself staring, she refocused on Alex. "You're responsible for his training?"

"A good part of it. There's a formal program for the entire K-9 team and their handlers, but we're paired. He lives with me and works with me."

She glanced down at the now-sleeping puppy and considered what that must be like. Fun, in a way, but what a responsibility. "What will he be able to do?"

"Once he's fully trained? He'll run the gamut on what he can find, including humans, drugs and bombs."

"Wow."

As she eyed the jean-clad form that even now leaned against her counter, she had to admit Donovan Colton made an impressive figure. And it wasn't just his body, though she could hardly deny that she found him attractive.

Wow was right.

There was an intensity about him. Some indefinable quality that intrigued her.

He was *interesting*. And she'd often found the opposite of attractive men, especially if her sister's long list of past boyfriends was any indication. It was as if somehow masculine features, a firm jaw and a sparkling smile negated any sense of humanity or interest in the world around them.

But not this guy.

"The K-9 team is designed to work across cases so we can go where we're needed. There are six others in the APD. Alex and I will make seven."

"It's impressive. And while he's obviously got great promise, you've got a big year ahead of you. I wish you the best."

"Thanks." Donovan's gaze dropped toward the sleeping puppy before lifting back to her. "So if you don't work here, what do you do?"

"I'm an employee at Lone Star Pharmaceutical. I'm just helping out here since my parents had plans tonight."

"LSP. That's impressive. Are you a chemist or something?"

"No, I'm in finance." Ignoring the whisper through her mind of Maggie's continued admonitions to showcase herself in the best light, Bellamy pressed on. "They're wise to keep me away from beakers. Other than warming things up in a microwave, I avoid anything that involves cooking or open flames."

"Maybe I should consider inviting you to dinner, then, instead of risking you making anything behind that counter for me."

"Maybe."

"What time do you get off tonight?"

"I close up at ten and this is small town Texas. Nothing's open then."

"What about next week?"

"Sure. I—" She broke off when a distracted air came over his face, his hand dropping to the phone clipped at the waist of his jeans.

"I'm sorry. I'm getting a dispatch."

He excused himself and moved around the counter toward the door, his gaze morphing from friendly and sexy to straight cop.

Alex stirred, his senses on immediate alert at the emotional change in the atmosphere. He was on his feet and scrambling toward Donovan in a heartbeat. When he reached Donovan, he sat immediately, his little body arrow straight.

Bellamy marveled at it, the ease and trust she could already see between the two of them. If the dog was this responsive to training at ten weeks, she couldn't imagine what he'd become once fully grown.

The low tenor of Donovan's voice pulled her from her thoughts. Something had happened. Something bad, if his clipped responses were any indication.

"I'm sorry. I have to go. Can we take a rain check on that dinner?"

"Of course."

The sexy cop and his trusty sidekick were out of the store as fast as they came in and for several moments, Bellamy simply stood and watched the door where they'd disappeared, wondering if the evening had actually happened.

It was only when she got the call a half hour later that she knew the exact accident Donovan Colton was called to. And that the people he'd helped pull from two tons of wreckage were her parents.

Chapter One

The last strains of "Jingle Bells" faded out, giving way to "All I Want for Christmas Is You" as Bellamy Reeves clicked the last email in her inbox. Despite the multicolored lights she'd hung in her office and the music she'd determinedly turned on each morning and kept on low throughout the day, nothing seemed to get her in the holiday spirit.

Losing both parents over the summer had left a hole in her life and in her heart. She'd braced herself, of course, well aware the holidays would be a challenge. But even with the knowledge the season wouldn't be the same, she'd diligently clung to the belief she could find some sense of joy, somewhere.

How wrong she'd been.

The days seemed to drag, no matter how busy she made herself, and her job at Lone Star Pharmaceutical—a job she'd worked hard at for several years—couldn't fill the gaps.

"One more email," she whispered to herself on a resigned sigh. "I'll do the last one and cut out early."

The company was estimated to finish out the year with stellar earnings, and management had given everyone an extra day of comp time as a reward for all the hard work. Most people had used the time to go shopping for presents in nearby Austin or to take in the pretty decorations scattered throughout downtown Whisperwood. She'd done none of those things, not up for walking the sidewalks and making small talk with her fellow townsfolk.

Which had also meant she was still sitting on the extra time. Perhaps an afternoon off would provide a chance to recharge and shake the malaise that seemed determined to hover around her shoulders.

She missed her parents terribly, but it was also the first holiday in more than she could remember that wasn't encumbered by illness. Her father's loss of mobility five years before had taken a toll on all of them and her life had been filled with pill bottles, a wheelchair and ramps throughout the house, and bouts of belligerence that telegraphed DJ Reeves's frustration with his body's betrayal.

It hardly spoke well of her, that she was relieved that stage of life had passed, but in her quiet moments of honest reflection she could admit it was true.

Illness. Suffering. And an endless sort of wasting away that stole the joy out of life. All of it had affected her mother as surely as her father's loss of mobility in the accident had decimated his. Where her mother had once found joy in simple pleasures—gardening or cooking or even a glass of wine—watching her husband deteriorate had caused a matched response. Ginny Reeves had wasted away as surely as her husband had and nothing Bellamy had tried could coax her out of it.

The kidney failure that finally stole him from them in June had been the final straw for her mother. Her mental health had deteriorated rapidly after that, and the heart attack that took her in late July had almost seemed unavoidable.

"And here I am, right back to maudlin and depressed," she whispered to herself as she reached for the bottle of water she kept perpetually refilled on her desk.

The water had been another nod to health, her recognition of mortality—a fact of life with her parents, and an equally relevant fact of life working for a pharmaceutical company. Lone Star Pharmaceutical had hired her out of college and she'd steadily worked her way up through the ranks, responsible for any number of financial projects. For the past two years, she'd been part of the team that managed the costs to bring new drugs to market and had honed her skills around price elasticity, working with insurance companies and ensuring LSP had a place on doctors' prescription lists.

The role had been meant for her, honing her accounting knowledge and expanding her contribution to the overall business and its bottom line. She'd loved LSP already, but coupled with the professional advancement, her employer had also been understanding of her family situation. They'd allowed for flexible scheduling when she'd needed it and hadn't asked her to curtail the care and attention her parents needed.

She'd met enough people in waiting rooms at the hospital to know that flexibility was a gift beyond measure. The fact she'd also had an opportunity to still be considered for and receive promotions had cemented her sense of loyalty to LSP that was impossible to shake.

The company was a good one, with a focus on making life better for its consumers, its employees and even the community where it made its home—Whisperwood, Texas. Their CEO, Sutton Taylor, was a longtime resident and had stated on many occasions how important it was to him that his company have the same deep roots as he did.

Deep Texas *roots*, he usually clarified with a wink and a smile.

She couldn't hold back a faint smile of her own at the image of Sutton Taylor, standing tall in his suit and cowboy boots, proudly telling the employees how strong their year-end numbers looked. It wouldn't bring her parents back, but she could at least take some small joy in knowing she'd worked hard and contributed to a job well-done.

Satisfied she might leave the office on a glimmer of a bright note, Bellamy returned to her email, determined to tackle the last one before leaving for the afternoon.

The missive still bold because it was unread, Bellamy scanned the subject line, registering the odd description. RE: Vaccine Normalization.

Normalization of what?

The sender said INTERNAL, a company address she didn't immediately recognize, but she clicked anyway. A quick scan of the header information didn't show a named sender, either, nor was there anyone in the "To" list. Intrigued, Bellamy leaned forward, searching for anything that resembled usable details to describe what she was looking at.

Was it a virus?

That subject never failed to make her smile, the fact they had a department that battled real viruses housed in the same location as one who battled the digital kind. The humor quickly gave way to the sobering details that filled the content of the note.

Bellamy caught the subject in snatches, the words practically blurring as she processed the odd, bulleted sentences.

LSP's virus vaccine, AntiFlu, will be distributed in limited quantities, with release schedule held in the strictest confidence.

Quantities are throttled to highest bidder, with market pricing increased to match quantity scarcity.

Management of egg supply has been secured.

If those points weren't bad enough, the closing lines of the email left no question as to what she was reading.

Lone Star Pharma has a zero-tolerance policy for discounted distribution of AntiFlu for the annual flu season. There will be no acceptance of annual contract prices with existing accounts.

Bellamy reread the email once, then again, the various details spiking her thoughts in different directions.

Throttled availability? Controlled pricing? Fixed scarcity?

And the fact there was mention of the egg supply—the incubation engine for production of the vaccine—was shocking.

What was this?

She read the note once more before scrolling back up to review the header details. The sender was veiled, but it did originate from an LSP email address.

Who would send this to her? And worse, why would anyone possibly want to keep the very product they created for the public's good out of that same public's hands? She knew for a fact they had more than enough flu vaccine for the season. She also knew the scientific team had followed the CDC's guidelines for which strains of flu needed to be included.

She scrolled through the details once more, daring the words to change and prove her interpretation incorrect. But one more reread, or one hundred more, wasn't going to change the information housed in the email.

If this email was to be believed, the company she loved and believed in had turned to some dark and illegal practices.

"WELCOME BACK TO WHISPERWOOD, Alex. Quintessential small town Texas, from the tippy top of the big white gazebo smack in the middle of the town square, to the string of shops on Main Street."

Donovan Colton glanced over at his companion as he passed the gazebo and turned from Maple onto Main, unsurprised when he didn't receive a pithy response or even acknowledgment of his comment. As a matter of course, he'd have been more concerned if he *had* received a response.

His large black Lab possessed many talents, but a speaking voice wasn't one of them.

What Alex—short for Alexander the Great—did have was a nose that could sniff out explosive materials and he knew exactly how to translate that knowledge back to Donovan so he could in turn secure help. The fact Alex had several hundred million scent receptors in his nose—and had been trained almost since birth to use them in support of police work—meant Donovan had a powerful partner in their work to capture the bad guys.

It also helped he got along far better with his canine partner than he ever would have with a real live human one.

Donovan had been an animal lover since he was small. His various chores around the Colton ranch never seemed like chores if an animal was involved. Whether it was horse duty, mucking stalls or collecting eggs from the coops, he hadn't cared or seen any of it as work, so long as he got to spend time with the furry and the feathered Coltons who shared space on the large ranch that sprawled at the far west end of Whisperwood.

That love ran ever deeper to any number of mutts who had called the Colton ranch home.

Just like me, Donovan added to himself, the thought a familiar one.

Shaking it off, he focused on the gorgeous dog next to him. Donovan had loved each and every canine that had graced his life, but Alex was something extra special. Alex had been trained since puppyhood for life on a K-9 team; the two of them had bonded quickly, one an extension of the other. Alex looked to him for security, order, discipline and the clear role as alpha of their pack. In return, Donovan stroked, praised, and directed the animal into any number of search and rescue situations, confident his companion could handle the work.

And Alex always did.

From bombs to missing persons, Alex did his job with dedication, focus and—more often than not—a rapid wag of his tail.

Yep. Donovan would take a four-footed partner over one with two feet any day.

Not that he could technically complain about any of the fine men and women he'd worked with in the past, but something just *fit* with Alex. They had a bond and a way of working that was far easier than talking to someone.

Their trip to Whisperwood had been unusually quiet, he and Alex dispatched to an old warehouse site to confirm the Austin PD hadn't missed any drugs on a raid the prior week. The cache they had discovered had been worth millions and Donovan's captain wanted to ensure they hadn't overlooked anything.

Donovan's thorough site review hadn't revealed any missed stashes but it was Alex's attention to the crime scene that reinforced the fact the initial discovery team had found all there was to find. Donovan would bet his badge on it.

If Alex couldn't find it, it's because it didn't exist.

What it also meant was that his trip to Whisperwood was over far earlier than Donovan had planned.

And disappearing back out of town—especially after greeting the local chief of police at the crime scene—wasn't going to go down very well. If his mother knew he'd come through and hadn't stopped by, no amount of excuses could save him.

"You're just too damn good, Alex."

The dog's tongue lolled happily to the side while he

maintained a steady view of the passing scenery outside the car. The use of his name had Alex's ears perking but even the warm tone couldn't distract the dog from the holiday wreaths hanging neatly from each lamppost in town.

Donovan took in the view, his memories of his hometown not too far off the mark of the real thing. The wreaths came out like clockwork the Monday before Thanksgiving, hanging until precisely the third day after the new year. A town committee changed out the ribbons on each wreath every week so they remained perfectly tied throughout the holiday. Red, green and gold, they alternated in a steady pattern, accompanied by bright, vibrant banners that wished people the happiness of the season.

His gaze drifted toward the corner store, an old memory pushing against his thoughts. A night, several Christmases past, when he'd had a sick little puppy and had flirted with a woman.

She'd been kind, he remembered, and pretty in a way that wasn't flashy, but that intrigued all the same. There was something solid there. Lasting, even. Which was silly, since he hadn't spent more than a half hour in her company before heading out on a call.

He'd thought to go in and ask about her a few times since, but training Alex had provided Donovan with a good excuse to stay out of his hometown; by the time he came back a year and a half later it had seemed lame—and far too late—to stop back in and ask about her.

But he did think of her every now and again. The slender form that filled out a pair of jeans with curves that had made his fingers itch and just enough skin showing at the top of her blouse to shift his thoughts in interesting, heated directions.

Dismissing the vague memory of pretty gray eyes and long, dark hair, he refocused on the pristine streets before him and the large ranch housed at the edge of town.

He needed to go see his mother. If he was lucky, his father would be out for the afternoon and he could avoid the lecture about coming to visit more often. He found it odd— funny, even—that it was his father who was more determined to deliver that particular guilt trip than his mother.

At the edge of the town square, Donovan looked at the large gazebo that dominated the space before putting on his blinker to head toward the Colton ranch. "Pretty as a picture."

At his comment, Alex's ears perked again and he turned from the view out the passenger window, his head tilted slightly toward Donovan.

"You don't miss a trick, do you?"

Donovan took his role as alpha in their relationship seriously, and that meant avoiding tension, anger or panic when speaking and working with Alex. Donovan had always innately understood an animal's poor acceptance of those emotions, but his K-9 training had reinforced it. He needed to stay calm and firm in the face of his furry partner, never allowing random, spiking emotions a place in their partnership.

Which meant the emotions that had the deepest of roots— established in the very foundation of his childhood—needed to be avoided at all costs. Especially if the prospect of visiting the Colton ranch was transmitted by his tone.

Extending a hand, he ruffled Alex's head and ears, scratching the spot he knew was particularly sensitive. A low, happy groan echoed from his partner when Donovan kneaded the small area behind Alex's ears, effectively erasing whatever tension he'd pushed into his police-issued SUV.

And on a resigned sigh, he made the turn that would carry him to the large ranch that sprawled for over a thousand acres deep in the heart of Texas Hill Country.

Home.

BELLAMY FOUGHT THE steady swirl of nerves that coated her stomach, bumping and diving like waves roiling on a winter's day as she walked the long corridor toward the human resources department. Lone Star Pharmaceutical had a sprawling campus and HR was three buildings away from her own, connected through a series of parking lots as well as overhead walkways for when the weather was poor or just too darn hot during a Texas summer.

She'd thought to call ahead and share her concerns but for reasons she couldn't quite explain to herself, ultimately decided on a surprise approach.

Was she even supposed to have the email?

The sender was veiled, but so was the distribution list. She didn't even know why she'd been targeted for such information.

Snatches of the email floated through her mind's eye, each destructive word adding another pitch and roll to those waves.

Limited quantities...throttled to highest bidder...quantity scarcity...

No acceptance of annual contract prices.

Was this the reason for the exceptionally strong year at LSP? Were they all celebrating extra time off and assured holiday bonuses at the expense of human lives?

She'd worked in finance her entire life and monitoring the ebbs and flows of the business was a part of her day to day. She understood balance sheets and marketplace pricing. She understood profit and loss statements. And she understood what it took to run an ethical business that still remained profitable.

And creating a scarcity in the market—*deliberately*—was not legal.

But it could be very, very profitable.

All the drugs LSP produced were essential for the individuals who needed them. They led the market on several fronts, with specialties in diabetes, heart disease and cholesterol reducing medicines. LSP had also done wonders with drugs designed to improve motor skills, several of which had been essential to her father's well-being.

But the flu vaccine was a whole different issue.

For anyone suffering from an illness, access to proper care and medicine was essential, but the flu affected everyone. A bad season could kill a large number of people, especially those at highest risk.

Just like her parents.

Had her father forgone a flu vaccine for the last several years of his life, he'd surely have been at higher risk of dying from the virus. And the fewer people vaccinated, the higher the risk.

Was it really possible LSP was attempting to profit from that?

Technically, they were late in the season to get the vaccine, but even as late as the prior week she'd run the numbers and realized that immunizations were down versus the prior year.

Was that because too many people felt they didn't need protection?

Or because there wasn't any protection in the market?

She tamped down on another wave of bile cresting in her stomach and knocked on the open door of the HR department. She'd been at LSP long enough to know several members of the HR team but wasn't acquainted with the head of HR, Sally Borne.

A light "come in" echoed through the cavernous outer office. Bellamy understood why the voice sounded so far away when she saw only one person seated in what appeared to be a sea of about six desks. She headed for the woman, taking in the office along the way. Decorations celebrating the holiday season peppered the walls and filing cabinets, and a bright string of lights hung from the ceiling over a table that held a pretty menorah as well as a beautifully carved wooden kinara holding the seven candles of Kwanzaa.

This holiday sentiment was matched throughout the five buildings of LSP and reflected Sutton Taylor's stated goals of inclusion and celebration of diversity. It had been yet one more facet of life at LSP and one more reason she loved where she worked

Could someone who believed so deeply in humanity and culture and individuality be so soulless as to withhold essential drugs for the good of others?

"Can I help you?" The lone woman smiled, her voice kind as she stood behind her desk, effectively welcoming Bellamy in.

"I'd like to speak to Sally Borne."

"What's this regarding?"

"It's a private matter."

There was the briefest flash of awareness in the woman's bright blue eyes before she nodded. "Let me see if Sally has a few minutes in her schedule. I'll be right back."

Pleasant smile for a watchdog, Bellamy thought.

The idea struck swiftly and was at odds with the sense of inclusion that had welcomed her into the human resources department.

The woman disappeared toward a wall of frosted windows that allowed in light but made it impossible to see through. The windows covered what appeared to be one large office that extended across the back of the space. While it was to be expected—Human Resources dealt with any number of private matters—something about the glass made her think of a prison.

Which only reinforced just how far gone her thoughts had traveled since reading the email.

This was Human Resources, for Pete's sake. The depart-

ment in all of Lone Star Pharmaceutical that was designed
to help the employees.

Bellamy had worked with HR during her flex time requests when she was caring for her parents and they'd been
kind and deeply understanding. They'd been in a different
building then, only recently having moved into this space
in the main building that housed the LSP executive staff.

Sally Borne was new to the company, as well. She'd replaced their retiring HR lead in the fall and had already
implemented several new hiring initiatives as well as a
new employee training program that was rolling out department by department. The woman was a leader and, by
all accounts, good for Lone Star Pharmaceutical. Painting
her as some fire-breathing dragon behind a retaining wall
wasn't going to get Bellamy anywhere.

Especially as those waves in her stomach continued to
roil, harder and harder, as she waited for the meeting.

The sensation was so at odds with her normal experience at work. She'd become accustomed to the frustration
and fear that came from managing her father's care, but
LSP had always been a safe haven. She loved her job and
her work and found solace in the routine and the sense of
accomplishment. At LSP, she was in control.

So why did she feel so *out* of control since opening that
damn email?

"Are you ready?" The lone HR worker reappeared from
Sally's office, her smile still firmly intact.

"Thank you."

Bellamy ignored the sense of being watched, and headed
for the inner domain, hidden along the back wall. There
was neither a fire-breathing dragon nor anything to worry
about. *She*'d been sent the suspicious email. Coming to HR
was simply about doing her job.

More, it was about being responsible to it.

"Hello." Sally Borne met her at the door, her hand extended and that same bright smile highlighting her face. "I'm Sally."

Bellamy introduced herself, then provided a sense of her role in the company. "I'm part of the financial team that manages the process of bringing new drugs to market."

"Andrew Lucas's team?"

"Yes, Andrew is my boss."

Sally nodded and pursed her lips before extending a hand toward her desk. Bellamy followed her, settling herself in a hard visitor's chair while Sally took her position behind a large oak monstrosity that looked like it belonged in Sutton Taylor's office.

Sally scribbled something on a blank legal pad, her attention focused on the paper. "Is Andrew aware you're here?"

Bellamy forced a small smile, unwilling to have the woman think she was here to complain about her boss. "Andrew's not the reason I'm here."

"But does he know you're here?"

"No."

"How can I help you then, Ms. Reeves?"

The prospect of sharing the details of what she'd discovered had haunted Bellamy throughout the walk from her office to HR, but now that she was here, the reality of what she had to share became stifling. Whether she'd been the intended recipient or not, the information she held was damning in the extreme. Anyone within LSP who would make such a decision or declaration would surely be fired. Worse, the possibility of jail time had to be a distinct consideration. They might be a for-profit company, but they still worked for the public good.

Was she really sure of what she'd come to discuss with HR?

Even as she asked herself the question, the memory of what she had read in the email steeled her resolve.

She was sitting on a problem and rationalizing it away at a personal moment of truth was unfair at best, flat out immoral at worst.

"I received an odd email today and I felt it was important to discuss it with you directly."

"Odd?" Sally's hands remained folded on top of her desk but the vapid smile that had ridden her features faded slightly.

"There wasn't a named sender, for starters."

"We have effective spam filters on our email but things can slip through. Do you think that was it?"

"No, no, I don't. The email just said 'internal.'"

"And no one signed it?"

"No."

Something small yet insistent began to buzz at the base of Bellamy's spine. Unlike the concern and panic that had flooded her system upon realizing what the email held, this was a different sort of discomfort. Like how animals in the forest scented a fire long before it arrived.

A distinct sense of danger began to beat beneath her skin.

"Here. Look at this." Bellamy pulled the printout she'd made out of the folder she'd slipped it into, passing it across the desk. "If you look at the top, you can see it came from the LSP domain."

Sally stared at the note, reading through the contents. Her expression never changed, but neither did that vague sense of menace Bellamy couldn't shake. One that grew darker when Sally laid the paper on her desk, pushing it beneath her keyboard.

"This is a poor joke, Ms. Reeves."

"A joke?"

"You come in here and suggest someone's sending you inappropriate messaging, then you hand me a note that's something out of a paranoid fantasy. What sort of sabotage are you intending to perpetrate against LSP?"

"I'm trying to prevent it."

"By forging a note and tossing it around like you're some affronted party?"

Affronted party? Forgery? The damn thing had popped into *her* inbox a half hour ago.

"This was sent to me."

Even as Bellamy's temperature hit a slow boil, Sally Borne sat across from her as if she were the injured party. "Are you sure about that? It would be easy enough to make a few changes in a photo alteration program and muster this up. Or perhaps you're even more skilled and able to hack into our email servers."

"You can't be serious. I received this email. Pull up the server files yourself if you're so convinced they've been tampered with."

"I'm sure that won't be necessary."

Bellamy sat back, her ire subsiding in the face of an even more unbelievable truth. The director of Human Resources didn't believe her. "You do understand the implications of something like this?"

"I most certainly do."

Although this wasn't the same as losing her parents, Bellamy couldn't fully shake the sadness and, worse, the acute sense of loss at Sally Borne's callous disregard for her word. Her truth. With one last push, she tried to steer the conversation back to steady ground.

"Who could possibly be sending messages like this? What are they trying to accomplish? And who else might have received something like this?"

"You tell me." Sally waved an idle hand in the direction of the email now lodged beneath her keyboard. "You're the one in possession of the mysterious email. No one else has called me or sent me any others to review." Sally's gaze never wavered as she stared back from her side of the large desk, her words landing like shards of ice as they were volleyed across that imposing expanse.

"Which I'm trying to get your help with. Could you imagine if this were really true?" Bellamy asked, willing the woman to understand the gravity of the situation. "We'd be putting millions of lives at risk."

Only when Sally only stared at her, gaze determinedly blank, did the pieces begin to click into place.

"So it's true, then? LSP *is* tampering with vaccines." The words came out on a strangled whisper.

"What's true is that you're a financial leader at this company determined to spread lies and disruption," Sally snapped back.

"I'm not—"

A brisk knock at the door had Bellamy breaking off and turning to see the same woman from the outer office. "Ms. Borne. Here are the details you asked for."

A large file was passed over the desk and Bellamy saw her name emblazoned on the tab of the thick folder.

Her employment file?

"Thank you, Marie." Sally took the folder as the helpful, efficient Marie rushed back out of the office.

It was only when the file was laid down that Bellamy saw a note on top. The writing was neat and precise and easily visible across the desk.

10+ year employee.
Steadfast, determined, orderly.
Both parents died in past year.

She was under evaluation here? And what would her parents' deaths have to do with anything?

Sally tapped the top before opening the manila file. Thirteen years of performance reviews and salary documentation spilled from the edges, but it was that note on top that seemed to echo the truth of her circumstances.

For all her efforts to make a horrible situation right, something had gone terribly wrong.

"Is there a reason you felt the need to pull my personnel file?"

"A matter of routine."

"Oh? What sort of routine?"

"When an employee is behaving in a suspicious manner, I like to understand what I'm dealing with."

"Then you'll quickly understand you're dealing with a highly competent employee who has always received stellar reviews and professional accolades."

Sally flipped back to the cover, her gaze floating once more over the attached note. "I also see a woman who's suffered a terrible loss."

While she'd obviously registered the note about her parents when the file was dropped off, nothing managed to stick when she tried to understand where Sally was going with the information. "I lost my parents earlier this year."

"Both of them."

"Yes."

"Were they in an accident?"

"My father has been ill for many years, the repercussions of a serious accident. My mother's health, unfortunately, deteriorated along with his."

"It's sad." Sally traced the edge of the damn note again, the motion drawing attention to the seemingly random action. "Illness like that takes a toll."

A toll? *Obviously.* "Dying is a difficult thing. Nothing like the slow fading we see on TV."

Sally continued that slow trace of the paper. "It's also an expensive thing."

"You can't possibly think—"

"It's exactly what I think." The steady, even-keeled

woman was nowhere in evidence as Sally stood to her full height, towering over her desk like an avenging cobra. "And you think it, too. You dare to come in here, convinced you can blackmail this company into giving you money for some concocted lie of immense proportions."

"You can't think that."

"I can and I do. And I want you to pack your office immediately. Security will escort you there and off the premises."

"But I—"

Sally pointedly ignored her, tapping on her phone to summon Marie. When the woman scrambled in, Sally didn't even need to speak. Marie beat her to it. "Security will be here momentarily."

"Excellent." Sally shifted her attention once more, her gaze fully trained on Bellamy as she pointed toward the door. "Don't expect a reference."

Dazed, Bellamy stood and moved toward the exit. The meeting had been nothing like what she'd expected. Surreal at best, even as she had to admit it was fast becoming a nightmare.

Lone Star Pharmaceutical had been her professional home for more than thirteen years and in a matter of moments, that home had been reduced to nothing more than rubble and ash.

Chapter Two

Donovan glanced around the large, welcoming, airy living room of the main Colton ranch house as his mother settled two glasses of iced tea on the coffee table. She'd already bustled in with a tray of his favorites—cheese and crackers, a bowl of cashews and a tray of gooey Rice Krispies Treats—and had topped it off with her world famous sweet tea.

Perhaps that was a stretch, but she had brought her tea to every gathering ever held in Whisperwood. Someone had even asked him about it at work one day, rumors of his mother's special recipe having reached as far as Austin. Donovan reached for his glass and took a sip, more than ready to admit every sugary drop deserved its near-reverent reputation.

"I'm so glad you're here." She glanced down at Alex, her smile indulgent as she pet his head. "Glad you're both here. Though to what do I owe the pleasure?"

"Alex and I had a job that finished early. I thought I'd come over and visit before heading back to Austin."

"I'm glad you did. Our last dinner ended too early. And I—" She broke off, shaking her head. "I'm glad you're here."

Memories of his last dinner with his family still stuck in his gut and Donovan avoided thinking about it. He loved them—he always had—but he couldn't be who they wanted

him to be. And he'd long past stopped trying. Their defini-
tion of family was different from his and he'd spent a lifetime trying to reconcile that fact.

And was coming up damn short, truth be told.

He reached for a handful of cashews and ignored the
guilt that poked beneath his ribs with pointy fingers. He
was here, wasn't he? That had to count for something.

Even if his presence was grudging at best.

"He's so good."

His mother's words pulled Donovan from his musings
and he glanced over to where she'd settled Alex's head onto
her lap, his gaze adoring as he stared up at her. "All this
food and he hasn't even looked at it."

"Oh, he's looking. Don't let him fool you."

"But he's so good and doesn't even attempt to make a
play for anything. Remember Bugsy. That dog could find
food if you wrapped it in plastic and buried it in the back
of the pantry. He'd find a way to get to it, too."

Unbidden, memories of the small, crafty mutt they'd
had when Donovan was in high school filled his thoughts.
Bugsy was a good dog—as friendly as he was tenacious—
and his forays into the Colton pantry had become the stuff
of family legend. "He didn't miss much."

"I always assumed all dogs were that way, but Alex is
amazing. He hasn't moved an inch."

"He's a formally trained police dog. It wouldn't do to
have him nosing into pockets at crime scenes or roaming
through the pantry on home visits. He's trained to sniff out
bomb materials and illegal drugs."

"Yes, he is. A dangerous job for a brave boy." Her attention remained on the dog but Donovan was acutely aware
the comment was meant for him.

"When the bad guys stop being bad guys, he can slow
down."

"I suppose so." His mother patted Alex's head. "But for

the record, I am all for a dog being a dog. I did enjoy documenting some of Bugsy's escapades."

"There aren't many like him."

"Remember that Christmas he ate all the cookies? Oh boy, was that dog sick."

Donovan remembered that holiday—along with the mess the dog vomited up in the barn later that morning—but true to form Bugsy had been back in business in no time. The wily dog raided the bacon and black-eyed peas on New Year's Day, barely a week later.

"He was a character."

The shift to a safe topic put them back on neutral ground and they fell silent again, his mother's soft smile focused on Alex and the large black head snuggled in her lap. She might not be his biological mother, but Donovan had always known he'd gotten his love of animals from Josephine Colton. Her gentle nature and genuine pleasure with the furry or the feathered had always been a hallmark of her personality.

His mother had never met a stray she didn't love or an animal she couldn't whisper sweet nothings to. And since he'd been a stray himself, Donovan had innately understood the value in that personality trait.

"Dad keeping busy?"

"As much as the doctor allows. Your father is frustrated he can't do the things he used to."

"There's no shame in asking for help."

His mother sighed, trouble flashing in her warm brown eyes before she dropped her gaze back to Alex. "There is, apparently, when your name is Hays Colton."

"He comes by that one honestly, don't you think? In fact, I'd say he comes from a very long line of stubborn Coltons, starting with Uncle Joe and working his way down."

The words were enough to vanquish the spot of trouble in her eyes and she smiled at that. "For someone who claims they can't remember the names of so many aunts, uncles and cousins, you sure can pull them out readily enough when making a point."

"The beauty of a large family." *An adopted one*, Donovan added to himself. He'd managed to hold those words back this time. Coupled with the fact that he and his mother were having a cordial afternoon, Donovan figured he might actually get out of his childhood home without offending anyone or causing a fresh bout of tears.

Because, try as he might, there wasn't any amount of love or extended family or years-old shared stories that could change one fundamental fact: Josephine and Hays Colton weren't actually his parents.

And while Donovan would be eternally grateful for their care, their upbringing and their name, he'd never quite gotten past the circumstances that had put him in their barn one cold Christmas morning, abandoned and alone.

BELLAMY MARCHED THE return trip back to her office building from the human resources department. The walk had been long enough that she'd already worked her way through the first stage of grief—denial—and was fast barreling toward number two.

Anger.

How dare they? Or how dare *she*? Despite the reputation that had spread quickly about Sally Borne's competence since her arrival at LSP, Bellamy still couldn't get over the woman's gall. Nor could she see past the horrifying thought that Sally thought she was somehow responsible for that awful note.

"Are you okay, Ms. Reeves?"

She turned at the sweet voice of Gus Sanger, doing his level best to keep up with her long strides through the above-ground corridors that connected the buildings.

"I'm fine."

"I've known you a long time, young lady. You're not fine. And that was no simple visit to HR."

"It's a private matter."

"Meetings in HR usually are." Gus tugged at his ear, but kept pace next to her now that they'd slowed a bit. "I've known you since you were small. Your parents' store was a key stop for me every morning on my drive to LSP and more often than not, you'd find your way behind that counter, fixing me a coffee and a muffin. You're a good girl, Bellamy Reeves, and whatever that private matter was about, you don't deserve an escort off the grounds."

The tears that had prickled the backs of her eyes intermittently since leaving Sally's office spiked once more but she held them back. She'd cried enough tears for a lifetime the past six months and refused to shed the same emotion over a situation that she hadn't caused, nor was she responsible for.

"Thanks, Gus."

"I don't care what HR says about me watching you like a common criminal. You go back to your office and take a few minutes to pack up. I'll wait for you in the lobby. It'll give me a chance to get some coffee."

"But what if HR catches you? Won't you get in trouble?"

Gus waved a hand. "If HR has a problem with me, they're going to have to go through Sutton. He may have his moments, acting like a damn fool ladies' man, but he and I went fishing in Whisperwood Creek when we were both seven years old. Been fishing there off and on ever since together. No one's firing me."

Bellamy smiled at the image—the grizzled Gus and the erudite Sutton Taylor, casting lines off the side of the creek. The "ladies' man" comment was a bit bold, even for Gus, but Bellamy was hardly unaware of Taylor's reputation.

"You've known each other a long time."

"A lifetime. All it would take is a few words to him and we can fix this."

"No, Gus." She shook her head before gentling her tone at the sincere offer of help. "I can't tell you how much I appreciate it, but I need to take care of this myself."

"If you're sure?"

"I'm sure. I'll find a way to fix this. To fix it all."

Gus nodded before using his badge to open the door to Bellamy's building. "Okay, then. I'll get my coffee and wait here. You take your time."

"Thank you."

A large staircase rose out of the lobby toward the second floor and Bellamy started up the stairs toward her office, another one of her daily concessions to health and wellness. The hallways were even emptier than when she'd left for Human Resources—had it really only been an hour?—and she passed a few pockets of conversation and could hear one of her colleagues talking in muted tones from inside his office.

What would they tell Andrew?

She liked her boss. They'd worked well since she'd been put on his team two years prior and she'd like to tell him in person what was going on. Share her side of the story. But he'd already departed a few weeks early for the holidays, taking his family on a long-planned trip to Hawaii.

The fleeting thought of texting him faded as she imagined what she'd even try to say.

Sorry to bother you on vacation. I just got fired because we're tampering with the flu vaccine supply chain here at LSP.

No way.

Even if she did want to bother him, what would he do from four thousand miles away? What she needed to do was take stock and evaluate what had happened. Then she could decide the best course of action. She was a well-respected employee at LSP and a member of the community. She'd find a way through this.

Even if Sally's comments at the end had taken a toll. Bellamy's father's accident and subsequent financial troubles weren't exactly a secret. She'd even had to sell the family business—the long-standing corner store her father had opened in his twenties—to pay for his medical bills.

No matter how sympathetic or understanding people might have been, it wasn't a far leap to think they'd believe Sally's innuendo.

It's sad.

Illness like that takes a toll.

It's also an expensive thing.

Each miserable word had stamped itself in her mind and Bellamy was hard-pressed to see how she'd come out in the best light should Sally decide to spread those rumors.

On a resigned sigh, she reached for the box Gus had handed her before departing for his coffee. Thirteen years, and she was left with a brown box and the few items she could stow inside.

The photo of her parents out front of the store—one of her favorites—came off her credenza first, followed by her calendar, a silly glass elf she'd purchased a few years before and the small radio that was still playing Christmas songs. She added a personnel file she'd kept her records in, a handful of cards given from coworkers through the years and, last, a few copies of the email she'd printed for herself.

Although she suspected even the affable Gus would have to take back any files she attempted to remove from her desk, she did a quick sweep of her files to make sure she hadn't missed anything.

And saw the framed photo of her sister, Maggie, she'd shoved in the bottom drawer. A dazzling smile reflected back at her, the remembered warmth there stabbing into Bellamy's heart.

She missed her sister. Desperately. And far more than she probably should, even as she blamed Maggie for all that had gone wrong over the past five years.

Her sister's abandonment had stung, but it was the cold shoulder Maggie had given her at their parents' funerals that had hurt the most. When had her bright, beautiful, vibrant sister become such a cold witch?

The urge to toss the photo into the garbage, along with a few of the folders that held out-of-date information or pamphlets on some of their older drug introductions, was strong, but in the end familial loyalty won out and she shoved the frame facedown on top of the small pile of items in her cardboard box. If she was going to toss the picture, she could do it properly at home, not in a snit in what was soon to be someone else's office.

Shaking off the personal reminder of her relationship with her sister, Bellamy finished placing the last few items in the box. The printouts of the email that had started it all were the last to go in and, on impulse, she took the printouts from the box and secured them in her purse. "At least I have something."

The copy wasn't much but it did have a time and date stamp on it, and if she were able to secure a legal representative who could subpoena the company's electronic records, she might be able to prove the fact the email had been sent to her and was not a result of her own tampering.

With a hard tug on the closure of her purse, Bellamy stopped herself and fell into her chair.

Subpoena? Electronic records? Legal representation?

How had she gone from a fiercely loyal employee to someone ready to instigate legal action in a matter of minutes?

The vibration of her phone caught her moments before

the ringer went off, her best friend Rae's name and picture filling the screen. She toyed with not answering when the overwhelming urge to talk to someone who believed her struck hard.

"Hey there."

"What's wrong? You sound upset."

Bellamy smiled despite the horrible weight that had pressed on her chest since leaving Sally Borne's office. The quick response after a simple greeting was straight-up Rae and at that moment, Bellamy couldn't have been more grateful.

"Well. Um." The tears that had threatened on the walk back tightened her throat once more. "I'm packing my office."

"What? Why?" The noise of the Whisperwood General Store echoed in the background, but nothing in the noise could dim Rae's concern. "Who would do that? You're one of their best employees."

"As of a half hour ago, they began treating me like Enemy Number One."

"What? Wait—" Rae broke off, the din in the background fading even as she hollered at someone to come help her at the counter. "Okay. I'm in my office. Talk to me."

Bellamy laid it all out—the email, the walk to HR and the weird meeting, even Gus's kindness in letting her have a few minutes.

"Gus'll give Sutton Taylor what for. Why don't you let him?"

"I need to process this. Something's going on and the faster I figure out what it is, the faster I can get my job back." *If I even want it.*

The thought was so foreign—and such a departure from who she'd been for the past thirteen years—Bellamy nearly repeated the words out loud.

Was it possible the damage of an afternoon could remove the goodwill of nearly a decade and a half?

"Who do you think did it?" Rae's question interrupted the wending of Bellamy's thoughts.

"I wish I knew. It's dangerous, Rae. If it's a joke it's a horrific slander on the company. And if it's true—" Bellamy stopped, barely able to finish the thought. "If it's true, it's a problem beyond measure. We serve the public good. We can't take that good away from them, especially in flu season."

"I've already had a few people in complaining about it. I'm tempted to drag on a surgical mask each morning before I open up."

Rae would do it, too, Bellamy thought with a smile. That and a whole lot more, she had to admit.

"Look, Rae. I need you to keep this to yourself until I understand what's going on."

"Bell, come on, you have to tell someone."

"I will. But. Well. Look, just don't say anything, okay? Please promise me."

The quiet was nearly deafening before she heard her friend acquiesce through the phone. "Okay. I'll hold my tongue for now."

"Thank you. Let me get my feet under me and I can figure out what comes next."

"So long as it entails a visit to the police at some point."

Since her thoughts hadn't been too far from the same, Bellamy had to admit Rae had a point. "I'll call you later. I need to finish packing up and get out of here. Even with Gus's willingness to give me time, the dragon in HR is going to expect me off the grounds."

"Okay. Call me later."

They hung up with a promise to do a good raging girls' night, complete with margaritas and a gallon of ice cream.

It couldn't erase her day, but as promises went it was certainly something to look forward to.

Bellamy glanced down at her box, her meager possessions all she had as evidence of her time at Lone Star Pharmaceutical.

Securing the lid, she took a deep breath and pulled her purse over her arm.

She'd already lived through the loss of her family, both through death and through abandonment. She would survive this.

Resolved, Bellamy picked up the box and walked out of her office. She refused to look back.

THE MID-DECEMBER AFTERNOON light was fading as Bellamy trudged toward her car. She'd snagged a spot in the far back parking lot, beneath an old willow that she loved for its sun protection and the added benefit of more daily steps, to and from the front door. Now it just seemed like more punishment as she put one foot in front of the other, her box completing the professional walk of shame.

Thankfully, the parking lot was rather empty, the impending holiday and the general spirit of celebration and success at LSP pushing even more people than she'd expected to knock off early.

Gus had been kind when he met her in the lobby, his expression sorrowful as he took her badge and her corporate credit card. Sally Borne hadn't shown up for the proceedings but her office lackey, Marie, had been there to take the badge and credit card before bustling off back where she'd come from.

It was unkind, but Bellamy hadn't been able to dismiss the image of a small crab scuttling back to its sandy burrow the way the woman rushed off.

And then it had just been awkward with Gus, so she'd given him a quick kiss on the cheek and a warm hug, prom-

ising to visit with him in town at the annual tree lighting
in the town square the following week. She'd already committed to Rae that she'd go and she'd be damned if she was
going to hide in her home like the same crab she'd mentally
accused Marie of being.

Shifting the box in her arms, Bellamy laid it on her rear
bumper as she dug for her keys. After unlocking the car,
then pressing the button for her trunk, she juggled the box
into the gaping maw of her sedan, only to fumble it as she
attempted to settle it with one hand while her other held
her purse in place.

A steady stream of expletives fell from her lips when
a brisk wind whipped up, catching the now-loose box lid
and flinging it from the trunk.

"Damn it!"

The temptation to leave the lid to fly from one end of
the parking lot to the other was great, but she dutifully
trudged off to snag it where it drifted over the concrete.
She might be persona non grata but she wouldn't add lit-
terbug to the litany of sudden crimes she'd apparently per-
petrated against LSP. Nor would she put someone at risk
of tripping on it inadvertently.

Box lid in hand, she crossed back to the car, dropping
into the driver's seat and turning on the ignition. The car
caught for the briefest moment, then rumbled to life. She put
her foot on the brake, about to shift into reverse, when her
gaze caught on the rearview mirror and her still-open trunk.

Resigned, she opened the door once more and crossed
back to the trunk. That damn cardboard box stared up at
her, the lonely receptacle of her professional life and—finally—she let the tears she'd fought all afternoon fall.

Lost job. Lost family. Hell, even a holiday that was shap-
ing up to be a lost cause. All of it seemed to conspire against
her until all she could see or think or feel was an overwhelming sense of loss.

Frustrated, Bellamy stepped back and slammed the lid.

Instantly, a wall of heat flared up, consuming her before she felt her body lifted off the ground and thrown across the parking lot.

DONOVAN WAS MIDWAY down his parents' stone-covered driveway when the call from Dispatch came in. He answered immediately, responding with his badge number and his location.

"We have a bomb called in at Lone Star Pharmaceutical. Your location indicates you're closest to the site."

LSP?

An image of the imposing corporate park on the edge of Whisperwood filled his thoughts, along with the pretty woman he'd met a million years ago who worked there. Who was bombing the town's largest employer? And why?

"I am," Donovan confirmed. "I can be to the site in three minutes. What are the known details?"

"LSP security called it in. Initial report says a car on fire and a woman shaky but standing."

"She walked away from a car bomb?"

"Reports say she was outside it and tossed back by the blast."

"I'm on my way."

"Thanks, Officer. Backup will meet you there."

Donovan took a left out of his parents' driveway instead of the right he'd planned. Flipping on his lights he headed out over the two-lane Farm to Market road that lead back into town and on toward the corporate headquarters that stood at the opposite edge of Whisperwood.

He'd already spent the morning with the town's chief of police and now it looked like he'd spend his evening with him, as well. The town was big enough to keep a sizable force, but they had to tap into the Austin PD for specialties like bomb squad support. As LSP had grown along with the town, Donovan had often wondered why the local PD hadn't been given more resources, but knew that wasn't always an easy battle.

It was one that big companies readily fought when they preferred to employ their own security.

Perhaps that folly had come back to bite them?

By all accounts LSP's owner was a local maverick who was as delighted to be a pillar of the community as he was to rub the town's noses in it when he wanted to do things his way. Bold and daring, Sutton Taylor had favored the town he'd grown up in to set up his world-renowned pharmaceutical company.

Donovan turned onto Lone Star Boulevard, the well-paved road that ran in front of LSP's headquarters. The scrub grass and occasional ruts that made up the drive across town vanished as he came onto LSP land.

The guards at the main entrance waved him through the gates before he'd barely flashed his badge and Donovan headed straight for the billowing smoke still evident at the back of the parking lot. Alex sat sentinel beside him, his body strung tight as a bow as he waited for his orders.

Even from a distance, Donovan could tell the scene was contained. Two LSP security vehicles were parked near the still-smoldering car and a crowd had gathered at the edge of the parking lot, obviously evacuated from the building. The security team seemed to have it under control, the individuals corralled far enough back to avoid any additional fallout from the wrecked car. With the destruction already wrought on the burning sedan, the car was the least likely source of any remaining danger.

Instead, he and Alex would go to work on the scattered vehicles still in the lot.

He parked, his already alert partner rising farther up on his seat. Within a few moments, he had Alex at his side, leashed and ready for duty. One of the security guards moved away from a huddled woman and walked toward him. The man was grizzled, his body stiff with age, but his clear blue eyes were bright and alert.

Sharp.

The man nodded. "Officer. I'm Gus Sanger. I'm in Security here at LSP."

"Donovan Colton. This is Alex." He motioned for Alex to sit beside him, the move designed to show his control over the animal yet ensure no one missed the dog's imposing presence.

"You got here fast. K-9's out of the Austin PD."

"I was in Whisperwood on another assignment." Donovan shook the proffered hand before pointing toward a pretty woman covered in soot. "Is she hurt?"

"Claims she isn't. That's Ms. Reeves. Bellamy Reeves. She's banged up and has a few scratches on her elbows and a bigger gash on her arm the EMTs bandaged up, but I'd say lucky all in all."

At the utterance of her name, Donovan stilled. Although he hoped it didn't show to Sanger, Alex recognized it immediately, shifting against his side.

Bellamy Reeves? The same woman he'd spoken to so many years ago in the Whisperwood corner store...

"Do you mind if I go talk to her?"

Sanger nodded, his gaze dropping to Alex. "Does he go everywhere with you?"

"Everywhere."

"Good."

Donovan walked to the woman, taking her in as he went. She was turned, her gaze focused on her car, but he could make out her profile and basic build. Same long legs. Same sweep of dark hair. And when she finally turned, he saw those same alert gray eyes, that were mysterious and generous, all at the same time.

She was still pretty, even beneath a layer of dirt and

grime from whatever happened to her car. Which he'd get to in a moment. First, he wanted to see to her.

"Ms. Reeves?"

She had her arms crossed, the bandage Gus mentioned evident on her forearm and her hands cradled against her ribs as if hugging herself. She was drawn in—scared, by his estimation—and doing her level best to hide it. "Officer?"

He ordered Alex to heel at his side, then extended his hand. "I'm Officer Colton. This is Alex. We're here to help you."

Whether it was the use of their names or the fading shock of the moment, her eyes widened. "You."

"It's me. How are you, Bellamy?"

Those pretty eyes widened, then dropped to Alex. "He's so big. Just like I knew he would be." She instinctively reached for Alex before pulling her hand back.

"You can pet him if you'd like. He's not formally working yet."

She bent, her gaze on Alex as her hands went to cup the Lab's head and ears. Donovan didn't miss how they trembled or what a calming effect Alex seemed to have on her as she petted that soft expanse of fur. "You grew just as big as I knew you would. But I hope you've learned some restraint around plastic toys."

"Grudgingly." Donovan smiled when she glanced back up at him, pleased that she'd remembered them. "We nearly had a repeat incident with a few Barbie high heels but I managed to recover them before he swallowed them."

"He's a little thief."

"One who fortunately matured out of the impulse."

She stood back upright but kept a slightly less shaky hand on Alex's head. "You're here because of this?"

"I was in town on another assignment today and hadn't left yet. Are you okay?" The assignment was a bit of a stretch but somehow, saying he had to visit his mother or risk her wrath didn't seem like the most comforting comment.

"I'm fine. Gus looked at me quickly and I don't feel hurt other than the scrapes. Shaken and sort of wobbly, but nothing hurts too bad or feels broken."

"How close were you to the car?"

"I'd gotten in and realized I hadn't closed the trunk. I was behind the car when it just—" She broke off, the disbelief still clear in her eyes. "When it just exploded."

"We're going to take a look at it but first I need Alex to sniff the rest of the cars that are still here so we can get these people out of here. Can you wait for me?"

"Where else am I going to go?"

For reasons Donovan couldn't explain, he sensed there was something more in her comment. Something that went well beyond a car bomb or the shaky aftereffects of surviving a crime.

Something terrible had taken the light out of her beautiful gray eyes.

And he was determined to find out why.

Chapter Three

Bellamy stood to the side and watched the chaos that had overtaken the parking lot. Several cop cars had arrived shortly after Donovan and Alex as well as two fire trucks and the EMTs. At one point she'd estimated half of Whisperwood's law enforcement had found its way to LSP. The scene was well controlled and she'd been happy to see how the local police handled the press who were already sniffing around for a story. They were currently corralled on the far edge of the property, clamoring for whatever scraps they could get.

She'd ignored them, even as one had somehow secured her cell phone number and had already dialed her three times. It was probably only the start and she'd finally turned off the ringer. There would be time enough to deal with the fallout once she knew what she was actually dealing with.

And it might be to her advantage to have a working relationship with someone from the press if she needed to tell her side of the story.

If? Or when? a small voice inside prompted.

Sighing, she let her gaze wander back over the assembled crowd of law enforcement. Would they help her if she truly needed it? Or would they bow to whatever pressure LSP might put on them?

Like a bucket of errant Ping-Pong balls, the thoughts

winged around in her mind, volleying for position and prominence.

She'd already taken the proffered water and over-the-counter pain meds from the EMT attendant and had finally begun to feel their effect. The pain in her arm had subsided to a dull throb and the headache that had accompanied her since the accident had begun to fade, as well. But the endless questions in her mind continued.

The EMTs had pressed repeatedly to take her to the hospital for additional observation but she'd finally managed to push them off after submitting to several rounds of "follow the light" as they looked into her eyes, searching for a possible concussion. It had only been Donovan's input—and assurances that he'd keep a watch on her—that had finally quelled the discussion about removing her from the premises.

Not that she exactly wanted to stand around and watch her car smolder in a pile of burned-out metal. Or question who might have wanted to harm her enough to put it in that condition.

It had taken her quite a while to come up with that conclusion, but once she did the sentiment wouldn't shake.

Someone had done this.

Cars didn't just explode when the ignition turned over. And innocent people didn't just get fired from jobs they were good at and loyal to.

So what was going on and what mess had she fallen into? And had she really left her home that very morning thinking it was just another day?

And how was it that Donovan Colton was the one who arrived to rescue her?

She'd thought of him intermittently over the past five years. Most of the time it was a good memory—a sweet, flirty interlude with an attractive man. But there were other moments—when the memory stung and instead of leaving her with a smile it left her with a strange ache. The painful reminder of what she'd lost that night that went beyond a lost date.

Could things have been different?

In the end it hadn't mattered. If she were honest with herself, it still didn't. Her father was horribly injured that night and her life—all their lives—had irrevocably changed.

"Bellamy?" Gus shuffled up to her, his bright blue eyes hazed with concern. "You've been awfully quiet standing here all by yourself. Are you sure you don't need to go to the emergency room?"

"I'm sure. I'm made of sturdier stuff."

"If you're sure?"

"I'm sure." She glanced at the dissipating crowd. "Did they find any other bombs?"

"It doesn't appear so. The damage from this hooligan seems confined to your car."

Hooligan?

While she had no wish to alarm an old man—and she suspected his use of the word was meant to comfort—the casual term wasn't nearly the correct one for what had happened to her. This wasn't a prank. Or a sick joke. Someone had attempted to kill her. And the sooner she got off of LSP property, the better she'd feel.

"Will I be allowed to go home soon?"

"I overheard Officer Colton talking with the chief. You should be able to get out of here right soon."

"Thanks."

Since her purse had been on her arm when she'd gotten out of the car to close the trunk, she still had many of her personal items. Best of all, she'd been pleased to find her cell phone undamaged where she'd had it zipped in a side pocket. The purse was ripped and headed for the trash but the fact it protected the rest of her personal items was the only saving grace of the evening. Especially seeing as how the car and her small box of memories were destroyed.

"Ms. Reeves?"

Donovan Colton took a commanding spot beside her and Gus, Alex immediately sitting at his side. There was something comforting about the presence of both of them and Bellamy felt a small bit of the stress and strain of the day ebb. "Yes."

"I'd like to ask you a few questions but perhaps you'd prefer to answer them after you've had a chance to clean up. Or maybe eat?"

"You can decide that? I mean, I can leave here."

The edges of his eyes crinkled in a small smile before he nodded. "I think I'm allowed to take you to a more comfortable place and out of the increasing cold. It may be Texas, but it's still December."

She had gotten chilled, the air growing cool once the sun set. "I didn't have lunch and now that you mention it, I am hungry."

"Why don't we leave, then?" Donovan turned to Gus and shook his hand. "You and your team have been incredibly helpful here. Thank you for keeping everyone at the edges and not allowing anyone else to leave until we had a chance to check their cars."

Gus stood taller, his chest puffing just like the dog's. "Of course."

"I'll see that Ms. Reeves is escorted home now. I'll be back tomorrow to finish a review of the site with the chief."

"We'll be waiting for you."

Now that she'd given her agreement to leave, there was little keeping her and Donovan on the property. In a matter of moments, he had her in his SUV and was driving them toward the exit on the back side of the property, in the opposite direction from the press. She wasn't sure if the strategy would work, but refused to turn around to find out.

"I'm sorry for the dog hair. Alex usually sits on the front seat."

A strained giggle crawled up her throat, at odds with the exhaustion that racked her shoulders the moment she sat down. "I think a few stray dog hairs are the least of my worries right now. And since I don't mind them on a good day, it's no bother."

"Are you warm enough?" The heater was on full blast, rapidly warming the car as they drove toward the center of town.

"I'm getting there." As days went, December in central Texas was often mild bordering on warm. She was rarely cold, but since being tossed from the car she'd had a weird, aching numbness that had settled in her bones and refused to let go.

"You're probably dealing with the lingering effects of shock. I should have thought of this sooner. Here." He pulled to the side of the road and shrugged out of his coat, handing it over. "Put this on."

The jacket enveloped her, a mix of body heat and a scent that was distinctly male. She could still smell the cold air that had wrapped around them in the parking lot, only instead of being tinged with the lingering, acrid taste of smoke and burned-out car, in its place was a musky, pleasing warmth. She also caught the faintest whisper of dog and smiled to herself.

Clearly Alex wasn't at a loss for hugs and affection.

That thought warmed her beyond the car or the coat, filling her with that years-old memory of a large man cradling a sick puppy in his arms. Her father had always told her you could tell a man's character by the way he treated animals and in the case of Donovan Colton, she had to admit the expression was spot on the mark.

"How are you feeling?"

"Better. Warmer." She took in his profile, not wanting to stare but unable to fully look away.

Goodness, was he handsome. She'd thought so that night in her parents' store and saw it even more now. The firm jawline. The close-cropped dark hair. And the thick, corded forearm muscles now visible where he gripped the steering wheel.

"Make a right when you get to the stop sign at the end of this road."

"That's not the way to the diner."

"You don't need to take me to dinner. Home's fine."

"I promised you a meal and I aim to deliver. In fact—" his gaze flashed toward hers before he resumed his focus on the road "—I believe I promised you dinner some time ago."

"That's not... I mean—" She broke off, feeling silly. "I'm covered in parking lot dirt and smell like the undercarriage of a car. Home's fine."

"I'll take you home but I'm not going to leave you right now. You've had an ordeal and I'd like to stick around for a bit."

"I know you have to question me. Can we just do it at my house?"

He frowned before reaching out a hand to lay over hers. "This isn't about questioning you. You're not a criminal, Bellamy. But I will respect your wishes and take you home on one condition"

"What's that?"

"You let me order a pizza from Chuck's."

"How DID A scrappy little guy from Brooklyn end up in Whisperwood, Texas?" Donovan peeked inside the oversize cardboard box of pizza before dropping the lid into place. He'd called in the order as they drove, hoping to minimize their time in town. In retrospect, the decision was a good one when he'd seen a local TV news truck wending its way down Main Street as he pulled away from Chuck's parking lot.

It was too much to hope she wouldn't be found by the press—or worse, whomever had put the bomb in her car—but if he could give her even an evening's peace, then he wanted to do it.

What he hadn't fully reconciled was how much he was looking forward to having dinner with her.

His offered dinner invitation had gone unfulfilled for so many years, it was humbling to realize how anxious he was to see it through. Which was ridiculous because she was now on his caseload and dealing with a horrific trauma.

Bellamy glanced over her shoulder as she grabbed sodas from the fridge before hip bumping the door closed. "Thank Cupid. Chuck met his wife, Maria, on a cruise and decided he couldn't live without her. New York's loss is Whisperwood's gain."

"And Maria's, obviously," Donovan added.

"You seem familiar with the pizza?"

"I'm from here originally. And you don't have to spend much time in Whisperwood before someone makes sure you have a pizza from Chuck's."

While technically true, his mother preferred food cooked in the Colton kitchens by her extensive staff instead of ordering in. Chuck's pizza had been a fortuitous accident one early evening after he'd ducked out of his parents' house and headed home to Austin. Since then, even though he avoided spending a lot of time in Whisperwood, he'd stop off at the small pizzeria after his sporadic visits to his parents' house. He could always make room for a fresh slice and the pizza was almost better the next day, cold, when it came straight out of the fridge.

A small, amused smile tilted Bellamy's lips. "Plates are in the cabinet above the sink."

She stood by her small kitchen table, her dark hair damp from the quick shower he'd encouraged her to take. She was fully dressed, an oversize long-sleeved T-shirt falling over jeans, but something about the look had him doing a double take. There was something fresh about her.

He'd noticed it five years before and was struck anew by that same fact. Even with the horrible events she'd experienced that day, there was a light in her. It had been dampened since their first meeting, but it was still there. Hovering.

Hoping.

Which made the situation she found herself in that much worse. Although he and Alex would go back tomorrow and do a more thorough search of her car, his initial take was that, while deliberate, the bomb had been planted with a degree of amateur crudeness. Crude or not, the work had been effective, the one who planted it only miscalculating the timing device.

And Bellamy's extraordinarily lucky miss by not closing the trunk.

He buried the thought that she was only standing there by the grace of an accident and finished his quick perusal of her, head to toe. It was a skill he'd honed on the job and he used it to his advantage before his gaze alighted on her bare feet. Where he'd have expected her socks to be a soft pink or maybe even a fun red, the distinct shade of burnt orange that covered her toes had him smiling.

"What's that look for?"

He let his gaze linger one more moment on her toes before meeting her eyes. He owed it to her to apprise her of his thoughts on what she was really dealing with, but he wanted time.

Just a bit of time with her.

"It looks like someone's a Longhorn fan."

"As every good graduate of the University of Texas

should be." She wiggled the toes on one foot, followed by the other. "I bleed orange, if you must know."

"A pastime around here."

"Pretty much." The mention of her alma mater had her standing a bit straighter and he was pleased to see a smile persisting on her lips as she crossed the small expanse to the stove. She lifted the lid on the pizza and bent closer to inhale the scent before nodding her head. "Oh yeah. Brooklyn's loss is definitely our gain."

They fixed plates and Bellamy grabbed the two sodas from the counter on their way to a dining alcove just outside the kitchen. The house was modest in size, but cozy, and it was easy to see that she'd made a life for herself here. Her taste wasn't flashy, but he caught subtle hints of whimsy in her home. A superhero cookie jar on the kitchen counter added to the decor and her dining room tablecloth had penguins around the rim.

Alex had laid guard outside the kitchen while they fixed their plates and then repositioned himself after they settled at the table.

"He's so good around food."

"Part of his job."

"It's amazing, though." She shook her head. "I had a dog growing up that made it his business to eat anything he could find, scrounge or flat out steal."

"I had a similar conversation with my mother earlier. I grew up with one of those, too. Alex is special, though. He knows his job and with it, his place."

The flow of casual conversation seemed to do its job. Their easy tumble from topic to topic, from Chuck's love life to the discussion of the Longhorns to ravenous dogs, had left that small, persistent smile on her face.

"Will he eat tonight?"

"I'll feed him when we're done. I keep food in the car

ecause I never know if we'll be out late. He's working now so he can eat once I'm done."

"Working?"

"Absolutely. You're in his care now. He hasn't taken his eyes off of you."

She laid down her pizza and turned her full attention toward the dog. Although Alex never moved, the tip of his tail started to thump against the floor. "He's watching over me?"

"Yes. Has been ever since we walked over to you in the LSP parking lot. He's going to protect you." *And so am I.*

The thought rang so clearly in his mind he nearly dropped his pizza. Of course it was his job, and by taking the call Bellamy Reeves had absolutely become his responsibility.

But something else called to him.

He had thought about her through the years. The easy moments they'd shared in her parents' store that lone December evening. The sweet way she had with Alex and the quick way she'd leaped to help them.

He'd remembered.

And he'd thought of her every time he'd passed the corner store on his way out of town.

The store had changed hands since then. He was curious about it and was about to ask when she interjected a fresh thought into the conversation.

"I think we get the better end of the deal."

"Of what deal?"

"The human and pet deal. They give us so much and we just sort of take it." As soon as the words were out, she seemed to catch herself. "Not that you treat him poorly— that's not what I meant. But they give from a special place. It's one I don't know humans have."

"I know what you mean. We think we're superior but there's an awful lot we can learn from animals. They live in the moment. They're loyal. And there's an honesty to them that we can't ever hope to aspire to."

"You're smitten."

"With Alex? Definitely."

"He was such a cute puppy and he's grown into such a handsome dog. Is he good at his job?"

"The best."

"Let me amend my earlier comment. You're smitten *and* biased."

The lightest whisper of heat crawled up his neck. "I suppose I am. He really is good, though. He consistently wins the drills we run across the K-9 teams. And he's got a special sort of alertness. Like now. He looks like he's casually sitting there but he's totally focused on the two of us and on his surroundings."

"What was your takeaway of today?"

The shift in question caught him off guard and Donovan couldn't help thinking that Bellamy Reeves was totally aware of her surroundings, too.

And the danger that threatened her in ways he couldn't begin to imagine.

BELLAMY WANTED TO hover in the warm cocoon of her house and her most comfy clothes and the incredibly able strength of Officer Donovan Colton and his sidekick, Alex. More, she wanted to lose herself in all of it and shut out whatever lurked outside her door.

Which was the very reason she had to ask the question.

And accept that the darkness that came into Donovan's already dark brown gaze had nothing to do with her question and everything to do with the answer.

Something terrible had happened today and pretending it hadn't wasn't going to set her up very well.

Just like her parents.

Where her sister had been insistent in believing things

weren't "that bad" after the accident, Bellamy had pressed on, well aware of what difficult times faced them. Her father's resulting paralysis—and the difficulty of trying to have a seventy-five-year-old body bounce back against that sort of crushing destruction—was nearly impossible.

And she'd met it head-on.

She hadn't hid, nor had she run.

Then why was the urge to do so now so overwhelming and urgent?

And what was she going to do about what she'd found?

"My takeaway?"

She nodded. "I know you haven't written a formal report, but you've obviously done this for some time. What was your initial impression?"

"I still need to question you. I also need to share my thoughts with my commanding officer."

"I see."

And just like that, he went into cop mode, shutting her out of what was clearly her own problem to deal with. Just like the doctors. Just like her sister. Hell, even just like her mother.

Life had careened out of control once again and the only person left to manage it was her.

Standing, she took her empty plate into the kitchen and placed everything in the sink. The rich scents of tomato sauce and cheese still wafted from the closed cardboard but she'd suddenly lost her appetite.

It was unfair to paint Donovan with the same brush as others in her life—she hadn't even told him of the email yet or the events of the day—but his reticence to share with her still stung.

"Bellamy, I'm sorry." She wasn't surprised he'd followed her, but she was stunned to feel the wall of heat that emanated against her back. "I'm not trying to keep you in the dark."

"Spare me."

"It's my job and I need to report my thoughts to my boss. I owe it to him. But that doesn't mean I won't tell you what I know. Nor does it mean I'm going to keep you in the dark. But I need to follow the correct chain of command and management of evidence."

"Evidence?"

"Your car is evidence. That's what I asked the chief to move into police custody. Alex and I will look at it tomorrow and we'll have a better sense of what we're dealing with."

That wall of heat seemed to grow warmer, if possible, even though he didn't touch her. Despite the lack of contact, she could feel him. Could practically sense the beat of his heart.

And even as she hated being kept in the dark, she couldn't deny how good it felt to have him stand there. To have him in her home, filling up the space.

To have someone nearby.

"I won't keep you in the dark. But please let me do my job."

"I got fired today." The words slipped out, as embarrassing to say them out loud as they'd been to digest in Sally Borne's office.

"What for?"

"Reporting an email I wasn't supposed to have received in the first place." She reached for a nearby dish towel, twisting the material beneath her fingers. "Or maybe I was. Who knows?"

Large hands settled on her shoulders, lingering there briefly before turning her around. "What's this about? I need you to tell me. Tell me all of it."

She knew this moment was inevitable. Had even expected it as she'd worked to process all that had happened since opening that stupid email earlier.

What she hadn't expected were the tears. Hot and sharp, they filled her eyes and tightened her throat like fingers wrapped around her neck. Worse, once she let them out, there was no way to pull them back.

"I—" She swallowed the hiccup, even as another hard sob swamped her.

And then it didn't matter. There was no need for words or explanations or even apologies as Donovan pulled her against that broad, capable, gloriously strong chest. He held her there, his arms around her and his hand nestled against her head where he stroked her hair, seeing her through the uncontrollable rush of emotion and raw adrenaline that finally had a place to land.

Sobs racked her frame as the hot tears continued to pour, unchecked, from her eyes. Abstractly, she thought to be embarrassed, but the sheer relief of expelling all that pent-up emotion kept her from dwelling on anything for too long.

As the tears finally subsided, those lingering moments of embarrassment bubbled to the surface. On a hiccup, she looked up at him, attempting to slip from his hold. "I am sorry."

He didn't budge, a wall of heat and man and solid strength. "Don't go anywhere."

"I... I mean... I—" A horrified squeak fell from her lips as she realized she stood in her kitchen, crying her eyes out in front of a virtual stranger. "I'm so sorry."

"Don't be sorry. And while you're at it, forget embarrassed, anxious or silly. You had a bad day. A really bad day. This will help you start to feel better."

As pep talks went, his admonishments did the trick. The embarrassment was already fading and in its place came that subtle tug of attraction her body still remembered from all those years ago.

Donovan Colton was an impressive man, and not just for the solid physique and commanding presence. The man had layers. She'd sensed it five years ago and she sensed it now, even as she had no reason for the observation.

Yet something was there.

Her mother had always teased her about being border-line psychic but she'd never paid it much mind. Bellamy had always believed instead it meant taking the time to observe her surroundings. She wasn't shy, per se, but she wasn't the first person to leap in and begin talking. Rather, she appreciated the opportunity to sit and observe before being called on to say anything.

Appreciated the opportunity to get her bearings around people.

The side benefit was that she'd learned to read people. She'd developed a sense of what made them tick and, often, what motivated them.

And that's where Donovan Colton tripped her up. It was obvious he was crazy about his dog. Along with that she took him at face value as a good, honorable cop. Even his reticence to share his thoughts on her case were steeped in following protocol, which she could—and did—respect.

So why the subtle sense that he was almost desperate to prove his place in the world?

She'd thought it earlier when he'd spoken of the pizza. He might be from Whisperwood but there was a distinct note of dissonance, that he clearly felt he didn't belong here. Nor did he have much love for his hometown. Again, she couldn't define how she knew that, she simply did.

"Are you all right now?" Donovan asked.

"Yeah. I feel better."

"Do you want anything else to eat?"

"No." She rubbed her stomach, the crying jag having left her raw and hollowed out. "I'm good."

"You mind if I feed Alex, then? And we can talk after."

"Go ahead."

Donovan ducked out of the kitchen and after some murmured words to Alex, she heard her front door click shut. Alex trotted into the kitchen in the wake of his master's departure, his tail wagging and his gentle brown eyes alert as he took her in.

"You're such a pretty boy." Bellamy picked up a plastic bowl she'd filled for him earlier and freshened the water. His nails tapped on her hardwood floor as he walked over to the bowl, his gaze on her until he dropped his head to the water and drank his fill.

Even in something so simple and natural, she knew the dog was alert and keen to his surroundings. What fascinated her was how attuned he was to her. It didn't take much to know Donovan's directive to the animal had been to watch over her. What she didn't know was what she was going to do when they had to leave.

Or how she'd fight back against the inevitable threat when it came at her once more.

Chapter Four

While Alex dived into his dinner, Donovan left his partner to his food and walked back into the dining room. Bellamy stood arrow straight, her head slightly bowed as her hands trailed over a small sideboard. She stared down at a series of photos and even from where he stood he could see she focused on one in particular.

"Are those your parents?"

"Yes." She tapped one of the photos. "This was their fiftieth anniversary."

He did the quick math in his head, surprised to realize they had been so old. "Do you have a lot of brothers and sisters?"

"No, just me and my younger sister, Magnolia. Maggie," she quickly added.

"Then your parents were older when they had children? Because there's no way you're close to fifty."

She turned away from the photo, the aimless energy that seemed to grip her at the sideboard fading as he asked her about her life. "Yes. And that photo was taken about six years ago. Before my father—" She hesitated, then continued, "Before his health declined. My mother's followed on the heels of that."

"I'm sorry for that."

And he was. While Donovan took full credit for the personal challenges he had with his own family, he loved them. It had been hard to see his father struggle the past couple of years as he was naturally forced to slow down from his normal routine—racing around the ranch, flying places for his business interests or evenings out entertaining. And his mother, for all her bright and happy chatter, carried the burdens of age, as well. She'd let go of a few commitments over the past few years, preferring events that didn't have her driving at night.

He supposed it was the natural order of things, but it didn't mean it hadn't been a transition.

"What about you?" Bellamy asked. "Any brothers or sisters?"

"Oh, the Colton family is a prolific one. I'm one of four, all older than me, and I come from a family that's even larger."

"That must be nice."

"Most of the time." Donovan avoided mentioning when it wasn't, especially since he had relatives who'd both spent time in jail for heinous crimes. While he knew his extended family didn't reflect on him, he was well aware there were places in Texas and beyond where the Colton name didn't win any fans.

How funny, then, that his parents were the antithesis. They'd been more than willing to take him in, nearly falling over themselves to make him part of the family. To save him, that poor little abandoned soul, dropped into their midst.

"You don't like coming from a big family?"

I don't like feeling like an outsider with all those eyes watching.

He never had. But like the black sheep branch of his family, he refused to mention anything. Instead, he focused on the positive and the values his mother had impressed upon him.

"It has its moments. I can do without everyone being

in each other's business. But it is nice knowing I have so many people to count on."

Her gaze flitted back to the photos at the edge of the sideboard before shifting determinedly back to him. "People to count on. That must be nice."

Alex trotted into the room, his dinner at an end and his guard duties back in place as he took a seat facing the two of them. The overwhelming events of the day—and the danger that lurked beneath—still seemed like a dream. Because she wanted to keep it that way for a few hours more, Bellamy focused on the dog. "I should probably let you both go. I'll be fine for tonight and then I can come in and make a statement tomorrow, if that's okay? I'm suddenly not up for getting into a recounting of my afternoon once again."

Exhaustion rode Bellamy's features, with dark smudges settling beneath her eyes postcrying jag. He didn't want to leave her but he hardly had a reason to stay, either. "I'm scheduled to meet with the chief tomorrow morning at ten. I would like to get your statement before then."

"How about if I come into the station at eight?" A hard laugh escaped her chest. "It's not like I have to go into work, after all."

She'd mentioned the job earlier, right before she was overcome with the emotions of the day. "You sure you don't want to talk about it now?"

"Can it wait? I promise I'll tell you everything. Including anything that may become clearer overnight."

"You have a deal, then."

"Oh. Wait." The bum's rush wasn't lost on him, so he was surprised when she stopped him. "I don't have a car."

"Alex and I can swing by and pick you up. I'll even include a stop at the coffee place in town."

"You don't have to—"

He reached for her hand, the move meant to reassure, but the sudden stop of her words hung heavy between them.

"It's okay. I can give you a hand. And it's not like Whisperwood is this sprawling metropolis. You're like a two-minute detour after I turn into town."

"Okay, then."

In moments she had him bustled out her front door, the rest of the pizza in his hands. As he opened the door of his SUV for Alex to hop in, Donovan couldn't avoid the impressions that had bombarded him over the past few hours. Where he'd initially seen a woman dealing with a difficult circumstance, those moments when she stared at her photos suggested something else.

Something more.

Bellamy Reeves was a lonely woman. And if his instincts were correct, she was dealing with something far beyond her understanding.

JENSEN TAYLOR SCROLLED impatiently through the news articles on his tablet, hunting for anything that might mention the incident in the parking lot at LSP. His father, Sutton, had been touch and go in the hospital for the past few weeks, a private matter Jensen had deliberately kept from the employees at LSP, but the old man had rallied over the past few days.

He'd inevitably be fielding phone calls if Sutton caught wind of a bomb detonating in the LSP parking lot.

He and his father did well keeping their distance—emotional and, when Jensen could manage it, physical—and the hospital stay had helped that even more. Jensen saw no reason to change that. He played the devoted son when it was warranted and then went about living his life the rest of the time. Now that Jensen's mother was dead, the situation worked well for them both.

Of course, cars blowing up in the LSP parking lot were likely to draw the old man's attention, no matter how poorly he felt. His father had been lingering at a private facility south of Austin, but he hadn't died. Public problems at LSP might give Sutton the ammunition to recover fully and that was the last thing Jensen needed.

All he had to do was convince the old man he had it under control.

It was his only choice.

He had little interest—actually, make that *no* interest—in pharmaceuticals, but he'd be damned if any of his father's bastards would get a piece of his legacy. The old man had already suggested he wanted to open up a new position on the leadership team for the moment one of his brats finished business school.

Oh, that was a big, Texas-sized *hell no*.

This was the only way to manage things and ensure his father's far-too-generous heart didn't ruin Jensen's future.

The entire situation had a funny sort of justice to it. His father had always played the field, his simpering mother just living with it while she flitted around as society matron of their hick town. Then his mother died and instead of publicly playing the field after an appropriate mourning period, poor Sutton was all sick and weak.

Justice at its finest.

LSP might have turned Whisperwood into one of the largest suburbs outside of Austin but it was still central Texas. Small freaking potatoes. But that hadn't stopped his father. The man had worked his playboy magic from one end of the Hill Country to the other. His mother had ignored it all, seeming to believe all that mattered was the large house Sutton had built for her, visible to anyone who drove a few blocks off of Whisperwood's main drag.

They really were a pair.

Jensen hadn't spent much time worrying if the two of them loved each other, but he had taken a few notes for himself on the type of woman who'd make a good partner. He could do with one who had his mother's penchant for living in ignorant bliss. Sadly, the last few women he'd dated hadn't fit the bill.

Resigned to worry about it later, Jensen shot a quick email to his father, assuring him all was well and to continue to rest and focus on getting better.

"Wanted you to hear it from me. Absolutely nothing to worry about. A holiday prank gone bad," Jensen muttered as he typed up a quick note and shot it off. He'd know by morning if the old man had bought it.

In the meantime, he wanted to do a bit of digging.

And figure out just what Bellamy Reeves knew.

BELLAMY GATHERED HER hair up in a twist, clipping the dark brown mass. Then she added a few quick swipes of mascara to her eyes for good measure. She'd spent a restless night and was well aware there was no amount of makeup that could cover the bags beneath her eyes.

"More like potato sacks," she acknowledged to herself as she added one last swipe of the mascara wand.

Standing back to assess her image in the mirror, she was pleased to see the mascara had at least made her look a bit more human. Zombie TV shows might be popular but no one wanted a monster walking down the Main Street of Whisperwood at eight in the morning.

The lack of a car was a problem, but she'd deal with that after she made her statement to Donovan. She'd already logged in the night before and started the claim process with her insurance company. The automated email she got back confirmed someone would call her today to keep the process moving.

Making one final effort to look human with a pass of her lip gloss, she grabbed a light jacket from her closet and went to wait in the front room for Donovan. The oppressive weight of the day before faded a bit as she thought about the strong, capable man and his dog.

They were an impressive pair. The dog was both obedient and clearly in love with his master, the big eyes and devoted stare something to see. She couldn't stop the small smile at the image they made, the affection in Donovan's eyes for the large black Lab proof he was equally smitten. It was sweet to see. And made a good-looking man even more attractive.

Along with her dad's advice, she'd also read once on a dating blog that three signs to watch for in a prospective mate were how they behaved with waiters, how they spoke in conflict and how they treated animals. From what she could see, Donovan Colton passed all three tests with flying colors.

It had been one of the things she still remembered about that night so long ago when he'd come into the store with a sweet little puppy. That mix of concern and care for an animal was an obvious clue to his personality.

Unbidden, the rest of that long-ago evening filled her thoughts. The easy conversation and subtle flirtation. Even the clear stamp of interest in his gaze. She'd been more interested than she could describe and had wanted to see him again.

Of course, all that had been forgotten once the news of her parents' accident was delivered. And all that had come after had changed her life in ways she never could have imagined.

So how odd that he was back. That he was the one who'd been in Whisperwood and taken the call for her car. And that he was the one she'd now share her story with.

Engine sounds purred from her driveway and a glance out the front window indicated her chariot had arrived. She picked up her things and let herself out of the house, surprised when either Donovan or Alex were nowhere in sight.

"Donovan?" When he didn't answer she hollered. "Donovan!"

His voice was muffled but came back from the opposite side of the yard. "Be right there! Stay at the door."

She stood still, curious to where he and his K-9 partner vanished to, but willing to follow the direction. She was nearly ready to go looking for them when Donovan reached her just as she was turning the key in the lock.

"Good morning, Bellamy."

"Oh!" She'd expected to meet him at the car, so the large frame and imposing presence was a surprise. "You didn't have to... I mean, I could have come to you."

"This is door-to-door service, ma'am. Even when I make you wait while Alex and I check the perimeter." He smiled and mimed tipping an imaginary hat. "It's part of the Texas gentleman's code."

She swallowed hard around the idea her perimeter even required checking and opted for a shot of dark humor. "The Texas gentleman's code? Is that a euphemism for politely escorting a suspect to the police station?"

The moment the words were out of her mouth, she knew they'd missed the mark. The anxiety that had kept her company throughout a restless night—including the fear that something horrible at LSP was somehow being blamed on her—had taken root and wouldn't let go.

But it was the frown that marred his face—matched to an equally disappointed light in his eyes—that had her rethinking the remark.

"This is nothing but routine."

"It may be for you, but it's not every day my car blows up and I follow it up with a visit to the police to make a statement."

"Did you do it?"

"What?" The sheer shock his question gave her had her mouth dropping, her momentary concern at possibly offending him fading away. "You think I did that? To my car? To my stuff? Why would I do that? And possibly kill myself in the process?"

Donovan had already walked her to his SUV, his expression turning serious as he put his hand on the car door handle. "I don't think anything of the sort. Or I'm trying hard not to, even though my instincts as a cop are to question everything."

"So you do think I did it?" The words came out prim and stiff and she wanted to sink through the driveway at the small shot of hurt that burrowed beneath her breast.

"I'm asking questions. Just like the chief will do. Just like reporters will do. Keep that hot core of righteous anger and you'll be just fine."

Bellamy was about to reply when Donovan pulled the door open. Alex was already in the back seat and she could see the depression marks of a sweeper head over the entire seat, from the back panel to the portion where she'd rest in her neatly pressed clothes. "You vacuumed?"

"Of course. I love Alex but I'm well aware no one wants to wear him."

"But… I mean…." She stopped, the weird conversation and the added awkwardness of her reaction to his questions slowing her down. She climbed into the SUV seat, but laid a hand on his arm before he could close the door. "Why don't I try this again? Good morning, Donovan. It's nice to see you. Thank you for picking me up."

He smiled once more, a small dimple winking in his cheek when the corners of his lips tilted upward into a relaxed grin. "Good morning, Bellamy. It's my pleasure."

He closed the door and she watched him walk around the front of the SUV, more than willing to look her fill unnoticed. He was still as attractive as that night he'd come into her parents' store, but he'd aged, as well. The rounder cheeks that marked a younger man were gone, replaced with a slight hollowing beneath the bones that set off his features. His jaw seemed harder than she remembered and there was a solidness to his frame that was rougher. Worn.

No, she amended to herself, *experienced*.

Age worked itself on every person in a myriad of ways, but experience left a different sort of mark. It stamped itself on the body by way of bearing and attitude, words and gestures.

He fascinates me.

The words popped into her mind, unbidden, but she gave them room to grow and the space to breathe.

Donovan Colton did fascinate her. He was attractive, obviously, but there was more. And what seemed to tug at her the most was what she sensed lay beneath the surface.

Unaware of her close scrutiny, Donovan hopped into the car and turned toward her. "Coffee first?"

"Sure."

"Then here." He reached behind his seat and pulled a cardboard container from the floor. "I didn't know what you liked but figured I couldn't go wrong with a latte."

"Thanks. And you guessed right."

The scent of coffee drifted from the cup in her hand and she wondered that she hadn't smelled it the moment she got into the car.

"You've been busy this morning. First the vacuum. Then the coffee. Did you catch a few bad guys while you were at it?"

"Alex and I are early risers. And I wanted to beat the traffic out of Austin so it worked."

"You didn't just stay at your parents'?"

"No."

Although she'd fumbled her first few comments, she'd gotten them back on track once she took her seat. For that reason, it was surprising to see his gaze shutter so tightly at the mention of his family. Her mother had always teased her that she was intuitive, but she didn't need a lick of extra awareness to know that there was a no-trespassing sign on Donovan's relationship with his parents.

What she wanted to know was why.

The Coltons were well-known in Whisperwood and throughout the greater Austin area. She had been so busy with her own family the past few years she hadn't paid a ton of attention to community gossip, but she wasn't completely immune, either.

She knew of the Coltons. To Donovan's comments the prior evening, he came from a large clan, with several branches spread across the state. The Colton family had been in the news recently, in fact, when serial criminal Livia Colton had escaped from prison. Public knowledge or not, it seemed bad form to mention that, so she relied on the manners her mother had drilled in from childhood and changed the subject.

"I know Austin's not that far. And it's always nice to sleep in your own bed."

"Exactly."

Donovan started the car, the weird moment seemingly forgotten as he navigated down her street and toward the main road into town. At a loss over what to say, Bellamy twisted in her seat, petting and praising Alex as she told him good morning.

Energy quivered beneath the dog's fur but he held his position in the back seat. She ran her fingers over the extra soft areas behind his ear, finding a sensitive spot that had his eyelids dimming in pleasure.

It was so simple, she marveled to herself. So easy. Alex wanted praise, attention and a reason to give his trust.

As Donovan's evasion over his family ran once more through her mind, she acknowledged to herself that people were far more difficult to figure out.

DONOVAN MADE THE turn into the parking lot at the Whisperwood police station. Bellamy had kept up a steady conversation on the short drive from her house, but quieted as they turned into town. The air seemed to shift and Donovan saw Alex shift with it, his already straight posture going even stiffer where he stood guard in the back seat.

Unable to delay the discussion, Donovan instead chose to treat it with the same casual care he'd managed at her house. This wasn't designed to be an interrogation, but they did need to understand what had happened to her and why Bellamy was targeted. He'd already sent the materials he'd collected on scene at LSP to the bomb squad and would oversee their review personally.

But none of that would assuage her anxiety or make this morning's discussion any easier.

Chief Archer Thompson greeted them personally, authority stamped in his bearing. In moments he had them seated in his office, his own coffee in hand. Donovan liked Archer. He was a good guy, took the law seriously and had always been a collaborative partner. The man reinforced that belief in the way he set up the conversation and explained to Bellamy what they needed to understand.

"Ms. Reeves, thank you for coming in today."

"Of course." She nodded and while her shoulders were still set in a stiff line, her hand no longer clenched her coffee cup in a death grip, which Donovan took for an improvement.

"I'm going to ask you several questions and some of them I'm going to ask more than once to see if you remember things from a different perspective."

"I understand."

With her head nod, Archer started. He took her basic information, even how long she'd been in Whisperwood, peppering in pleasant comments along the way and easing her into the discussion. Although Donovan knew his way around an interview, the ease with which Arch managed the conversation was impressive.

"How long have you been at Lone Star Pharmaceutical?" Archer asked.

"For a little over thirteen years. I started with them out of college."

Donovan digested that point. Thirteen years in her profession put her around thirty-five if she did college in the standard timing. He was thirty-one and had estimated her to be around the same age, so it was intriguing to know she had a few years on him.

You'd do better with an older woman, Donovan. You're far too serious for a younger woman to stay interested.

His sister had said that to him recently and he'd been amused and vaguely offended. Too serious? Since she was kind to a fault, he quickly saw his way past it, but the underlying intention in his sister's thoughts had stuck.

He had dated younger and none of those relationships— for the ones that could even be called a full-on relationship—had had much life in them. He had Alex and his work and while the initial weeks of a relationship went well, the moment things turned serious and his schedule wasn't fully aligned to theirs, the women he dated chose to walk.

Bellamy Reeves didn't strike him as a woman who walked. From what she described of her parents' needs, she had stuck around, taking care of them and seeing to their well-being. She'd been loyal to a job when far more people were jumping from company to company for greener pastures. Even the night they'd met, she'd been at the store helping out.

It was an impressive trait, one he couldn't deny appealed to him.

Hell, Colton, might as well just suck it up and admit it. Everything about the woman appeals to you.

"Did anything unusual stand out about your day yesterday?"

Donovan keyed back into Archer's questions, the basic pleasantries of job history and life in Whisperwood long past.

"The whole day was unusual."

"Did something happen?" Archer leaned forward, his already sharp focus growing visibly more pointed. "Something besides the car?"

"It was… Well, I mean, I found something. On email." Her fingers fumbled as she reached for her purse where she'd set it beside her. "I have an email. I printed a few copies."

Archer kept his cop's eyes focused on her purse, his attention unwavering until she pulled the promised piece of paper from her bag. Although Donovan had no qualms her purse held nothing more than what she'd said, he couldn't blame the man for staying on his guard.

If she sensed the heightened attention, Bellamy never indicated it, instead handing over a piece of paper folded in half. She handed a second copy to Donovan and he quickly read through the terse, telling statements, bulleted out in list form after a cold, lifeless salutation.

Donovan scanned the page again, his gaze going to the header that had printed out along with the content of the note. Her name was printed in the "To" line, along with her full email address, but no named sender was visible in the "From" line, just the word INTERNAL. The date was yesterday, the timing late morning as she'd already shared.

He wasn't an expert in technology and programming, but he had enough working knowledge to know something was manipulated in the note. A masked sender was a problem.

A problem that could be easily created if one simply altered a printout.

The thought struck fast and hard, nearly knocking his breath. His gaze shot to Archer's and he saw the chief had already traveled down that path and fast.

"Ms. Reeves. Tell me a bit more about this email. Do you know if anyone else received one?"

"I think it was only me but I don't know. We're on a lighter work schedule with the holidays so there were fewer people around. Not that it would have mattered." She shrugged, her vivid gray eyes dulled with the troubling memories of the day before. "I didn't go around asking anyone. I thought it was wrong to do that until I'd spoken to Human Resources."

"And what did they say?"

"They fired me."

"Yesterday?" the chief clarified, before pointing to the lone sheet of paper in his hands. "After you reported this email to them?"

"Yes, that's correct."

"Based on what you've described, you're a loyal employee."

"I thought so, too. But I wasn't even given a chance to explain. HR refused to support me or even listen to my side of the story."

"Have you been working on any special projects? Anything that would have given you access to the details in this email?"

"Of course not. That email's about price-fixing, market manipulation and harming our customers. If LSP did that, I'd have quit on my own a long time ago."

"So this is a malicious rumor, then? Something to harm the company."

Bellamy stilled at the suggestion, her eyes going wide. "This is a terrible rumor to go spreading. It could ruin the company."

"I agree," Archer said.

Donovan had remained quiet, allowing the chief to do his work, but he couldn't stay silent any longer. "Do you know who sent this? Someone who had a vendetta against the company? A disgruntled employee or maybe someone else let go recently?"

"I don't know anyone who'd do this. LSP is a reputable company. I've worked in the finance department for thir-

teen years. We file our reports properly and on time. We
manage all government requirements and standards the
industry is held to. Nothing about this email, or the practices it suggests, makes any sense. Too many people would
know if something like this was happening. LSP provides
vaccines to the entire Southwest. You don't just cover up
something like this."

"Then it does sound like a vicious rumor designed to
seed doubt and destroy the company's reputation."

"Maybe. I don't know."

"Don't you, Ms. Reeves?" Archer left the thought hanging, the impression of an affable, easygoing town leader
fading in the space of a heartbeat. "Because it would be
easy enough to manipulate a printout like this. Even easier for someone with such a lauded history at the company
to whisper to a few people and seed a whole lot of doubt."

"You think I did this? Me?" Her voice squeaked on the
last word.

"I have to ask those questions. It's my job."

Whatever nervousness carried her into Archer Thompson's office vanished as Bellamy rose from her chair. She
stood tall, her gaze direct as she stared the chief down
across his desk.

The same alertness that had filled Archer's eyes returned, matched by Alex's sudden readiness beside Donovan. They all seemed to hang there, the moment stretching
out in a weird tableau of mismatched power, authority and
frustration.

"I lost my job yesterday, Chief Thompson. In the span
of an afternoon, I lost my professional home, my reputation
and nearly my life. I don't know what sort of cruel, vicious
game someone's playing with me but I did not write this
email, nor did I manipulate its contents."

"No one's suggesting you did."

"Oh no? I came in here to freely discuss what happened

and in moments, you managed to make me feel as if I was responsible for this." She shook her own copy of the email, the one she'd retained for herself. "I'm lucky I even printed this out, but it was a last-minute thought before I blithely marched down to Human Resources, thinking they could help me. Or at minimum listen to my concerns and give me a fair shot. But they failed me and now so have you." She sat back down, her gaze remaining steady before it flicked over to him. "Both of you."

Donovan wanted to argue but said nothing. She wasn't wrong.

And he had failed her. He'd promised her a safe space and instead had brought her into the lion's den.

Bellamy's gaze returned to the chief, her attention so focused Donovan might have left for all she'd have noticed. That same loneliness he'd sensed the night before was back, her posture shuttered and protective as she turned fully in her chair to face Archer.

"Ask me whatever you want, Chief Thompson. Ask me however many ways you want to. The truth remains the same."

Chapter Five

Bellamy couldn't get out of there fast enough. She'd walked into Chief Thompson's office a trusting soul and walked out disappointed and once again unsure of herself. Why had she even listened to Donovan Colton in the first place? Had she really been taken in by the big, bad protector routine? The hot cop with the cute dog.

Was she really that lame? Or that hard up?

Obviously she was both.

With the interview at an end, she'd already left the chief's office a free woman.

For now, that small, scared voice inside whispered. She'd done her level best to keep it quiet, but she couldn't deny the raw, mind-numbing fear or the surreal nightmare she seemed to have fallen into, like Dorothy into Munchkinland. Why didn't anyone believe her? Or, at minimum, listen to her without judgment?

Was LSP so powerful that no one believed anything could happen there? That an employee could possibly discover something that was at best below standard and at worst, nefarious and deliberate?

Even as she asked herself the questions, she knew the truth. Had it been anyone else, she'd have questioned them, too.

What really stung was Donovan. She'd placed her already fragile trust in him and what had she gotten for it?

Just like Maggie.

Her hands fumbled as she stood in the lobby of the Whisperwood police station, punching a request for a car into an app on her phone.

Like Maggie?

Whatever this situation might be, it was nothing like her relationship with her sister. Nothing at all.

Maggie had left her and their parents when they needed her most. Instead of providing the familial support and understanding their family needed, Maggie had chosen a life with her rich new husband, James, and came around as little as possible.

Bellamy had given Maggie the benefit of the doubt at first. Newlyweds should have a chance to start their marriage off right, spending time with each other and cementing their relationship. She'd said those words to her mother often, especially on the occasions when Maggie turned down invitations to Sunday dinner or couldn't come by the hospital when her father got too sick, disabled beyond her ability to care for him. She'd been adamant that her sister needed that time until the day she realized she was adrift at sea, caring for her parents all by herself.

It had been those times that had created the rift that had never mended.

Get out of there, Bell. They're suffocating you.

They're our parents. How can you even suggest that? Worse, how can you walk away?

I'm not walking away. I'm talking about legitimate care that can handle Dad's needs and whatever it is that's got Mom fading away more and more every day.

They're my parents.

They're my parents, too. Yet you've done nothing I've asked. You refuse to even listen to reason.

The conversation had changed as their father's condition worsened, but only about where her parents should be for the optimal care. As if it mattered. The type of facility her father belonged in wasn't anything they could have afforded, even if they'd wanted to. So Bellamy had scraped together what she could for daytime care and had swallowed her pride and taken her sister's husband's money to fill in the gaps.

And they'd gotten by. Her father might not have had perfect care, but he had his family around him and he'd lived in his own home. The house was small, so it hadn't been too difficult to make the needed changes to help him get around. And they'd all gotten used to the hospital bed in the front room after a while.

The images were still so vivid, yet at times they seemed like another lifetime, they were so distant. The house had become hers after her parents' life insurance settlement and it no longer resembled the home of an invalid. Wheelchairs, hospital beds and the endless rows of pills were long gone. The scent of illness no longer lingered.

At times she was relieved and at others she wished she could bring it all back, would do whatever it took to have even one more day.

When she went to her last physical in September, her doctor had told her these swings in emotion were the natural cycle of grief. Even knowing that didn't make the days easier or the memories any less weighty.

The ping of her phone announcing the arrival of her driver pulled her from the maudlin thoughts. She'd fought so hard not to be a martyr over her parents, so it was disheartening to realize how quickly those feelings could creep in, especially when she thought about Maggie.

It was negative energy and she didn't want it or need it in her life. Just like she didn't need to be the object of a criminal investigation into why she might have decided to blow herself up.

As if.

Shaking it all off, she got into the car that pulled up to the curb. For as small as they were, even Whisperwood had adopted personalized transportation apps and she'd never been more pleased about that. She'd get home on her own and could assess the damage from her kitchen table.

With the police station firmly behind her, Bellamy focused on the driver's route through town and toward her small home.

Her haven.

She'd hole up and assess the damage.

And then she was going to figure out just what the hell was going on and why she'd somehow been targeted as the one to take the fall.

"THAT WENT WELL." Chief Thompson stared at the closed office door in the direction Bellamy just departed.

"Please tell me that's your special brand of sarcasm." Donovan eyed Alex where he lay on the floor across the room and could have sworn the animal let out a small sniff of displeasure.

"Justice may be blind but I'm not. If that woman's guilty, I'll eat my hat."

Donovan thought the same but was curious about Archer's sudden assessment. "You didn't act like she was innocent."

"Appearances. I can't have my constituents thinking I'm soft or unable to ask the tough questions. But there was some pure, righteous anger there the moment the tone changed. She was well and rightly pissed at both of us and I'm glad. She's going to need that bit of fire to get through whatever is going on here."

"You believe the email?"

"No reason not to."

Donovan glanced down at the paper he still held in a tight grip. "Emails can be doctored."

"Lots of things can be doctored. What I don't see in this situation is why. She's got a good job. She's well liked and well respected. I did some preliminary digging. She's not in debt or trouble and there's nothing to suggest she's got some sort of vendetta and is looking to ruin Lone Star Pharmaceutical. Nothing clicks there."

"No, it doesn't."

It didn't make any more sense an hour later as Donovan worked over Bellamy's car. The chief had had her vehicle towed to a small impound area the man kept for police business and Donovan had gone straight there with Alex after leaving the station. Her gray gaze still haunted him, the whispers of "traitor" and "coconspirator" stamped so clearly in those depths they might as well have been written out.

And hadn't he contributed to that?

He'd brought Bellamy to the station himself, hand delivered to the front door. He'd genuinely believed she was the victim in this situation, but the moment she'd pulled out that email the tenor of the meeting had changed. Archer might be working the bad cop routine but that didn't exactly leave Donovan as good cop.

And he still had questions.

Was Bellamy responsible in any way for what had happened? And if she wasn't, then why was she targeted with such incriminating information?

Worse, what sort of scam was LSP running against the market?

The chief had promised to start looking into those elements, especially since the case was on his turf, but Donovan knew well that wasn't an easy investigation for anyone, let alone a small police department that had grown on the goodwill and funding of the town's largest employer.

Donovan had almost used that level of conflict to transfer the investigation to his own precinct in Austin when Archer took matters into his own hands. The chief sent all notes and information to the Austin PD chief himself, CC-ing Donovan in the process.

Nothing about this situation made any sense. Instead, it felt like mysteries wrapped in mysteries, with no discernable threads or entry points.

By all indications, Bellamy Reeves was a solid, well-respected employee. Responsible, but not a part of the company's upper echelon. And yet she'd somehow been granted access to information that created a quagmire of doubt.

What could she possibly know?

If she were higher up in LSP, he might explore a whistle-blower angle, but she didn't have the power to affect that sort of change.

Shaking his head to dislodge the roiling thoughts, Donovan caught sight of Alex from the corner of his eye. The dog was still seated in the position he'd instructed, his gaze never wavering as Donovan searched the car with a flashlight.

Was that accusation he saw in his partner's eyes?

Alex had been his usual obedient self, but he'd deliberately sniffed the front passenger seat of the car before they climbed in and headed for the impound lot. He'd also taken the back seat, refusing to sit in his normal spot in the front.

Loyalty to Bellamy?

If it was, he'd take Alex's judgment more seriously than many others.

But even with the positive canine reinforcement, it didn't change the situation. Bellamy Reeves was in a heap of trouble.

"It's about damn time you figured out why, Colton."

Whether it was the muttered instructions or the simple twist of a moment, he had no idea, but his flashlight tilted over a quick glint of something lightly colored. Repositioning the light, he searched once more for the source and saw a small, thin button, the sort used on men's fancy dress shirts. He flashed the light fully on the object, a momentary pang that a man might have lost a button in Bellamy's car burning through him like wildfire.

The woman *was* entitled to date. To have relationships. Hell, she could make out in her damn car if she wanted to, buttons flying in all directions in the heat of the moment. What business was it of his?

At the bark from behind him, Donovan turned to see Alex, that firm stare still in place. "Okay, fine. No jumping to conclusions."

Even as the odd shot of jealousy lingered, Donovan refocused on the evidence he'd collected. He carefully picked up the button with his gloved hand, anxious to preserve whatever prints might be on the flat disc as part of the investigation. After dropping it into an evidence bag from his field kit, he stood back to assess the car once more.

With a light pat on his thigh, he motioned Alex closer and was comforted when that large body scrambled to join him, resettling himself at Donovan's side. Together they stared at the remains of the car.

It was a simple, serviceable sedan, about four years old. Nothing flashy, but it had been kept clean. Even beneath the grit and residue of the explosion, he could see there weren't items left scattered throughout the car like an extra storage space or trash receptacle. He hadn't even found the normal junk stuffed in the armrest, only the charred edges of a few napkins.

The car was neat and orderly. Just like her home. And just like the office he suspected he'd find when he headed over to LSP later.

On a resigned sigh, he continued the review of the car, layer by layer. He'd need more time to take all the samples he wanted, but he did have enough to start the process. He needed to apprise his chief of what he'd discovered so far, so he'd kill two birds and drop the materials off at the lab himself. Maybe with some space and distance, and the idle time on the drive back to Austin, something would shake loose.

It was only ten minutes later, both he and Alex back in his SUV and headed for the highway, that it hit him. Whatever possible involvement Bellamy had in the situation unfolding at LSP, one thing was clear.

She'd been the target of a car bomb.

And since the perpetrator hadn't been successful, what would stop him from trying again?

Donovan skidded to a stop and took a hard spin on his steering wheel, whipping the car around before heading back into town and in the direction of Bellamy's house. Adrenaline lit him up like the Christmas lights on Main Street as he raced toward the small home.

Why had he let her walk out by herself? Worse, how had he been so blind to the needs of someone on his caseload?

The woman was at risk and in very clear danger.

And he'd been worried about a damn button and who she might be dating.

He pressed harder on the gas, bumping over the slightly uneven road that lead to her home. With yet another hard turn of the wheel, he spun onto her street. Relief punched through the adrenaline when he saw her in the distance, on her knees around the flower beds that surrounded the front porch, a hat on her head.

The scenario of smoke and fire that had accompanied him on the wild drive through town was nowhere in evidence. Instead, all he saw was a pretty woman on a cool Texas afternoon digging in her flower beds.

He'd never been more relieved.

Even as he couldn't shake the hard, insistent slam of his pulse that suggested he'd arrived just in time.

"Everything's fine, Dad. Really, it was nothing. It was an unfortunate accident, is all."

Jensen paced around his office, the faint voice of his father, Sutton Taylor, echoing from the speakerphone on his desk.

And everything *was* fine. Hadn't he been trying to tell the old man for half an hour already? Even confined to a bed, the old man could natter on and on.

"Bombs in cars? In our parking lot at headquarters?"

"An incident, nothing more."

"How can you say that, Jensen? It's an employee in danger. On our property."

In danger because I put her there. Voluntarily.

The retort was so close to the edge of his tongue Jensen nearly had to bite it, but held back. Gloating over his plans would get him nowhere and would prematurely tip his father off before he'd completed the work.

But he satisfied himself with a small smile, pleased that he'd found a way to get exactly what he wanted, all while pinning it on an unsuspecting victim.

Even better, no one would question the line of succession from Sutton to Jensen Taylor when the inevitable handoff of LSP finally came. He was the rightful heir to the Taylor family fortune and to Lone Star Pharmaceutical. His father might have enjoyed sowing every oat he had, but there was no way one of his bastards would get a single piece of what Jensen had worked for.

What he deserved.

"Dad, let the police do their job. Bellamy Reeves has been a loose cannon for some time."

"The sweet girl in finance?"

Jensen had to give his father credit—he did know his employees. Or maybe it was more that his father never forgot a pretty face. Whatever the reason, he'd pegged Jensen's scapegoat with surprising accuracy.

"She might have been sweet once but she's had a rough

go these last few years. Her father was the one paralyzed in that accident several years ago."

"I knew Daniel-Justice Reeves, Jensen. I know what happened to the man."

Even with the sickness that had gripped him with increasing severity over the past few weeks, his father's withering voice was as clear as ever.

"Then you know he died a terrible death. Lingered there at the end way too long. That does something to a person, Dad. I don't know what I'd do if I was in the Reeves girl's position. If I lost you that way."

Sutton paused for a moment before continuing on in slightly quieter tones. "You need to help her. Find out who did this."

"Of course."

"And keep me posted. I'm not that far away."

"I know that. I know you can be back at any time." *Any freaking time*, Jensen thought. "I want you to focus on getting better. I'll figure out what's going on here and keep you updated."

"You can still come here for Christmas, you know," Sutton said, his voice quiet. "I'd like to see you."

The comment was almost sweet, for a man who'd never shown a large degree of fatherly care. *Nice time to try and mend fences, dear old Dad.*

But he said none of it. Instead, he forced that calm, capable tone into his voice, his focus on getting through the call. "I know I said I'd cover things through the holidays but that won't keep me from coming down to see you. You can count on me."

"All right. We'll talk tomorrow. Get Chief Thompson on this. I make sure that man has a rock-solid department with all the latest tools and tech for a reason. I want him taking care of this."

"Of course, Dad."

After a few more minutes of blustering, Jensen heard the voice of a nurse who'd puttered in to take Sutton's vitals and his father made excuses to hang up.

Jensen hit the end-call button on the speakerphone and stood there, staring out the window of his office at the view of the parking lot and the hill country beyond. He could still see the spot where Bellamy Reeves's car had been parked the day before, yellow police tape flying from a nearby tree. Even at this distance, a large black spot was visible on the ground from the remnants of the burned-out car.

His clueless little scapegoat.

She was the perfect choice. The absolutely perfect scapegoat for what he needed to do.

LSP would turn a shockingly enormous profit.

His father wouldn't be around to see any of it.

And one lonely, unlucky woman would take the fall before suffering a painful, lonely death.

How could he lose?

BELLAMY HEARD THE bark first, immediately followed by the solid poke of a squishy nose on her hip. She turned to see Alex playfully teasing her, his master standing about six feet away, hands on hips.

Her heart gave an involuntarily hitch at the sight he made. His thick, powerful shoulders were set off and backlit by the winter sun that rode low in the sky. The light breeze ruffled the edges of his hair, and his eyes were a warm, gooey chocolate-brownie brown as they stared down at her.

"We need to talk. Alex and I will check the grounds again and then we can discuss this morning."

Was that apology she saw reflected there? Remorse? Or neither, she quickly scolded herself as she dropped back on her rear and focused on Alex. Donovan was probably just here so he could scold her again.

"You checked the grounds this morning. Talk to me."

"It's important that I check things out."

"And it's important to me to talk to you."

To punctuate her point, she pulled off her gardening gloves and gave Alex a vigorous pat down, from the top of his head, down over his back and on toward the lower part of his spine as he wiggled in ecstasy. It didn't take much after that to push him to his side so she could give him the added joy of a belly rub.

"Careful. He might quit my team and join yours."

"Then I'd say he's one smart cookie." She patted Alex's chest before giving in and looking back up at Donovan. "I'm not sure I'd want to work for a suspicious brute, either."

"Suspicion comes with the territory. What did I do to get 'brute,' too?"

"You really don't know?"

"I'd rather hear it from your perspective."

Whatever she might suspect in his gaze, it was impossible to miss the sincerity, especially once she matched it to his voice. "You played the whole white knight routine this morning. Picking me up. Bringing me coffee. Even reassuring me it would be okay. And instead I walked into a firing squad."

"Chief Thompson wasn't quite that bad."

"He thinks I'm guilty. And so do you."

"Where'd you get that from?"

"The moment the two of you jumped all over those email printouts. I thought I had evidence of something horrible and all anyone who's looked at them has done is accuse me of doing something wrong. First Human Resources at LSP, right before they fired me. Then the two of you. I received that email and I have no idea who sent it or why."

Donovan dropped onto the grass beside her and reached for one of the garden gloves she'd dragged off to pet Alex. Toying with one finger, he twirled it in his hand and she tried her level best not to imagine him playing with her instead. Her hand inside that glove, her fingers trapped in his.

He would be warm, she imagined. His touch strong and capable. And how nice it would be to hang on in every one of those moments where she had no one to lean on except herself.

It'd be nice to hang on in all the other moments, too.

The thought was a surprise, the warmth that flooded her even more so.

Donovan Colton was the enemy.

Or at bare minimum a wary adversary, working at cross-purposes. There was no way she should even be entertaining thoughts of him in her life. Absolutely no reason at all to give them free rein.

"So talk to me, Bellamy."

"Why? So you can grill me again and make me feel like a common criminal?"

"No. Let's talk it through so we can try and find answers. Both the chief and I heard you today, though I'd like you to tell me again. But when I ask you questions, even the hard ones, don't assume it's because I don't believe you."

That sincerity was back, along with a subtle plea in his voice that tugged at her.

"Where do you want me to start?"

"At the beginning."

THE SUN BEAT down over his back as Donovan held his breath. He had driven over to Bellamy's like a madman, determined to get to her to make sure she was safe. Now that he was here, he'd done nothing but watch her, as smitten as Alex.

What was it about this woman?

She was beautiful, that was without question. Slim and lovely, she had a warmth about her that was hard to resist. It was funny, though, because he suspected if he asked her to describe herself she would outline a much harsher, tougher woman than the one who sat before him.

He imagined she saw herself as hard, maybe, because of the challenges she'd managed the past few years. But where she likely saw rough edges, he saw a diamond.

"What beginning?"

"Wherever you think this starts. You keep saying the email you received yesterday. Do you think that's the right spot?"

"Isn't it?"

"It depends."

"On what?"

Did he tell her what he thought? He was a man who played his life close to the vest and police work had simply been a natural extension of that. He knew the roots of it all. More, he knew it was laughable how his worldview was steeped in every moment of his childhood. And from his continued embarrassment that he wasn't a true Colton.

He'd made the mistake of letting those feelings slip the year he turned fifteen, when he'd made an unsuccessful attempt to find his birth parents on the internet. Hays and Josephine and his siblings had spent the last sixteen years trying to change his mind.

Attempting to convince him he was as Colton as they come.

Oh, how he wished that were true. But he'd just gotten left in their barn one Christmas morning. Heck, he had better knowledge of Alex's lineage than his own.

"It depends on what, Donovan?"

Bellamy's intense focus and near breathless request caught him up short. This wasn't about him. Nor was it about whatever asinine issues he couldn't get over.

This was about her and her life and whatever lurked in the shadows, seemingly focused on her.

"Okay. Three things come to mind when I read that

email. Either you inadvertently got information you shouldn't have or you've got information someone's using to embarrass LSP and were specifically targeted with it. Or you did it."

"I didn't!"

He raised his hands in a stop-don't-shoot gesture. "We're taking that one off the table, okay?"

"Okay." She nodded. "But even if we go with the first two, why do either? The company is a significant employer in this area. Their stock has risen year after year for over a decade. They've been on the leading edge in several health categories." Her gaze drifted to Alex as a small smile edged her lips. "We even have a robust veterinary medicine program in partnership with Texas A&M. I just don't see why the company would manipulate the drug supply or why someone with an intent to do ill would suggest they were. None of it rings true."

"Why not?"

Her eyes widened, the smile fading as her mouth dropped open. "Because it's illegal."

He fought his own smile at her innocence. Legality and illegality were lines far too many crossed easily and with impunity, nonplussed by the risk of consequences. For far too many, illegal activities were framed in one way only— don't get caught.

"Let's also table that it's illegal for now. Why don't either of those options ring true for you?"

She stilled, her eyes drifting over the flower beds as she thought over his question. Alex stared up at her, an enraptured expression on his face when her deep thoughts brought on additional belly rubs.

He seemed even more grateful when the belly rubs continued once she spoke again. "Sutton Taylor is our CEO. He's a good man and a great leader. He's not the sort to fix drug prices and throttle supply. It's just not possible."

Donovan wasn't quite ready to give any CEO such carte blanche for benevolence, but he wasn't ready to debunk her instincts there, either. "Okay. Anyone else?"

"I don't know. A disgruntled employee, maybe?"

"You have layoffs anytime in the recent past? It is the holidays. People out of work at Christmas have a lot of fair and well-aimed anger."

"The company hasn't had a single layoff since we brought a major Alzheimer's drug to market a decade ago."

"Okay. Who else? A landowner or a manufacturer? Maybe a government official? There are any number of worlds LSP plays in during the normal course of business. Lots of places an enemy could be lurking."

"Maybe. I guess." She shrugged at that. "I guess I could see it, but I simply don't have knowledge of all those areas. But—" She broke off, something alighting in her face. "Why would I get the email and be possibly framed if it were an area I had no knowledge of? I don't work in real estate or manufacturing. I don't even manage the finances for that area."

"What areas do you manage?"

"Drug trials, drug launches, go-to-market strategies and the relationships with our supply chain."

"There you go. So you are connected there."

"Connected to the degree that I know how it works. I know the players."

"So if someone were framing you, you'd be a person who others could believe might be involved."

"No!" Her hand stilled where it rested over Alex's fur. "Yes, maybe. I guess."

"That's where we need to focus."

"But who would do that to me?"

"We're going to find out."

A light breeze kicked up and with it, Alex shifted into motion. One moment he was flat on his back, tongue lolling in ecstasy, and the next he was on all fours, his nose buried in the ground as he took off through the grass.

"What's wrong?"

"I don't know." Donovan was up and after Alex, his partner's alert focus and intermittent barking all he needed to know.

Alex had found a scent.

Bellamy's property wasn't large and it didn't take Alex long to cover the ground, stopping before a small toolshed.

"What's wrong with him?" Bellamy nearly ran into his back before she stilled, her hand going to his shoulder to steady herself.

"He's fine. It's what he's found that's not. I need you to move back."

"You think he found something? In my shed?"

Since she hadn't moved, he did it himself, walking her back several steps to stand at the corner of the house.

"When was the last time you were in here?"

"An hour ago. I wanted to get my gardening equipment."

"And you didn't see anything odd or off?"

"No." She let out a long, low sigh. "I'm not sure I'd have seen much. I was angry and…well, I just slammed in and out of there without really looking at anything."

Donovan fought the shudder at what might have happened to her if she'd stepped the wrong place and instead focused on the matter at hand. "I need you to go to my car and get my equipment in the back. I need to make a call."

"For what?"

"Backup in Austin."

"Backup?" Her voice faded on that word, her eyes widening in dawning horror.

"If Alex's nose is right, and it always is, it looks like you've got a bomb in your shed. The last thing we need to do is set it off this close to the house."

Chapter Six

Bellamy fought the rising tide of panic that filled her stomach and crept up her throat.

A bomb?

In her shed?

She'd blithely walked past a few hours before.

A *bomb*.

One discovered by a sweet dog she'd been petting two minutes ago.

The anger and frustration she'd carried home from the police station vanished in full as she stared into the back of Donovan's SUV. Protective gear just as he described it filled the space, and she lifted out the thick jacket and headgear so he would be safe.

For her.

Shivers gripped her at the idea his life was in danger. She had a healthy enough self-image to know that she'd not asked for this or wished it on herself, but it didn't change the fact that Donovan was in danger on her behalf. Alex, too, for that matter.

"Bellamy! Did you find it?"

Her woolgathering at an end, she grabbed the gear and ran back to him. The materials were heavy and she was slightly winded by the time she got to him. "Here."

He took them easily, lifting them from her arms. "Go stand by the car, please."

"I can't leave you here."

"Go now. You can't be here. I'm protected and I know what I'm doing."

"I know, but—"

"I'll send Alex with you. He's good company and can stay with you until backup comes."

"Of course."

He ran a finger down her cheek in one long stroke. "I know what I'm doing. But it's easier to do it without worrying about you."

The movement was so unexpected and so very sweet she went with impulse. Without checking herself, she leaned in and pressed a quick, hard kiss to his lips. "Be careful."

The color of his already dark eyes deepened, drawing her in. "I will."

With quick instructions, Donovan ordered Alex to stay by her side. The black Lab trotted beside her, so close they nearly touched, all the way to the front yard. Sirens echoed in the distance and Bellamy braced herself for what came next.

More danger.

More suspicion.

And even more proof that someone was out to kill her.

DONOVAN HEARD THE sirens in the distance, mentally timing when his backup would arrive. He'd already calculated what might lay beyond the door and took some solace in the fact that she'd already entered and exited the shed once without detonating the device.

Dumb luck?

Or further proof they were dealing with an amateur?

The car bomb had been crude, the lapse in detonation time a pretty solid indicator they weren't dealing with an expert. But lack of skill didn't diminish the risk that the bastard would get lucky at some point.

There was the alternative—that someone was trying to

scare Bellamy more than hurt her—but why? Even for experts, bombs were tricky things. If the goal was to frighten, there were a hell of a lot easier ways to accomplish that.

Which took him right back to an amateur, and the question that seemed to swirl at the center of all of this: What was going on at LSP?

The email had been quite clear. LSP was fixing prices and managing the supply of necessary flu vaccine. It seemed like an odd choice—surely there was more money to be made on other drugs. But flu was also ubiquitous. So many took the vaccine that keeping it out of circulation would incite panic.

And where there was panic and chaos, you had the right mix to put an object in demand.

Wasn't that the heart of all supply and demand? Make it seem irresistible and you made the product a must-have.

Only in this case, lives were at stake. The elderly and the infirm and small children all needed the vaccine to prevent an outbreak or to diminish the severity of one. How many people were ultimately protected by vaccines supplied by LSP?

Were there other pharmaceutical companies that could provide the needed supply if Lone Star couldn't?

Donovan didn't know enough about the specifics but made a mental note to ask Bellamy later. If the supply chain really was damaged in all this, there had to be reasons it wasn't simply a matter of changing course and getting more vaccine from someone else.

His questions faded in full as the Whisperwood PD pulled up to Bellamy's house, the fire department in tow. Although they depended on Donovan's team in Austin as well as the K-9 unit for the majority of their bomb works, the local team was trained in basic detonation work and could support him as he walked through the proper procedures.

"What do you have there, Colton?" Chief Thompson hollered the request as he strode across Bellamy's yard.

"A hot one, if Alex's nose is any indication."

"Isn't his nose always an indication?"

"That's why you're here, Chief, while that hot sub you bought for lunch is getting cold on your desk."

"It's a cold sandwich today. It'll keep."

It was dopey banter, but it kept the situation moving forward until Archer could reach him. The man was already in protective gear that matched Donovan's, sans the helmet.

"What do you have?" The question was quiet, not meant for any potential bystanders or the small crowd gathered around Bellamy.

"Not sure yet. I don't think it's tied to the door, as Ms. Reeves went in and out about an hour ago, but I figured I'd wait to test that theory."

The chief nodded before asking a few more questions, then ordered his team forward to help set the scene. The fire department had already run their lines so they could quickly put out any potential blazes and an ambulance was on standby a bit farther down the road.

"It looks like Ms. Reeves is in a heap of trouble." The chief eyed the door before his gaze slipped back toward Bellamy. "A rather big heap."

"Sure seems that way." Donovan agreed.

"It also seems like a lot of trouble for someone to set this little scenario up all on their own."

"I was thinking along the same lines. Especially since she's so pale, it's a wonder she's not reflecting light right now." Donovan avoided turning back to look at that confused face for fear he'd lose his concentration. But even without looking, he knew she was scared.

And alone.

That thought had kept him company since his race across town and his discovery of the lone woman tending her garden. She didn't appear to have a support system, as she'd not mentioned anyone since he discovered her yesterday, huddled in the LSP parking lot staring at her car.

Was it really possible she was that alone?

He'd given her space the night before, even as his instincts kept suggesting she was into something they didn't fully understand.

But was it possible she'd been targeted specifically because she didn't have a support system? Or someone nearby paying close enough attention?

He wasn't exactly the poster child for familial happiness, but he could always count on his parents and siblings if he needed something.

But would you go to them?

The mental intrusion had him fumbling his hold on his helmet and he fought to put it out of his mind as he righted his grip on the face cover.

This wasn't about him and he'd do well to keep his damn head in the damn game.

"So what do you say, Chief? Ready to open this one up?"

"I'd say. That sub's not going to eat itself."

Donovan hollered a few instructions to the assembled team, then reached for the shed door. Like a shiny present sitting under the Christmas tree, a small pressure cooker sat in the far corner of Bellamy's shed, easy to miss if you weren't paying attention.

Which she hadn't because she'd stomped in here, still mad at him and Archer.

A chill ran the length of his spine as he imagined what could have happened if the bomb was attached to the door, but forced it out of his mind. He could worry himself into a cold sweat later.

Right now he needed to get it handled.

The bomb was crude, reinforcing his impression that an amateur had made it. It had the same look and feel as the bombs that had littered news stories over the past decade, especially acts tied to homegrown terrorism. More than that, it was a device someone could easily discover how to build online and hastily put together, with the intention of doing localized harm.

Donovan moved closer, quickly cataloging the device before scanning the detonation mechanism. A small burner cell was wired to the device, its face dimly reflecting the fact that it was on and charged.

"You see the detonator?" Archer's voice was thick behind his mask but Donovan heard him and nodded.

"Yep. Burner cell."

"You know how to manage it?"

"Yep."

"Then let's get to work."

BELLAMY STOOD AT the end of her driveway, a crowd of EMS professionals surrounding her, and had never felt so alone or scared in all her life. Even with her parents—even at the very end—she hadn't felt this absolute sense of emptiness.

What had happened to her life?

Had she somehow brought this on herself? Pissed someone off at work so badly that they'd decided to make her pay?

Because whatever this was, it was highly personal. First her car and then her home. Which meant whoever was doing this knew what she drove and where she lived.

Unbidden, an image of Sally Borne's hard face popped into her mind. HR would have access to her personnel files, including her home address. They also knew her license plate because it was needed as part of the documentation to receive a badge to the LSP property.

Alex leaned against her leg, the heavy weight of his body a reassuring comfort as she stood there, puzzling through all the implications. She laid a hand on this head and stroked the soft fur that grew even softer where it ran down the backs of his ears. He seemed to understand what she needed, pressing his head into her hand when she stilled, insisting she keep up with the soothing, steady strokes.

The dog was a marvel. She'd always loved pets but had never found time to own one. In the years before her father's accident she'd been busy with work and never felt she could give an animal the proper attention. And after, once there were pills and wheelchairs and a constant focus on keeping him well, it didn't seem like the right time.

Perhaps that had been more shortsighted than she realized. Her father would have responded well to a pet, a gentle friend to keep him company each day. And for herself, it would be nice to have a companion to come home to now. A warm, furry body who was happy to see her.

Maybe if she had a dog they'd have warned her of whatever was lurking around the house and putting bombs in her shed.

Alex laid his head against her thigh and let out a soft sigh. He was a funny creature, she thought as she took comfort in his large body, with a fierce devotion and gentle personality. It was easy to see what he was thinking and she had no doubt he *was* thinking. It might be veiled through the lens of canine understanding, but there was something going on behind those dark brown eyes.

More, there was a fierce protection there that promised the dog knew his purpose in life and would carry it out without fail.

Purpose.

Understanding settled over her, a soothing balm in the midst of the chaos that surrounded her. She'd had purpose once. A focus on the life that stretched before her and the goals she'd set for herself.

Somewhere along the way, she'd lost that. Yes, her parents had needed care and attention. At times, that had taken precedence over other choices in her life.

But she'd been solely responsible for losing her sense of self. For allowing what was happening around her to take possession of her dreams instead of keeping them firmly in her sights.

Whatever her future held or however long she had, it was time to make a change.

Alex let out a large bark at her side, a funny punctuation mark to the definitiveness of her thoughts. But it was the quivering beneath her hand and the immediate thump of his tail that had her smiling just as Donovan came around the corner of the house.

He held a small silver bowl in his hands that took shape as he got closer. A pressure cooker? She had one herself, buried in the back of the cabinet on the rare occasions she decided to cook rice for a week of meals. What was one doing in her shed?

It was only as she saw the wires dangling from beneath his gloved hands that she understood. That was the bomb. Positioned in her shed and ready to cause irreparable damage.

Ready to kill her.

A wave of nausea flooded her stomach as she took in the innocuous kitchen appliance turned into a device that could end her life.

With a gentle push, she urged Alex forward. "Go see him." The dog seemed to waver only a moment before she patted his back and pressed him forward. "Go!"

He ran to Donovan, his focus on the device in his partner's hands. Donovan bent over, allowing the dog to sniff the contents, praising him for his understanding of the threat. His tail wagged at the praise, and again, Bellamy was amazed at all the animal communicated without words.

Where his tail had thumped with the excitement of seeing his master, now it wagged with the determined understanding of the job they did and the risk to the people around them.

The dog *knew*. He understood on a base level that was fascinating to watch.

But it was the body language of his master that had Bellamy taking a step back. Even encased in the heavy protection gear, she could see the purpose and determination as he walked across her yard. He innately understood the danger in the device in his hands—more, he knew the danger it posed to her—and with that knowledge he carried the responsibility for fixing it.

SALLY BORNE SCANNED the email on her phone before tossing the device onto her desk. "Merry freaking Christmas to me."

What had she gotten herself into? Worse, what sort of ridiculous sweet nothings had Jensen Taylor managed to put into her ear that had made her think any of this was a good idea?

She was smarter than this. Had *always* been smarter than this.

So why had she listened to the little slimeball?

Especially since it had become increasingly obvious his father was neither on the verge of turning over the company nor getting ready to enter into his dotage. Hell, she'd have been better off seducing Sutton Taylor. If she was fifteen years younger, she might have tried, but those rheumy old eyes could still pick out a stacked twenty-five-year old at fifty yards. She had a complaint file from several sales reps in her top drawer to prove it.

Unable to hold back the sneer, she thought of the last one who'd pranced in and complained about Sutton's less-than-subtle attentions.

Ridiculous.

When you had assets, you used them. Those same reps weren't above using a little T & A when they visited doctors, selling in LSP's latest offerings. You'd think they'd be

more appreciative when the head of the company appreciated the same thing they were flaunting to fill their pockets.

Brushing it off, she picked up her phone and read the
email from the police one more time. The friendships she'd
cultivated at the Whisperwood PD had paid off and the up-
date on Bellamy Reeves's visit to the station that morning
was detailed and thorough. The little bitch had a copy of
the email and had freely handed it off to the chief.

Sally reread the last line of the message, heartened that
the ploy might end up working in their favor. The lack of
sender and the strange nature of the missive had put some
doubt in the chief's mind, suggesting that poor little Bellamy Reeves had gone around the bend and was setting
this all up for her own benefit as a way to defraud and manipulate the company.

Curious, Sally sat down and pulled out the Reeves file.
She flipped through the personnel records, the praise for
Bellamy clear on every review and evaluation as well as
the input sheets tied to her past promotions.

The woman had a stellar reputation. She was well liked,
kept to herself and avoided causing any drama at work. A
model employee.

Of course, there was the matter of her family. A loss
like that was something that changed a person. It erupted
in the middle of life, taking everything you once knew and
turning it upside down.

There was power in that. A story she could weave, tightening the threads until they were impossible to unravel.

Shifting to her laptop, Sally began her reply to the Whisperwood PD. No reason not to seed a bit more doubt about
poor, sad Bellamy Reeves, preparing to enter the holiday
season all alone.

DONOVAN STRIPPED OFF the protective gear and laid it in the
back of his SUV. He'd already turned the evidence over

to Archer, tagging it with the necessary markers from his side and calling it in to his own chief to keep the man updated. He'd been given the order to stay in Whisperwood until this was handled, the focus on Lone Star Pharmaceutical ensuring his chief didn't want any blowback from the investigation.

If he hadn't been given the go-ahead to stay, he'd have asked anyway, the risks to Bellamy too concerning to leave her alone. But now that he was here, he needed to figure out how to get her to agree to his plan.

Not only was he not going to leave her alone, but he and Alex would stay to guard her. He'd nearly made up his mind on the drive over, but now it was a done deal, especially when it was more than obvious that whoever had targeted her wasn't above escalating their tactics to her home.

Once again, the crudeness of the bomb struck him as he nestled his gear into its proper place. A pressure cooker bomb? It was far from elegant and the fact that they'd been in the news as incendiary devices gave further credence to an amateur picking up on something and running with it. Easy to purchase and easy to build, it made the perfect device for limited range, deliberate hits.

He and his fellow K-9 team members had seen an increase in the devices and the lunatics who thought a homemade bomb made a nice, clean, easy way to deal with a problem. It was a coward's way to kill, far removed from the point of impact, the perpetrator safe at a distance.

And it was easy because no one had to stick around and face the damage.

Just like your mother, dropping you off in the Colton barn, abandoned on Christmas morning.

His hand shook as he laid his headgear on top of his flak suit, the connection between his own birth and a bomb was one that hit way too close to home. Yet even as he rejected the maudlin thoughts, something about them stuck.

It was easy to do the wrong thing when you didn't have to stick around and face the consequences.

"Donovan? Are you all right?"

He turned to see Bellamy, her hands still against her sides as she took him in. The moment struck him, her slender form clad in a simple T-shirt and yoga pants backlit by the afternoon sun. That same breeze that had tipped Alex off to the bomb in the shed whispered around them once more, a bit cooler as the afternoon edged toward evening, a bit wilder as it blew her hair against her face.

"I'm good."

"How do you do that? You walked in, not knowing what you were going to find."

"It's part of the job description."

"Yes, but it's—" She broke off, her beautiful mouth dropping down into a frown. "But you didn't know what was behind the door."

"Believe it or not, you inadvertently helped there."

"How?"

"While it gives me the chills to say this, you'd already gone through the door. And even though that wasn't a foolproof method, it did indicate the bomb wasn't pressure sensitive to the opening of the door."

She seemed to shrink in on herself at that and he reached out to take a hand, squeezing the slim fingers. "Thanks for the assist. Try not to do that again, please."

"Okay."

Her hand was cold in his and it dragged at him, twisting him up even further about the fact that something could have happened to her. Without checking the impulse, he tugged on her hand, pulling her forward so she was flush against him. In one long move, he seated himself on the back bumper of the SUV, pulling her between his legs as he dragged her mouth down to his.

His seated position gave her the height advantage, but

he had the benefit of surprise. When she'd kissed him in front of the shed earlier, she'd surprised him with the power of the simple gesture.

Something inside of him—something hungry and raw and the slightest bit scared—wanted to feel that again. Wanted to feel the heat and the life and the sheer beauty of her pressed against him.

It was with a hunger for all those things and something even more—something distinctly Bellamy—that had his tongue pressing into her mouth, satisfied as she granted him ready access. If this kiss had surprised her, she'd quickly caught up, her tongue meeting his stroke for luscious stroke.

And then she turned the tables on him, her hands wrapping around his shoulders and neck, her fingers lingering at the base of his neck. What had been cool to the touch heated quickly, those exploring fingers also pressing his head to hers, fusing their mouths as each plundered the other.

His hands moved over her hips, tracing the length of her tantalizing curves as the kiss continued to spin out, a sensual web of feeling. It was erotic, the meeting of tongues, the light winter breeze over their skin and the simple touch of their hands on each other.

Donovan knew he should pull away. Knew even better that this was not only ill-advised, but a massive conflict of interest.

Yet, even with the sense of duty that drummed beneath his skin, he couldn't walk away. Couldn't tear himself back or pull away from something so lovely and tantalizing and *real*.

It was the last that gripped him in tight fists.

She was real. Yes, she was beautiful and sensual and appealing as a woman, but she was so much more. He respected her bravery and her determination. Even more, he valued her belief in her truth and her refusal to back down or be cowed by what was happening around her.

"Donovan." Her whisper against his mouth broke the

kiss and he tried to nip her bottom lip once more, unwilling to end the sweetly sensual moment.

"Donovan." She whispered it again, even as her lips curved into a smile.

"What?"

"The chief is still here."

He surfaced quickly at that news, combined with Archer's hard cough as Bellamy slipped out of his arms and moved to stand a few feet away from the SUV.

"Archer."

"Donovan."

Donovan knew the man's blue eyes were twinkling, even though he couldn't see them behind the dark lenses of his sunglasses.

"I think we're wrapped up here," Archer said.

"I thought we already were."

"I'm going to need another statement, but seeing as how I was here as it all unfolded, I think I can write up the majority of what we need for the report. Perhaps you could escort Ms. Reeves to the station tomorrow to provide any needed details."

"That will be fine," Bellamy quickly added from where she stood beside Alex.

Archer obviously sensed his presence was no longer welcome and he made a hasty retreat, a tip of his hat before he took off.

A light flush covered Bellamy's face before following a lovely path down her neck and over her collarbone. "He certainly got here quick."

"Shame he couldn't leave as quickly." Donovan's hands still itched and he heard the hoarse, husky notes in his voice. He'd forgotten where he was. Utterly and completely, as he'd fallen into that kiss.

And Chief Thompson had known it, his eyes twinkling as he'd said his goodbyes.

Twinkling, for Pete's sake.

Donovan glanced at Alex, unsurprised to see a large grin painting his furry face as he panted into the breeze beside Bellamy.

The entire situation would have been funny if he hadn't diffused a bomb in Bellamy's shed. A point only reinforced by the high-pitched cry of a woman who peeled to a stop in front of the driveway, running toward Bellamy as the car still idled in her wake.

"Are you okay? I just heard the news." The woman was attractive, a tall, thin blonde dressed in needle-sharp heels, elegant black slacks and a silk blouse that likely would cost him a week's salary. It was all set off by flashy jewelry that seemed to drip from her, including a large diamond that lay against her collarbone.

Donovan gave the woman credit—she moved in the heels—and watched as she flung her arms around Bellamy's shoulders, pulling her close. He wouldn't have believed it if he wasn't standing there watching, but Bellamy stiffened up so much she could have been a poker standing beside the small fireplace in her living room.

But it was the ice that dripped from her tone that truly caught him off guard.

"Hi, Maggie. What are you doing here?"

The woman pulled back, her shoulders slumping at the greeting. "I'm your sister. Of course I came. What I don't understand is why you didn't call me right away."

"Because I'm fine."

Fine?

The diffused bomb even now being driven to the Whisperwood police station suggested otherwise, but it was the distinct sense of unease and anger telegraphing from Bellamy's rigid frame that truly pulled him up short.

What was going on here?

And what sort of issue could Bellamy Reeves possibly have with her sister?

Chapter Seven

"I'm fine, Maggie. Really. How many times do I have to say it?"

Bellamy heard the coarse, stilted words that spilled from her lips and wanted to pull them back. She wished that she could find a way to get past the anger and the confusion that marked her relationship with her sister.

It hadn't always been like this. No one had been happier to have a baby sister than her. She'd welcomed sweet little Maggie along with her parents and the two of them had been inseparable as kids, even with a five-year age difference.

Maggie had always seemed so fragile and waifish, and Bellamy had developed a mix of protectiveness and encouragement for her sister that she gave to no one else. That gentle, fragile nature had changed over the years and by the time Bellamy graduated from high school, Maggie was getting ready to enter, already the belle of Whisperwood. People spoke of her beauty and their parents doted on her, willing to give their precious baby anything she wanted.

The sweet little soul Bellamy had cared for and protected suddenly didn't need her any longer and it had hurt to realize, as she went off to college, that she wasn't the center of her sister's world anymore.

It had taken several years and making of new friends with fresh perspectives while she was away at school for

Bellamy to realize her sister didn't need a second mother, but a friend. But by the time she'd returned to Whisperwood, Maggie's life had shifted in new directions, including spending time with the popular crowd, riding around town in her convertible and winning the heart of half the boys in school.

She'd been happy for Maggie, even if she was forced to accept that her own life had turned out very differently. The job at LSP had provided another fresh perspective and after immersing herself in work and a new group of friends and colleagues, the distance with Maggie didn't seem to matter so much.

Or maybe she'd just stopped caring any longer if it hurt.

She'd had a life and a job she loved and a future to look forward to. Life was good and if she didn't have a strong relationship with her sister, then it was something she'd live with.

"Bellamy, did you hear me? What is going on around here? First I hear about a bomb that blows up your car and now I hear there's one in the shed, too?" Maggie settled three glasses of iced tea on the small drop leaf table Bellamy kept in the corner of her kitchen, handing one over. "And hurry up and tell me before the always attractive Donovan Colton comes back inside. Goodness, I remember him from high school. He was a year ahead of me but what a looker."

Something in the casual assessment of Donovan spiked her ire once more and Bellamy fought to hold her tongue. Whatever her relationship with Maggie, spitting at her like a she-cat—a *jealous* she-cat—wasn't the way to handle things.

"He's part of the K-9 team out of Austin. He's been assigned to my case."

"He's done well for himself. I'd heard he was getting into K-9 a few years after joining the Austin PD."

"How'd you hear that?"

Maggie shrugged, her perfect blond hair rising and falling with the motion. "The Coltons are always the subject of local gossip. People talk, Bell, you know that."

"Is that all people in this town are to you? Gossip? Is that why you rushed over here? So you'd be in the know."

Maggie's glass stopped halfway to her lips, her mouth drawing down in a frown. Carefully, she set the glass back on the table before shifting her cool blue gaze fully to Bellamy's. "I realize you and I have had our differences, but I don't understand how you could think I don't care about you."

"You've never seemed all that interested in taking part in my life."

"You shut me out! Just because I saw how we should be caring for Mom and Dad differently than you did, doesn't mean I'm some horrible person."

"You wanted to put them in a home."

"No, I wanted them to get the proper care they deserved while taking the burden off of you."

"They're my parents. I did it willingly."

"And are now playing the martyr because you did."

That unpleasant rebuttal settled in the middle of the table between them, an oozing pile of resentment and anger that only seemed to grow bigger and more acidic.

How was it that things had gone so badly between them? They'd barely spent ten minutes with each other and were already fighting. Yet even as it bothered her, she couldn't fully kill the resentment and the anger.

"Why are you really here? I can't imagine James would be happy with you putting yourself in danger by being so close to a crime scene."

"James doesn't much care what I do." Maggie ran a hand over the cold condensation on her glass, her cornflower blue gaze averted. "Our divorce will be final in early January. Just after New Year's Day, as a matter of fact."

"Your what?"

The resentment and anger grew smaller and faded in the face of Maggie's news, before vanishing away as Bellamy moved around the table to take Maggie's hand. "When did this happen?"

"Earlier this year."

"But why? How? I thought you were so happy being married."

"We were married. Happiness wasn't a big part of it. A situation that got worse when he informed me he wasn't interested in having children."

"Oh."

She'd not been a part of her sister's life for some time, but the finality of that statement left its sting, chunking away a bit more of her years-old anger. "I'm sorry, Maggie. Really sorry."

"It's fine. We've said a lot of horrible things to each other and now we've just become numb. The New Year can't get here fast enough."

Bellamy wanted to say more—felt she *should* say more—but had no right. Whatever frustrations she might have over Maggie's behavior the past several years, she wouldn't have wished the dissolution of her marriage on her.

Neither would she ever have suspected there was anything wrong in the first place. James Corgan came from one of the wealthiest families in the state and had always seemed smitten with Maggie. Their marriage had happened quickly, but Bellamy had always assumed it was a love match.

Was she wrong about that? Or had things simply gone wrong, the same way her relationship with Maggie had changed into something neither of them recognized any longer?

"I guess we've both been keeping secrets."

"I'm not keeping secrets."

"Oh no?" Maggie raised a lone, perfect eyebrow. "Then what's going on that has you the target of bombings?"

"I have no idea."

"Come on, Bell. This is real life, not TV. People don't just walk out to their car after work and nearly get blown up."

"I'm well aware of that. It still doesn't mean I have a clue to what's going on."

The lie tripped right on out, practically skipping around the room. For the first time in a long time, she wanted to open up to Maggie—wanted to tell her about the email she'd received—but she had no idea how. If she said something, would she put Maggie in danger, too?

And if she told her, she would also have to admit that she was out of work. She still hadn't figured out how she was going to handle the taxes on the house her parents had left her or what she was going to do about getting a new car. She had a little bit saved, but nothing that was going to see her without a job indefinitely.

Especially if Sally Borne made good on her threat to blackball her from getting another.

"This is ridiculous." Maggie drummed one painted fingernail on the table. "Surely you have to know something. Or we can ask around and find someone who might know what this is about."

"I'm not making my personal life gossip fodder for the town."

"But if someone can help you…"

"No. I will handle this and deal with it myself."

"Just like you always do."

Whatever subtle truce they'd arrived at vanished completely as Bellamy got to her full height. "Yes, Maggie. Just like I always do. I can handle myself and whatever comes my way. I've been doing it for years."

The door to the kitchen opened at that moment, Donovan and Alex barreling into the room in a rush of feet and paws. The echo of Bellamy's retort still hovered but even if Donovan had missed the words, there was no way he missed her standing up, hands fisted at her sides.

"Everything okay?"

"Fine. Absolutely fine." Bellamy stepped away from her seat, extending a hand to Donovan and gesturing him to sit in her place. "Let me just get some fresh water for Alex."

The ploy was either enough to divert attention or Donovan was simply too polite to say otherwise, but he took the offered seat as Maggie thrust his glass of iced tea on him while Bellamy busied herself with some water for Alex.

The awkwardness of the moment was quickly covered up with Maggie's questions, her voice a sensual purr now that she was in the presence of an attractive man. As she listened, settling a large bowl of water on the floor, Bellamy felt herself closing up even further.

It didn't matter how badly she wished things were different with her sister; it wasn't possible.

And just like the loss of her parents, she was simply going to have to find a way to accept it.

DONOVAN PLACED HIS empty glass of iced tea back on the kitchen table and counted off the number of minutes until he could make a polite excuse and leave the room once more. If he'd known what he was walking into, he'd have found a way to stay outside with Alex a bit longer.

But they'd already done two perimeter sweeps of Bellamy's small property line and found nothing. Nor had they found anything else inside the shed, even after Donovan ran Alex through the drill a second and third time. He'd finally given in and gotten a fresh treat out of the car, sorry that he'd put Alex through such rigor over an obviously clean site.

Which was one more proof point that he was too far around the bend over Bellamy Reeves. He trusted Alex implicitly. The dog was well trained and had never let him down. That wasn't about to change.

What he now needed to figure out was how he was going to get Bellamy to let him stay. There was no way he was heading back to Austin and leaving her alone. He briefly toyed with the idea of leaving her at his parents' home. He would consider it if things went truly sideways, but wasn't quite ready to give in and bring his family into this mess.

Which left him and Alex as her newest houseguests.

He'd met the woman who'd arrived earlier, remembering her after the basic introductions. Maggie Reeves had been a year behind him in high school but he still recalled her reputation as one of the most popular kids. Funny how it hadn't mattered to him then and mattered even less now.

Yet somehow, in looking at Bellamy's sister, he sensed it was deeply important to how she saw herself.

"It's been a long time since I've seen you," Maggie said, her smile broad.

"High school, probably." Donovan nodded after taking a sip of his iced tea. "I haven't spent much time in Whisperwood since then."

"What brings you here now?"

"I'm part of the APD's K-9 unit. We support the surrounding communities in addition to Austin and I'm here to help the chief."

"On Bellamy's case?"

"Among others."

Donovan heard the genuine interest in Maggie's voice, but couldn't shake the underlying tension that hovered in the kitchen. He was the last person to criticize family dynamics, but there was a stiffness to Maggie and Bellamy's relationship that struck him as sad.

Not your business, Colton.

And it wasn't. But knowing what Bellamy had been

through in the past few days, he couldn't understand why she wouldn't lean on her sister.

"What you do must be fascinating. Law enforcement. And working with your sweet dog, too."

Maggie kept her distance from Alex, but Donovan had seen how her gaze kept darting to the large form currently slurping water in the corner of the small kitchen. Even that was curious. Bellamy had warmed to Alex immediately, but Maggie kept looking at him as if he were going to attack her at any moment.

"Alex is my full partner. We work together to find and diffuse bombs as well as missing persons and drugs."

"Wow." Her gaze shifted to the dog once again, but her tension seemed to ebb ever so slightly. "He can do all that?"

"He's pretty amazing. His nose can find far more than we can ever understand. And his training ensures he knows how to tell me what he's found."

Jiggling the ice cubes in his glass, Donovan glanced over at his partner, now seated on his haunches with his tongue lolling. "We're going to leave you two alone. Alex and I have a few more things we need to cop outside."

Before anyone could protest, Donovan made his escape, a quick nod all the dog needed to follow along. They weren't outside more than ten minutes when Maggie found her way to the back of his SUV. Donovan finished reordering his gear and turned at her quiet greeting.

"Hello, Ms. Reeves."

"It's Corgan. Maggie Corgan. For at least a little while longer." She muttered that last piece, even as a bright smile remained firmly on her face.

"Of course. What can I do for you?"

"Bell and I have a tough relationship. We haven't agreed on a lot of things for a long time and it's chipped away at what we used to have."

While he couldn't deny his loyalty to Bellamy, something in Maggie's words tugged at him. He knew what it was to have a distance between him and his loved ones. More, he knew what it was to want to close that distance but have no idea where to start.

"I love my sister," Maggie continued. "I care for her very much and I hate to think that she's in danger. Please take care of her. And please keep me posted if there's anything I can do."

"This is an active investigation but I'll do my best."

"Thanks. I guess that's all I can ask."

He watched her walk away, her physical look at odds with what he sensed lay beneath the surface. Maggie Corgan was a beautiful woman. Her hair was perfect, as were her body, her clothes, her car and her jewelry.

Yet beneath it all he sensed a woman who had very little.

As Maggie started her car and drove off, Donovan wondered if Bellamy understood that at all.

BELLAMY PUTTERED AROUND the kitchen, at odds with herself. Donovan and Alex were still outside—his SUV was visible in the driveway—but she didn't want to go out to see what they were doing. Maggie's visit had hit hard and she was still raw over the way they'd left things.

Her sister's news was unsettling, as well. It was the holidays and here Maggie was anticipating a divorce in the next few weeks. A small voice whispered that she should have invited her to spend the holidays together but she'd ignored it. And allowed the years-old anger and pain to prevent her from saying anything.

Wherever she'd once expected to be in life, thirty-five and alone, with no relationship with her sister, was so not it.

Which meant she needed to do something.

She retrieved the empty glasses from the kitchen table and washed them all in the sink, and was drying the last one when Donovan and Alex returned to the kitchen.

"We've swept your yard and shed three times and haven't found anything. You're clean."

Clean? Just like the glasses, only instead of washing out a bit of iced tea, he was hunting for bombs. Items designed to maim and kill. On a hard swallow, Bellamy nodded. "Thank you."

"I'd like to discuss what's going to happen next."

"Of course."

"You can't stay here. Not by yourself."

"Where do you think I'm going to go?"

"Your sister's would be a place to start."

Whatever ideas she had about making things better with Maggie, dragging her into this mess wasn't one of them. Bellamy pushed back from the counter and crossed the kitchen to face Donovan. "Absolutely not."

"She cares for you. And she's worried."

The thick lines of his body projected capable strength and something inside of Bellamy melted. How easy would it be to just move in, wrap her arms around him and sink in? The imprint of his lips lingered on hers, the heady sensation of their kiss still in the forefront of her mind.

But much as she wanted to talk to him and tell him how she felt about her relationship with Maggie and all that she desperately wished she could make right, it wasn't his problem.

None of this was his problem.

And a few kisses couldn't change that.

"I'm not bringing her into this." Bellamy said.

"But we can put protection on you both. Can make sure no one harms either of you."

"I'm staying in my house. That's non-negotiable."

"You can't stay here alone. That's why Alex and I are moving in until this is handled."

"You can't move in." The words came out on a squeak, even as a sly sense of delight curled beneath her skin.

"Since you seem to feel similar about going to your sister's, it's the only way."

Bellamy ignored how neatly Donovan made his argument and searched for some way to push back. "But this is my house. And you're assigned to my case. You can't live here."

"This is Whisperwood. The town is small and I'm from here. The department is well staffed but they don't need to put someone out here full-time. And I can work from here as well as Austin. On the few times I need to head into the city you can come with me."

"You can't upend my life this way."

Donovan glanced down at Alex, his smile broad as he placed a hand on the dog's head. "We just did."

THE UPENDING OF her life began immediately, and with surprising regularity. True to his promise, Donovan and Alex kept close watch on her and their days together had taken on an odd sort of routine.

Four days into life with her new roommates, Bellamy found herself once again heading down I-35 with Donovan and Alex, straight into Austin. The afternoon traffic was thick, with cars bumper-to-bumper as they approached downtown.

"This is ridiculous."

"No more ridiculous than a woman who's fighting off bomb threats to her life."

"I meant the traffic," Bellamy said. "I sort of thought the rest of it all had moved into the realm of the absurd."

His grin was broad as he glanced over at her. "Consider it an absurdity I'm determined to end."

She was grateful for that, the quick confidence that he could fix things going a long way toward soothing the nerves that refused to abate. She'd forget about the situation at LSP and her car and her shed for a few moments, and then it would all come streaming back, like a film on constant replay.

She wanted to believe it was over—a temporary madness that had descended in her life and vanished just as quickly—but the presence of man and dog suggested otherwise.

As did the unshakable feeling that things weren't over, no matter how badly she wanted them to be.

"You really believe you can stop whatever's going on?"

"Of course. That's my job. That, and keeping you safe in the process."

"Isn't that the chief's job?"

"We work together. Archer Thompson's a good man. If it's on his caseload, he's committed to handling things."

"For the biggest employer in Whisperwood. Isn't that a conflict?"

The easy smile vanished. "You always go around accusing the police of being in people's pockets?"

"I'm not—" She broke off, aware that was exactly what she was doing. "No, I'm not trying to suggest that. But I do know that much of his funding comes from the fact that LSP is such a huge business in Whisperwood. The tax contribution alone is significant. It can't be easy for the chief to have to investigate them."

"There's nothing easy about his job. Doesn't mean he can't handle it."

The quiet stretched out between them once more and Bellamy was forced to look at her behavior through Donovan's eyes. What must he see when he looked at her? A lonely woman, living in a small house all by herself. No obvious ties to anyone to speak of, made more evident by what he'd observed between her and Maggie. And now she was going around accusing the Whisperwood police of corruption.

The thought had whispered through her mind more than

once over the past few days, but now that it had taken root, something had the words spilling from her lips.

"I wasn't always like this."

"Like what?"

"Suspicious and unkind."

"Is that how you see yourself?" Donovan kept his eyes firmly on the traffic but it took no less power out of his question.

"Some days. Others I feel like I'm drifting through life on autopilot, not sure how I got there."

"You suffered a big loss. You're entitled to grieve."

"Am I? Or has it become a convenient excuse to stop living?"

SOMETHING IN BELLAMY'S words tugged at Donovan. He wouldn't have called her unkind—hadn't even considered her through that lens—but he did see the suspicion and the anger.

And the fear.

How did a person deal with that, day in and day out? Yes, the bomb threats were new, but dealing with ill and infirm parents, then losing them, had been a part of her life for far longer. That sort of pressure would change anyone.

"I'm the last person qualified to answer that question."

"Why?"

"I've lived on autopilot myself for an awfully long time. Gets to a point where you stop noticing it anymore."

He hadn't expected to say that much and the words left a bitter aftertaste on his lips.

Bellamy didn't immediately respond. It was only when he felt the light touch on his hand, where it lay over the center armrest, that she spoke. "What are you running from?"

"The same thing I've been running from my entire life. I'm not a Colton and my family refuses to see that."

"What do you mean, you're not a Colton?"

"I'm not. I was left in the Colton stables Christmas morning thirty-one years ago. Hays and Josephine took me in but I'm not their son."

"Of course you are. They're your family. Adoption or biology doesn't change that."

Her ready defense was sweet but Donovan had lived a lifetime feeling like an imposter. A poser. The truth haunted him and only grew worse this time of year.

"It changes everything. I'm not one of them, no matter how much they want to believe otherwise."

"Biology doesn't dictate your relationships. Look at Maggie and me. We're sisters and we can't seem to find common ground. What matters is the relationships you have. The love you have for each other. The family you make."

"You don't love your sister?"

"Of course I love her."

The emphatic response gave him heart that there was a path for Bellamy to move forward with her sister, but the dichotomy of their familial situations wasn't lost on him.

"So you have a family you can't seem to reconcile with, and I have a family who wants me in it and I keep walking away. Is that it?"

"When you put it like that, I suppose so," she agreed. "Family's hard. It's messy and emotional. That's why I love animals so much. They take you just the way you are."

"From what you've said, the Coltons took you just the way you were. You're the one who doesn't want to accept that."

Bellamy's words lingered long after they cleared Austin traffic and entered downtown. Donovan didn't want to believe them—didn't want to accept that he was the one who'd rejected his family's love—but the lingering guilt that had accompanied him since he was young glommed on to her statement.

And way down deep inside, he knew she was right.

Chapter Eight

The K-9 training center was quiet for midafternoon, but Donovan hardly noticed it as he unclipped Alex's leash and let him bound off into the large grassy area they used for training. He'd always encouraged Alex's socialization time with the other dogs and smiled as his partner headed toward two other members of K-9 teams. Loud barks and leaps onto each other's backs indicated both greetings and the time to play, and Donovan couldn't help but smile at the happy tail wags of his partner.

It was a huge contrast to his own confusion.

Confusion that sat squarely in the knowing eyes of Bellamy Reeves.

She'd already headed for one of the trainers and a group of puppies scampering around the yard. Her diverted attention gave him the reprieve he needed to analyze his thoughts.

What had happened on the drive down?

He and Alex had been with her for four days. Four agonizing days in which he'd diligently ignored the interest that simmered between them in favor of focusing on the task at hand.

Keeping her safe.

Clearly the sexual tension must have gotten to him because here he was, less than a week in her company, and he was like a singing canary.

He never spoke of his family or his feelings of inade-
quacy as an adopted member of the Colton clan. Yet there
he went, spilling his guts to Bellamy like he'd known her
for years.

*The Coltons took you just the way you were. You're the
one who doesn't want to accept that.*

Her words continued to roll through and roil up his
thoughts. Was it merely a matter of acceptance? Or was
that too convenient an explanation?

No matter how much love his parents had lavished on
him, they couldn't change the fact that his biological parents
had left him. The people who were supposed to love him
most had abandoned him in some rich family's barn, hoping
and depending on the kindness of strangers. Wealthy ones,
who could easily take on another mouth and who would be
unlikely to abandon him a second time.

That wasn't a slight on Hays and Josephine, but a fact
of his existence.

So why did it so often feel like punishment to the people
who'd promised to love him the most?

Here he was, encouraging Bellamy to take the comfort
and help of her sister, yet he'd been unable to do the same.
Biological or not, his parents had shown their love in myriad ways since his infancy. The day they'd taken him in
and given him a home was only the first.

So how did he begin to change? The helplessness he
sensed in Bellamy—that question of where to start with
her sister—was the same for him. He'd been distant for so
long he had no idea where to close the gaps.

No idea of even where to try.

With one last look at Alex, Donovan headed back into
the main building. His desk at the K-9 center had all the
same equipment and latest software as police headquarters
and he was determined to do some digging on Lone Star
Pharmaceutical. The company had an outstanding reputa-

tion, but the contents of Bellamy's email continued to nag at him. It was a clue that couldn't be dismissed or ignored.

If the corporation was involved in some bad dealing, he owed it to the investigation to tug that line and tug it hard. Deliberately mismanaging the vital supply of vaccines was a crime and a health hazard and no one, no matter how powerful, should be allowed to get away with that.

Since Bellamy was still in the courtyard, safe with the trainers, he wanted to take a few minutes to tug those lines.

In moments he had several articles pulled up on Lone Star Pharmaceutical and its founder, Sutton Taylor. The man was well-known in and around Whisperwood, and Donovan was humbled to realize he only recognized the man peripherally. That knowledge only reinforced his earlier thoughts of his family, another proof point that he was out of the loop with his hometown news, gossip and local politics.

Donovan scanned article after article, getting a sense of the man, before shifting to some of the more telling websites. Anonymous reviews on those job sites where people said what they really thought of their employer, Austin area gossip sites and even a few posts on *Everything's Blogger in Texas*, a blog that had shown zealous attention to his extended family in the past.

The additional sites provided layers and context to his profile of Sutton Taylor, including a subtle thread of the man as something of a lothario.

He supposed it went with the territory—a powerful man with a powerful job—but it smacked of cliché at the same time. He wasn't a man who'd ever understood the appeal of cheating. You either wanted to be with the person you were with or not. It seemed awfully low to string them along when it was easier just to get out of the relationship and start a fresh one.

Was it pragmatic?

Or maybe it was a sign he thought relationships were too disposable?

Either way, Donovan knew it was how he was wired. He'd had several relationships over the years that had simply run their course. Nowhere during that time did he feel he needed to look elsewhere, but when it was time to leave it was time to leave.

Unbidden, an image of Bellamy the first time he met her filled his mind's eye. Bright-eyed and welcoming, she'd helped him with Alex and had been content to stand there in the general store parking lot as his small puppy had gotten sick. The moments that had followed had been even more special, talking and laughing and getting to know each other. He'd never forgotten that evening, nor the number of times he'd thought of her since.

Maybe it was those moments together that helped him see the person beneath the current pain. Or maybe it was just an attraction that hadn't been dulled by the ensuing years. Either way, he was attracted to her. It was inconvenient and not ideal, seeing as how he was working her case, but he *was* interested.

And he'd like to see where things might go between them.

A flash of awareness skittered through his mind as the night he met Bellamy came fully into focus. He'd been called away at the end to go to a nearby accident scene. Shifting gears on the computer, he minimized the articles on Sutton Taylor and pulled up his case files, logging backward until he found that night five years ago. In moments he had it up, the particulars of the accident coming back to him as he recalled the scene.

A drunk driver racing and swerving home from a holiday party. An older couple returning from an evening out. A small patch of road just off the main highway that lead into Whisperwood.

His gaze scanned the screen but Donovan already knew what he'd find.

Airlifted to Austin Memorial due to severe injuries: Daniel-Justice Reeves. Moved by ambulance to Austin Memorial for minor cuts and scrapes and further evaluation: Virginia Reeves.

He'd left Bellamy that night to go to the scene of her parents' accident. That was why he'd never seen her again.

It was the night her life shattered.

BELLAMY HELD THE now-sleeping puppy in her arms, loathe to let the little guy go. He was a smaller version of Alex, the K-9 facility trainer confirming for her that they had a lot of success with Labradors in the program. They'd rescued this one from a small flop in Austin and decided to raise him as their own. The trainer had already assured her they'd find a home for him if he ended up not being focused enough for the K-9 program and, on impulse, Bellamy had given the woman her phone number.

Her thoughts earlier in the week about having a dog had clearly taken root. She smiled ruefully as she headed into the building to find Donovan, but took joy in the idea that the pup had a future, no matter what happened to his time in K-9 training. They'd already named him Charlie and she thought it fit him to a T. That warm little body cuddled closer into her chest as she rounded the corner toward a large open-office area, and she bent down to smell his sweet little puppy head.

Oh yes, this was the right idea. And if Charlie ended up being a fit for K-9, Bellamy had been promised visiting privileges and the name of a rescue organization in Austin that would love to have another ready adopter on their list.

She entered the staff room and saw Donovan hunched

over a desk. Winter sunlight streamed into the room, back-
lighting his broad frame as he focused on his screen. It
made for an odd tableau and something in the set of his
shoulders pulled her up short.

"Donovan? Is everything okay?" The puppy stirred
lightly at her voice but quickly snuggled back into her arms.

He turned from the screen, his dark eyes shuttered. His
expression was enough to have her moving forward. Something *was* wrong.

"What is it?"

"I'm sorry."

"For what? Did something happen?"

The puppy did stir then, either sensing her confusion
or from a subtle tightening in her arms. He wriggled as
his head lifted and she pulled him close, attempting to
soothe him.

Since Donovan's attention had been on his computer,
she veered there, surprised when he backed up to give her
access to the screen.

"Bellamy, I'm sorry."

She scanned the screen and recognized the words, but
didn't understand why Donovan had the record of her parents' accident pulled up. "Why do you have this?"

"It's my case file. That night. The night I met you when
Alex got sick. We were talking and then I had to leave
abruptly to go to an accident scene."

His words rattled around her brain like a loose pinball
racking up points against the bumpers. "You? You were
there?"

"I never realized it was your parents."

Her gaze roamed over the words once more, disbelief
battling with the facts on the screen.

Drunk driver. Daniel-Justice Reeves. Virginia Reeves.
Austin Memorial.

And the date all their lives changed.

Had he never put it together? Donovan had been called out to an accident, which was why he'd needed to rush off. There hadn't been one as massive as her parents' in years.

For the past week she'd simply assumed he knew and didn't want to hurt her by bringing it up.

But he'd had no idea.

She dropped into a nearby seat, the puppy now fully awake and squirming in her arms. He licked her face in obvious concern and she hugged him close, taking the comfort he offered.

"Are you okay?"

"I thought you knew. I took comfort that you were there."

"You did?"

"Of course. You saw them that night."

"Yes."

She'd always had a picture in her mind of what the accident must have been like, but didn't know the reality. She couldn't know what it smelled like or what it sounded like to hit another car with such force. She couldn't even begin to imagine.

For all his injuries, her father had seemingly moved past that point—past those horrid memories—but her mother never did. She'd struggled to sleep ever since the accident, to the point that Bellamy had considered a week with only one nightmare a good week.

And Donovan had been there.

"Did you help them?"

"We did all we could to keep your parents comfortable and steady until ambulance arrived."

"You were there for them."

Donovan only nodded, his lack of words somehow fitting.

What was he supposed to say?

It had been the same with everyone else in her life. People cared—they wanted to help and they definitely wanted to express sympathy—but in the end, there wasn't anything for them to do. Grief left a person helpless, but she'd learned it was no easier to comfort a grieving person. That had been the oddest part of her journey with her parents and had left the largest craters in her heart.

It had also served as the fuel to push others away.

She'd lost contact with her friends. She kept her colleagues at a distance, always claiming an excuse when she couldn't attend a happy hour or an event outside of work. Even her relationship with Maggie had suffered.

Years lost, along with some of the most important relationships in her life.

She hugged Charlie close, her attention shifting to Donovan. She'd been attracted to him five years before and a few days in his presence hadn't changed that. If anything, the concentrated time they'd spent together over the past week had only reinforced that initial attraction.

Was it coincidence that he'd come back into her life at a point where she needed a friend?

More to the point, did she want a friend, or did she want something more?

"Are you okay?" Donovan reached across and ran a finger over the top of Charlie's head. The little guy preened under the additional attention before lifting a paw to swat at Donovan's hand.

"I am. I've had a long time to get used to what happened. On some level, it's comforting to know you were there with them when they needed you. I've seen how capable you are. And I know how good it felt to have you there at LSP when we were dealing with my car." She reached out and laid a hand over his. "I'm glad you were there. Thank you."

"You're welcome."

Their gazes met and locked and Bellamy wondered, with all that had happened in her life, how the world just fell away. The rest of it—her job, her car, even the threat at the house—it all seemed so far away.

In its place was something real and *present*.

She'd put off having a life for so long, it was startling to realize just how good it felt to be the object of someone's attention. To be the object of Donovan's attention.

"So you're okay?"

"I'm okay," she murmured, already anticipating the feel of his lips pressed to hers as he leaned in closer.

"Who's your friend?" His eyes dipped between them, the perusal intimate.

"You mean Charlie?" Her gaze dropped to the puppy, his excitement at having two humans so close causing him to wriggle even more.

Donovan kept a soothing hand on the dog's head, the steady attention holding him still, the back of his hand tantalizingly close to her breasts. "That's a good name. A good partner's name."

"He's the newest recruit for the K-9 program."

"Can you can give him his first lesson?"

"His lesson?"

Donovan moved even closer, his lips drawing nearer. "You think you can hold him still while I kiss you?"

A shot of heat traveled the length of her spine before spreading through her entire body. "I'll do my best."

The last coherent thought she had was that Donovan Colton was doing *his* best.

The press of lips against hers was both firm and yielding, the perfect mix of give-and-take. He kept a calming hand on the puppy, his other hand settling against her hip. His fingers teased the top of her slacks where her waistband met flesh, a tantalizing brush against her skin.

But his mouth. Oh, the wondrous responses he could create with the greatest of ease.

Bellamy fed on his attentions, the sweet push-pull of

desire fueled by their sensual play of tongues and the light moans each drew from the other. His fingers continued to trace light patterns against her skin, featherlight yet deeply powerful as her body heated at the simple touch.

She briefly questioned if her response was tied to how long it had been since her last relationship, but even she wasn't silly enough to think any man could compare to Donovan. Strong. Sure. Safe.

Capable.

Those attributes and so many more.

Charlie had stayed still, somehow sensing the humans needed a moment, but the waiting finally got to him. The combination of active puppy and a body that was going limp from Donovan's sexy ministrations got the better of her and Bellamy stepped back from the kiss before she lost her hold on Charlie.

"Whoa there. Hang on." Donovan took him easily, transferring the bundle of energy into his arms and holding the dog as if he weighed nothing. He lifted him up and stared him in the eye but kept his voice gentle. "Way to ruin the mood, little man."

Charlie only wagged his tail even harder, his tongue lapping into the air as his little body wiggled from his excitement.

"He looks very remorseful." Bellamy giggled, the small, wiggly body too cute to resist.

"I think we may also be getting the universal signal to go outside. I'll be right back. There's something I want to show you anyway."

Bellamy watched Donovan go, struck once again by his gentle nature with animals. Even at the risk of wearing puppy pee or something even less desirable, he had a soothing way about him and kept Charlie close.

She stood there for a few moments, absorbing what had just happened. The intensity of the kiss. And the pure joy of being in Donovan's arms. Even the solicitous way he'd worried over her parents.

The computer screen still had all the information on her parents' accident and Bellamy scanned it again, doing her level best to read it with detachment. She knew the case well, but read through Donovan's impressions of the night and what he'd contributed to the report. His description of the scene matched the final crime report. So did the on-scene reconstruction.

"You sure you're okay with that?"

"I'm good." Bellamy glanced back over her shoulder, pleased to see Donovan was still dry. "No accidents before you got him outside?"

"It was close but Charlie showed admirable control. He also ran off to play with the big guys after doing his business so I'll leave it to Alex to keep an eye on him for a while."

"Alex is good with other dogs."

"He is. The socializing is good for him and so's the time outside. We're lucky to have pretty decent winter months here in Austin but I never take them fully for granted. Every opportunity to get him out here is time well spent for him."

The time at the K-9 facility obviously did Donovan good, too. He was more relaxed here. More at ease. Was that because this was his professional home or was it because he wasn't comfortable in Whisperwood? His earlier comments about his family still lingered, but Bellamy chickened out before she could ask him about them.

There was a sweet vibe between them for the moment, a by-product of the kiss and the puppy, and she was loath to mar that in any way.

"Was there something you wanted to show me?"

"What do you know about Sutton Taylor?"

"The CEO of LSP?"

Donovan dragged over a chair from a nearby desk and pulled it up next to her and took a seat. "The same."

"I know him peripherally. Once a year all the departments present to him. Given how long I've been at LSP, he knows my name. I've had a few encounters with him at annual meetings and at the company picnic and I had to take him through a financial file once all on my own."

"What were your impressions of him?"

"He's incredibly well respected. He built LSP from the ground up, using some seed money he'd made early on in pharmaceutical sales. He's grown the business from there."

"That's good." Donovan nodded. "But what are your impressions of him, who he is as a person?"

"Oh. Well, I'm not sure I ever thought about it." She stopped as one of those rare meetings came back to her. "That's not entirely true. I remember this one time. We were waiting for a meeting to start and several of us were in line to get coffee and breakfast."

Donovan's attention never wavered at what she felt was a silly story. "Go on."

"So we're in line and because I had fiddled with a few pages of my presentation I was at the back of it. And I could see how Sutton admired one of my colleagues. I know men look at women. Heck, women look at men. It's natural. But most people aren't so—" She did break off then. "Most people aren't so obvious about it. And all I could think was that this was the founder of the company and he was ogling this woman like he was a fifteen-year-old boy."

"Do you think others noticed?"

"If they did, no one said anything. But there was just this quality about it all that I found disappointing. Like he should be above that somehow."

"Do you think he's behind the supply management and price-fixing?"

Bellamy wanted to dismiss it but gave the question her attention. "Why would he do that?"

"One of the two greatest motivators in the world. Money."

"What's the other?" The question was out before she could check it and his answer came winging back on a wry grin.

"Sex."

"Of course."

"Which brings me to my other question about Mr. Sutton Taylor. Take a look at these." Donovan clicked through several browser windows he'd opened, pointing out various elements that had caught his attention on each page with the mouse. "See here and here and here. All suggest, either in a veiled manner or in the case of that blog right out in the open, what a ladies' man he is. All reinforce the story you just shared."

Bellamy considered the assessment, weighing her answer. "I guess others have seen what I have."

"You're not ruining his reputation to answer honestly. Especially not if it will help us get to the bottom of what's going on."

It still felt like a betrayal of some sort, but Bellamy knew he was right. More, she was in the middle of this now whether she liked it or not and she had a right to take care of herself.

"He's very highly regarded for all he's built LSP into, but if I'm being honest, people do talk about his wilder side. Apparently he's had a wandering eye for decades now. His wife passed a little over a year ago, but rumor has been that she always turned a blind eye."

"Behavior like that might be enough to piss someone off."

"And give them access to our drug supply chain?" She shook her head, the notion simply not possible. "No way. There are too many people involved. Too many steps in the process. The sheer amount of government reporting we do on the various drugs we produce makes that virtually impossible."

"So we're back to the email as a way to ruin corporate reputation, not as fact."

She held up a hand. "Wait a minute. There's an easy way to find out if this is reputation or reality. Hang on."

Fifteen minutes later, Bellamy hung up the phone and tapped the notepad she'd scribbled onto. After five calls to pharmacy chains she knew LSP provided flu vaccine for, all confirmed they were out of it.

"Five for five?"

"Yep." She tapped the pad. "No one has the vaccine. Once they got past their initial supplies in September and October, all were asked to pay highway robbery to reorder. And I know there's plenty of vaccine. Our supply is manufactured to ensure it."

"And no one at work has mentioned this?"

Bellamy considered Donovan's question, reviewing it through the new lens uncovered by the calls. "The office has been on a lighter schedule because of the holiday and I didn't give it much thought, but one of my colleagues was complaining in the lunch line a few weeks ago. He mentioned how he'd fielded several calls from field reps complaining about problems with orders. Only when he went back to look at the manifests, everything appeared to have delivered in full."

"So where's the gap?"

"Exactly."

Her gaze drifted back to the computer screen and a small link at the bottom of the article currently facing them from Donovan's screen. "What does that say?" She pointed to the link before reaching for the mouse to click on it.

A new window popped open out of the existing one, a small blurb on the blog they were already looking at.

Sutton Taylor in hospital with mysterious illness. Family worried the Hill Country's most powerful CEO is at death's door.

"Death's door? What?" Bellamy scanned the article quickly, trying to decipher through the gossip and the innuendo to see what she could discover. "It says here he's been ill for some time until being checked into a private facility between Whisperwood and Austin earlier this month."

"This site is known for stretching the truth. Has he been seen at work? Or has anything been mentioned about an illness?"

"Not at all. Last I heard his son was boasting that his father was headed out on a well-deserved Mediterranean vacation for the holidays."

"Could be a cover-up."

"But why hide that from the employees?"

"Maybe they don't want anyone to panic or get upset? Or feel they can get away with anything if the boss is ill."

Bellamy stilled at Donovan's theories. While all were sound, they seemed so foreign.

So at odds with the company she'd known and loved for the past thirteen years.

"Did you remember something?"

"No, it's just that this doesn't seem possible. I've worked there for so many years. Maybe my loyalty to them has blinded me to their possible faults, but what we're talking about...corporate price-fixing? Putting millions of lives at risk? How could I possibly have worked for a company who saw that as a way to turn a profit?"

"I'm sorry, Bellamy. Really, I am. You've lost a lot and this is only adding to that burden."

While she appreciated the sympathy more than she could say, it was way more than a burden. Had she truly spent nearly all of her adult life working for a company that was so profit driven they'd violated the core tenets of their business—to make people well?

"It's a lot to digest, that's all."

"Then why don't we do something to take your mind

off of it? Staring at these articles isn't going to bring any
answers. Maybe something fun and different would be a
better idea."

"Like what?"

"There's a neighborhood down off Lake Travis full of big
beautiful homes that's known for their Christmas decorations. They're also known for their friendly neighborhood
competition of putting holiday inflatables on the front lawn."

"Sounds classy."

"Apparently it started as a prank from one house to another and morphed into a neighborhood joke. Now that they
get over twenty thousand visitors a season, everyone decided to get in the act. Especially when they started charging admission for a local charity."

She hadn't been full of a single drop of holiday cheer
this season, but something about the promise of goofy in-
flatable lawn decorations and bright, shiny lights felt like
the right idea.

"Can Alex come along?"

"As if I'd leave him behind. Though I have to warn you,
he's a bit of a spoilsport."

"Oh?"

"With all the running around he's done today, he's going
to be asleep before we leave the K-9 training center."

"Poor baby. He'll miss all the fun."

Donovan leaned forward, a grin on his face as he whispered in a conspiratorial tone. "Shh. It's probably for the
best. There's one house with a decoration of a dog dressed
like one of Santa's reindeer that will give him nightmares
for a month."

"Then it's good I'm along. I can make sure his eyes are
covered from the horror of lawn decorations gone awry."

Chapter Nine

It *was* good she was along. Even better, Donovan thought, it was nice to see a broad smile on Bellamy's face as they drove slowly past the brightly decorated houses and the laughable lawn decorations.

"That is not a pig in angel's wings."

"It most certainly is."

Bellamy's laughter filled the car, a soothing balm to what they'd shared earlier. Even with the difficult discussion of her parents at the K-9 center, she'd kept her equilibrium, but he hadn't heard her laugh. The sound was enticing. Sweet.

And thoroughly enchanting.

Is that what the kids were calling it nowadays, Colton?

Bellamy Reeves might be enchanting, but she was also sexy as hell, a fighter and a woman who had come to occupy far too many of his thoughts in far too short a time.

Had she ever fully left?

That notion had dogged him on and off, taking root fully when he reviewed the case file on her parents. He *had* thought about her over the years. He'd be a liar if he said it was a strong, desperate sort of yearning, but he hadn't forgotten her.

He'd also remembered the easy conversation and sexy chemistry from the night they'd met with a certain sort of fondness. It was a sweet memory and he'd enjoyed pulling it out every so often, polishing it off and reflecting in the glow.

But seeing her again was something else entirely.

She was a beautiful woman and despite the understanding that her life was in tremendous turmoil, he couldn't keep denying his interest.

"There's a Santa decorating a tree in his boxer shorts. And over there is another pig but this one is in reindeer antlers. What is with this neighborhood?"

"I think it's a combination of fierce competition and a lot of money to burn. A lot of these lawn decorations are custom-made. This is one of the wealthiest neighborhoods in Austin."

"It sure is fun." She hesitated for a moment, and he might not have realized it if he weren't stopped behind a line of cars that had already slowed in front of them. "And I don't know. It's frivolous but they're obviously excited to share it with others. I think if you have money it's not so bad if you're willing to share it."

"Not everyone feels that way."

"No, I suppose they don't," she mused. "I'm certainly not wealthy. My parents got by at best and the only reason I have my house is because my parents' insurance settlement paid for it for me. But it seems that if you are fortunate enough to end up provided for, it's only right to share what you have. I love that all this fun also contributes to charity."

They drove on in quiet contemplation, occasionally pointing out a certain house or a specific decoration, but otherwise not speaking. Donovan appreciated that they could spend time together silently, but also wondered what she was thinking.

He waited until they'd cleared the traffic and pulled out onto the road that would lead them back to Whisperwood before speaking again. "I know it's not much, but maybe it is a little burst of Christmas cheer."

"Thanks for that. It was nice to forget for a little while."

"Is that all?" A small shot burrowed beneath his breast-bone. He'd hoped to do more than just allow her to forget for a while. Donovan had been intent on helping her make a new memory—something to hold close to her heart—even if the rest of her life still had more holes than she'd ever imagined.

"You know, your life's not over."

"Excuse me?"

"Your life. Your opportunity at happiness. It's not over because your parents died."

The warm moments they'd experienced on the drive through the pretty neighborhood vanished, melting away like ice on a summer Texas afternoon. In its place was a layer of cool that would give that same ice a run for its money.

"Are you actually lecturing me on grief?"

"I'm suggesting you have a right to live. Is that wrong?"

"Not at all. In fact, I think it makes perfect sense coming from you."

Donovan heard the warning signs. They all but leaped out at him, yet he pressed on. "Why's that?"

"Do you honestly think I'd take advice on grief and the loss of my parents, at the holidays no less, from a man who can't be bothered to spend time with his own?"

"My family is my business."

"Yes, they are your business. They're also alive and well and interested in sharing your life, yet you hold them at arm's length."

Again, Donovan saw the red flag waving boldly in front of him and he barreled right on through, heedless of the consequences. "Like your relationship with your sister?"

"Maggie abandoned us."

"I was abandoned!"

The words slipped out, harsh and violent in the closed

cabin of his SUV. Up to that moment, Alex had lay sleeping in the back seat, but he sat up at the rising tenor of their words. But it was the harsh emotion that ripped from somewhere around Donovan's stomach that had Alex nosing forward, poking at his triceps where Donovan had his arm resting on the console.

"Shh, buddy. Go back to sleep."

Alex was undeterred and sat straight and tall in the back seat, unwilling to lay down.

Neither he nor Bellamy said a word as he drove steadily on toward Whisperwood, and it was only when they neared the city limits that she finally spoke. "I'm not suggesting your feelings aren't legitimate. You've lived with the knowledge of being left by your biological parents. But what I don't understand is why you punish the family who loves you. They're a gift. And there will come a day when you can't take any of it back. When they won't be here any longer."

"They took me in out of duty."

"Isn't duty a form of love?"

The framing of that caught him up short. Duty as love? "It sounds like a chore."

"Caring for Alex is a duty. Yet you love him and you do it willingly. My parents were infirm and it was my duty to help them. Yet I did it with love. Helping others, taking them in, seeing them through the things that are hard—they're the *duties* we take on for the people we love."

Her words humbled him. All the way down deep, in the places he'd kept buried for so long Donovan had convinced himself they'd finally vanished, was a rising sense of remorse.

Had he been that selfish?

Yes, he had.

Worse, he'd thrown his family's love back in their faces, claiming that it was somehow less than or unworthy. He'd rejected them and they'd done nothing but love him. The knowledge was humbling. But more than that, it was enlightening.

The reality he'd spent his life running from was the one place where he truly belonged.

SUTTON TAYLOR SCROLLED through the news on his iPad and tried to make sense of what he was seeing on the screen. He'd felt like warmed-over bull crap for the past month— a sensation that had only grown worse by the day—but he was determined to rally.

Determined to get some of his damn strength back so he could figure out what was going on at his company. Jensen claimed to have everything under control, but if everything was under such tight reins, why did he have four emails on his personal account from longtime distributors asking where their flu vaccines were?

They'd shipped it months ago, the moment the vaccine came off the lines.

How were people out? Worse, he read the supply details himself. Signed the manifests for the eggs they needed to incubate the virus for the vaccines several months ago. They had *enough*, damn it.

So why was he sitting on multiple emails asking where the supply was? One even complained about pricing, which made no sense. They'd decided that back in March.

Head suddenly fuzzy, Sutton laid his tablet on the rolling tray that had become his constant companion and lay back into the pillows. He was so weak. He had moments of clarity but they were interspersed with long windows of fuzziness when he couldn't seem to grasp anything.

But he needed to grasp this.

Why were there no vaccines? Where had they gone?

Had he asked Jensen about it? The last time they

talked—was it yesterday or today?—had he mentioned it to his boy? Or had he decided to keep it to himself?

The questions roiled in his mind, growing fainter like an echo that died out over the rolling Hill Country, but still he tried to hang on to the threads. Maybe he didn't ask the question. Maybe he wanted to see if Jensen asked him about suppliers calling looking for their vaccine.

Was that right?

The exhaustion that had dogged him for weeks finally gripped him in sharp claws and Sutton gave in.

He'd think about it tomorrow. He had to feel better tomorrow. It would all be clearer tomorrow.

It had to be.

BELLAMY STARED OUT the front window of Donovan's SUV and looked at her house, now lit up as man and dog traipsed through her small haven. Was it safe to go in?

And did she have any choice?

Every time they came home, the routine was the same.

Donovan and Alex had already gotten out to reconfirm the perimeter, then started in on the interior, leaving her with strict instructions to stay inside with locked doors and wait for them to come back. He'd also instructed her to keep her phone in her hand with his number already programmed in and her hand near the horn to quickly alert him to anyone outside.

It was a semicrude warning system, but she figured it would do the job if someone approached.

What she hadn't quite figured out was what had happened earlier. She'd pressed his buttons on their evening jaunt around Austin, that was for sure.

The real question, upon reflection, was why.

His relationship with his parents was none of her business. And even as she knew that—accepted it—she called BS on it, too. He'd started it all, poking around at her grief with an emotional stick. She'd simply defended herself in the age-old technique learned on the playground.

When mud's slung at your head, sling it right on back.

Which said very little about her if she was still employing playground tactics as a grown woman.

Donovan opened the front door and waved at her, hollering for her to stay in the car until he got there. She did as he asked and tried to juxtapose the protector marching toward her with the man who'd frustrated her less than an hour ago.

Your life. Your opportunity at happiness. It's not over because your parents died.

It was the holidays, for heaven's sake. The holidays were supposed to be hard for people who'd lost loved ones, and this was her first time through them without her mother or her father. A few bright lights and goofy lawn decorations couldn't change that.

Even if he'd tried really hard to give her something fun to focus on.

That thought caught her up short and whatever playground mud pie she was about to mentally sling died mid-toss.

He'd *tried*.

And didn't that count for something? Something quite special, if she were being honest.

The door clicked open with his keyless remote and he opened her door. She swung her legs over, but stayed put in her seat.

"All clear. You got the Alex sniff of approval."

"Thank you."

"It's what we do."

She got out of the car but took his hand before he could move on. "For before. Thank you. You tried to show me a fun evening and I repaid you by saying some unkind things. I'm sorry for that."

"You don't have anything to apologize for."

"No, I think I do. The past months have been hard. Way harder than I expected, even, and I had more than enough time to prepare for this. But it was nice to escape for a while. To go see something fun and silly and happy."

The breeze that had swirled all day chose that moment to kick up, a sign that even with the warmer Texas days, it was still winter. She wrapped her arms around her waist at the sudden shot of cold. Donovan took her arms and pulled her close, the heat of his body an immediate balm against the wind. His head bent near hers, not quite touching, and she reveled in the loss of personal space.

A warm, manly scent filled her senses. A bit musky, a bit smoky, it made her think of warm fires on cold nights and she would have happily stood there in his arms for hours, if only for the opportunity to breathe him in.

"I think about the night we met," she murmured. "Not often, but I have thought about it."

"I have, too."

Ribbons of pleasure wrapped around her, delight at his words settling in her chest. "I can still see poor little Alex, sick on a few Legos."

"He did learn his lesson that night. He rarely picks up anything that's not food."

"That's good."

"And ensures far fewer messes in my house."

Once again, Bellamy marveled at how easy and freeing it was to be with Donovan. Their argument in the car had faded, and instead of creating a rift, it gave them another opportunity to connect. One of those small steps that paved the way toward a relationship.

Could something good come out of this confusing time? The small tingle that hovered beneath her skin reinforced just how much she hoped that might be possible.

A whisper of sound echoed from the direction of the

darkened street and Donovan shifted, instantly alert. He pressed her back into the open car door before looking around, Alex leaping to attention. When man and dog remained still, neither moving, Bellamy whispered, "What is it?"

"I'm not sure. Let's get inside."

Her home was small, the driveway a modest distance from the front door. She often ran the length when she came home during a rainstorm and unless it was a soaker, rarely got too wet. But suddenly the stretch between the car and the front door seemed endless.

"I'll walk behind you and cover you to the front door."

"You can't—" She stilled at his unyielding gaze.

"Behind you. Let's go."

Bellamy respected his wishes, nerves racing the length of her spine and back again as she moved swiftly toward the front door. If something really was out there, wouldn't Alex have already started barking?

The thought had barely had time to land when a loud clatter cracked through the air, lighting up the night with noise. Donovan crushed her body to his before dropping them to the ground, absorbing the impact with his body.

Her breath whooshed out on a hard burst as Donovan quickly rolled over her, continuing to shield her with the length of his body. The heavy weight pressed her before it vanished. Then, before she could even register the rapid sensory changes, Donovan hollered instructions as he raced down the driveway, Alex at his heels. "Into the house, Bellamy! Now!"

She did as he asked, even as worry for him and Alex nearly blinded her as she fumbled her way through the front door. The precautions he'd taken to sweep the house upon their return had seemed silly at the time but now gave comfort. Her home was free of traps.

On the inside.

But an intruder lurked outside, and they seemed determined to find her, no matter where she was.

DONOVAN FOLLOWED ALEX, his partner's nose down and his focus solely on the hunt. Donovan kept up a steady stream of instructions to keep Alex focused on the scent, yet by his side. He didn't want to let him go and risk getting his partner shot.

The gunshots had been a surprise and they shouldn't have been. *Nothing* about this situation should be a surprise. Yet for reasons that defied description, the faceless threat to Bellamy continued to catch Donovan off guard.

She'd been targeted by a killer and it was time he not only accepted that fact, but took it for the serious threat it was. The crude construction of the bombs might suggest an amateur, but it also denoted determination, focus and a willingness to get the nefarious job done.

The escalation to gunshots only reinforced that determination.

He'd learned long ago that second-guessing himself in the middle of an op was the quickest way to lose focus, but the recriminations continued to pound in time with his steps. They'd been so focused on understanding why Bellamy was a target and what she might possibly know about the inner workings of LSP that they'd lost sight of the bigger concern.

Maybe she was simply the scapegoat.

The thought chilled him, but as the idea took shape and form in his mind, it grew clearer and more defined. By all accounts, the email that started this all shouldn't have even found its way to her. HR had paid no attention to her claims or even given her the benefit of due process. And perhaps the most telling, the initial attack against her happened on LSP property.

Everything centered on Lone Star Pharmaceutical and someone operating from behind its walls.

The online search earlier around Sutton Taylor played through his mind. Was the founder behind this? He'd built a successful company and could easily be maneuvering something like this from a distance. Money bought influence but it also bought professionals to do your dirty work.

Yet the job had smacked of an amateur from the start.

He paced behind Alex, moving off into the wooded area that surrounded her property line. He'd already reholstered his gun when they'd arrived back at Bellamy's home to do the property sweep and he kept a firm handle on it now. Even with that layer of protection, he was exposed. They'd barely cleared the woods when he called Alex to a halt.

He wanted to find his quarry but he was no good to Bellamy if he and Alex became sitting ducks for someone who saw them far more clearly than they could in return.

Alex stilled immediately, his training outweighing even the lure of the scent. With careful steps, Donovan backed them toward the road, his gaze roaming the area before him. Other than the briefest glimpse of their prey shortly after the gunshots, he had been totally blind to their assailant's whereabouts.

As his foot hit macadam, Donovan gave one final scan of the area. Then he turned and ran, zigzagging across the road to make himself harder to sight.

He didn't stop until he reached Bellamy's front door.

Jensen lowered the night vision goggles and watched the cop disappear into the night. The other hand that held the gun still trembled at his side, the realization the man had a dog an unexpected development. Those beasts knew scents and now the animal had his.

And that wasn't even his biggest problem. He knew the cop and remembered him from growing up in the same town.

Donovan Colton.

They hadn't been in school together, but everyone in town knew the Coltons. The Colton family regularly competed for their share of Whisperwood headlines, especially because of their black sheep cousins who lived a few towns over in Shadow Creek. Hays Colton had always downplayed that branch of the family, but family was family.

Wasn't that what this was all about, anyway?

He was the rightful heir to LSP. The company was his and nothing would stop him from securing his legacy.

Bellamy Reeves had been the perfect target. But as he watched Donovan Colton fade into the night, he knew the game had just taken on a new dimension. Cops didn't drive their caseloads around town in their cars. Nor did they hover over them in ways that suggested a far more intimate relationship than that of a protector.

But what were the odds?

The question both amused and frustrated as Jensen considered Donovan Colton. The man was a bright, shining example of why Jensen had started on this path to begin with.

It was time to go to ground, regroup and figure out how to manage this added dimension. He needed more information about Colton.

And then he'd take out the woman and the man who'd become her shadow.

Chapter Ten

Bellamy had hot coffee waiting and about a million questions.

"Are you okay? What happened? Was someone out there? I didn't hear any more gunshots."

Donovan had braced for the questions but hadn't prepared himself for the rush of need that poured through him at the sight of her.

"Donovan? Did you see anyone?"

With careful movements, he ensured his gun was safely holstered and removed the piece, setting it on the middle of her dining room table next to the mug of coffee. He scanned the room, pleased to see the curtains were already drawn on all the windows. Then he released Alex so his partner could get to the water and food that already occupied a place of prominence on Bellamy's kitchen floor.

Only when he'd done all that and realized his blood still pounded and his hands still shook with nervous energy did Donovan take what he needed. On a groan, he reached for her and dragged her close, burying his face in her neck and inhaling her. She was safe. Whole.

Untouched.

"Donovan." His name was a whisper where she brushed her lips against his hair. "You're okay. I'm so glad you're okay."

He moved fast, the moment of comfort flashing over to

a desperate, achy need that threatened to consume him as he took her mouth. She matched him, her lips meeting his in immediate surrender. He captured her hands, linking his fingers with hers, and gave the mutual need between them free rein.

There was power in the surrender, he realized as the kiss spun out. A power he'd never known or understood before. Dating. Relationships. All that had come before had been satisfying, yet functional.

But for Bellamy he burned.

Passion flared and Donovan kept his hold tight as he moved them both toward the couch. Dropping to the soft, well-worn cushions, he held her close as he draped her over his body so she straddled his lap. Their bodies pressed together intimately, a sign she was real and gloriously, physically present.

By unspoken agreement they never broke the connection of their lips, even as each explored the other. Her hands roamed over his chest, smoothing the lines of his T-shirt before dipping to pull the material from the waistband of his cargos. It gave easily, slipping over his body as her hands tugged the cotton higher and higher.

They broke the kiss only long enough for her to slip the shirt over his head, her mouth returning to his as her hands moved unerringly over his skin. Her explorations were tentative at first but grew bolder as the tips of her fingers circled the flat area of his nipples. Shots of heat moved from his chest to his groin, insistent darts of pleasure that both fulfilled even as they demanded more.

He wanted all of her.

But for the moment, he'd settle for touching her, feeling her skin beneath his fingers and pressing her to his chest.

His hands traveled the same path as hers, dragging the silk of her shirt from her slacks before shifting to work the line of buttons. One by one, those small pearls fell away to reveal soft skin. He grazed the swells of her breasts over the cups of her bra, the demands of his body building ever higher, ever tighter.

He wanted her. With everything he was, he wanted this woman who was so warm and responsive in his arms. Yet it was because he wanted her so much that he needed to hold back.

But heaven help him, he couldn't stay away from her.

Just a few minutes more. A bit more time to share what flared to life between them and reassure himself she was safe. A few more touches would hold him.

They'd have to.

His hands roamed over her breasts, the weight of her flesh heavy in his palms. He moved his thumbs over her nipples, the sensual play drawing a moan from deep in her throat.

The knowledge they needed to stop—that whatever flared to life when they were together couldn't be acted on further—nearly vanished like smoke at what pulsed and demanded between them. Donovan nearly gave in—nearly acquiesced to desire—when a loud bark echoed through Bellamy's living room.

Alex's war cry was fierce and immediate, effectively breaking the spell of desire that wound around him and Bellamy.

Need glazed her beautiful gray eyes, but rapidly gave way to the moment as she scrambled off his lap. Her motions were stiff but she moved quickly so he could get to Alex. His partner was already at the door, his bark deep and full as he stood guard.

"Alex." Donovan ordered him to quiet as he crossed to the dining room table and picked up his gun. He briefly thought to grab his shirt but refused to waste the time if their quarry lurked outside the house.

He'd already scoped out safe points in the house on his

earlier sweep and knew the walls that framed the edge of the dining room were the most secure place. There were no windows in the room, and the short walls that set off the entrance archway would provide additional protection from the front door.

"Bellamy, please get behind the dining room wall. I'll let you know when it's safe to come out."

"Get behind—"

"Now, please."

The adrenaline that had carried him into the house fewer than twenty minutes before spiked once again, a heady cocktail that fired the blood. Alex had remained in place at the door, a ferocious protector who would go through the entrance first to protect his humans. The thought humbled Donovan as it always did, the animal's courage dwarfing that of many people he knew.

"Colton! It's Archer. Let me in."

The order was clear and at confirmation it was the chief, Bellamy scampered from behind the dining room wall toward her clothes.

"Bellamy—"

"I'm half-naked, Donovan, and the chief is here." She hissed the words, color high on her cheeks, and Donovan couldn't quite hide the grin. She did make an awfully pretty picture, her skin flushed a sweet pink while those gorgeous breasts pushed against the cups of her bra that he hadn't managed to get off.

A quick glance down reminded him of his own decision to forgo his shirt and he pulled the door open to let Archer in before striding back to get his clothes. Archer was a quick study and likely would have known what he and Bellamy had been doing, clothing be damned, and there was no way Donovan was leaving his friend to stand at the front door like a sitting duck.

Archer made a fuss over Alex, his gaze averted as Donovan righted himself. If Bellamy's sudden appearance from the corner of the dining room was at all a surprise, Archer was too big a gentleman to show it.

"A neighbor down the way called in gunshots. You wouldn't know anything about that, now, would you, Colton?"

HEAT RACED FROM her neck to her face and back down in increasing waves of embarrassment as Bellamy smoothed her shirt over her hips. It was bad enough she'd fallen into Donovan's arms like a woman starved, but to be discovered by the chief of police added an extra layer of mortification.

She and Donovan had been shot at and how did she respond? By attacking him like some sex-starved fiend.

Although embarrassing, Chief Thompson's arrival was perfect timing before she'd made an even bigger mistake. She barely knew Donovan Colton. Yes, they'd been thrown into a crazy situation. And yes, there was a base attraction.

But to act on it so quickly?

That was the recipe for a serious heartache once her attacker was caught and life went back to normal. She'd already accepted life had changed with the passing of her parents. Even her job could be overcome as she looked to find a new one.

But getting over Donovan Colton? Somehow she sensed that would be a near impossibility.

The man she'd met five years ago and had hoped to get to know better at the time had grown even more attractive and interesting. But their circumstances made it difficult to tell if there was truly something there or just the heat of close proximity in the midst of danger.

"Ms. Reeves? Are you okay?" Chief Thompson crossed to her, his concern evident. If he did have any thoughts about what she and Donovan had been doing—and she had no doubt he knew *exactly* what they'd been doing—it didn't show.

"I'm fine. Scared, but doing okay."

"Did you see who shot at you?"

"No. After we arrived home earlier, Donovan and Alex did a sweep of the house while I waited in the car. It was only after they came out with the all clear that we were shot at. Donovan took off after the shooter but he was gone."

The chief's attention shifted to Donovan. "Did you see him?"

"Nothing more than a fast-moving silhouette. I held Alex back as we didn't know what we were dealing with, although the suspect did have a man's build. Alex caught the scent and we'll follow it again in the morning and see what we turn up."

"I'll come back out to help you myself."

"We're leaving at first light."

"I do know how to wake up early, Colton."

Bellamy sensed the tension beneath byplay and knew there was something beyond the words. Donovan was embarrassed that he'd missed his quarry. On a base level, she understood that.

The chief, on the other hand, had increasingly impressed her. She'd believed him insensitive to her situation based on their first meeting, but now realized she'd misjudged his questions during the interview for something other than due diligence.

"I owe you an apology, Chief Thompson."

"Me? Why would you say that?"

"You seem upset about this situation."

"Of course I'm upset. There's a dangerous threat to my town and my people. I take that threat seriously and so does my entire department."

She nodded, her anger from that morning a distant memory. "After you questioned me. I thought you believed I was responsible. Now I see you were doing your job."

"You've come around pretty quickly."

"My father was a simple man, but he was quick to teach my sister and me that if you misread someone you owed it to them to fix the error."

Chief Thompson doffed his hat on a head nod. "Daniel-Justice was one of my favorite people in town. I was sorry when he was no longer able to manage the store and even sorrier when he passed. You have my promise I will do all I can to find who is doing this and to make sure you stay safe."

"I believe you will." Their subtle truce in place, Bellamy extended a hand. "I know it."

Feeling his firm handshake, Bellamy saw the promise in Chief Thompson's eyes matched the solemnity of his words. "Thank you, ma'am."

The chief left as fast as he'd arrived, promising to return at first light to go out with Donovan. He also assured her he'd bring along a deputy to stay with her while he and Donovan hunted for who was responsible. It was only after he'd left that Bellamy was left to face her earlier actions, the heat creeping up her neck once more.

She was alone with Donovan. Again. And while her clothing might be firmly resettled on her body, the memory of their flushed skin pressed intimately together was still fresh in her thoughts.

Too fresh, if the quivers that beat in tempo with her pulse were any indication. "You didn't need to do that. Before."

"Do what before?" Hesitation marked Donovan's tone even as his gaze shifted to the couch where they'd so recently explored each other.

"Racing off. Chasing the shooter. You could have been hurt. Or—" She broke off, the reality of what it meant for him to go off after a threat like he had. "Or worse. You could have been killed."

"I had Alex. We're a pretty good pair."

"Neither of you are a match for a crazy, determined person with a gun." She rubbed her hands over her arms, suddenly cold in a way she'd never experienced before. It pierced her skin and invaded her bones, a bleak sort of chill that made her wonder if she'd ever be warm again.

"That's why we only followed to the edge of the woods beyond your property. I know what I'm doing. And despite the threats so far, I will keep you safe. And myself in the process."

He moved closer as he spoke, each step punctuating his points, but Bellamy moved back in matched time, unwilling to give in to the nearly overpowering desire to return to his arms. She had to be strong—had to stand up and do this on her own. Donovan would catch whoever was doing this—of that she had no doubt. It was what would come after that time that worried her. Donovan would catch the perpetrator and then she'd be alone again.

The nearly desperate need for self-preservation had kicked in and she had to protect herself. When this was all over, Donovan would go back to his life and she to hers. It was time to start focusing on that.

"I, um. I should turn in."

"Of course." The small light in his gaze vanished, replaced with a subtle layer of confusion. "It's been a long day."

Bellamy grasped at the peace offering, clawing to keep her head above water and not come off like the most ungrateful bitch in the world. "Too long."

"I'm not tired yet, so I'll hang out here for a while, if that's all right?"

"Of course. Help yourself to the coffee or anything else you'd like."

"Sure. Thanks."

Then she made a run for it, the short trip to her bedroom seeming endless as she felt Donovan's gaze on her back. It was only when she closed her door and leaned back against it that Bellamy finally let the tears come.

In her entire life, she'd never needed anyone more than she needed Donovan Colton. But that way lay madness.

And a heartache she knew she'd never recover from.

DONOVAN SETTLED DOWN on the couch, Alex hopping up to curl at his side. The large blanket he kept for Alex was spread out beside him and his partner obediently stayed on it, his tail thumping lightly as he stared up at Donovan.

"Busy day, my friend."

The tail thumped a bit harder, whether it was agreement or the simple joy of sharing the day together. Donovan wasn't ever quite sure, but he appreciated the companionship all the same. He scratched Alex behind the ears, the dog's soulful brown eyes nearly rolling back into his head in ecstasy. He added a few additional belly rubs and a neck massage and in moments had a partner who snored like the dead perched beside him on the couch.

"And another one lost to Morpheus's powerful brew."

Donovan snagged his tablet from his bag and did a quick scan of his email, sending in a few updates on two of his cases in progress. His caseload was unusually light and he appreciated the extra time it gave him to watch over Bellamy, even as he struggled to find the right balance with her.

Had he scared her off? Or been too aggressive with the make-out session on the couch? Their stolen moments together had seemed mutual, but then she checked out after Archer had arrived, his tempting companion fading behind a very clear wall.

It served him right. He had no business taking advantage of her at such a vulnerable time and a bit of distance would be good for both of them. He'd allowed himself to think otherwise after spending several days in close proximity and the danger of the moment, but it was good Archer had arrived.

Wasn't it?

Well aware he didn't have the mental energy to figure it out, Donovan focused on the lingering questions that still dogged him about LSP instead. Whatever was going on, it had to be tied to Bellamy's job. The email. The car bomb placed at work. Even the way she was summarily fired without even a moment's consideration for her side of the story from Human Resources. All pointed toward something rotten at Lone Star Pharmaceutical.

Donovan pulled the same articles from earlier on Sutton Taylor, reading through the material, looking for any new insights. The man had helmed LSP for over thirty years. He held numerous patents in the field and was responsible for providing lifesaving drugs throughout the US and globally.

What would he gain from manipulating pricing on one of the most basic vaccines LSP produced?

Opening up a fresh search bar, Donovan tried a new angle. If there weren't overt answers with LSP, maybe there was something in the Sutton Taylor's personal life that would provide better insight. He tapped his way through a few searches before finally hitting pay dirt in an Austin lifestyle magazine article from about ten years before.

Donovan abstractly scratched Alex's head as he read the salient points out loud. "Married to high school sweetheart. One son, arriving later in their marriage. Provided extensive grants to the University of Texas medical school."

He kept scanning, the accolades for Taylor impressive. By all accounts the man was a veritable saint, his insistence on working for the public good a consistent mantra even as LSP accrued massive profits year over year.

Benevolence and profit. Was it really possible to maintain the two?

Donovan had a suspicious nature—he'd always believed it was what made him a good cop—and his senses were on high alert for what Taylor might be hiding. It was only as he clicked on yet another link that he remembered the blog from earlier. Toggling back to the *Everything's Blogger in Texas* post, he read through the list of gossip items that had followed Taylor throughout his professional life. Every article suggested the same thing, and all reinforced Bellamy's impressions, as well.

Sutton Taylor was a womanizer.

The blog was full of his conquests, with names, dates and, where those weren't available, a litany of insinuations. The lists also included three known illegitimate children, all claimed by Sutton Taylor as his own. Donovan read through the details, then clicked on the various links the blog provided. It was that last one that stopped him. An image of Taylor, dressed in a hunting outfit with a dog at his side.

The man's hand settled on the animal's head, his gun held against his hip with the other. The dog stared straight ahead, a faithful companion to his master. While the scene was different, it was such a clear match for his own photo for the K-9 team Donovan could only sit and stare.

Sutton's hair was longer where Donovan kept his short and cropped close to his head, but other than that the stance was the same. The jawline was the same. Even the shape of the man's hand where it cradled the dog's head was the same.

A subtle sense of awareness tightened his gut and Donovan flipped back through the other tabs he already had open, scrambling to find the blog and the list of dates. The tablet bumped against his knee as he swiped through various screens, jittery nerves jumping beneath his skin.

Was it actually possible? Could it be this obvious? Had the mystery of his birth been here in Whisperwood all along?

The blog provided confirmation and details on Taylor's three illegitimate children, all born over a ten-year period during his marriage and all provided for through legal means with a piece of his fortune. His son Jensen was the only child produced during his marriage.

Donovan vaguely remembered Jensen Taylor. The two of them didn't go to school together but Whisperwood was a small town and Taylor may have hung out with Donovan's older brother a time or two. Even with his limited memory, he did remember Jensen Taylor as one of the golden kids. Part of Whisperwood's elite, the younger Taylor had enjoyed the freedom his father's wealth provided and had run with a fast crowd. He and Donovan's brother hadn't stayed friends for long.

Was it possible the man was actually *his* brother?

It was a strange, disturbing punctuation mark to his weird thoughts about Sutton Taylor.

Had the man regretted one more illegitimate child and sought to deal with the problem by disposing of him in the Colton family barn? Even as he toyed with the idea, Donovan couldn't get any real enthusiasm behind it. Sutton Taylor was a powerful, wealthy man. He could do far better for his offspring—even the illegitimate ones—than dropping them off in a barn.

The wealthy had options, from farming unwanted children out to families or disposing of them through private adoption. Regardless of the path chosen, Taylor could have avoided ever having his name associated with an unwanted child—he didn't need to abandon a newborn infant to do it.

Nor did abandoning a baby follow pattern. The articles all reinforced the fact that Sutton Taylor had taken care of the children conceived outside his marriage.

Alex stirred next to him before lifting his head and placing it on Donovan's thigh. Warm brown eyes stared up at him, full of support and a devotion that never failed to humble him.

"Do you think it's possible?" Donovan whispered the question, testing it on his tongue and allowing it to expand and take shape in his mind's eye. Even with all the reasons against it, there was no accounting for human nature. Taylor was a wealthy married man with a reputation to protect. A family of his own he wouldn't want to expose to scorn or ridicule. Even if he hadn't cared for either of those things, thirty-plus years ago Sutton Taylor was still building his empire. It might not have set well with investors if the young owner and businessman couldn't demonstrate even the slightest bit of control to keep his baser needs in his pants.

Hays and Josephine Colton were well-respected members of the community. They had a young, growing family of their own and were well-known residents of Whisperwood. They'd easily have the financial wherewithal to take on another child, and would be local so someone could keep an eye on the baby as it grew up.

Donovan considered the scenarios, testing them out to see what might stick. It wasn't a perfect theory, but it had some weight. Maybe what he needed was a good night's sleep and a fresh perspective after sleeping on it. When he woke up, perhaps he'd have answers. Like whether or not Sutton Taylor was his real father.

The one who'd abandoned him in a barn on Christmas morning, left to be raised by strangers.

Chapter Eleven

Donovan had no more answers at dawn than he'd had when he crawled into the small double bed in Bellamy's spare room six hours before. What he did have was a raging headache after a sleepless night and more questions than answers.

If Sutton Taylor was his father, who was his mother?

And if Sutton had abandoned him, had the woman spent the ensuing years looking for him?

Alternatively, what if Sutton didn't know at all? Maybe his mother had been the one to abandon him, leaving him to his fate in the Colton barn.

"You look like hell, Colton." Archer handed off a steaming to-go cup of coffee, his gaze irritatingly bright for 6:00 a.m.

"Thanks."

"You don't even look like warmed-over hell. You actually look like that special sort of tired reserved for first-year medical residents and parents of brand-new babies."

Donovan took a long sip of hot coffee and barely winced as the brew scalded his tongue, such was his need for the caffeine. "How would you know about either of those scenarios? Last time I checked you got queasy at the sight of blood and your ugly mug hasn't had a date in a year."

"Six months, but thanks for checking." Archer took a sip of his coffee and glanced toward the woods. He'd already left one of his deputies as backup in a cruiser parked in Bellamy's driveway before reiterating his intention that he wanted to go on the search himself. "I know Alex is good and all, but you think he can catch the scent again?"

"I know he can."

Donovan dropped to a crouch, his gaze level with Alex. "You ready to go to work?"

Alex's thick tail began its fast metronome thump against the ground and Donovan couldn't help but grin up at Archer. "Alex is ready. The real question is if you can keep up."

"Lead the way."

"Let's go get 'em, Alex."

The three of them took off in the direction of the copse of trees that surrounded Bellamy's property. The area was thickly wooded, though not nearly as overgrown as it had looked in the dark. Alex navigated it with surety, trailing over leaves, twigs and the occasional downed log as he pushed them onward, farther into the trees.

Donovan took it in, the air growing quiet as the foliage grew thicker. While a big part of him would have preferred to end this all the night before, he was still sure of the decision to return to Bellamy. Barreling into the trees, heedless of a man with a gun who potentially had a better view on them than they had in return, was a suicide mission.

"You come up with a motive yet?" Archer asked.

Donovan kept tight hold on Alex's leash, his focus on the dog's small signals that confirmed a change in direction or an increase in the intensity of the scent he tracked. His partner saw the world against the dimension of smell and Donovan had learned long ago to let him work against the pictures that world made.

"Money or power's my pick."

"Money's usually a good one. They teach you that at the academy?"

Donovan ran a tired hand over the back of his head.

"First day, I think. Funny how it's a lesson that keeps repeating itself."

They tromped in silence for a few minutes, the only sounds Alex's thick sniffs and occasional whines from the back of his throat as he caught a fresh direction.

"I put in a warrant for access to LSP's tech," Archer spoke. "But I am hitting a wall so far. Between the holidays and a 'flimsy case' as Judge Carson told me, I'm not getting very far on diving into the LSP email server."

"Carson's tough."

"Yeah, but he's not wrong. I need something more than a printout of a suspicious email to go on."

"You been looking at anyone else? You and I both know Bellamy Reeves is innocent in all this." It was on the tip of Donovan's tongue to ask about Jensen Taylor but something held him back. His questions from the previous evening and his hunt for information on Sutton Taylor had left him exposed and raw, and Donovan wasn't quite ready to poke around that one.

Especially not with someone as astute as Archer Thompson.

"I've got notes to call Human Resources today. Something about Bellamy's description of her time with the director kept ringing my bell. It feels funny, you know? Who gets fired on the spot for bringing something to HR's attention?"

"A guilty someone?" Donovan asked.

"Guilty on which side is my concern."

Archer's comment pulled Donovan up short and he tugged lightly on Alex's leash to pull him to a stop. "You think HR's got something?"

"I think it's awfully strange that Bellamy goes to HR to make a formal complaint and is not only fired but walks out to an explosive device in her car. I'm not much into coincidences, nor do I like situations where our victim appears to be bullied."

"So why'd you give her a hard time in your office?"

"To make sure she is a victim and not the puppet master behind the scenes."

Donovan chewed on that idea, the opportunity to bounce things off the chief a welcome distraction from his own thoughts. "I'm not a big conspiracy buff but the puppet master angle has legs."

"Don't you mean strings?"

Donovan only shook his head and wouldn't have been surprised to hear Alex groan at that one. "They clearly didn't make you chief on your rockin' sense of humor. But they did make you chief on your nose for bad guys. Who's in a position to pull those strings?"

"Offhand? I'd say bigwigs at LSP. Maybe a few enterprising drug distributors who have some of the biggest accounts in hand and already locked up. Maybe even a disgruntled employee who manages the supply chain high up."

"I've looked but haven't found anything to suggest LSP is in dire financial straits."

"Me, either." Archer crushed his coffee cup in his hand before shoving it into his back pocket. "Wall Street's happy with their quarterly and annual performances and their stock remains strong. Something like this puts that performance at risk instead of enhancing it."

"Not including the profit they might make in the meantime."

Archer shrugged. "Still seems awfully shortsighted. Why ruin the company reputation and long-term health for the sake of a few bucks in the short term? Especially if you're profitable to begin with."

"Back to our original motive?" Donovan asked. "Money."

"Short-term money versus long-term success, aka money. Still seems shortsighted to me."

Shortsighted, illegal and overconfident. Each description fit and suggested a person who had little self-control and more than their fair share of arrogance.

Which only brought Donovan right back to Sutton Taylor. The man had proven himself out of control and arrogant when it came to his personal choices, but in his business, he'd seemingly exercised control and long-term vision.

So why ruin that now?

Sutton ran his hands over the thin hospital blanket, his fingers tracing the weave over and over. He'd begun counting the interlocking squares, desperate to stay awake and focused. It was so hard to concentrate and he *needed* to concentrate.

Needed to stay alert.

More, he needed to figure out what was wrong.

He'd have windows of time when he understood something was the matter and then would fall back to sleep, groggy and unfocused, his body exhausted from the mere effort of thinking. But it had to stop.

Twelve. Thirteen. Fourteen.

He couldn't afford to sleep anymore. Like last night. What was he thinking about? And what had filled his dreams with oversize cars that floated in the air before exploding, their parts shattering like a firework?

Twenty. Twenty-one. Twenty-two.

Jensen. Wasn't he worried about his son? Sutton tried to focus on that as he kept counting, forcing himself to stay awake with the repetition.

Where was Jensen?

Forty-four. Forty-five. Forty-six.

Jensen was watching over LSP. But why was Jensen in charge? He hadn't shown a great aptitude for the business. In fact, some of his ideas were flat out wrong.

We need to focus on managing our production. Too much product floods the market, Dad. Scarcity is our friend.

We produce the drugs people need to get well. Why would I throttle production? We need to find opportunities to expand. To push past our production limits to get more into supply. To help more people.

Profit. Jensen had slapped him on the back with a barely concealed eye roll. *Profit is why.*

When had they discussed that? A few days ago? Or was it months?

Sutton stopped counting squares, his hands going still on the blanket. It *had* been months. Back in the spring when they were finalizing the formulary and the orders on the flu vaccine.

And now their suppliers didn't have enough vaccine?

Their suppliers. The emails. He'd read the emails last night.

Sutton reached for his phone where it lay on the rolling tray that sat beside the bed. He lifted the device, his hand shaking as he tried to turn it on. Damned phone, what was wrong? His hand shook as he stabbed at the small button at the base, only to see the phone screen black and lifeless.

Out of charge.

His hand shook harder as he tossed the phone back onto the tray. A loud beep started from the machine behind his head as his entire body began to shake. The dim lights in the room quavered, shimmering in and out of focus as several nurses came running through the door.

BELLAMY AVOIDED ONE more look out the front window, well aware of what she'd find. The deputy's car would still be in her driveway, the man perched behind the wheel with his gaze on the road. She was impressed by his diligence, even as she questioned how horribly bored he must be just sitting there.

For her.

Once again, that thought struck her. It had hit hard when she realized how focused Donovan was on keeping her safe and protected, but it extended to the broader Whisperwood police force. So many people trying to keep her safe from a killer.

Would they succeed?

Was it even possible to succeed against someone so determined?

Sick of pacing and worrying, she crossed her arms and tapped her fingers on her biceps. What else could she do? She'd already cleaned up the kitchen and freshened Alex's water and food for when he and Donovan returned. The beds were made and the living room had been straightened up. She'd even toyed with mopping the kitchen floor, which meant her boredom had reached unprecedented heights.

Still, her thoughts flipped and tumbled, one over the other and back again.

Who was behind all of this? And why had they targeted *her*?

When she stopped asking that question through the lens of the victimized—*Why me?*—she'd begun to ask different questions. It was less a question of why was this happening to her and, instead, why had she been targeted.

Did she know something? Or had she been inadvertently exposed to some sort of information that had made her an easy target?

Her laptop was closed and still sitting on the edge of the kitchen counter. She'd nearly glanced past it, her eyes roaming over the floor once more as she considered pulling out the mop when she refocused on the laptop.

Was it possible?

Reaching for it, she opened the lid and waited for the computer to come out of sleep mode. In moments, she had a browser window open and tapped in the familiar remote address that would put her into the cloud.

And access into her email.

Butterflies dive-bombed her stomach as she walked through each step. Technically she was no longer an em-

ployee. Which meant she had no right to log into the system
and even less right to hunt through her email.

Which made it all the more imperative that she take what
she could while she could.

Her latest password—HOLIDAYSSUCK, all one word—
spilled easily from her fingers. She hit the return key,
shocked and extraordinarily pleased when her email filled
the screen.

She was in!

In HR's rush to fire her, they'd forgotten to go through
the proper protocols to turn off her email and remote access. All standard when an employee was terminated.

Yet they'd forgotten to dismantle her accounts.

Well aware diving into her email didn't put her in a good
light, Bellamy shrugged it off as the least of her problems.
She sorted through the unread emails that had come in
over the past few days. She passed notes about the holiday
schedule, the latest financial reports for the prior week
and even a note about using up benefits before the end of
the year, scrolling toward the email that had started it all.

Staring at it with fresh eyes, she noticed there wasn't a
named sender in the chronological listing of email. Instead,
all she read was the word INTERNAL. Which was odd. She'd
been at LSP long enough that she knew the form their email
addresses took. There was no sender called INTERNAL.

Of course, no one sent anonymous email detailing corporate greed and illegal behavior, either.

Yet someone had sent this one.

She opened the email again, quickly sending a copy to
her personal address before looking once more at the details she'd not paid enough attention to upon first viewing.
She was no tech whiz, but she'd used enough software programs throughout her career that she figured the naviga-
tion bar at the top was the place to start.

The information command didn't provide any detail beyond the date and time sent. Ticking through the other op-

tions, she tried to open the actual sender's email address, only to find a string of gibberish that read like a garbled line of code.

Was there something in that? Something an expert could track back and use?

The peal of her cell phone pulled her from the screen and Bellamy practically dived for the device, desperately hoping it was Donovan telling her he was on his way back. Instead, her friend Rae's name flashed on the screen. They'd texted recently but hadn't spoken. Bellamy regretted her hasty info dump of what had happened the other day and wanted to minimize Rae's involvement in what was going on.

But ignoring her friend wasn't fair, either.

"Hey."

"You're lucky this week's one of the busiest at the store or I'd be camped out on your front lawn as we speak."

"Good morning to you, too."

"Your sister was in here last night. Told me that your car blew up."

"It didn't—"

Before she could protest, Rae pressed on. "Bell. The bomb squad was called and you've got protection detail at your house. What am I missing here?"

"I didn't want to worry you." *Or risk involving you in something that grows more dangerous by the hour.*

"I'm your friend. Of course I'm worried about you. And Maggie is beside herself."

"Maggie already read me the riot act."

"Good for her."

A small gasp caught in Bellamy's throat. "Don't tell me you're on her side."

"In this I am. I don't care what's in the past or how far apart you two have been. She's your sister and she's worried. Rightfully so."

Bellamy toyed with the track pad on her computer, the cursor circling the screen in time to the sweep of her finger.

Rae had always been her rock, her supportive champion who was always on her side. To hear her defend Maggie was a major departure from her usual stalwart defense.

"Does the silence mean you're mad at me?"

"Of course not."

And she wasn't. But it did sting to hear her friend so easily defend her sister. She and Maggie had been on opposite sides for so long, it was startling to realize the sands beneath her feet might have shifted.

Did Maggie actually care about her?

She'd believed it once. The baby sister whom she loved and adored could do no wrong and Bellamy had believed their sibling bond would keep them close forever. Then her father had gotten ill and Maggie had grown more and more distant. It was easier to blame her or think poorly of her instead of trying to see her side of things.

And that was on her, Bellamy acknowledged. She had a right to her opinion and an even bigger right to disagree, but her unwillingness to hear Maggie's side sat squarely with her.

"So what's going on?" Rae's question pulled her back from her thoughts, and Bellamy pictured her friend up to her elbows in holiday inventory as she worked to get the general store open for the day.

"I wish I knew, Rae. Really, I wish I did. Things have gotten weird and scary."

"Is Donovan Colton with you?"

"You know about that?" Why did that bother her so much? Donovan wasn't her personal property and it wasn't exactly a secret he was helping her. Even with the pep talk and the silent acknowledgment not to get flustered about it, Bellamy couldn't quite hide her frustration. "Let me guess, Maggie told you."

"I didn't need Maggie to tell me. Marie in HR at LSP was in here yesterday. You were all she could talk about. You and the hot guy helping you."

Bellamy caught on the name, cycling through the people she knew at LSP. Marie was the woman who'd brought her files into Sally's office the day she went to HR.

"You know Marie? Do you know anything about her?"

"No more or less than I know about most people. She and her husband settled in Whisperwood about three years ago."

"And she told you what happened?"

"Quite happily. Told me some stuff had gone down at LSP and that HR took an employee to task. Unfairly, too." Rae's smile traveled through the phone. "I put two and two together that it was you. And when she started telling me about the hot cop seen around town with his dog, I took my two and two and multiplied them even further. Donovan Colton doesn't make it to Whisperwood all that often. The fact that he's stuck around is a testament to you."

"Why me?"

"There's no love lost between him and his family. Most of his trips through town are quick and functional at best. But from the gossip swirling around town, you've given him a new reason to stay."

"That's just silly. He was the one who got the dispatch call on my car and he's been helping me out. Nothing more."

"Are you sure?"

"Of course I'm sure."

"Then why do I hear that funny note in your voice?"

Bellamy flushed any sense of surprise or outrage from her tone, focused on keeping things as nonchalant as possible. "I don't have any funny notes."

"Yes, you do. You're sort of squeaky at the edges, like that time in freshman year you asked Bill Monroe to the Sadie Hawkins dance."

"I do not."

"I heard it again. You squeaked at the end of your protest. Which means you've got something juicy and interesting to share."

It was on the edge of her lips to protest before Bellamy

pulled it back. Rae knew her well and would only take joy in continuing to push her buttons. So she switched gears and focused on why she hadn't called in the first place.

"Please promise me you'll be careful. Keep your ears open but don't ask any questions and don't give anyone the idea you and I have spoken."

The laughter that had characterized Rae's voice up to then vanished. "What's going on, Bellamy?"

"Promise me. Please. You need to be careful and you don't need to let on to anyone that we've communicated. Not until this is all taken care of."

"Taken care of? Who's taking care of it?"

"Please, Rae."

"Okay. I promise."

"Thanks. Now go do what you need to do and I'll call you in a few days."

"If you're sure?"

"Positive."

They said a few goodbyes and then hung up. As her phone switched off, Bellamy couldn't hide her concerns. The person who'd targeted her had made it clear they knew what she drove and where she lived. It would stand to reason they'd know who she was friends with, as well. And who her sister was.

Fear struck low in her gut, raw and icy cold. Not seeing eye to eye didn't mean she didn't love her sister. But could she get to Maggie in time? Reaching for her phone once more, she dialed Maggie's number and counted off the rings.

And wondered what it meant when her sister didn't pick up.

DONOVAN TOSSED HIS gear in the back of his SUV, frustrated with the wasted morning. They'd been out for over three hours and, other than going around in circles, Alex hadn't found anything useful. Or more to the point, their quarry had covered his tracks.

Even with a disappointing trek, Alex always got his treat when he was done. Donovan hunted for the container of bones he kept packed in the back of the car and pulled one out for his partner.

"I'm going in to work on the tech angle." Archer looked as frustrated as Donovan felt, and once again, he was struck by the man's commitment to the community of Whisperwood. "I still don't believe we haven't found a thing."

"Me, either." Archer waved his deputy on before crossing Bellamy's driveway to meet him.

"Wait." Donovan patted his gear, suddenly remembering the button he'd found in the sweep of Bellamy's car and tagged in an evidence bag. "I pulled this when I swept her car and tagged it."

"A button?"

"Off a man's shirt. A fancy one, I think."

Archer turned the bag over in his hands, tracing the thin disc. "I don't have the resources to hunt this down but it is another notch in Bellamy's favor. Where'd you find it?"

"Buried beneath the seat. I would have ignored it except for the fact that she was genuinely surprised to see it. Claimed that it didn't match anything she owned."

"You mentioned earlier this felt like an amateur job." The chief eyed the button once more. "Here's one more example that reinforces the point. No one even halfway decent at their job would risk losing something like this."

"It's clumsy. Lazy, too." Donovan nearly mentioned his suspicions about Sutton Taylor but held his tongue at the last minute. He had suspicions and nothing more. You didn't go around accusing men of Sutton Taylor's stature and standing in the community on a hunch.

Nor did you go around suggesting he was your missing father.

So Donovan waved Archer off instead, mulling over all

he'd discovered. And while he considered all of it, he had a woman waiting for him.

One who might have the answers to his questions. And one who might help him figure out the mystery of his father. Donovan finished stowing his things when the sound of tires on pavement had him turning to see Maggie Corgan pulling up.

The woman was out of the car and around the hood, her perfect blond hair waving around her face in the morning breeze. "First it's a bomb and then it's gunshots? What is going on, Officer Colton? Who's after my sister?"

Donovan was struck once again by the sincerity in Maggie's eyes. The relationship between her and Bellamy might be strained, but he didn't think it was because Maggie didn't want one with her sister. "I'm working to find that out, ma'am."

"Why has she been targeted? None of this makes sense. She's the kindest, gentlest person. She's a hard worker and she's always loved working for LSP. I hate that she lives out here all by herself, but I know it's what she wanted. It's why—" Maggie broke off, her eyes widening.

"It's why what?"

"Nothing." Maggie waved an airy hand, the motion dismissive. "Nothing at all."

"Ms. Corgan." Donovan moved closer, curious to see a look of utter defeat in the woman's eyes. "Do you know something?"

Maggie shook her head, her gaze dropping to the sidewalk. "About what's happening to her? No."

"Then what are you talking about?"

"I tried the only way I knew how."

She broke off again, her slim form agitated as she twisted her hands and shifted from one high heel boot to another. "Tried what, Maggie?"

"I tried to marry the right person to have money for my father's treatments. It was the only way I knew how, and I

thought James and I would be a good fit. He wanted a tro-
phy wife and I never minded being a trophy all that much."
She sighed, brushing her hair back. "I'm butchering this.
Why don't I try again?"

Donovan waited as she gathered herself, suddenly curious to see the parallels between Bellamy and her sister. While he wanted to hear the entire story, he'd already
sensed where Maggie was going. It was humbling to see
what had changed that lone night he went off to an accident scene and all that had played out since. Two sisters,
each driven to help their family.

Each stymied by pride.

There's a lesson in there, Colton.

The thought struck hard, an uncomfortable parallel to
his own family relationships that he wasn't quite ready to
explore.

"Things didn't work out the way I planned and James
wasn't all that free with the checkbook. He gave me a bit
as an allowance that I could funnel to my family after I
bought the requisite clothing and shoes and my mother-
in-law took pity and helped a bit once she knew what was
going on. It wasn't enough, but it was something. And it
gave me enough to get this house for Bellamy. Before it
all—" Maggie hesitated again, her gaze roaming toward
the house. "Bellamy thinks my parents left this to her, but
they didn't. There wasn't any money from their estate left
to leave her and I didn't want to take this from her. I know
how important this house is to her. How important these
memories are. So I worked with the lawyers to make it so."

"Why can't you tell her?"

"Because I can't. And you can't, either. Bellamy isn't
interested in what I have to say and I'm not going to grovel
for my sister's affection."

If Donovan thought the knowledge would put Bellamy
at risk, there was nothing that would keep him silent, but

he could hardly fault family relationships or go against them. "I won't."

"Thank you."

"But I do think you should tell her. There's love there. Between the two of you. It'd be a shame to miss an opportunity to build a relationship as adults."

Maggie's eyes narrowed, her mouth firming into a straight line. "I know your sister. She and I both worked on a Junior League project a few years back."

"Oh?"

"She mentioned her family on several occasions while we worked on that project. I know how important her family is to her and how much she'd like adult relationships with her siblings. I got the sense that she had that with all but one of them."

"I don't—"

"Things aren't always as simple." She laid a hand on his arm. "Even when they should be."

Bellamy chose that moment to come outside, her eyes shielded against the morning sun. Maggie waved at her, her smile bright. "Just catching up with Officer Colton. He's got things well in hand."

She moved back around to her car and climbed in, starting the car and pulling out before Bellamy had even crossed the yard.

"What was that about? Why did she leave?"

"I think she came to visit me. To make sure I'm handling your case well."

"Was she satisfied with what she found out?" Bellamy's gaze remained on the departing car as it sped down the street.

"I have no idea."

Donovan walked Bellamy back to the house, Maggie Corgan's parting words still heavy in his heart.

Things *weren't* always simple.

Even when they should be.

Chapter Twelve

Bellamy left several messages for Maggie over the next few days but hadn't managed to reach her sister. They exchanged a couple of texts every day and she tried to probe what Maggie's holiday plans were, even going so far as to invite her for Christmas dinner, but got a vague excuse about being busy.

Which stung.

She'd tried, hadn't she? Extended the olive branch and attempted to repair things and got a big fat slap in the face for her efforts.

It was one more layer of frustration overtop of the rest of her life. Donovan and Alex had been in her home for nearly a week and they were no closer to finding the person behind the attacks on her than they'd been since man and dog moved in.

Other than the pervasive sense of being watched, nothing else had happened to justify Donovan and Alex's ongoing presence in her home.

And the lack of information or movement on her case had everyone on edge.

She, Donovan and Alex made daily trips into Austin, spending time at the K-9 center and getting some distance from Whisperwood, but each night they'd return, no further on her case than when they'd started. It was maddening.

Even more frustrating was the fact that each night they

went through this weird, awkward good-night that sent her to her room alone while Donovan and Alex headed for her spare room.

Maddening.

Bellamy snapped the lid of her laptop closed. She'd just paid off her last remaining December bill and was angry by the ever-dwindling number in her bank account. She couldn't be without a job forever, nor could she stand sitting around much longer.

But for the moment she was in a holding pattern.

Her LSP email still worked and she and Donovan had explored all they could find from a distance, but the system was fairly locked down in terms of using it as a mechanism into the inner workings of LSP.

Donovan had sent her email to one of their digital forensics experts to work through the signatures that sat behind the data but the woman had found precious little to go on, and without a warrant for LSP's data they didn't get very far. Which only added to the soup of frustration that was her life.

"It's Christmas Eve. Would you like to go look at lights again? I hear they've got a big holiday festival south of Austin as you head toward San Antonio." Donovan padded into the kitchen, his feet bare beneath jeans that hugged his backside and a black T-shirt that made her mouth water. The man had limited tastes and he'd already washed and recycled several T-shirts that hugged his chest, but the jeans were a mainstay.

Which also only added to her general sense of irritability.

The man was mouthwateringly attractive and he hadn't laid a hand on her since their interrupted make-out session on her couch. Where she'd first thought that was a good thing, as each day went by she'd grown less and less convinced.

"I know it's Christmas Eve. And attempting to cheer me up with shiny lights isn't the answer."

"Okay." Donovan shrugged and poured himself a fresh cup of coffee.

"And you can get rid of the attitude while you're at it. I know it's boring as a tomb around here. Why don't you go back to your family or just go home? It's silly for you to sit here day after day. No one's going to attack me for Christmas."

She'd rehearsed the speech in her head, desperate for her life to return to some sense of normalcy, but had to admit to herself that it didn't come out quite as she'd planned. In her mind, it was competent and confident, setting the tone for how they'd move forward. In reality, it had come out edgy and whiny, with a side of bitchy that didn't speak well of her, especially when she'd stood up and fumbled the chair behind her.

No, it didn't speak well of her at all.

"You want me to leave?" Donovan asked.

"Do you really want to stay?"

"I want you to be safe."

"Since the incidents stopped, it's hard to feel like I'm in danger."

"You didn't answer my question." He left his mug on the counter and moved closer, his hands firmly at his side even as he moved up into her space. "Do you want me to leave, Bellamy?"

"I don't—" The words stuck in her throat when his hand lifted to her stomach, the tip of his finger tracing the skin there. The touch was light but it carried the impact of an atom bomb, fanning the flames of attraction that she'd tried desperately to quell over the past week.

Whatever had happened on the couch was a moment in time. A crazy moment of abandon that didn't need to be repeated.

Hadn't she told herself that over and over this past week? More than that, hadn't she seen firsthand how hard Donovan worked and how committed he was to her and to his case-load? He stayed with her, uprooting his own life while still digging into her case. Even with all that, he remained focused on his other responsibilities, as well. Their daily drives to the K-9 center had shown his dedication to Alex and keeping him fit and well trained. Even the things he'd shared with her over coffee each evening had pulled them closer.

He'd opened up about his family a bit more, usually in the guise of probing her about Maggie, but it was sharing all the same. And a few nights before he'd blown her mind when he shared his theories about Sutton Taylor. His comments hadn't moved far from her thoughts, the image of the man she knew as leader of LSP as Donovan's biological father. She struggled to put the two together, yet as she listened to his points, had to admit his theory had merit.

The fact they couldn't find Sutton Taylor to speak to the man directly had only added to the questions around LSP's leader. The chief's inquiries to Lone Star Pharmaceutical had gone unanswered, Sally Borne's dismissal of requests growing increasingly uncooperative.

Where was the man? Holidays or not, CEOs never went so far away as to be unreachable. Yet the man seemed to be off the grid and every outreach made to local hospitals— even the exclusive ones—hadn't turned up any leads.

All the questions and conversation had brought them closer, yet until this very moment, Donovan hadn't so much as touched her. Nor had his dark gaze turned heated, not once. And neither had he attempted to kiss her again.

So what were they doing here?

Yes, she was under his protection, but she'd never heard of anyone getting a personalized police protector who moved in. He'd gone above and beyond and it was getting more and more difficult to understand why.

"What are you doing?"

A small smile tilted his lips as he continued pressing his finger slightly against her stomach. "Nothing."

"Are you bored?"

"You seem to be."

"Are you?"

"Whatever I am, Bellamy, I can assure you it isn't bored."

She lifted his gaze from the mesmerizing play of his finger. "Then what are you?"

"Truth?"

"Of course."

"I want you and I'm not sure I can do the right thing by you any longer."

"You're—"

The right thing? Had he been purposely keeping his distance?

He waited while she worked through the details, punctuating his point when she gazed up at him once again. "You're under my protection. You're my responsibility. It would hardly do to act on our attraction."

"Why not?"

"Because it's unprofessional. And a conflict. And—"

She moved into his body, wrapping her arms around his neck to pull him close. All the confusion and anger and frustration of the past week faded as he opened his arms and pulled her close. "And completely wonderful, Donovan Colton."

"It's nearly killed me this past week. Everywhere I look, there you are." He framed her face with his hands before shifting to push several strands of hair behind her ear. "I want you. And I want to see where this goes. But I know it's a bad time."

"Maybe it's the perfect time."

And as his lips met hers, Bellamy knew she'd never spoken truer words.

It was the perfect time.

DONOVAN PULLED BELLAMY close for a kiss, the motion achingly beautiful. Hadn't he dreamed of doing this for the past week? Every time he looked at her, he imagined her in his arms. He saw himself peeling off her clothing, piece by piece, until there was nothing between them. And then, once they were both naked, satisfying this hunger that had gripped him and refused to let go.

She'd been so brave. He saw the toll the sitting and waiting had taken, yet she'd remained hopeful. Focused on the future and their ability to find whoever was behind the attacks on her. It had only been today, after she'd finished up on the computer, that he'd finally seen the cracks.

And he had more than a few cracks of his own.

He wanted her. He knew there were consequences to taking this leap but heaven help him, he couldn't walk away.

"Donovan?"

"Hmm?" He kissed her again.

"Stop thinking and take me to bed."

He lifted his head then and stared down at her, a seductive smile lighting her up from the inside. "You're sure?"

"I've never been more sure. I want you. And I want to make love with you. Let's take what's between us and not worry about anything else."

Had he ever met anyone so generous? Or wanted a woman more?

All the questions that had swirled around his life for the past week—heck, for the past thirty-one years—seemed to fade in the face of her. She was warm and generous and she took him as he was. That was a gift beyond measure and he swore to himself he wouldn't squander it.

Her home was small and he was grateful for that when

they arrived at her bedroom a short while later. They'd stripped each other along the way, a path of shirts and pants and a sexy bra forming a trail from the kitchen to the bedroom. And after he laid her down on the bed, her arms extending to pull him close, he sank into her, reveling in the play of skin against skin, the full press of her breasts against his chest a delicious torment.

Slipping a hand between them, he found the waistband of her panties, the last piece of clothing to come off. The warm heat of her covered his hand and he played with her sensitive flesh, gratified by the sexy moans that spilled from her throat and the gentle writhing of her legs where they pressed to his hips. She was amazing. Warm. Responsive. And as in the moment as he was.

Long, glorious moments spun out between them as the dying afternoon light spilled into the room. They had all they needed there, just the two of them, as their touches grew more urgent. As fewer words were exchanged. As soft sighs expanded, growing longer before cresting on a gentle breath.

They didn't need anything else, Donovan realized as he jumped up on a rush and raced for his discarded jeans. Her light giggle had followed him out of the room as he ran for protection and her smile was pure and golden when she opened her arms for him and welcomed him back to the bed.

Welcome.

The thought struck hard as he rejoined her, making quick work of the condom before fitting himself to her body.

She was the warmest, softest welcome and it nearly killed him to go slow and take his time. To make the moments last between the two of them, as powerful as a tornado, as delicate as spun sugar.

The demands of her body pulled against him as he moved inside of her, her delicate inner walls indicating her release was nearly upon her. He added a firm touch to pull her along, gratified when she crested mere moments before he followed her.

Pure pleasure suffused his body as he wrapped himself up in her. And as he rode out wave after wave, he knew nothing in his life would ever be the same.

Bellamy had changed him.

And he had no desire to go back to the way he'd been.

JENSEN FITTED THE small hunting cabin at the edge of the LSP property with a strip of explosive. He fashioned the claylike material around the needed wires and then worked backward toward the detonation device.

His father had kept this place, private land adjacent to LSP, as a small getaway right in the heart of the Hill Country. How apropos that a place used to destroy God's creatures had become a human hunting ground, as well.

He'd waited for this, carefully mapping out how he'd secure Bellamy Reeves's arrival at the cabin. In the end, he had no idea it would be so easy as snatching her sister as an incentive to come without a fuss.

Maggie Corgan was hot, but damn, the woman was a sad sack. She'd been moping around Whisperwood like a bored prom queen and it had been easy enough to grab her and bring her here. He'd made a point to run into her in town and made a fuss about some details they'd found at LSP on Bellamy's car. Despite the holiday, the woman had practically jumped into his passenger seat, anxious to find the details that would exonerate her sister.

The chloroformed cloth had knocked her out just after they passed the gated entrance to LSP property and she'd been asleep ever since.

"Do you know what you're doing?" Sally's voice echoed from the small front room slash kitchen, her tone growing increasingly naggy and whiny as they got closer to finishing this. He'd seriously misjudged her. He thought he had a partner in his efforts to secure his future—and he was paying her off well enough for that partnership—but she'd gotten increasingly worried over the past few days. She wouldn't stop asking him if he knew how to handle things and she was convinced his old man was going to make a magical recovery from his blood poisoning.

What good was it to own a pharmaceutical company if you couldn't co-op a few of the products for your own use? The chloroform fell into that category. So did the experimental drug he'd used on his father. That had been the easy part.

Setting up Bellamy Reeves to take the fall while he initiated his "brother" Donovan into the family? Now that took real planning.

"It's fine, Sally. I've got it all under control."

"You said that a week ago and since then I've fielded daily calls from the police nosing around. You're lucky I know my rights. They can't get in without a search warrant and so far they can't get one."

"Good."

"So far, Jensen. It's only a matter of time if I keep blocking."

"The problem will be gone by then and you'll be long gone. Calm down."

She gave him a side-eye but marched back into the front room. He was glad to see her go. The nagging was driving him crazy. They said men looked for women like their mothers, and in that respect he had to agree. His mother might have been a passive soul, but she knew her place and didn't harp and harangue every chance she got.

No, Jensen thought with no small measure of glee. *His* mother had taken notes. Detailed notes she'd left behind for him to find and pore over. She'd not mentioned Donovan Colton by name but it had been easy enough to note the

Christmas date and the reference to Sutton's latest "bastard left in the stables across town like a discarded piece of trash."

He'd read that passage more than once, pleased to know his father was oblivious to the brat's existence. It would make it that much easier to ensure Donovan Colton never got a piece of the Taylor inheritance.

Jensen snipped an extra length of wire and tested the hold. It was only a matter of time until Bellamy Reeves showed up, her knight in shining armor in tow.

And then Donovan Colton would understand, once and for all, what a discarded piece of trash he really was.

DONOVAN LEVERED HIS hands behind his head and watched as Bellamy flitted around the room. She was full of nervous energy post-sex that he found incredibly adorable and he was enjoying just watching her. Especially since he felt like every muscle in his body had just had the best, most effective workout. It was a treat to lay back and watch her beautiful frame and whip-quick energy light up the room.

"Maybe I should have gotten a tree? I know I didn't want one, but it'd have been nice to have the color. And the smell. I love that fresh tree smell."

"We can still get one if you'd like one."

She stopped midpace, a hand going to her hip. "You wouldn't mind doing that?"

"Not at all. Let's do it."

She glanced own, her eyes widening. "But we're naked."

"So we'll get dressed and then get naked later."

"Later?"

He smiled at the slight squeak in her voice. "I'd like that, if you would."

Bellamy crossed to the bed, her nervous energy fading as a soft smile spread across her face. "I'd like that, too.

Even as crazy and scary as this time has been, I wouldn't change it."

"Me, either." Donovan reached for her and pulled her close, nestling her against his chest. "Not one single second."

She pressed her lips against his skin before lifting her head. "I'm glad you're here."

"Me, too." He tickled her before rolling her over on her back. "Let's go buy a tree."

"Now?"

"Maybe in an hour."

And then he proceeded to show her just what he could do with an hour.

BELLAMY PRACTICALLY DANCED through the kitchen, gathering up her purse and her phone where they still lay on the counter. She couldn't believe what a difference an afternoon could make in her spirits and her attitude. She'd spent the morning morose and frustrated and had spent the afternoon in Donovan's arms.

And what an amazing afternoon it had been.

Catching herself before a sigh escaped her lips and already imagining the cartoon hearts that were floating above her head, she took her phone firmly in hand and hit the home screen out of habit. A text from her sister showed up, followed by a phone number she didn't recognize, along with a voice mail prompt.

She'd been waiting for insurance to call her back about her car and had to catch herself a good ten seconds into the voice mail before she realized the message wasn't from her insurance company at all.

A muffled voice, disguised with some sort of filter, echoed against her ear. "Come to the LSP grounds alone if you want to bring your sister home."

She fumbled the phone and listened to the message once more, a desperate sense of urgency forcing her into action, as the message also outlined an appointed time and meeting place. She had to leave. She had to get to Maggie.

Why hadn't she tried harder to talk to her this week? Instead of being persistent and trying to win her sister back, all she'd done was curl into her usual shell and get angry. It was always someone else's fault. She was never the one to blame.

And where had it gotten her?

With Maggie's life in danger, all because of her.

Donovan's voice rumbled from the hallway, where he talked to Alex, and Bellamy quickly cataloged what to do. Tell him where she was going and put Maggie's life at risk? Or take his car and go alone?

This was about her. For reasons she still didn't understand, she'd been targeted by someone inside LSP and all that had ensued was directed at her.

She needed to be the one to fix it.

Her hand closed over Donovan's keys, where they lay on the counter near her purse. She had them in hand, their heft and weight firm in her palm. She would do this. She'd face this nameless threat and handle it. She had to.

The door beckoned but Bellamy stilled, her resolve wavering.

She *could* do this. She could do anything she set her mind to.

But she could also use the help. Qualified help from an expert trained in crisis and criminal behavior.

"Donovan!" He and Alex came running the moment she screamed.

And as man and dog rounded the corner into her kitchen, Bellamy took solace that she'd not have to act alone.

THE NERVOUS ENERGY that had carried her from the house to the drive to the far end of LSP's property faded as Bellamy caught sight of Sally Borne in the distance. "She's behind all this?"

Bellamy supposed it wasn't all that big a revelation, yet somehow she hadn't seen Sally at the heart of everything. A lackey, maybe, taking orders from the inside, but not as a mastermind behind what had happened to her or the decision to throttle drug production.

The disguised tones on her voice mail hadn't suggested a woman, either, yet Bellamy couldn't argue with the tall, feminine form traipsing and tromping around outside the small hideaway bordering the edge of the LSP property. It was a hunting cabin, as she recalled. Something Sutton Taylor had used for years as a place to let off steam on the weekends.

"She looks mad," Donovan whispered in her ear as he lowered night vision goggles. "A plan unraveling?"

"Or a crazy person at the end of her rope."

"That, too." Donovan took her hand in his and squeezed. "We'll take her down and we'll get Maggie back."

"You seem awfully sure about this."

"It's my job to be sure. It's also my job to pin criminals in their dens so we can haul them in."

His certainty helped, as did the knowledge that he had been through something like this before. All she could think of was that Maggie was inside the cabin, but Donovan had a broader purview. He knew how to manage an op and he also knew how to take down a criminal.

And he also had backup setting themselves up in the distance. The two of them hadn't walked into this alone, despite the clear warning on the voice mail to do so.

She'd trusted Donovan to do the right thing, but knew it wasn't going to be easy. They'd gotten in but they still needed to get out.

"I don't believe it's Sally. She was unpleasant and dismissed me from the company without giving me the opportunity to defend myself, but I didn't take her for a kidnapper and a killer."

"Maybe she got in over her head," Donovan suggested.

"Or maybe you did." The voice was low and quiet in the winter night, but the click of a cocked gun was unmistakable.

How HAD HE allowed himself to get so distracted?

That thought pounded through Donovan's mind as he covered the remaining ground from the LSP property to the cabin in the woods. He was responsible for keeping Bellamy safe and there was no way he could do that with a loaded gun at his back.

He hadn't seen his assailant's face, but had to give Bellamy points for gut instinct. She couldn't believe Sally Borne was responsible for what had unfolded, and she wasn't. Sally was in this up to her eyeballs, but she wasn't the mastermind.

Donovan toyed with turning on his assailant, but the proximity made it nearly impossible to get an upper hand. If he was by himself, he'd make the move and worry about any possible consequences in the fight, but with Bellamy by his side, it put her at too much risk. Which only reinforced why she belonged home in the first place.

He'd done his best to convince her to stay behind, but nothing had swayed her.

Including the promise that he'd bring Maggie home.

So he'd listened and believed they could keep her safe anyway, buying into her BS that LSP would only negotiate with her. He'd trusted that Archer and his backup fanning the perimeter would be enough and that he could keep her safe, no matter what.

Now he wasn't so sure.

"Come in, come in." The gun pressed to his back as the

jerk marching behind them pushed them inside the front door of the cabin. "We're going to have a family reunion."

Bellamy had stiffened each time the man behind them spoke, but it was only once they were inside the door that she whirled on him. "Jensen Taylor. You're behind all of this?"

Jensen?

Donovan's mind raced over his memories of Jensen Taylor. The paunchy man before him was a genuine surprise and he realized that any of the articles he'd read on the father had limited information about the son.

And old pictures.

Taylor had been a popular, good-looking guy, more than able to get his fair share of dates. But the man that stared back at them had changed. The degree of crazy in his eyes was concerning, but it was something more. He was in his midthirties, but he was already soft, his body doughy and neglected. If it weren't for the gun and Bellamy's close presence, Donovan would have immediately taken his chance at overpowering the man.

"Who were you expecting?" Jensen sneered.

Bellamy shook her head. "I'm not sure but certainly not the heir to the company."

"That's exactly why I'm involved," Jensen said. "I need to make sure I stay that way."

"Stay what way? You're Sutton's son. You already sit in on board meetings and you've got a big position inside LSP."

"It's not big enough. Nor is running distribution a sign that I'm being groomed for the CEO's spot. I decided I need to set up my own plan for upward mobility."

"So you fixed the prices of vaccines?" Bellamy practically spat out the words, her gray eyes nearly black in the soft lighting of the room. "And then tried to blame it on me."

"I did blame it on you. It's just my luck that my little brother over here showed up to play knight in shining armor. He kept rescuing you instead of letting you take the fall."

"Your brother?" Bellamy whispered, her gaze colliding with Donovan's. He saw the awareness there and the subtle agreement that he'd been right with his theory about Sutton Taylor's infidelities.

The question was, how did they all get out of there before his big brother imploded?

BELLAMY KEPT HER gaze on Maggie, willing her sister to wake up. She was tied to a chair, her head lolling at a strange angle from where she'd been knocked out. She wanted to go to her, but Jensen's insistence on keeping the gun cocked and pointed directly at her and Donovan had her staying in place.

They needed to talk him down and give Archer enough time to break in.

And they also needed to keep an eye on Sally. The instability that marked Jensen was nowhere in evidence with her. In fact, the more Jensen railed, the calmer Sally got as she stood there, stoically watching the proceedings.

"Why are you so convinced I'm your brother?" Donovan asked the question, his gaze revealing nothing. "I'm a Colton."

"A Colton discovered in the barn on Christmas morning. The whole town knows."

"It's not a secret I was adopted."

"Adopted because you're some stray they felt sorry for."

"Does Sutton know?"

"About you?" A small corner of spittle filled the edge of Jensen's mouth, his skin turning a ripe shade of pink around his collar. "My mother knew about you. A pithy little story, if you must know. Dear old Dad knocked up his secretary. It was my mother who orchestrated everything, convincing your simpering fool of a mother to hand you over to a family who could really take care of you."

"But does Sutton know?" Donovan insisted.

"No. And that's how it's going to stay. My father has already given enough money to his illegitimate offspring. I'm not losing one more piece of my inheritance to the fact he couldn't keep it zipped."

"Fair point." Donovan nodded, his face drawn in sober lines.

Bellamy watched him, fascinated as he began to subtly control the room. She could only assume he'd received some signal from the chief, because bit by bit, he maneuvered Jensen around the room, drawing the gun off of her and her sister.

"It wouldn't do to have more of your inheritance go to anyone else." Donovan's voice was even and level. Reasonable. "Especially since LSP stock stands to go through the roof with the vaccine price-fixing."

"Exactly."

"You had it all figured out. Work the system, blame it all on Bellamy and then get rid of the evidence."

"Yep." Jensen nodded, the dull red of his skin fading again to a warm pink.

"What about your father?"

"Don't you want to call him Dad?"

It was the first moment Jensen managed to get a rise and the smallest muscle ticked in Donovan's jaw. "Where's Dad in all this?"

"Fighting for his life across town in a quiet little facility that isn't on anyone's radar. He's unknowingly been the recipient of a new drug being developed to treat certain forms of cancer. It's a miracle drug, unless you don't have any cancer to cure."

Bellamy knew what Jensen spoke of and had seen the trial details a few months prior. The drug was powerful and had the potential to be a game changer, but it had to be used properly.

And there he was, poisoning his father with it?

"You're a monster."

"Yeah, sweetheart, I am." Jensen shifted his attention at her outburst, his eyes now wild with whatever madness had gripped him. "But you can take solace in the fact that I'm the last one you're ever going to see."

"You're mad."

"Mad at the world, yes." Jensen's gaze swung toward Donovan before coming firmly to rest on her. "I've spent my life waiting for my turn. To run the company. To earn dear old Dad's respect. To get my shot. Yet I was never good enough."

The roller coaster of the past days seemed to slow in the face of Jensen's anger. It was too simple to think of him as a crazy person to be taken down.

Far too simple.

What she saw instead was a man beyond reason. Whatever he believed was meant to be his—his father's love, his birthright, even the Taylor name—had somehow twisted over time. And as she stared at Jensen, Bellamy had to admit that under different circumstances, that could have been her.

Hadn't she spent the past five years resenting Maggie for choosing to live her life while poor little Bellamy stayed behind taking care of their parents?

And hadn't she buried herself in her job, shunning relationships—heck, even shunning the chance to own a pet—because she'd crawled so far beneath the rock of self-sacrifice?

Looking into Jensen's angry, disillusioned eyes, Bellamy saw it all so clearly. And in that moment, finally understood all she was about to lose.

Donovan and Alex had shown her the way. Even if what

was building between her and Donovan still needed time to grow roots, she was grateful for what he'd given her.

For what he'd shown her.

That she had a life and it was time to get living.

How horrifying it was to realize that far too late.

DONOVAN'S FINGERS ITCHED as he held his hands by his side. Brother or not, Jensen Taylor was going down. Assuming he could get them all out of there.

"Nice speech, Jensen."

The words were enough to pull the man's attention off Bellamy and it gave Donovan the briefest moment of relief. If he could keep Jensen's focus diverted, he had a chance of getting Bellamy out alive.

If.

"It's the truth."

"Your truth."

"It is my truth!" Anger spilled from Taylor's lips with a violence that shouldn't have been surprising under the circumstances. "And now it's yours, Colton. You think you've got a way out of here, but you don't. Even with whatever backup you inevitably brought along, I've thought of it all. This place is wired."

While Donovan didn't doubt Jensen's threats, taunting him might get the information he needed to defuse whatever lurked around the cabin.

"Like Bellamy's car? Because you were so good at that. A half-assed explosion rigged by an amateur."

"It was meant to be. It wasn't time to kill her. And if it gave the cops time to wonder why someone suspected of stealing company secrets would make herself look like an accident victim, it was that much better."

"And the bomb at her house?"

"Same. How does it look if the poor little woman peddling company secrets escaped death twice? It would be like a red flag—she's setting herself up."

"So killing her here? All of us here? How's that going to go down?"

"Ah, that's where Sally comes in. She's the one with Bellamy's personnel folder and she's the one who let her go. It stood to reason the stress of getting discovered and fired was the last thing Bellamy Reeves needed before going around the bend."

"All figured out."

"Except for you," Jensen sneered.

And the backup waiting outside the cabin.

Donovan calculated the odds—and the acknowledgment that Jensen Taylor had to have walked in here with a plan B.

"What are you going to do about me?"

"Same thing I'm going to do about all of you. I came out here to counsel a distressed former employee. And I'm going to get out barely alive from the bomb she's planted to blow me to smithereens."

Cold. Impersonal. Distant.

The very reason a bomb made an effective weapon for cowards stood before him.

And in that moment, Donovan knew there was no time to wait.

As he leaped forward, Donovan's momentum was enough to knock Jensen off balance. Donovan slammed Jensen's gun hand on the ground, a harsh cry in his ear proof he'd damaged bone, as well. As soon as the man went still, Donovan was on his feet, moving toward Bellamy.

Jensen's fall must have been what Archer was waiting for. The room erupted in gunfire and smoke, a series of officers rushing the room from outside. Donovan had a split second to register it all before Bellamy's scream had his gaze shifting back toward his half brother. The man lifted a small square no bigger than a lighter from his pocket, his hand flipping the top open.

"Donovan!" Bellamy screamed his name once more, just as Donovan leaped into motion. His hand closed over Jensen's, effectively stopping his brother from taking the final step of blowing up the cottage with all of them in it. Archer was the closest, and he twisted Jensen's wrist to retrieve the device that would no doubt blow them all sky-high.

All noise ceased, everyone in the room going quiet as Archer stepped back, the detonation device in hand.

"Tell me you know what you're doing with that, Thompson." Donovan gritted out the words.

"Underestimating me again, Colton?"

"Never."

"Good." Chief Thompson nodded, his hands calm and still. "Then I can swallow my pride and ask you to come handle this."

"Deal."

DONOVAN TAPPED THE back of the EMT vehicle in a signal that the crew could move on. Sally and Jensen had already been transported in handcuffs and the other EMT team had worked on Maggie, treating her for lingering effects of the chloroform and taking her in for an overnight of observation. The bomb beneath the cabin had already been removed, detonated on the far edge of the property where it couldn't hurt anyone. Archer and his men still worked the scene and they'd already called into the facility where Sutton was to get the doctors diagnosing him with the correct meds to get well.

"I had no idea it was Jensen. I never even considered him." That thought had kept her steady company since Archer's team had cuffed Jensen and even an hour later, she still couldn't believe it was true.

Everything that had happened had been engineered by Sutton's greedy—and clearly unstable—son.

"Archer asked me what I thought the motive was in all that was happening."

Bellamy took in his bedraggled form and the spot of blood that had dried on his cheek where Jensen had nicked him in their fight. "What motive did you give?"

"I went with the old standby. Money and power."

"I'd say you pegged them both."

Donovan pulled her close, folding her up against his chest. "I don't know what I'd have done if something happened to you."

He'd said the same thing off and on since Jensen had been taken away, and each time she'd stood patiently, wrapping her arms around his waist and holding him tight. "I'm okay. We all are."

"I never should have let you come."

"You didn't get much choice in the matter."

He shook his head at that, his warm brown gaze still bleak from the events of the evening. "I shouldn't have let that matter."

"Is that how it's going to be, Donovan Colton?"

"Be?"

He looked crestfallen as she pulled from his arms, her own hands fisting at her hips. "You tell me what to do and I just do it. I'm not Alex, you know."

"A fact I'm glad about."

"I have my own mind and I make my own decisions. It's why I stopped and told you what was happening instead of harking off on my own. That was big for me." She moved in and pressed a kiss to his chin. "Don't make me regret my decision."

"Why didn't you leave?"

Bellamy knew there were a lot of reasons she'd chosen to go to Donovan instead of heading out on her own, but one had stood out beyond all the rest. "Because it's time to stick."

"To stick?"

"I've been doing everything on my own for far too long. It's time to depend on people. To let people in and to depend on them and the support they can provide."

"Does this mean you want me to stick around?"

So much had happened in such a short time, it seemed nearly impossible to be having this conversation.

Yet here they were.

She'd spent too much time unwilling to voice what she wanted, now that the moment was here, Bellamy was determined not to fumble it. "Yes, I do."

"I'm not in a position to walk away from my job in Austin."

"I'd never ask you to."

"And Alex and I are a package deal."

"I certainly hope so."

"And I'm sort of surly and grumpy in the morning."

She smiled. "Believe it or not, I figured that one out all by myself."

"What else have you figured out?"

"That I want to spend time with you. I like having a surly, grumpy man and his furry best friend in my life. I'm tired of my own company and I'm tired of ignoring all the life going on all around me."

"If you're sure?"

She thought about those scary moments, when she stared at Jensen Taylor and saw the faintest outline of herself.

"I'm absolutely positive."

Donovan bent his head and pressed his lips to hers. The kiss was full of passion and promise and abundant joy. As she wrapped her arms around him and sunk into his kiss, Bellamy knew she'd finally found the partner to share her life with.

Two partners, she silently acknowledged to herself as she added Alex. And she couldn't be happier.

Epilogue

Six weeks later

Bellamy juggled the plate of cake and pot of coffee and headed for the living room. She'd come to look forward to these Saturday afternoons with her sister and was excited to share the recently discovered recipe with Maggie.

"Is that Mom's pound cake?" The words were said in a reverent tone as Maggie leaped off the couch to help her with the plate.

"I found the recipe back in the fall. She had it hoarded in the bottom of her jewelry box."

"Who knew?" Maggie's musical laughter was a balm and Bellamy couldn't deny how nice it was to share something funny about her parents.

"She was so proud of that cake. She preened every time someone commented on it at town events."

Maggie reached for a slice. "Then I'm glad it's not lost to us."

Her sister took a bite, her eyes closing as she chewed, and Bellamy screwed up her courage. She'd wanted to say something for a while now, but had struggled with how to express all she felt. "I'm sorry for all that's happened."

Maggie's eyes popped open. "What do you mean?"

"Mom. Dad. All of it. I was stubborn and unfair to you

and I'm sorry. I'm sorrier it took a kidnapping and an attempt on both our lives to realize it."

"I'm sorry, too."

"You don't have to be sorry."

"Yes, actually, I do." Maggie settled her plate back on the coffee table. "I thought I could fix everything. That marrying James would give me the financial tools to fix what was happening. I'm not proud of myself, nor was I fair to James."

"But you loved him first."

"Yes. Maybe." Maggie swiped at a small tear that trailed down her cheek. "It's the 'maybe' that's the problem. For a long time, I enjoyed being with him. And I liked being a Corgan. But I liked those things too much. My husband should have come first."

Since coming back into each other's lives, she and Maggie had danced around the subject of her sister's marriage. It was humbling to realize all that had gone on beneath the surface. "But you did care for each other."

"We did. And I'm glad we finally remembered that, there at the end. But James has moved on and in time, I will, too. And in the meantime, he helped me make sure you've got this great house."

"He… You what?"

A mischievous light filled Maggie's eyes. "You belong here, Bell. And I know it's what Mom and Dad would have wanted."

"But the will. The insurance. The house came from there—" Bellamy broke off. "Didn't it?"

"They actually came courtesy of the Corgan fortune."

A sinking feeling gripped her, and Bellamy felt the coffee she'd sipped curdling in her stomach. "I can't accept that. I mean, it's not my place."

Maggie reached over, her gentle touch stopping the torrent of words. "It's what James and I both wanted. He understood it was important to me and in a lot of ways, it was the final act of kindness that allowed us to let each other go. And we both decided to keep it a secret so you wouldn't say no."

"But I can't take it."

"Actually, you can. We both knew how much you sacrificed for Mom and Dad. More, you deserved something to cement your future. This is your home."

"But—"

"But nothing. I know you love playing the big-sister card, but on this one, I win. It's what I wanted. James, too."

The generosity was nearly overwhelming, but in her sister's words, Bellamy sensed healing, as well. "You're okay with the divorce?"

"It's best for both of us." Maggie reached for her plate again. "Speaking of best, how are things with Donovan Colton?"

She knew her sister, and Bellamy suspected the rapid change in topic was deliberate. But she also understood how important it was to Maggie to stand on her own two feet. Vowing to take the issue of the house up with her later, she let the joy of being with Donovan wash over her.

"Things are good. He's good."

"You're spending a lot of time running back and forth to Austin."

"We're enjoying each other's company."

"First you make her pound cake and now you're using euphemisms like Mom?"

Bellamy swatted at her sister's leg. "I like being with him."

"Then tell me what you're doing for Valentine's Day."

LATER THAT DAY, her earlier conversation with Maggie still lingered in her mind as Bellamy cleaned up the plates and mugs. The time they'd spent together since the holidays was helping to mend their relationship and it was wonderful to have her sister back.

She heard the bark moments before a nose pressed into her hip, a large, wiggly body prancing at her side. Donovan followed behind Alex into the kitchen and Bellamy fought the urge to lay a hand against her heart at the sight of him. She bent to lavish praise on Alex instead, willing her pulse to slow down.

How did the man manage it?

"Where's Maggie?"

"She had a date with a sale at the mall."

He moved in and pulled her close. "And you didn't want to go?"

"I'm getting used to having some money back in my bank account. I'd like to revel in that glow a bit longer."

Concern lined his face. "Sutton's made good on everything that happened at LSP. Your job, your good name *and* a raise."

She wrapped her arms around his waist, unable to hold back the truth. "Okay. I admit it, then. I wanted to stay home and spend the afternoon with you."

The worry faded, replaced with a cocky smile. "Well, then, Ms. Reeves. What did you have in mind?"

"This."

The kiss had her pulse racing again, a wild thrill ride that she couldn't imagine ever tiring of.

How things had changed since December. Her lonely, quiet life had vanished and in its place was something more wonderful than she could have ever imagined.

She was in love.

The thought hit so swiftly—and came from a place so deep—it had Bellamy pulling back from the kiss.

Love?

"Bellamy?"

"I... Um... I..." She grasped at the first thing that came to mind. "Do we need to feed Alex?"

"What?" Confusion furrowed a small line between his eyebrows before Donovan glanced toward Alex, who even now lay curled up on the floor, fast asleep. "He's fine."

"Good."

"And he doesn't eat until six."

"Right."

"It's one."

"Sure." Bellamy silently cursed herself for her inability to think on the fly. "Of course."

"Are you okay?"

"Yeah. Sure. I'm fine." She moved back to the sink and snatching up a dish towel to dry the mugs from earlier.

"What's wrong?"

"Nothing."

"Something's wrong. One moment I'm kissing you and the next you're pulling away like you got burned. What's wrong?"

She dropped the dish towel as the cup banged against the counter with a discordant thud. "I love you."

The words were out before she could check them and it was enough to have her holding her breath. Had she really just told him she loved him?

It was stupid and impulsive and about as well thought out as the "let's feed Alex" line.

"Bellamy."

The second, urgent use of her name had her looking up, turning to face him. To face the reality of her impulsive words. "Look. Just ignore me. That kiss scrambled my brain and I sort of short-circuited. It's noth—"

He laid a finger over her lips. "It's not nothing."

The soft press of his finger turned tantalizing as he ran the pad over her lower lip. "Believe it or not, I have a few thoughts on this subject you seem hesitant to voice, too.

It's not particularly original but I think it fits in these circumstances."

"You do?"

"I love you, Bellamy Reeves. I love everything about you. I love that you don't mind my attitude in the morning before coffee. And I love that you've been quietly encouraging me to visit with Sutton *and* my parents. And I love that you're mending fences with your sister."

"Those are good things."

"They are. And they're good because I can share them with you."

Whatever she'd been expecting, a declaration of love was the farthest thing from her mind. "You love me back?"

"I sure do."

"I love you, Donovan. And I love your furry partner, too."

"Alex is a lot smarter than me. I think he already figured it all out and has been waiting for the two humans to get on board."

The heavy thump of a tail had the two of them turning at the same time. The sleeping lump in front of her fridge was wide-awake, his dark eyes full of knowing and endless wisdom.

Bellamy smiled, surprised at how easy it was to believe the dog knew all. "I guess that means he approves."

As if on cue, Alex leaped up from his favorite spot and jumped up, completing the small circle in Bellamy's kitchen and pressing eager kisses on both of them.

Bellamy laughed as Donovan tightened his hold.

"Oh yeah," Donovan whispered against her ear. "He definitely approves."

* * * * *

MILLS & BOON®

INTRIGUE
Romantic Suspense

A SEDUCTIVE COMBINATION OF DANGER AND DESIRE